BRAND CHASER

DARK RANGE BOOK ONE

RANDI A. SAMUELSON-BROWN

WOLFPACK
PUBLISHING
— EST 2013 —

Brand Chaser
Paperback Edition
Copyright © 2022 Randi A. Samuelson-Brown

Wolfpack Publishing
5130 S. Fort Apache Rd. 215-380
Las Vegas, NV 89148

wolfpackpublishing.com

Paperback ISBN 978-1-63977-791-4
eBook ISBN 978-1-63977-790-7
LCCN 2022936550

The location of Stampede, Rimrock County, Colorado is a make-believe place, although hopefully it captures the essence of true places within the state. All characters portrayed are products of my imagination and any similarities to real people are a coincidence.

ACKNOWLEDGMENTS

I would like to thank Brand Commissioner Chris Whitney and Brand Inspector Terry Florian, for speaking with me and sharing their perspective, the history of brand inspectors in the State of Colorado and describing some of the current challenges they face. Any mistake made in the portrayal of Brand Inspectors is down to me.

I would also like to thank a fabulous group of friends and readers for their feedback and input—Natalie Bright, Jane Little Botkin, Michelle Ferrer, Karen Jones and Cindy Quibell.

Also, a special thank you to Mike Bray and Paul Bishop of Wolf Pack Publishing for their support and enthusiasm for my stories.

BRAND CHASER

PROLOGUE

1888

THE STEER LAY DEAD AT THEIR FEET.

Blood seeping into the ground, and the parched dirt drinking up the sacrifice.

A stand of three wranglers considered the still-warm carcass, one cradling the rifle that brought it down. A quick check of the brand made one thing certain—it didn't belong to their outfit. They had known that going in. But verification had a way, even after the fact, of bringing comfort to the proceedings. Only dudes and flatlanders killed their own brand for food. Well, these three men all knew better. They weren't dudes, and they weren't flatlanders. Or at least they hadn't been, not for a very long time. Colorado had a way of changing men. Especially if they stuck around.

The steer in question had wandered onto the ranch from a section where the fences weren't complete. A lot of land needed fencing on the Lost Daughter. Until recent history, it had been known as the Cross Ranch.

The Crosses, and by extension the wranglers, wore the tragedy that caused the name change as an emblem of wary pride. An undeniable stamp of ownership paid for by a girl's death, although no grave stood waiting to receive her body. Only the lonesome mourning sound of wind catching on the peaks gave a hint of what had transpired.

No body, no grave.

That remained the dying proclamation of the matriarch, Polly Cross, a woman made of the same flint as her husband. A woman who had dwindled down to little more than skin and bones with a wasting sickness that had no name. Thin parchment skin stretched tight, holding her skeleton together.

"I'll dig a grave once I know my girl is dead," she had pronounced whenever the matter arose, and her pronouncement carried that same tone that allowed no argument.

Polly Cross held that determined and unyielding stance until her ragged breath ran out. Seven months, almost to the day, after her daughter disappeared.

From that time, if not even before, it became apparent that the Lost Daughter would prove hard on women. An unspoken curse carried in the river cutting through the land. The men sensed it hanging in the air. The women sensed it more deeply, a dread carried as certainty, in the cords of their spines.

A LONE RIDER approached the outcropping of wranglers, loping across the meadow and up the slope to join them.

They waited as he neared, knowing his fondness for

dealing out instructions. The rider wheeled his horse around, as he gazed down upon the carcass.

"Good work. Cut 'im up, and pack 'im down," Hank Cross instructed.

Two of the wranglers pulled out skinning knives and proceeded to carve incisions along the cattle's hindquarters. The slits would meet under the steer's stomach: the hide split along the length of beast's underside then cut free at the neck. It took all three men to heave the beeve over, the horse pulling drag. They pulled the hide down the length of the body—ripping free and tearing the membrane. The men inspected the underside. A clear image of a deeper brand showed, pronounced.

"Would you lookee here," one of them said.

Sure enough, the original brand had been altered somewhere along the line. Vented, in the local terminology.

They held it up for Hank Cross to see.

"Well, ain't that interesting," he said, wryly. "Give it here."

One of the wranglers presented it to the boss, who didn't dismount.

He addressed the senior wrangler. "Bring it back down to headquarters when you come in."

He rode off, and the men set to butchering in short order. There would be fresh beef for dinner that night. A filled belly was a fine thing. Bellies filled with free beef even better. Such plunder was one of the founding codes in their corner of the West.

Founding codes often proved profitable.

AN HOUR OR SO LATER—NO one kept much store by their timepieces but rather tracked hours by the movement of the sun and light—the head wrangler knocked on the ranch house door holding the hide and not exactly overjoyed about the matter.

The boss opened the door and stood there, silent and waiting.

"Checking to see where you want this stored."

A shrug and a flick of the boss' head. "Hang it in one of them outbuildings."

The wrangler nodded, still troubled. "You mind if I ask why? That's evidence, is what that is."

Hank Cross considered the question. For a long moment, it seemed like no answer would be forthcoming. In the end, he decided to trust the man. "Yup. That's a fact."

"Then why do it? The law would say we vented the brand. Most would get rid of the hide and get rid of it fast."

Cross' pale eyes scanned the distance. "How many lawmen do you reckon are going to travel over here without good reason?"

The ranch hand chewed on that question, normally unwilling to second-guess his employer. "I'd have to say none. Not, as you say, without good reason."

Hank Cross considered the rimrocks and the mountains beyond. Seeing something far out of reach; something beyond the two of them standing there discussing a hide.

"One day my descendants will run this ranch, when I'm long gone and buried. There's lessons to be learned from that hide. The last man to draw usually is the one who dies. To fight for what's ours, even if it means fighting to the death."

The wrangler considered what he held. "That's a lot to expect from one hide that ain't even our work."

"Maybe. But I want whoever he is to be tough and to learn that if he sees an opportunity to take it. Like whoever vented this brand. Same as how we took that steer. We took him, because we could. I want that future Cross to understand that we owned this land and we held it. He owes it to us to do the same."

"Yeah. Put like that, it makes sense."

"Let me know where it ends up, and there's no reason to go waving a red flag. Should any of the hands be dumb enough to ask, it ain't none of their damned business."

"Consider it done." The wrangler turned to walk away, tipping his hat.

"Stuart? If you find a hide in one of the outbuildings that's been made over into the Lost Daughter brand, put that along with this one. Give and take, I call it." The boss' laughed came out dry and ended in a cough.

History hung heavy between the two men. "Sure thing," the cowboy replied.

Both knew that Susan wouldn't have approved of their actions. Gentleness likely proved her undoing. It still troubled the outfit not so much that she had died, but in the manner of her passing. Her disappearance troubled them fierce, and likely would for the rest of their lives.

The unspoken bottom line held firm. They thought she should have had enough fight in her to best the river.

But any fight had sunk to the bottom of the river when daughter Susan drowned.

To her father's way of thinking, that meant the remaining Cross sons needed to be a far sight tougher than she had proven. His three boys needed to grow into strong, hard men and raise strong, hard sons. The fate of the ranch depended upon their determination. Perhaps more importantly, their willingness to fight.

That altered brand on the hide would provide a clue and a tangible lesson through the misty reaches of time.

The Cross name would carry because they weren't afraid of blood. They didn't owe any apologies. And if someone tried to take what was theirs, they would have one hell of a fight on their hands. They held that land by right. Their right. Sealed by the disappearance of Susan.

Susan's mother rested in the only marked grave on the property. Sure, there were some unmarked ones scattered around, but there was no reason to go shooting their mouths off about those.

Adele "Polly" Cross. Dead at age 37.

That about summed it all up.

PART I

1

RIMROCK COUNTRY

2020

PURPLE SAGE MY ASS.

The scrub remained the same greenish gray since time immemorial, and the coyote willow branched out dense along the banks of the river, swollen and running fast from the Never Summer Mountains in the distance. Heavy late season snows caused an even later run-off, the rivers flowing higher than in a typical July. Nevertheless, a hot wind blew in from the west; a hot wind pressing down like an iron drying everything into kindling as the summer wore on. But for now, the sage and willow flashed silver underbellies, sparkling in the sunlight and dancing in the dry gusts rattling through the land and blowing roughshod over the sage and cottonwood trees alike.

A black-antlered pronghorn stood sentinel on a hillock, turning his face into the wind, sensing unfettered freedom. Alert for the slightest of changes, his large dark eyes would miss precious little. Pronghorns didn't need water or so the local knowledge claimed, but that amounted to just another fact to research. Just the same as how Emory Cross had felt compelled to look up Zane Grey although at the time, she couldn't have explained why. Just a nagging curiosity and a thread that kept bothering, like a loose thread running through her brain.

Full well knowing that sometimes, it was best to leave things alone. Unknown and untainted by fact.

Teachers in school had encouraged her curiosity, but following those threads often led to disappointment. Take Zane Grey for instance. While his name couldn't exactly be called a sham, it didn't strike as quite honest, either. Named *Pearl* Zane Grey, he'd changed that up right quick, and she couldn't exactly blame him on that count. Kind of like a *Boy Named Sue*, that would be a hard name to live down. He'd changed the spelling of his last name too, and that only added to the tally he had running against him. But the main source of her irritation stemmed from the fact that not only was the sage not purple, old Pearl was a dentist from back East. Just another flatlander who fell in love with an imaginary West, trying to make the land and the people out to be something they were never meant to be. A larger-than-life legend none lived up to, nor did they even feel the need to try.

True westerners left that image-building to the newcomers and the tourists. And people who insisted that sage grew purple despite all evidence to the contrary.

Too much time on her hands.

Time in the saddle gave her plenty of opportunity to debate and ponder any number of things. Scanning the landscape with a practiced eye, nothing in particular snagged her attention, so she returned to the question of Mr. Zane Grey, Ohio dentist with an eye for the ladies. His wife had to be one understanding woman, or a sucker. The verdict remained out on that one. Nevertheless, Mr. Zane Grey, Ohio dentist turned all-around western champion and spokesperson became a legend. *Riders of the Purple Sage.* That title sure sounded good, but the summer heat bleached everything out as the season wore on.

Nothing like arguing over a hundred-year-old point and bothering a notion to death while riding the fence line and searching through ravines. Under a sky as wide and blue as a body could imagine, life came just as independent as a person cared to make it. The problem with independence was that it carried dangers that travelled alongside. Most people just didn't think that far or that deep. Or that dark.

Often on the receiving end of critical judgements herself, why, she liked a good Western movie or book as much as the next person. So, she tried again to reframe her opinion. *Perhaps Zane Grey had been imagining the sage at twilight, when the setting sun had a way of painting in its own palette.* But even allowing for the waning light, the prospect of purple sage amounted to nothing more than poetry lingering on the page or a notion in the air; but either way, once examined, the evidence to support his claim simply wasn't there, or at least not in Colorado.

In other words, none of it rang true to her. No matter how pretty the strung-together words sounded.

"Well, Kai," her gelding's ears flicked back to listen, "maybe he was talking about Arizona or Utah. Nothing here purple. Nothing but scrub."

The horse licked and chewed and blew in response. She patted his neck. "You're a good boy," she murmured, meaning every word. "At least I can talk to you while we ride and round up cattle. You like rounding up cattle, don't you?"

And no matter Mr. Zane Grey's opinion or descriptions about the West: substance mattered to the locals. Or so it used to be.

Like the pronghorn who still watched; waiting for the spirit—or a flash of danger—to move him. King of the scrubland, that scrub basin bled out into the valley and unfurled beyond the line of sight. That meeting point, an uncertain edge where the mountains rose cold and dark and met the flats never would cause the pronghorn to balk. And for now, they travelled the scrubland range together. The pronghorn no doubt catching the scent of her and Kai as they rode along the rimrock, peering into the wash below and across at the slopes covered with scrub.

Looking for strays.

The midday sun beat down upon the world, flattening out the shadows. Temperatures rose and heat shimmered low in the distance summoning rippling mirages that held no consequence. Odds remained that smart cattle would seek relief alongside the river, but it was the dumb ones she scouted for.

Still, the sun beat down. Emory pulled off her hat, swiped at the sweat on her forehead and pushed strands of her long brown hair out of the way.

"You know Kai, cowboy poetry and a whole lot of songs come out of what we're doing right here and now."

She put her hat back in place, and the horse nodded his agreement. Or maybe that was a figment of imagination like those dang mirages, but she'd take it for an answer. Otherwise, she talked to no one other than herself and the sky. That's what crazy people did. Or people working cattle. Riding the range without a damn thing to do but chase cattle tails and sit in the saddle, scanning the endless open expanses and riding the wire fence lines down. Making sure nothing had changed and finding only mind-numbing boredom.

Distractions often proved deadly.

There wasn't a ranching family out there that didn't have a litany of accidents that befell the unwary: the daydreaming uncle or that girl who hadn't known how to handle a team when they spooked. Emory's own family passed down the story of the Hapless Susan who'd started out to cross the river, never to be seen again. The team and the wagon arrived on the other side, but that Susan never did.

Body never located, never retrieved.

Probably the water ran high back that day, like it flowed right now. Singing forcefully in the distance.

The image of a wet wagon and team drying in the sun, reins dropped and hanging loose seared itself into her everlasting imagination. The team, found in their harness and traces were perfectly fine, waiting on the other side of the crossing for the young driver who never struggled out from the river. No one ever said why she drove out there alone on the day. Probably going into town, but that remained just another detail sucked into the sink of time.

Emory imaged Hapless Susan as delicate and small, whereas she was built sturdy and solid, and able to swim and to take care of herself.

Nevertheless, life could turn stark and unfair with the toss of a coin. And that tale of a drowning rang undoubtedly true.

Whoever found the team must have searched the area with mounting concern. Wondering where the driver could possibly have gone and listening for clues. But when no human sounds were detected—the finder calling out at first calm, more desperate each subsequent try—that living person was met only by silence. They might have started screaming at that point and heard nothing except for the water rushing against the bushes and rocks. It was a hard and fateful decision to take the team back to the Cross Ranch; it amounted to the gut-wrenching decision to leave a person stranded.

No doubt a search party was immediately raised. But the Hapless Susan never was found.

Local people marked the disappearance down as a strange, if not ominous, business. That inexplicable event turned out to be the first of many involving the Lost Daughter, and that dated back to 1890 or there-abouts. The legacy threaded through their lives unabated, evoking a darkness they couldn't quite shake.

The long reach of superstition zinged along her spine.

Skeletons weathered out there, both man and beast. Literally. Somewhere under the dirt and grit, perhaps even under a boulder or two, the Hapless Susan decom-posed if she hadn't disappeared altogether. She wouldn't be the first or the last, but her rare circumstances earned her a place in the legends of Rimrock County.

The family, for reasons of their own, did nothing to dispel it.

Bones.

Another topic presented itself for consideration when she noticed an old small vertebrae half buried in the ground.

Human skeletons where what most fixated on, but the bones of cattle meant a loss of income. The bones of pronghorn, elk, deer, coyotes and pica proved that predators abounded, but that summed up the nature of the terrain. They had to take note of death which surrounded them in one form or another. Skeletons belonged to either predators or prey who succumbed.

Most average people probably didn't think about that part, but cattlemen certainly did.

Cattle growers, she corrected herself with a nod.

Now that she had latched onto the notion of human skeletons, pondering the fates of those two-legged varieties that travelled before and succumbed struck as pretty damned interesting. Her thinking didn't concern those in the family plot. Instead, her mind turned to travelers who had lost their way, perishing in the unforgiving elements. Reduced to a heap of bones scoured by the wind and by time. The more fortunate likely turned into an unmarked graves, shroudless bodies thudding into the shallow depressions and covered back up with varying degrees of concern. Holes filled in just enough to prevent the corpses from being chewed on by predators.

Or not.

Graves fading and melding into the expanse of sagebrush that never turned purple, no matter how the light might cast.

Rimrock County's claim to fame involved outlaws, and with good reason. Prime outlaw country, its canyon-riddled land held draws and crevices a-plenty to hide out in. That applied for both the four and the two-legged varieties.

A fair reminder that she'd best keep her mind on the task at hand.

Shifting in the saddle and pressing Kai to stop, they waited, listening and watching. Feeling small, the vastness didn't scare her like it should. Probably the wide-open vistas didn't scare any of them that had been raised out there, but in order to survive, they'd all learned to respect the dangers early on.

It was then she caught what she had been searching for. The faintest ribbon of a bawling calf carrying on the wind. Unfurling its cry—a clue in the vastness.

A vastness that could swallow them whole.

2

NO SUCH THING AS OPEN RANGE

IN THE SPACE OF A HEARTBEAT, MUSINGS FELL AWAY LIKE A dislodged stone. The bawling still carried.

From the higher vantage point near the rimrock cliffs, the washes and draws fanned out below. Similar to mine dumps, those landscape features formed by erosion persevered. Water running downhill in an endless cycle of years had chiseled the facets into the landscape. Who knew how long those features would last? Probably as long as she remained above ground, and a few hundred years besides. The drop-offs were all scree, dirt and dust. A few scraggly plants hung on to the soil out of sheer cussedness. Runoff emptied into the riverbanks from the melting snow above like they had every year since the Ice Age. Water meant life, money and livelihoods. Lack of water led to bloodshed, but that wasn't her concern at the moment. Rivers meandering through the bottom and flanked by stands of cottonwoods were a good thing. So were cattle.

Emory nudged Kai along a narrow switchback trail, reins loose to allow him to pick his own footing and to choose his timing. Only amateurs tried to force a horse's path, especially downhill. Anymore, there were plenty of those amateurs to go around.

But she wasn't one of them. Every morning her mirror reflected back a rancher, if she had any doubts on the matter. Capable, strong boned, and displaying a flattened nose bridge from the time a horse bucked her off into a fence. She'd always wanted to be a slim, wild beauty, but that wasn't how she could ever be described. Still her eyes sparkled when she smiled, but lately there hadn't been all that much to smile about.

They trekked in the general direction of the bawling cries building, but not of a particular urgency. Kai's ears pricked forward listening, a cattle horse at heart.

As they searched for those calves and following their calls, Emory expected a mother's answering response. But none carried. Horse and rider waited a bit longer, Kai's nostril's flaring. Still no response. They continued on with that slow, careful pace. At the mouth of the first draw, they paused. Emory took a good, hard scan. Nothing moved. An old worn track threaded deeper in, brush dotting and casting shade over the baked dirt in patches.

Still riding on, the calves fell quiet and the rhythm of Kai's hooves striking the rocky trail seemed the only sound. It didn't take long before she found evidence and spied visible tracks marked in the dust—tiny calf hoof prints outlined clear.

"See that, Kai? Here we go."

Emory patted Kai's neck as they hung back, waiting to hear the calves again and knowing full well that sounds had a way of ricocheting. Seated and still, they lingered as the sun pressed down. In time, the sound reached them again—the bawling caught on the wind.

She nudged Kai forward. Sure enough, a few hundred yards in, two calves huddled together near tall boulders that partially blocked them from view.

"Come on out babies, and let me get a good look at you," she crooned, calming them out of an ingrained habit.

Seemingly unlikely to bolt, one even took a couple of tentative steps toward the horse and rider.

Pointing Kai uphill and acting disinterested, they passed the calves to the left. The best bet was to push them from above—the hillside steep, the terrain rough. She turned Kai, and they came down to the calves from an angle.

Although Kai picked his footing, they still slid a bit, scree giving way downhill and startling the pair. The calves bounded away, all legs and angles and moving fast. Fast toward the mouth of the draw, which had been Emory's plan all along, even if the execution left a bit to be desired.

A nice pair of Red Angus. No markings or brands visible.

Hell, they could belong to anyone.

Never once did she think the pair belonged to the Lost Daughter: all their heifers had delivered and offspring counted. But that was one of the beauties of BLM land. Many outfits ran their stock on 'open range' and distinctions blurred, nice and easy.

Possession remained nine-tenths of the law, and that sounded about right.

Back out in the open with calves calmed down, she headed them toward the river's edge, satisfied that she wouldn't come away empty-handed.

The rhythm of the land reflected in the cattle's parade

as they strung along, and in the tradition from which she sprang.

She took stock of that feeling and wondered whether it provided an advantage or not; to that question, there was no clear-cut answer to find.

Emory dismounted, noticing a tear in her sun-scalded shirt as she dropped the reins, freeing Kai to eat his fill of the green river grasses. The calves edged up to the water in the flattened depression and drank. Just the same as countless other cattle over the years had watered and crossed before.

Billowing thunderheads rose in the searing blue sky, dwarfing everything below. Sticking two fingers into her mouth, she let 'em rip. Two sharp whistles cleaved the distance like an axe splitting a log. Strong enough to travel, strong enough to carry a respectable distance. Women weren't supposed to be able to whistle like that, but she could. Another dubious distinction, but one that came in handy especially where cellphones weren't always a sure-fired bet.

A single sharp whistle returned from the distance.

Cade's reply.

BEFORE LONG, Cade Timmons came into view—ranch hand and all-around smartass. Hair too long to ever be considered upright and his beard, a cross between a scruff and a five o'clock shadow, suited him and his bad-boy reputation fine.

There was a reason he attracted notice.

He drove seven head out in front of him and his mount, pushing them a bit hard. No one could accuse him of wasting time. Well, not when he was riding.

The hired hand's eyes flickered over the two calves waiting in the shallows.

"Mavericks," she said; that one, singular word opening the door on plenty of possibilities.

A glint of a deeper calculation ran through Cade's deep brown eyes. "I see. You figure on keeping them?"

"I do. They're common enough."

A partial shrug only half convinced.

"Got a few more ravines to flush," he told her. "Won't take long."

Turning his head to cue his mount, she caught it. Purplish-red marks blazoned upon his neck.

Cade intercepted her stare all right but tendered no explanation. Like the word maverick, 'hickey' landed square in the self-explanatory category, too. He wheeled his horse around in no uncertain terms and took off at a good clip.

He left her sucking in his dust and surrounded by cattle. Expecting her to wait. Wait for his thundering return.

To hell with that.

More importantly, to hell with him.

Her cheeks burned at the memory. Only a few days had passed since he had kissed her. He had turned away from her at the time and laughed at her surprise and confusion. Acting like her returned kiss meant next to nothing; and flirtations were just another game to play and a way to pass the time. To him, that kiss amounted to nothing at all.

With a yip and a haw, Emory moved those cattle along. She was of a mind to cut out the calves from Cade's cattle, leaving those to graze and free to wander at will. Anything with the aim of causing more work for the ranch hand.

But she didn't cut out the calves. Instead, she left them mingled in with the others.

Ranching remained a business, pure and simple. Any burgeoning retaliation shouldn't involve the source of her family's income. A bunch of unexpected profit had just wandered right into their ranch account. Sorely needed inventory as far as she knew, and she wasn't about to let that get loused up all on account of pride.

If she had ever entertained any notion of trying to locate the calves' mother, that got dashed to pieces right about that point. A decision that she could only conclude was the Crosses dark side taking over.

"Come on, Kai. Let's get everyone back home."

Emory headed back to the ranch, keeping a special eye on her prizes. The Lost Daughter cattle knew the way and kept up a good clip as she and Kai brought up the rear, riding drag.

Jaw clenched, she pulled herself up taller in the saddle to pretend she didn't care about Cade. Turning her attention on the surrounding Colorado landscape, the flattops gleamed almost white in the distance though late afternoon storm clouds had built up a shelf toward the west, slate gray and promising rain somewhere along the line.

Two mavericks for the taking seemed a fine proposition altogether, or maybe she just succumbed to another whisper from past history.

And while she might not know all that much about romance or men—in fact, she felt foolish for giving Cade any thought or encouragement at all—she did know about ranching.

Her blood quickened at the thought of having expanded the herd by two head, free of charge.

NOT FAR AWAY FROM the ranch's back gate with the last five hundred yards to go—strung out single file and pushed along by Kai—all neared the finish line. However, about halfway to the gate, the bunch pulled up short, snorting and lowing. Confused.

Startled, the calves turned at first stiff-legged, before bounding to the side. A rustling and a clanking sound came from the bushes, announcing the fact that they certainly weren't alone on the trail. A man in gaiters emerged, fishing poles and tack box in hand.

"Well, hello!" He ground to a halt, staring at the cattle, the cattle stared back at him and Emory stared at everyone from her vantage point on horseback.

"I'm trying to get to the river," the gaiters flashed a toothy grin and overly hearty greeting.

Probably a Texan, she concluded with a sigh.

3

TOURISTS AND LOCUSTS

"It's that way," she pointed, forcing an expression she hoped came out as sincere when it sure the hell wasn't. "Let me push these guys past so I don't have to round them up again."

Damn, a witness. Still, a witness who probably didn't know all that much.

"You visiting?" She tossed the question over her shoulder while she got the older cattle moving again, and the calves falling in alongside. Changing her approach and now halfheartedly trying to make her suspicions sound all friendly and nice. Sounding, more importantly, like the question amounted to nothing more than an afterthought.

She circled back toward Gaiters, momentarily.

"From Chicago," he puffed up. Like that would cut anything in Rimrock County. Being from Chicago was possibly worse than being a Texan, but that fact struck perfect in its own irritating way.

He eyed the rifle in the scabbard. "Planning on shooting something?"

The likelihood of him knowing anything about the rules governing livestock slimmed down with that clarification.

"Not unless I have to. Make sure you have a Colorado fishing license," Emory called, circling Kai around again.

He patted his bulging fisherman's vest—a multitude of gadgets, pockets and ties. A *logo* unfamiliar to her blazoned across the front and meant money. The man looked for all the world like he was preparing to wade his way into expensive and fashionable combat.

Just more overpriced shit, to her way of thinking.

"You want to see it?" He asked, turning a shade toward uncertain. Eyeing the rifle again.

Secretly pleased—or maybe not so secret—she shook her head, all false apologetic. "No need. I'm not a game warden. Just didn't want you to get in trouble, that's all. They check, you know."

The tourist nodded, relieved. "What's the rifle for?"

"Predators," she explained, "or cattle with broken legs."

The notion of *problems* clearly troubled him, never having considered the possibility on his western vacation.

With that clarification, she nudged Kai forward toward the Lost Daughter's back gate; Gaiters clanking onward toward the streambank, and likely scaring off any and all self-respecting fish that weren't deaf in the water.

"Hope you don't fall in," she muttered under her breath.

Tourists had become the locusts of the twenty-first century, no joke.

They flocked into town and tried to fit in for obscure reasons, baffling many. No, they didn't have green spring-mix salad in the two restaurants. Yes, they still ate iceberg lettuce. Beef, while it may have been a four-letter word in some locales, was still what was for dinner. And the land prices soared. The land prices scared her the most when she stopped to think about them. But wealth, or the lack thereof, remained an undercurrent that colored through their lives. The rest of the other ranchers, well hell, they thought they were rich. And they were. On paper.

The transplants, the flatlanders, and the right or left-coasters, sure as hell would swoop in and buy those hard fought-for homesteads with money a-flashing. Property taxes climbed as a result from all that flaunting. The transplants were welcomed by some in fact: the shop keepers and the hospitality workers. Just as long as they had big wads of money to throw around for the hell of it.

Spend, they all did. They spent stupid amounts of money.

But somehow true prosperity passed the locals right on by—families who had settled and tamed the land as best they could. Families like hers who did their level best to carve out a life in the rugged terrain—a land of high altitudes, deep snows, driving blizzards, and glorious sunny days smack dab in the middle of winter. Fabulous summer evenings and the golden aspen covering the mountainsides lured them in by the planeload.

Private planeload.

The dull thudding of hooves and a few deep-throated cattle protest calls approached and drew near on the same trail, pressing down upon them and narrowing the distance. Catching up, in fact. As they neared the last hundred yards, Emory picked up the pace from a sense of pride. She pushed the cattle a bit harder than her normal custom. She drove them right through the open metal stock gate.

The calves trotted on in, as nice as anyone could ask. She waited for Cade to drive his cattle through. He added another three head to the total. All the mature cattle were branded with the Cross L Lazy D blazoned on their left shoulders.

"See the fly fisher?" She asked.

"I saw 'im." His eyes flickered as he rode on by, pushing the cattle onward and leaving her to shut the gate.

He didn't even see the need to break his pace.

Common courtesy dictated that he should wait for her to close the gate and remount. That remained a rule out on the range, out in their part of the world. *Never ride off until the last person remounted.* Apparently, Cade didn't hold much in store with that rule. Or any others, for that matter.

True, the barn and house were a manageable walking distance, but still. That wasn't the point.

Irritated, Emory remounted without trouble, thinking how at times the Code of the West had turned to shit even among their own kind. She trailed along behind, feeling every bit as superfluous as Cade apparently judged her to be.

But he was wrong. Dead wrong. She was everything to the Lost Daughter, and the Lost Daughter was everything to her. A hired hand would never understand just how deep that association and history ran.

He rode on ahead competent, experienced, and oblivious, having swept up all of the cattle with the maverick calves included. Already in the process of cutting out the calves from the mature cows; he was poised to wrap up his portion of the day by getting the newest additions into the holding pen. The other head ambled out into the pasture, a bounty of grass spread before them thick and green. Of course, Cade didn't dismount but shut and chained the pasture gates while remaining seated on horseback.

Emory seldom took the easy way out, which at times made things harder than they had to be. Cade certainly took the easy way where he could, and much to her chagrin, it often paid off just fine.

"Need anything else from me?" he asked, not waiting for an answer as he swung down from his horse, straight-backed and at ease in the world. A little too at ease.

His smirk made her feel ungainly and slow, so she retaliated. "Yeah. I'm going to need you to stick around and help me with the calves."

"Mind if I unsaddle first?" The tone underscored the fact that it wasn't a genuine question.

She dismounted as well. "Nope. We're done riding for today."

He bit back a smart-ass reply no doubt parading around his brain. Instead, he unbuckled the bridle and freed the horse's face, slipping on a headstall and lead rope in one fluid movement. Uncinching the saddle, he thrust a hand through the gullet and hefted it over his shoulder, acting as if he found the weight inconsequential when in fact, that saddle weighed a good thirty-five pounds.

There he stood, the stereotypical picture of western virility in a denim shirt unsnapped a bit too low, every inch a heart throb. A dark kind of sexy and he knew it. He was of the cut that beckoned from billboards and magazine ads, and far too good to ever be true.

Using his free hand, he picked up the saddle pad and caught her watching. He winked.

Heaven help her.

Grinding her bootheel into the ground, she tried to recover her balance. There was no sense in going all moon-eyed over someone like him.

She turned her attention to Kai and loosed his cinch.

"What's eating you," Cade asked without the slightest concern one way or the other.

She stared daggers at the mark on his neck. "Ever hear the one about how you're supposed to wait until the last rider mounts?"

He found that plenty amusing but had enough sense not to laugh outright. "Well, did you have trouble getting back on? You could have whistled."

Yeah. Sure. Go whistle.

He walked into the barn, saddle still slung over his shoulder, pad and bridle in hand. Calling out and stride unbroken.

"I never took you for a lame-ass rosebud, but if you insist…"

But her insistence didn't amount to ineptitude on her part. It amounted to taking a stand for basic manners. Besides, on occasion, remounting proved difficult—a dangerous difficulty in unusual circumstances. But truth be told, anyone could use the gate to get back on, and they both knew as much.

So, she shouted in the direction of the open barn door. "I'm not a lame-ass rosebud, and we're paying your wages. Or did something change with that arrangement that I'm unaware of?"

He returned out to the hitching post, tongue stuck in his cheek. He brushed his horse using long, firm strokes where sweat had darkened its coat underneath the saddle and along the girth line. "Whatever you say, Boss Lady."

"I say get those calves ready, and load one into the chute and get the other in line," Emory snapped.

"Your wish is my command," he drawled, still brushing. "But let me finish my horse first."

His lack of regard had never been clearer. He made damn sure to get that point across without uttering another single word.

4

BRAND 'EM

Branding animals was nothing new to either of them after all.

Cross L Lazy D was the Lost Daughter's brand, and it had plenty of heft and history behind it. Sometimes on one side of the law, sometimes on the other. No one, however, disputed the quality of their cattle. Even if the provenance might raise a few eyebrows along the way.

"Provenance," she said aloud, liking the sound as the word curled itself around her lips, weaving a charm or a spell.

Hell. At least she knew the word.

They had all grown up working the spring and fall round-ups which involved branding, tagging, vaccinations and castrations. Speaking from a practical perspective, brands proved ownership first and foremost with plenty of rules and regulations surrounding the practice. A practice dating all the way back to when Colorado marked the frontier and sprang up as the Wild West. The State of Colorado didn't *require* branding, but every livestock grower in the area did it all the same.

"Inspectors say that a brand is an animal's return address, or something along those lines," Emory mused not exactly in passing.

Cade squinted. "Hang out with brand inspectors a lot, do you?"

"Nope," Emory replied. "But they do have a point."

She dagger-eyed Cade and the trophy on his neck. "Whatever girl gave you those hickeys probably thinks that she's branded *you*."

"Huh. That would sure be a mistake on her part. Shoot, these'll fade."

Cade had toyed with her, no sense in pussyfooting around that uncomfortable fact.

She had the upper hand on him and knew it. He did, too.

"I'll be right back," she said, dismissing Cade and his female conquests without complete success.

He didn't bother an answer.

She turned her thoughts to *her* conquests. Any cow momma's would be damned near impossible to find if she even wanted to try. Which she didn't. Those new calves would soon be card-carrying members of the Lost Daughter outfit in a matter of moments.

The Crosses stored the branding options in the barn: the electric iron and the traditional iron brand. The running iron kept hidden and out of sight in one of the old tool sheds for historical, and somewhat obvious, reasons. The electric one heated the fastest, so she plugged it in and ran the extension cord outside next to the chute. Four thirty-five in the afternoon.

She sized up Cade, who came across as a bit twitchy and disgruntled.

He had good reason. The Lost Daughter's branding had been carried out a full two weeks earlier; all those brands scabbed over and in the process of healing. Fresh brands would prove a dead giveaway.

"Get the first one into the squeeze chute, would you?"

Cade made no move toward her. In fact, he took a step away. "I'm getting a beer first. You want one?"

"Nah," she frowned, taken off-guard.

While Cade went off in search of his refrigerator, Emory stood in the pen waiting, stamping her heel. She doubted Cade would go off in search of a beer if her father was the one kept waiting.

Hell, her father would have accepted that damn beer and there they'd both go, drinking on the job.

Shaking her head at the thought, she waited for the iron to heat hot enough and considered the moral precipice she approached. A precipice that had nothing at all to do with beer.

Nonchalant, Cade returned from the bunk house, set his bottle on one of the fence posts, and grabbed a flag. With a quick flick, he popped one of the calves on the butt and drove it down the alley where it darted into the chute as planned. He snapped the flag a couple of extra times single-handed to keep the heifer calf in the squeeze chute as he pressed the levels down.

"Who's the girl?" Emory asked, cursing herself for showing any interest at all.

Cade grinned. "Which one?"

A dismissive half-wave. "Sure hope you remember her name."

"Always do, darlin'."

Calf loaded and the squeeze locked into place, Cade deadpanned. "And to think some places even have hydraulics."

The branding iron heated up and burned red, ready to go.

Cade apparently wasn't finished. "They have electrical outlets built into the squeeze chutes, too."

"We can get that too, if we ever buy new ones," Emory snapped, knowing that day would be far distant, if at all.

Cade eyed her close, serious on the matter. "There's no turning back after this point you know."

"Bothered?" Her conscience prickled, but she smothered any misgivings back down.

It would be next to impossible to call all the fence-line neighbors that bordered the BLM land.

"I'm just the hired help, like you said." He spat out the words like tobacco juice.

"Uh-huh. That's mighty convenient. If you have any objections, state them now or forever hold your peace."

"Nope. Nothing here," he replied. "Let's get this over with. Time is a-burning."

She eyed him, and he eyed her back. Partners in crime, if nothing else.

But dammit, her pride hurt. "Am I slowing you down, getting into town?"

She earned the stink-eye by way of response.

The brand was ready to go but she stalled, taking her own sweet time. Intentionally deliberate and slow.

Cade swore under his breath.

She settled the ear tag into the puncher, inserting into the first calf's ear before shooting it up with vaccine. None of which was in the least bit damning. The tag could be removed, and the vaccine was an accepted matter of heath.

The long reach of family history pressed down as she held that heated brand against the hide; rocking it back and forth so the mark would take. The calf struggled against the rails; the familiar, putrid smell of burning hair.

In less than forty-five seconds, the operation finished solid. The first maverick released, crow-hopping out of the chute and bounding away.

The second calf proved harder to convince.

Those big brown eyes took in Cade and the flag. The heifer tried to stare the cowboy down, but when she realized that wouldn't work in her favor, she took off running.

On foot, Cade took a couple of fast strides chasing her, flag flicking and snapping. A bitten-off curse when she outfoxed him, but in the end, he got her turned into the chute.

Providing a nice wide opening for Emory to poke. "What do they say? Ground work is the foundation of everything."

"Yeah, well I didn't see you trying," Cade groused.

The process repeated itself, but without the delay of conscience this time around. One maverick branded in the eyes of the law probably carried about the same penalty as two.

Cade let the calf out of the chute, and the critter let loose with shit; timing impeccable as the muck hit one of his boots square.

Emory let a few snickers fly.

"It's not funny, Em," he warned.

"You planning on wearing those boots out tonight? They might be a bit too realistic for those tourist gals sitting at the bar."

"You need anything else?" His question came out pretty darn close to a growl.

"No," she replied smirking. "You are free to go."

5

WHEN WRONG AND PRIDE GET TANGLED

THE TV VOLUME BLARED TOO HIGH, THE EVENING NEWS belting out to her father like they'd all turned stone deaf. Sounding, for all the world, like the news played on constant repeat. Emory stood in the dirt yard and listened for a moment half-way embarrassed, but of course, no one heard other than her and Cade, if he even paid attention to things such as those. No outsider to notice that things weren't as they should be. No one to guess the dark world belonging to the Cross patriarch threatened to win.

She paused outside the screen door, noticing the weathered floorboards that needed a few good hammer whacks. Come to think of it, the wooden door frame needed a lick of paint as well. Then she took into account the gapping screen that let in biting horseflies and required mending. Shoot.

Everything, everything, everything needed repairs.

And there her father sat, plaid shirt two sizes too small, buttons playing a losing tug-of-war against the fabric, the skin of his fat belly visible, six buttons down and above his waistline. Hard to believe he'd once been a fine figure of a man. But there he now sat, slouched in his recliner with stuffing oozed out in cotton tufts and the room darkened against the outside world.

The only consolation Emory could find being that gloom hid the dirt far better than prying sunlight.

The TV flickered and the reception came through ghost-like and shadowy.

The head of the ranch, a bloated ghost of his former self, made his way through his sixth approximate can of beer, judging from the empties jumbled around. No money for cable, but plenty of money to piss away for booze. He didn't even bother to meet her eyes.

"How many'd you bring in?"

Emory didn't remove her boots but tracked around the mud and manure like her father. Like anyone else who ever entered as of late. What the hell, that floor hadn't seen a mop in months. The Lost Daughter remained a staunchly *working* ranch. Working meant plenty of dirt and manure to go around.

"Ten of ours, and two mavericks. Branded them already and turned them loose in the upper pasture."

His bleary eyes registered that last piece of information. "That a fact?"

"Two angus, just like ours. Nothing remarkable about them. Ran into a fisherman on the way back. A tourist."

A flash. "Huh. They don't know their asses from their elbows."

Her father sounded confident, but nothing felt certain. That tourist might be an investigator of some type, or maybe she was just turning paranoid. "For the most part, you might be right."

She eyed him. "You know, chasing strays is more than a two-person job. Don't suppose you'd consider riding out with us tomorrow…"

A half-snarl. "When I want your opinion, I'll ask. Now, who else knows about the branding?"

"Cade."

He cocked his head in a reluctant way, not completely sold on any of the proceedings. "Keep an eye on him, and don't fall for any of his bullshit."

Emory reared back. "You're the ranch boss. What do you want *me* to do?"

"And here I always thought you was a smart girl. I mean, he's too smooth for his own good. Whatever he's up to better not mean you."

The TV flickered images from the rest of the world. Images that didn't apply.

"It's not like there are a whole parade of men to choose from out here," Emory grumbled.

For a moment she swore her old man softened, but that brick wall went right back up.

"Find a good worker…someone who is not too enterprising. We need new blood to keep this place running and that part is down to you."

"Maybe one day I'll just up and move away." She floated that notion by at least once a month, but nothing would come of it.

"Not without my permission you won't," he snarled, but it came across as tired. Like everything else.

His reaction never varied. She'd mention the possibility of leaving, he'd slap it down, and so the challenge went. Time and time again. Truthfully, more than anything, she didn't want to be an outcast for the rest of her life. But that would mean trying her luck in the wider world and seeing if the shadow hanging above her family name lifted. Of course, she had nowhere else to go. Her desire might have been there, but she chose her words to get a rise out of her father. To prove that he still cared about something, anything. Well, he still cared about his perceived authority. An authority proving anemic, if nothing else. But he would fend off challenges, even from his TV chair if needed. At least fifty pounds overweight and counting, his time might not be long in coming before a heart attack struck him down dead.

"Fresh air would do you some good," she said.

"Bullshit," he replied.

Beyond the window, across the holding pens and the pastures, the towering shadowed mountains stood guard. Not purple, but *blue*. Maybe even slate. Yes, slate described the color. The dusk even managed to soften the sorry state of the outbuildings, shadows grown long and blurring the edges. The waning sun illuminated the barn's roof as the evening scaled the walls, but its reaching radiance mellowed and drained down into a golden hue. Like everything else, that gold would soon get spent, swallowed up by the hour. Swallowed up by the dense velvet darkness of night.

She stopped mooning about. Ranches didn't run on moon shadows and fairy dust. Casting a critical eye over the here-and-now, the barn, for the most part, remained sound. Sound might have been a bit of a stretch. Make that serviceable by the Lost Daughter standards instead.

The battered old bunk house burrowed down in a slight depression, a structure little more than an old rail-road car with dirt packed up against the edges. Still, it provided four walls with two tiny windows cut in as an afterthought. The window frames had boards nailed on for decoration. Probably the work of some long-since departed cowboy, bored out of his mind on any given day or year. A stovepipe poked through the roof and listed askew. A roof that kept most of the elements at bay.

At least *she* hadn't heard about it leaking.

She turned to her father, half-way and in profile. "And here I thought you'd be pleased there's two more head to add to the tally."

A grumbled, "You done good, all right?"

That would have to count as praise, no matter how grudgingly given.

"But no," he went on, "I ain't roundin' up cattle for you. I've spent enough years doing that shit. I'm just going to stay behind in headquarters here and see that everything runs right. Problem with that?"

More words strung together than he usually bothered, that discourse counted as darn near a speech. Still, he turned nasty if pressed too hard. Badgering, he called it.

And Emory knew enough not to badger.

"No, no problem," she said, backing down and figuring to pick her battles. There was no sense in kicking the bear, even if the bear actually had it coming. She'd ride the line, and so would Cade. Only two riders meant more trips would be required to round up the herd, track the strays and bring them all back into the pasture.

They weren't given a choice, or another option.

"Any particular reason why we're moving the cattle off the BLM land that I should know about?"

"Nope," came the expected reply.

She had her suspicions but held them close.

Those suspicions would involve getting into deeper waters than where she already swam.

Half of her wanted out, in no uncertain terms.

The other half figured she was exactly right where she belonged.

6

THE REFRIGERATOR
PROPHECY

EMORY REMOVED THE PLASTIC TRAY FROM ITS CARDBOARD box and slid the frozen dinner into the microwave, setting the power on high.

"I bought one of those family sizes," she called out to her father, who couldn't have cared less. "Macaroni and cheese."

"Bring me a beer," he replied.

Breathing out a sigh, she considered the refrigerator purchased sometime in the early nineties. A hulking big white rectangle marked up, banged around and generally ill-used on occasion. The top freezer needed defrosting. Funny how that relic from the last century still kept on working, plugging along with an industrious, misplaced hum. A half-chuckle recalling the memory of her grandmother's wonky, yet astute, advice:

Most women put more thought into the refrigerator they want to buy, than into the man they're going to marry.

There might be something to that notion after all.

Amusement fading, her mother might have heeded

the warning had she ever heard of such a notion, but her paternal grandmother had delivered that piece of advice. A woman definitely and squarely in the enemy camp, as her mother once saw it. The feeling ran mutual as far as Emory could tell. Likely her father had gotten the worse end of that deal, but apparently the topic of 'refrigerator suitability' proved only a one-way instruction. Grandma never once considered that men might have need of the durability talk, too.

Emory embodied the living result of that particular refrigerator purchase and didn't want to dwell on any of that ancient history. None of the hard feelings were worth resurrecting anyhow.

She pulled out a beer, noticing the dirt embedded beneath her fingernails. Delivering the Coors with a helping of disapproval on the side, she held the bottle by the neck and stuck out the bottom toward him. Condensation rolling.

Her timing into the front room coincided with Cade's bunkhouse departure—visible through the window and all spruced up, swaggering over to his dark blue Ford. All male, plenty of fine and fancy and having someplace to go.

The comparison between the two of them and their situations struck as pronounced and unfair. Him going out for a good time and a meal in town, while she remained stuck standing there in a sweat-stained, dirty faded shirt delivering a sweaty beer to a man who'd already had too many. Expecting nothing more exciting than a flipping microwave dinner after working hard all day long.

That wasn't all. The TV might be on loud, but not loud enough to drown out the sound of Cade getting into his blue pick-up truck, turning the radio on full-blast and peeling out of the yard.

Sure. Bound for the Ace-Hi, he had plenty of places in town to hang his hat. Not to mention his tight-seated jeans. All of which amounted to plenty of beds to stick his boots under.

"You planning on sitting at the table to eat?" She asked her father.

"In here," he grumbled, never once taking his eyes off the TV screen.

Taken for granted as a ranch hand that he didn't even have to pay was the obvious conclusion in the situation. Two ranch hands for a ten-thousand acre spread that needed more.

"You might say 'please'," she chastened.

That time he looked at her and looked at her full. Beer-eyes red and glaring.

"I might say a lot of things," he growled.

Yeah. And so could she.

The tap in the kitchen sink kept on slow drip, drip, dripping. A rust brown streak stained the avocado green enamel, travelling from where the faucet dribbled down to the drain. A constant assault that a wrench and a new washer might fix, but that struck as damned unlikely to occur. But outside the window above that dripping sink, the landscape unfurled in full glory. The sinking sun spangled the sky in techno-colored brush strokes—gold set against the draining blue, all cast in a backlit glow. For the briefest of moments, the world showed bright inspiration edged with hope. Like life in the west, however, the night gathered around the edges as the sun sank lower and the green grass faded darker and darker still. The cattle lowed, calling to one another as the final rays dipped behind the jagged mountains. The west-facing cliffs remained in the gentling light, standing sentry to the last. Holding the line.

Those rimrock fortresses guarded their way of life. The horse thieves and the outlaws who brushed shoulders alongside her ancestors must have felt that stirring, deep within and strong.

So, apparently, did the outsiders with money to spend.

She watched the light die out. Tomorrow would dawn, come hell or high water.

Discomfort needled as she turned to go to bed, pressing the antique light switch that had never once been updated since the nineteen-tens. A single, hanging bulb on a chain illuminated the stairs. Venturing down the narrow hallway, the naked walls came across as stained and dingy, as likely they were. Bare feet on a bare wooden floor, Emory dodged splinters in the thin slatted yellow pine, worn and wearing out from worry and time. The bathroom stood at the end of the hall. There the yellow pine succumbed to a rust-colored linoleum improvement, and one that almost covered the whole floor. It might have been fine if it hadn't been cut short, missing length to line up the edges flush against the walls.

But the original antique clawfoot tub remained good —nice and deep after a hard day's work.

The commode replete with an overhead water tank operated by an old, verdigris chain lorded over the room. She soaped up her hands and splashed her face in the chipped pedestal sink. Meeting her eyes in the mirror—hazel flecked gold—she tried to peer inside her life, searching for a clue. Same as every morning and night in fact, doing that same old routine. Unusually, she stared deep into her eyes for a long moment and wondered what lurked on the horizon. And the answer usually came back the same.

Not much of anything at all.

MORNING ROSE faint in the eastern sky, and she awoke without an alarm, the same as any other morning.

But this time, she snapped awake. Those two calves waited.

They were something new. A little bit too new, but there was no turning back. Not that she even wanted to. She'd slip out and feed them milk replacement by bottle or bucket.

Right after she got the coffee started.

Hopefully, Cade had made his way back to the bunkhouse in one piece. His private life ran akin to a car accident, the type that you couldn't help but stare at. She'd do her best not to ask. But if she did, she wondered what his offered lie might be. This day, this time.

Hell. Maybe he'd feel like living dangerously and even tell her the truth.

Maybe they were both dead set against honesty like everyone else, living and dead, at the Lost Daughter.

Her father snored in his room past the time when serious ranchers were already up and about handling chores. She caught a glimpse of him through the crack of his bedroom door, flat on his back and mouth gaped wide. His rounded stomach rising and falling with each rattling breath.

She didn't linger long.

A tender-hearted revulsion rose up—a feeling that had no easy answers.

The morning rolled around as expected, pale streaks

of light fingering the eastern horizon. The sky brightening at first a dove gray before turning into a watered-down piss yellow. Pale starts were a prelude. A prelude until the heavens above pulled their act together and settled into a vivid, searing blue bolder than the clouds that faded.

7

ANYTHING CAN HAPPEN
TUESDAY

EVERY TWO-TRACK TOWN HAD A BANK STANDING ON A corner, a hardware store, a barbershop, a laundromat and whatever might reasonably pass as a grocery store. All with varying degrees of success. And every one of these Jack-and-Diane towns boasted a dark watering hole. Bearing the description of *bar* or *tavern*—writing slapped across its front or hoisted atop up a jerry-rigged pole, like a tribal flag flying its colors—it purpose spelled out clear to make sure that no one entertained the wrong idea.

Those signs, monikers, or what-have-yous, sure did the trick and lured people in. Cade Timmons was a card-carrying member of the bar dwelling fraternity.

Emory's own experience remained fairly limited, but she knew how the bar's front door stood propped open during the bright light of day in some sort of dark come-on. Everyone who passed by, took a quick glimpse into the overcast world that ensnared the shiftless, defied the hour, and heaven only knew what else. The bar stench spilled out and tumbled a ways down the sidewalk with a singular fragrance of beer-sodden carpeting, stale cigarettes, and Copenhagen chaw. Known as the Ace-Hi in their locale, the clientele sure didn't come across as riding on any winning streak.

Everyone in Stampede knew the people who frequented that place in the daytime hours. The pale and ropey hardcore drinkers—men whose sweating beer bottles rolled beads of condensation the left rings upon the bar's scarred counter. The kind that smoked endless cigarettes and bitched about the State of the Union pretending they might actually do something about it. Cowboys too lame to work, old men whose wives had up and left them one way or another, and those spending their government issued checks, all hopeless at the core.

Women didn't go in there much. Not, at least, during the day. Only one or two skinny old women sporting elaborate hairdos left-over from the 1950's. Eyes faded from heartache and faces wrinkled from cigarettes. Just lonely fixtures seated at the bar, nursing amaretto sours and chain smoking.

'No smoking' laws be damned—they didn't apply to patrons such as those.

Of course, Cade frequented that place.

Usually after working hours. But she wouldn't put it past him to sneak out, if he could get away with it, before the day's work ended.

Emory stood leaning against one of her house's porch posts, thinking about the Ace-Hi and wondering when Cade would make a break for it, like he did at the end of most days.

She didn't have to wait long.

Cade came springing out of the bunkhouse that used to house five men. "Going' into town," he shouted with a preemptive wave, not inviting her to go along.

She would have cramped his style.

Cade peeled out of the ranch in his pickup truck, country music thumping and twanging and windows rolled down. No doubt headed for the Ace-Hi.

Her father slumped in his chair; passed out and not poised to come around any time soon.

Well, what the hell, Emory thought. She had a car, too.

Quietly and without commotion, she eased upstairs and put her mascara on.

Ready to go out, checkin' up on Cade.

———

She pulled into an empty spot along Main street and parked, her white knuckles gripping the steering wheel, rigid. From that vantage point she had a fine view of what surely passed as an evening on the town. Neon signs flashed and beckoned, drawing in customers like miller moths to bright lights. The town's loose change arrived on foot or by car. A steady stream of customers unable to resist the flashing Coors signs, succumbed to the come-hither that wasn't all that seductive when she bothered to analyze it.

She had her misgivings.

"Are you just going to sit here," Emory said aloud, "or are you going to go on in?"

A smart girl would turn right around and go back to the ranch before something couldn't be taken back.

But like a dang miller moth, she felt drawn to bright lights or flames. Not smart enough to stay away from danger in any case, because she stepped out of her truck and straggled toward those fricking neon bar signs.

The jukebox belted out *Crazy* by Patsy Cline.

Yep, the lyrics sized up the situation pretty close.

Boot-toeing an outside wooden post, she pretended to be taking in the night air. *What kind of desperate would she come across as, going in there all by herself?*

The kind of desperate that proved she didn't have any friends to speak of, and she had no way of dressing that one up.

She'd been inside the Ace-Hi before but hadn't stuck around all that long. She'd left almost as soon as she had arrived that first time for the simple reason that nothing within held her interest. Not for any length of time. On that last go-round, she certainly hadn't been tracking anyone. Funny how time had a way of mixing things up in a torch-light twang.

Patsy Cline singing her heart out like it had already broken into two.

Stomach tightening and nerves jangling, she took a breath and ventured on inside. The music pounded out loud, the laughter and shouted conversations even louder. She lingered by the door a second or two longer than she should have.

Immediately, plenty of attention flowed in her direction. The term *fresh meat* ran through her mind, but maybe she simply flattered herself. It remained within the realm of possibility, that no one thought anything about her at all.

The bartender glanced up when she approached the bar for lack of a better plan.

"Hey there, Emory. What brings you in?"

The question came from a guy named Jeff. They'd been in high school together. He hadn't made it too far.

What the hell. Neither had she.

A half-shouldered shrug to hide the secret relief that she knew someone to speak to. "Nothing much. Just bored, I guess. How about a glass of white wine?"

He reared back a bit, startled. Remembering his place, he reached down to the refrigerator underneath the counter and pulled out a large green gallon jug. "We've got this here, but it's probably worse than the swill my parents used to drink. Masons, or something like that."

She eyed the jug, knowing he was right. Anything coming from a bottle that big probably amounted to swill. "What else do you have, other than beer?"

Relieved, he put that jug away right quick.

"Hard Lemonade, one of those Claw things, cider…"

"Whatever you suggest." She didn't have an arsenal of options prepared. With an inward cringe, she realized she might have planned that part out just a bit better.

"Depends on what you like." Jeff waited, ignoring her lack of barroom couth.

"I'll take a cider," she said.

She didn't happen in there for the alcohol, but she'd never admit as much. That would lead to questions, and questions might be difficult in the circumstances.

He pulled a bottle out of a cooler, twisted off the top and set the concoction down in front of her. "You don't usually come in here."

"As you've already said. That might tend to put your customers off; it seems like you don't think they should be here."

"Well, shoot, Emory. That's not what I meant and you know it. Just making conversation." A troubled expression. "Shoot."

Trying not to come across as obvious, she eyed the crowd. Plenty of cowboy hats to go around. Plenty of cowboy hats to block the view.

She reached for her back pocket to pull out the twenty she had waiting there. "On the house," he said, when he saw where her hand was going.

"You own this place?"

"Nah," he said. "My uncle does."

"How'd he feel about you giving the profits away like that?"

Jeff screwed up his face, disgusted. "Fine, if you want to be that way. Five dollars." He held out his hand and she gave him her twenty.

He counted out the change in a ten and five ones.

"Guess you expect a tip," she said, pocketing the bills.

"You're a strange one, even if you are kind of cute," he drawled in a foregone conclusion. Relieved to move off when some other customer called.

Hell. She'd never been too good at small talk anyhow.

She took a swig, and the hard cider didn't taste half bad. Still, there was no reason to go hog wild.

About forty people milled around inside that bar, and as the crowd shifted, she located Cade almost at once. There he presided in all his glory, surrounded by three girls in one of the back Naugahyde booths. To make matters worse, he wasn't just sitting there, hands front and center and wrapped around a beer bottle. Oh, no. He draped his arms across the back of that booth, brushing against the shoulders of one or the other blondes. Blondes who pressed into his side, batting their long false eyelashes and flirting.

Damn near close to buckle bunnies.

All having big, dumb cow eyes and plenty of peroxide hair, long fingernails and rhinestones to go around. Sure as shootin' they were tourists, or the next closest thing. They might even have been from Denver.

Obviously, Cade didn't act like one of those door scanners; and why should he? He had his attention completely occupied, and the entertainment seated at his table. For the briefest of moments, she considered disrupting the party. But what would that even prove?

Well, hell.

She didn't have to make up her mind right then and there. So, as an afterthought, she turned back to Jeff, but he had moved about serving others. Besides, she'd kind of been rude to him.

Hard to play nice when she'd already blown up the bridge.

She pulled out a barstool and took a seat, pretending a fascination with the rows of liquor bottles all lit up and glowing.

An attractive display, she supposed, in a tawdry way.

"Hi there," a male voice said coming up alongside her. "You here on your own?"

Emory frowned. "See anyone else seated here?"

The stranger laughed. "Kind of salty, aren't ya? It doesn't seem like you frequent bars much."

"Is that so? Well, no. No, I don't." She eyed him up and down. Kind of cute in a pushy sort of way.

"You're here tonight, so I guess it must be my good luck. Can I buy you another drink?"

Emory tipped back her bottle, and dang if he wasn't right. Empty. That had gone down a bit too fast.

"Sure, why not. Seeing as how it's 'Anything Can Happen Tuesday.'"

He laughed and raised his finger to get Jeff's attention. "Another cider for this young lady, and I'll take a whiskey."

"Ten dollars," Jeff replied.

The stranger gave him a ten and didn't leave a tip. But then again, neither had she.

He hadn't offered a name, and he wasn't from around there. That much was for damn sure. And he stared her in the face, too close to exactly be polite. "How'd you get that scar under your lip?"

Startled, she hadn't remembered thin line until just then. "I took a header off of a bike in high school and bit through my lip."

"Ouch. And here I thought it might have had something to do with horses."

"Nah," Emory shook her head. "A rutted dirt road, a friend's mountain bike, and a caught tire. Nothing more exciting than that."

"Well, I find it sexy." He smirked.

"You ain't from around here, are you?" She already knew the answer.

The flash of disappointment. "How could you tell?"

"We all know most everyone nearby. That, and your boots are too shiny and your jeans are too new."

His mouth took a downward turn.

"Now I see why you're sitting by yourself," he said, leaning against the bar like he owned the place. Handsome, too. He knew it. They *always* knew.

Emory took a sip of the cider. Beamed at him while glancing back at Cade.

"Is that your boyfriend?"

"No," she replied, a little too slow to sound convincing. "Just a ranch hand. I wondered what he was up to, and now I guess I've got my answer."

Uncertain, the stranger stared back at Cade. "Would you say he's good-looking?"

That took her back. "I would say he is." A pause. "Do *you* think he is good-looking?"

A bitter laugh. "I'm not gay, if that's what you are asking. I am interested in *you*." He threw his whiskey back and signaled for another.

Jeff poured him a drink. "Five dollars."

Again, the exact change offered. He turned his intent upon Emory and moved closer, pulling himself up tall to make her feel small; the way men did when physically trying to impress. "You're better off without him, I'd say. He seems to like bar-flies."

None of which made her feel any better.

"Hey," the stranger leaned in. "Do you want to leave this place and go get something to eat?"

"Everything's closed," she answered, taking a swig.

"Well then, how about coming back to my hotel or I'll come home with you. Don't tell me that you're not trying to pick me up."

She thought she misheard. "I'm trying to pick *you* up? I'm not trying to pick up anyone. I'm just here having a drink and trying to figure out what our ranch hand is up to. Like I said, and nothing more."

"Well, you let me buy you that drink…"

"So what," she asked, voice cold and sharp. "And you didn't even leave a tip. Short on cash?"

"Why you little bitch…"

He grabbed her arm and tried to pull her up to her feet—tried to kiss her.

She slapped him, the open-palmed crack against flesh sounding for all the world like a whip. That sure captured everyone's attention in nothing flat.

Before she knew exactly what happened, someone picked her up and moved her three feet to the side in nothing flat. *Cade.* And he stood between her and the tourist, squaring off.

"Don't you lay a hand on her, or you'll be picking your teeth up off the floor."

Cade reached out behind and pushed her further out of the way.

Jeff came out from around the bar. "We don't want

any trouble in here, you two." His eyes darted between Cade and the tourist, and back again. "Everyone going to play nice?"

The tourist's color burned high, and he looked like he might take a swing.

"Just being friendly," he claimed.

Cade, for his part, came across equally offended, and maybe even more so. The tendons and veins on the insides of his arms stuck out, taut as wire.

One of the blondes chose that moment to sidle up to the group. "Cade, I thought you wanted to sit with us."

He ignored her. "You OK here, Emory?"

"I can take care of myself, you know." Her words sounded rather dim, given the circumstances.

Cade took her by the elbow while the blonde pouted, sidelined. "You just get in your truck and go straight home. Do you hear me?"

He sure acted in his element.

"I'm leaving," Emory said. "Your admirers are waiting, and I don't want to get in the way of whatever it is that you've got going on there."

True enough, the blonde still lingered at Cade's elbow.

"Are you coming, Cade?" Her question came out like more of a pout and a purr.

Distracted, Cade stood up taller out of instinct, but stared down at Emory. "In a minute, darling. This here is someone I know: the boss' daughter."

Emory, deciding everything was turning stupid, headed for the door.

"Everyone count your money!" Someone called out, and snickers followed.

Yeah, she knew what they were talking about. Her father'd been accused of short-changing on a cash-only deal.

Which reminded her, she had forgotten to leave a tip.

Returning to the bar rail, she put three dollars on to the counter.

She glared at the table where the insult originated; a group of four locals huddled together, cracking themselves up at her expense.

Well, what the hell. She told herself that she didn't care, but in truth, it stung.

To the sound of Cheap Trick blaring out, she left. What kind of cowboy bar had the Ace-Hi turned into, anyhow?

A pretty shitty one, she thought.

That, at least, made her feel better.

8

MESSAGES FROM THE SPIRIT WORLD

EMORY SAT IN HER TRUCK FOR A LONG, HARD MOMENT FOR her nerves to quit jangling and her mind to stop racing. What was Cade to her, anyhow?

She watched the Coors sign blink on and off, on and off

Emory stuck her key in the ignition but sat back in the seat, contemplating.

Watching people come and people go—slightly rubber-kneed and soft around the edges. Others stumbling out and worse for the wear. Cade sure didn't bother to leave his bevy of blondes to come out chasing after her.

Guess he figured he'd done enough on her behalf.

An unknown girl rushed out and plopped down on the curb, crying. The saddest part of all came down to the fact that no one came rushing out for her either.

Not one blessed person cared enough to even saunter out for either of them.

Emory eyed the girl figuring it none of her business, but she kept watching all the same.

From her vantage point of the truck's interior, the girl didn't come across as entirely drunk. That measure of composure added weight to the scales of Emory's opinion, tilting in favor of the crying tourist.

Hard to say why Emory didn't just drive off like she ought to have done, but against her better judgement she pulled the key from the ignition, stepped back out of the truck and approached.

"You OK?"

Mascara ran down the girl's face in rivulets. She used both hands to swipe at the black streaks. Efforts that didn't help the mascara situation any.

"Do I look OK to you?"

Emory offered a half-shrug, a gesture snagged somewhere between a lie and the truth. "Well, your mascara is making a bit of a mess. You crying over a guy?"

"Yeah. What else could it ever be?"

"Don't know," Emory admitted. Gauging her from the corner of her eye and trying to be gentle. "Maybe the booze and the altitude are hitting you hard. It happens up here, you know."

The girl didn't need any more encouragement than that.

"I'm not a lightweight," she replied, like that made any difference to what Emory thought. "I had what turned out to be a one-night stand with a cowboy in there, but I didn't know that at the time. Stupid me, I thought it was more to it, but I was wrong. Especially seeing as how he's sitting with three other chicks. I have half a mind to go back in there and tell him what I think."

Dang nabbit—that description sure fit Cade.

Emory pretended to consider the deserted street, stalling for time. Trying to decide upon the best course of action.

The dark mountains beyond stayed silent and offered no easy solutions. They seldom ever did, and that remained the everlasting truth.

In the end, Emory decided to give the girl a bit of respect, already knowing the answer. "You new in town?"

"Not exactly," she sniffed. "Just visiting. Guess I was pretty stupid, falling like that. My Colorado cowboy. What a crock. Think he sleeps with tourists all the time? He said I was special."

Emory took a half step closer, sizing up the girl slumped on the curb, dramatic black streaks coming across like either war paint or something in a horror movie.

Take your pick, a voice replied inside her brain. But saying anything of the kind wouldn't help. Rude at best, or words for fighting at the worst. Emory cursed inside, mad at the situation and even madder at Cade.

The door to the Ace Hi opened and music spilled out into the night, muting back down as the door swung shut. The only game in town, and a crooked one at that.

Towering over a half-drunk and broken-hearted tourist in the street hadn't been her plan starting out that evening.

The girl's heart would mend in a week. Once she returned back home, where ever that might be.

"Don't suppose his name was Cade, was it?"

Her blue eyes widened. "Oh, please. Don't tell me you're his girlfriend." She struggled to her feet, eyes glued to Emory's face.

"No," Emory replied, gut twisting. "I'm his employer."

The girl blinked a couple of times.

"You're kind of young," was she all came up with.

"Don't let that fool you." Emory eyed the girl back.

A thought gleamed through her distress. "So, if you're the boss, why don't you just fire him?"

"On account of him leading girls on? No, good help is hard to find out here. And, although he might be an asshole, Cade is good at what he does."

The girl didn't appear convinced. "So that's what you call it. You know, I get the feeling that he's dealing."

That got Emory's attention, straight up. "Dealing?"

"Drugs."

"What kind of drugs?"

The girl shrugged. "How would I know? He passed along a small packet the other night to some guy, and the guy gave him folded up money in return. Doesn't that strike you like drugs?"

Her words sank like a stone. To make matters even worse, that tourist gal probably had no real reason to lie.

"Well," Emory said, edging away, "I've got to go. You gonna be OK?"

The girl nodded, head hug low. Still, she waved one hand over her head. Conversation concluded, and outcome unclear.

Whatever the case, that night sure felt like one for the books.

Darkness fell heavy and black on the drive back to the ranch, away from the dim and fading town lights. Literature tended to extol 'bright lights', but that's not how it worked out there.

Emory turned on the radio and let the night wind blow in, smelling of mowed green hay and of late summer nights. Innocent and wholesome and deceptive.

Deceptive like Cade.

Rounding a bend and driving too fast, a pair of amber colored eyes glistened straight in front of the truck. Right smack-dab in the center of the road.

Slamming on the brakes, Emory jerked forward hard and almost hit her head on the steering wheel. A coyote loped off into the land of night and shadows beyond.

Coyotes, in their part of the world, could be taken as warnings. That's what some of the regional tribes thought, and she wondered if they were right.

This time, she fastened her seatbelt and checked it. Just to be on the safe side. She didn't want one of those drunk driving signs put up along the wayside in her memory. While she might not be drunk, the dead had trouble defending themselves and their reputations.

She might have gone straight through that windshield.

Shaken and heart racing, she turned the radio off and continued on her way. But slower, and now erring toward caution. Watching straight ahead and scanning the sides of the road. Hands on the wheel and eyes on the road, driving like an old woman.

Other Native Americans considered coyotes as tricksters. She'd picked up those nuggets somewhere along the line, again wondering. Looking for clues where there weren't any. That particular coyote might have carried a specific message for her, a message she couldn't decipher.

Cade proved tricky all right.

With that inevitable conclusion, she turned onto the ranch road toward the house. The yard lights clicked on as Emory pulled up in front; the blue light from the TV still glowed and flickered in the living room.

Cade's bunkhouse stood empty and dark, and likely would stay that way until morning light.

Shaking her head, a serious dilemma had presented itself. Should she tell her father what she'd heard? Then she'd have to explain she'd been at the Ace-Hi, trailing Cade around. But what the hell, she was twenty-three.

The night hadn't cooled all the way off yet, the air warm as she approached the screen door.

Emory figured she'd tell her father and face the round of unwelcomed questions.

Stepping inside the screen door she paused, realizing no confidences would be exchanged that night, and that she'd worried for nothing. Her father sprawled passed-out and snoring in his recliner as the television droned on.

Her father travelled down a bad path, no lie.

But his passed-out condition gave her time and space to decide.

Upstairs in her room with the sickly green walls, she closed the door behind her and looked at nothing much. *Nothing much* summed up that entire room, possessions and perhaps even her life to date. Even her furniture was second hand—her grandmother's, a double bed and matching battered dresser and a cast-off chair summed it up. At least she had books and a few perfume bottles to place on top of that dresser. Her girlhood horse posters stared down from the same green walls. She didn't have the heart to take them down, although they felt very girlish for someone aged twenty-three.

More immediately, her clothes stank like smoke and beer, although technically no smoking was allowed in the Ace-Hi.

A shower was the best option she had going, so she high-tailed it down the hallway and into the bathroom and returned ten minutes later, hair dripping.

She slipped into bed anyways, picked up Zane Grey as the coyotes yipped in the dark. Prose so purple (ignoring the sage debacle, which she couldn't entirely) that she almost choked. Boy howdy, that man sure liked the color purple. In fact, it sure seemed he only recognized that singular color. Purple this, and purple that. Likely he never imagined that one day his prose would be deemed purple, too.

The novel opened to the hapless female Jane Withersteen begging to prevent her hired man from being killed by a Mormon elder named Tull.

Emory immediately decided that the woman must not have owned a gun. If she had, the story would have turned out a whole lot shorter.

Nevertheless, the hired man named Venters verged on a whipping or getting strung up from the nearest cottonwood, but the woman pleads, begs and goes all helpless in the process. At which point the fearsome gunman Lassiter arrives.

She stopped.

How did Cade see her?

Inexperienced but with a large, land rich inheritance? Few would deny the clout of the legacy ranch. Then again, few locals were willing to take on the long shadow of its history.

Emory stuffed those misgivings right back down, but that didn't mean such questions didn't require asking.

Just—not—now.

Concerned about the man passed out downstairs, she recalled how he once enjoyed *Riders of the Purple Sage* or any other western when he bothered to read. He used to read nighttime stories to her when she was nothing more than a slip of a girl. Before her mother absconded. Come to think of it, Emory hadn't seen a book in his hand in a few years—other than ranch accounts.

And those, not often enough.

She turned back to the pages in front of her. But that

overly floral prose got to her in the end.

More impossible and romanticized bullshit, no matter how much money Miss Jane Withersteen reportedly had.

The old men who ran the local museum swore to the fact that Zane Grey spent one summer in Stampede. He took a room in the local hotel, and reportedly chased some athletic heiress around the range. They insisted, those old men, that his saddle remained displayed in the museum barn along with plenty of other saddles. Mr. *Pearl* Zane Grey's didn't boast any sign or indicator.

Once again, the legend left everything up to interpretation.

And where was Emory's Lassiter or Venters when she needed one? Sure as hell, he didn't frequent the Ace-Hi. Or if he did, she might be further ahead just leaving him there where he rotted.

She cast the book aside and drifted to the window. The mountains stood out black against the deep midnight blue. The sky and stars twinkled sharp and clear like cold blue diamonds. A rustler's moon that cast enough light to get the job done.

She leaned against the window frame and stared out at the night beyond and listened to the coyotes in the distance. The cattle called to each other, low and easy.

And she wondered what the world held in store for the likes of her: able to see the beauty and argumentative enough to challenge what passed as fine literature.

One thing stood out clear. Life out in Rimrock County hid the blade of a knife, sharp and glinting. It was deadly beneath the surface.

Some of those lumps in the prairie attested to that fact. A hard-gained knowledge paid for with their lives.

Final resting places forgotten. One hell of a thing.

9

REPPING THE HERD

Of course, her father still slept it off in his bedroom. Somehow, he'd navigated the stairs in the middle of the night, and Emory took it for a good job that he hadn't broken his drunken fool neck along the way.

Ready before either of the men, Emory marked Cade as he eventually emerged from the barn, horse loosely saddled and headed for one of the hitching posts. There, he fussed with the saddle ties, back toward her.

"Cade?" Her voice called out low and soft.

Nothing.

Frowning and more forceful this time, her tone cut through the distance. "*Cade.*"

Stiffening, he turned around acting like his thoughts had lassoed him. "Sorry, Em. I was miles away."

"Hungover?"

Cade's light blue eyes sized her up. "Not even, but you look sour. Something got you riled?"

A cold, long-eyed stare cast in his direction should,

by rights, have made him squirm. But if it did the trick, he didn't exactly show it.

"What time did you get in?"

"Seems that you ought to be thanking me," he claimed in that sing-song way of his. "And when I got in is none of your business, darlin'."

She stiffened. "That guy was drunk."

A half-laugh. "That don't matter much. A drunk man can do harm. That all just goes to prove you're plenty green in such matters."

Too green for him, he meant.

Green wasn't exactly what she aimed at. At the very least, it made it seem like something was wrong with her.

To make matters worse, he eyed her close. Too close and studying her reaction.

"It's still a free country," she argued. "And just because I don't pick up guys in bars, doesn't mean anything more than I have better taste."

"Whatever you say," he smirked.

"I only popped in there because *someone* made mention of the tourist string you had going."

"So you were checking up on me?"

He'd already guessed as much, but the way he said it made her color.

Seeing no sense in lying, no matter how he took it, she offered the unvarnished truth. "Yes."

"And what *exactly* did you see?"

"I saw three bleached blondes and a girl who's now thinking about bleaching her hair, too. I can't help but wonder you have to talk to those girls about; what you say to them. Sure hope you aren't talking about cowboying over here."

He eyed her straight. "I talk about cowboying in

general. They really seem to go for that. You know, those women have more money than you and I will see in a lifetime of running cattle around. Cash money. Not this. Not acre money." He gestured around at the mountains, but she knew what he meant.

"You have a date with one of those bottle blondes?" Emory hated herself for asking, but the words burst out and couldn't be taken aback.

"As a matter of fact," he crooned at her, "I had one. All night long."

"Spare me the details," she chided.

"Oh, I don't kiss and tell," he lied.

Sure enough, he did. Time and time again.

She cocked an eye, tilted her head and stared at him. Hoping he caught the disdain she most certainly felt.

Predictably, he found her reaction amusing and perhaps a shade toward desperate.

Cade and Emory were already saddled up and heading back out to the BLM land by 7:30. Passing through the back gate for the second day in a row, Kai's steady gait remained comforting even if her world teetered on edge. Duty was one of those words that meant different things at different levels.

"You know what we're doing this for?" Cade tossed the question over his shoulder once he let her catch up.

True, she could put Kai into a lope, but she didn't. Not without a reason.

"Because he told us to," she stated.

She had a fair inkling of the real reason further in, but it was none of Cade's concern. Instead, she toyed with mentioning the topic of pot growing, meth usage and opioid distribution. She would shy away from the accusation of drug dealing. For the time being.

As an alternative, she offered something that might

partially smooth things over. "The least he could do is help run the ranch."

Cade snickered and shifted in his saddle. "Guess he don't have to. Not with you on hand."

Beyond the seemingly idle griping, Cade normally didn't question much because it flat-out made no difference to him. Maybe he had his drugs stashed somewhere on the BLM land. That would be preferable, all things considered.

Hickeys paled in comparison to the trouble drug dealing would kick off if the accusations were true.

"You good at growing things, Cade?"

Again, he shifted in his saddle and offered a strange expression, like she'd turned dingy on a dime.

"You mean hay? It grows itself. You know that."

"No flowers, huh?" She eyed the back of his shirt and those shoulders.

He waved that question off like a horse fly. "I don't give girls flowers, Em. Is that what you're thinking? Shoot fire. See? You are green. Just like I told you. Only saps spend money on flowers. Whiskey does the trick so much better."

Yeah. Probably in his world, it did.

THE MORNING BREEZE reeled down from the mountains, setting the cottonwoods and coyote willows to flashing and their silver underbellies to shining. The shining silver underbellies which reminded her of coins, and led to her thinking about serious money, or the lack thereof. Riding left plenty of time for thinking, especially when the cattle proved elusive. All of which meant Emory had plenty of time to consider what Cade was up to.

Perhaps even more puzzling, why her father ignored the cowhand's shortcomings.

She sensed trouble afoot in the currents flowing around her but couldn't quite pin it down with any certainly. Just vague notions swirling.

Cade was chasing tourists, one way or another. The likelihood that his actions boiled down to money likely claimed a large role, and none of it good.

"I heard on the NPR how rural America has got a drug problem. Opioids."

A half-hearted shrug that meant he cared less.

She pressed ahead. "You know those meth-heads with the gas pump?"

"Beanie and Dave," he snorted. "Hell, I don't even know what their last names are. Don't care, neither."

"You buy your gas from them?" That might explain a few things.

"Sometimes. They're cheaper. What are you on about today, anyhow?"

"Well, they're part of an epidemic," Emory claimed, sounding sanctimonious even to her own ear.

Cade snorted again, unsympathetic. "Yeah. Of their own making."

"They might say they were just trying to make money. Make ends meet."

"Bullshit," came his reply.

Maybe, just maybe, that tourist girl had gotten it wrong or liked slinging accusations around. Accusations about things that didn't exactly concern her. Emory didn't know that girl's name, but she did know Cade's.

That's where their loyalties were supposed to lie. With their own kind. Not half-drunk tourists horning in when they weren't particularly wanted in the first place.

They certainly weren't needed—well, other than for their money.

It always boiled down to the money.

And it seemed pure unlikely that Emory would receive a straight answer from her roundabout questioning of Cade.

If she had something to say, she ought to just come out and say it. Talking in riddles only returned murky responses. Asking someone if they dealt drugs proved difficult for Emory, and she knew better than most, how people didn't always want the answers they might receive.

MONEY.

Old or new, straight or crooked, clean or tainted, honest or ill-gotten.

Funny how money gobbled up everything in their part of Colorado as of late, and no one seemed to give a damn. Not until it came time to pay their taxes on rising valuations. That was a real problem for most of the ranchers, or at least the real ones with ongoing concerns. Hobby ranchers were another matter entirely, and one she didn't know much about. Not that she cared. For the Lost Daughter, coming up with hard cash for the tax bill wasn't a simple proposition. Maybe it never had been, and she had been too young to notice. But sure as hell, she heard plenty about it these last few years. Families faced tax bills that increased every year; come drought, avalanche, hell or high water.

The stark reality remained that the valley's way of life was changing. The way of life they had built was slipping away, Emory felt its loss and suspected others did the same.

But as long as the month wasn't March or April when the long-reach of tax time rolled around, the ranchers basked in their sky high valuations. Wealthy on paper and not much else, they still wore patched and worn through shirts.

Cade suddenly nudged his horse into a fast clip without any warning. "I'll be right back," he called, disrupting her thoughts.

Likely he tired of her company. Most definitely he grew dismissive of her attempts at casual conversation, which wasn't that casual at all, when it came right down to it.

Despite herself, she loved to watch him ride. He actually glided. Back ramrod straight, motion fluid and in control. Hell, anyone with an eye for skilled horsemanship admired him for that much, if little else. He'd ridden rodeo for a while. Bull doggin'. Safer than bull riding for damn sure.

"Do you see something?" She hollered at his back.

But her question went unanswered.

The denim shirt and strong profile of Cade Timmons riding up ahead had its standard toxic effect around her heart. He was too fast for Emory, and she was too forthright for him. Not to mention, too poor in comparison to those bleached blond buckle bunnies.

Unless he started respecting that acre money. But no one wanted to be loved for their land. But she wasn't naïve enough to know that certain deals couldn't be cut.

Out of the corner of her eye she still tracked Cade, loping along until he decided to rest his horse for a while. Only when absolutely nothing else claimed his attention, he thought to look back. Lifting his hand that everything was fine and as it should be further ahead.

And like any idiot schoolgirl, her stomach flipped as she raised her hand in return. Even knowing what she already did.

Even suspecting something worse yet to come.

A RENEGADE HISTORY

THE RANCH HOUSE AND BUILDINGS HUNKERED DOWN defiant, proud in a half-moon of natural basin surrounded by sand cliff and rimrock walls. The landscape provided a stone fortress on three sides except to the south where the pastures bled out into the sage brush and the lines blurred down. Their homestead, ranch, or whatever the phrase of choosing, consisted of a jumble of eras. The only constant to the land—altitude, wind, and snow—proved harsh and deadly. In other words, the collection of battered wood buildings called the Lost Daughter had held its territory over time.

A whole lot of time.

Sure enough, the Lost Daughter Ranch had a long history in the region. Hell, in the state for that matter. People took notice, if of that bent. And while her father, Lance Cross, might not concern himself about general appearances and upkeep, he kept dead straight on the fact that the ranch was his birth right to do with as he chose. To paint, or not to paint. To run cattle, or not to run cattle. To let uninvited guests onto the property or run them off.

Lance Cross sure had feelings about that last one.

The Historical Preservation people didn't appear to hold much store in his preferences, however. In fact, if anyone asked them, they'd likely say they had a wider legacy to protect. A wider legacy that involved the entire state, not just one family with a ramshackle outfit clinging onto their acreage.

"They have an *agenda,*" as her father put it.

True, they'd nosed around the previous year or so, 'gushing and fawning'—or so his story went. He kept their business card to prove his story.

"Shut the door in their faces," he claimed, puffing up. "Said they wanted to talk, but I didn't buy it. Trying to tell me how to manage this spread, like they'd even know the first thing about it. They left that damn card behind, and I'm keeping it as a reminder."

But the other day, they'd come back, harboring a greater mission and a refusal to cower. For the most part.

Rifles had a way of weakening resolve.

This second foray, Emory had been present in the house.

The sound of the car driving up their road carried. Both Crosses peered out from the large front window at the intrusion, lying in wait. When the car ground to a halt, they remained hidden from line of sight, sizing up the interlopers.

The Crosses watched as a cluster of people mounted the three ragged steps to the porch and attempted to capture their attention with a cautious rapping on the screen doorframe. Timid at first, they knocked louder making the old door rattle, determined to elicit a response.

The trespassers didn't fully understand what they were up against. They didn't know about the family's inbred ability to identify sounds out of the ordinary. A peculiar skill honed throughout the generations, the Crosses remained proud of their skill in identifying authority at the outset, if not a few steps before. Some claimed the family had a type of second-sense when it came to law enforcement. They sure as hell had the skill and the practice to avoid the law when needed. Their reputation, for the most part deserved, rippled through the family line and was prized as a valuable, requisite skill. These knocking interlopers—for that's how the Crosses considered them—had nowhere near the outright force of law.

Lawmen carried guns.

Preservationists didn't. In fact, they almost came across like librarians in comparison.

Emory and her father exchanged glances as the rattling continued, halfway toward amused.

"I'll get it," she said, voice low enough to slice through the chirping morning news.

She allowed herself to be seen through the screen. Biding her time and making sure they reached the conclusion of exactly who was in charge, and it wasn't them. When they blanched, she opened the door about four inches wide, surveying the people huddled together.

"Miss Cross?"

"Yes," Emory replied, stepping out onto the porch. "Can I help you?"

A heavy-set woman in a flowered dress took a half-step forward. "My name is Linda Paulson. We're with Colorado Historic Preservation. We've sent a few letters, which perhaps you didn't receive. In any case, they haven't been answered." She eyed Emory, shrewd and calculating. "Perhaps the bit about a designation came as a surprise…"

Emory held the woman's gaze. "I don't know anything about that."

A thin man, boasting an even thinner tie, spoke up. "Well, that's not all that surprising, I suppose…"

The heavyset Paulson shot him a warning glance. "We're here to speak to you or your father about your ranch. You see, we have documents outlining its historical significance. The Lost Daughter is deemed both a 'Centennial' and a 'Legacy' ranch because it has both stayed in the same family since inception over one hundred years ago. As you may know, the Lost Daughter is the oldest ongoing ranch in this county, and the oldest one remaining within the original family in the state. Do you understand how rare that is?"

"I guess I've never given it any thought," Emory replied. Her father stirred inside, the creaking floorboards a dead giveaway. The *visitors* missed the threat in her father's shifting weight.

"Not to mention," the thin man piped up, "this house here used to be an old stage stop. Not to mention the reported Bu…"

Another warning glare from Paulson, accompanied by a nudge from the silent woman cut him off short.

Emory knew what he referred to. Hell, everyone did. The purported Butch Cassidy connections, which hit a bit too close to the bone for comfort. Such associations fueled local lore and were taken as gospel. Good for the tourists, too. *Outlaw Country* had a certain ring about it that drew people like flies.

Emory heard another warning creak. "I guess I know

something about the stage coach part. What do you want?"

"A survey has been taken from the *county* road." The Paulson woman referred to a piece of paper on the clipboard she carried. "We couldn't get any closer. No one actually set foot on the property because we did not have permission. We asked for it in a couple of those letters. Anyhow," she sighed, "there is one house, one barn, an outhouse, a hay barn, a bunk house, the original house and seven miscellaneous structures all in various states of repair and completeness. One corral, several pens and aisles in varying stages of disrepair. Any way you want to consider it, that's quite a spread."

A warning zing traveled down Emory's spine. Those people might know something about the taxes that her father may or may not have figured correctly. "Well. Like you said, most of those old buildings are only half-standing and half-complete. Some will likely collapse in the next heavy snow."

"That's what I'm getting at. We'd like to speak to the owner of record about *officially* designating the Lost Daughter Ranch as a Colorado Historic Place. There's a tax incentive for your family to do so."

Emory sensed her father still listening. He hadn't come out to run them off yet, and that was saying something right there.

Her instinct had been half-right about the topic, but the direction veered unexpectedly. "A tax credit? What do we have to do for that, beyond letting you put up a plaque or something? And, how much are we talking about here?"

The third woman stepped forward a full twelve inches. "The amount of the grant depends on how much you spend. You'd get a twenty to thirty percent tax credit, matched on a dollar per dollar basis. That grant or credit is applied to any preservation work you undertake to keep these buildings in good historical condition."

So, the quiet one had a purpose other than moral support after all. Maybe she was the accountant.

Emory frowned.

The woman interpreted that frown correctly. "That means," she continued, "if your tax bill is $100,000, you would get a credit of $20,000 to $30,000, provided you paid that same amount of money for repairs or upkeep."

Emory eyed her. "And you, or someone, would come around to do inspections, is that right?"

A nervous shuffle.

"The tax credit can run up to one million dollars and is good for ten years. There are fees associated with filing for the grants. As a matter of fiduciary control, we would need receipts for the expenditures. With money of that magnitude, well, some oversight is required."

Emory nodded, stuck her hands in her pockets. "I don't know that we'd be interested in spending for filing fees. We've got enough fees to pay here with the livestock and all."

The bodies buried on the property flitted through her mind. On that matter, she sensibly held her tongue.

Each of the huddled three stood there blinking. Finally, the heavyset Paulson tried again.

"You seem to be a sensible girl. Why don't you talk to your father and see about his feelings on the matter? Last time, I believe, the people who approached the door were run off with a rifle, so we're doing better this time around."

Emory considered the barn. "Painting and everything count?"

"Yes," Paulson replied. "You don't have to make everything historically accurate, but the owners are required to preserve the historical features that already exist. A survey would be made up front."

"You already said you had one."

"A better one than possible from the road," the Paulson said. "Maybe we could even figure out a way to help reduce the filing fees if we had to. But we'd need to think of a legal and ethical way to do that. Like I've said, the Lost Daughter Ranch is culturally significant to the State."

The accountant held out a business card cautiously, as if Emory, or something else, might strike. *Smart woman.*

But Emory did no such thing. Instead, she took the card, made a point of reading it, and nodded that she understood.

"I'll talk to him about what you've said. No people would come onto the property without our permission, sightseers and that type of thing, would they?"

"Well," the thin man offered, "it might be nice to allow the tax payers to see their tax dollars at work, but we understand this is a working ranch and it may not be conducive to have people roaming around. Sometimes there is an open house day, which might be nice."

And there the house stood in its full glory: sagging porch, peeling paint and a corrugated steel roof rusting. That roof needed replacing outright but even a patch-job would do wonders. Most remarkably, those preservation people stood regarding the outfit like a gem in the rough. A rustic gem that only needed a bit of polishing to bring the shine out.

Right before they scuttled back into their car, heels thudding on the loosened boards. *Sensible* heels.

As they high-tailed it, and Emory turned to find the outline of her father standing behind the screen door.

"Were you drunk the last time you ran them off?" She asked.

He grunted something non-committal, which most likely meant he'd been soused. "It was Kid Curry."

"Who?" Emory asked, not following.

"The outlaw. Not Butch Cassidy. He was nowhere near here as far as anyone *really* knows."

"Never heard of any Kid Curry," she challenged.

"Then look him up," he growled.

She folded her arms, appraising her father. Seeing if he would rise to the possibility of more money just dropping into their laps. "Speaking of outlaws, seems there's up to $1, 000,000 for grabs, in case you didn't hear that part."

"I heard," he said. "Our tax bills ain't that high."

From his tone, Emory knew to leave well enough alone.

For the time being.

TALK IS CHEAP WHEN BOTTLED

EMORY PULLED UP TO THE PUMPS AT THE KUM-AND-GO on the road out of town.

Frankly, the spelling always got her hackles up and she objected to it out of principle. Worse, she was probably the only one in town that even noticed anything amiss. Depending upon the direction travelled, the convenience store was either the first or the last business on the fringes of town. Checking the price per gallon, it ran high. Priced at least fifty cents more than in the bigger towns, but cheaper than the full-blown tourist destinations. Still, gas prices remained a sore subject in rural Colorado, and they were fed the line about trucking costs, or so the gas station owners claimed. Nevertheless, the Kum-and-Go remained the best place to get gas, if one discounted the single-pump relic run by meth-heads on the other side of town. They might charge a nickel or so cheaper, but that cheapness came with a price. One went away with a decidedly sketchy sensation of having taken part in something not quite on the level. So whether Emory approved or not, like the rest of the town, she paid the going price for gasoline. Like everyone else, bitching about the prices passed as conversation when topics fell thin on the ground.

She stuck her credit card into the pay-at-the pump.

Card reader not working. See cashier inside.

"Shit."

Irritating, but no matter, really. She knew the lady who worked inside; a middle-aged woman whose none-too-great reputation preceded her, but for entirely different reasons than the Crosses.

"Hey, Josie. The pump rejected my card. Says it can't read it?"

"Yeah, they're switching systems. Everyone's been coming in saying the same thing. How you doin', honey?"

Emory shrugged. "Fair to middling, I guess. Anything new?"

She held out her hand for Emory's card. "Oh, the usual, I suppose." A glimmer of something, but for the moment, it was business as usual. "How much do you think you'll be putting in?"

"Say thirty dollars-worth, I guess. That should do it. Kind of expensive."

"I hear you, sister. Say, you know that ranch hand of yours?"

"Cade?"

"Since you asked what's new," she surveyed around the shop as if whatever she was about to depart held the greatest importance—and no one lingered inside but a tired mother dragging two kids around, arguing over candy choices—"he's been hanging out with a fast crowd. Or so I've heard."

Emory knew enough not to ask who'd been doing the talking. Or the noticing.

"What do you think that means?"

"Beyond the fact that there ain't a tourist tail he ain't chasing after, he's been seen taking to some strangers. Huddled up like."

"Any idea who they might be?"

"Well, you know Freddy the meth-head? He says he thinks they're one-percenters from over on the western slope. Grand Junction way."

"One-percenters?"

"Motorcycle gangs. Don't you watch them shows? Anyhow, your ranch hand has been splashing a bit a money around and buying drinks, if you know what I mean."

"You seen that yourself?"

"I have," she stood a bit taller, proud about something small. "I've seen him in a huddle in that back booth at the Ace-Hi. Looked like some kind of business meeting to me—either that or they was plotting something."

The harried woman and her children came up to the counter, candy clutched in tiny, grubby hands.

"Go ahead," Emory said, standing aside and displaying a forced politeness. "We're just shooting the breeze."

Josie rang up their quickly, dispatching the family in short order. She eyed their retreating backsides out through the glass doors before she continued.

"Now I know your family don't like to air their business in public; but let me tell you this. They even bought me a drink," she said all proud. "I asked Cade if they'd come into money, the way they was carrying on."

"And?"

"And that's the strange part. Your ranch hand winked, said 'not yet', and they left in a passel. Strange huh?"

Strange indeed.

"Maybe they were just being nice to you. Flirting." A

friendly shrug and a pause. A pause to make her words sound casual. "When was all of that? I sure hope not during working hours."

Josie cocked her head, reaching back for the memory. The specifics. "Maybe around 4:30 in the afternoon. I hate to be suspicious, but I'd say he's up to something. Wouldn't you?"

Yeah. She sure would.

But Emory didn't want to admit as much. Not to a gossip, and not about their ranch. A twinge of jealousy travelled up her spine, and down again.

"I hope he's not getting involved in things that he shouldn't—I'll grant you that."

But in truth, she thought more along the lines of those tourist girls. The ones who smelled clean and nice, to boot.

Emory took her card back and headed out the door, distracted enough that she almost left without putting gas in the tank.

"Stupid," she muttered, as she emerged back out of her grandpa's beat-up truck.

Flipping open the gas flap and spinning the cap, she fought the twisted hose to get the nozzle free and into the tank. She slapped the meter upwards. The man on the other side of the island regarded her strangely, but she ignored him. Just like she pretended not to notice the wind building and blowing her hair about her face and forcing loose strands into her mouth.

Emory jiggled the nozzle as if that would somehow make the gas come out faster. Like she had someplace in particular to be.

But of course, the flow remained the same as she waited out that thirty-dollar mark.

She slammed the nozzle back into the holder when

the magical number hit, climbed into the truck, and slammed that door too.

The radio started up when she turned the ignition. Trisha Yearwood belted out *She's in Love with the Boy*, and Emory flicked that radio knob right off. Pointing toward home, the winds blew insistent and the range sprawled far and wide and empty.

Suspicions didn't count for all that much in their family.

Guarding their ranch, however, did.

If she told her father of the prevailing suspicions, she might be saddled with all the work on her own until they managed to hire another hand who had a thick hide, wasn't overly-curious, and didn't mind bunking down in the next best thing to a railroad car.

In other words, they'd have to find another hand with fairly low standards who could also ride.

Anymore, that felt like a fairly tall order.

———

EMORY TURNED onto the dirt ranch road, rumbling along in silence. The ranch crossbar read Lost Daughter Ranch —although that sure wasn't what the locals called it when her family moved out of earshot. She and her father might consider adding a hanging sign saying *Established in 1888*. That might go a ways toward demanding respect and might even be the type of an improvement that the Historic Preservation group would champion. Such a declaration would put a stamp on their claim and presence, for damn sure. *Establishing provenance*, she thought the preservationists would say— and wondered where she'd ever come up with such a fancy notion.

The school library, or course.

Scanning the horizon for anything that struck amiss, nothing stood out to her. The riverbanks cutting through the ranch could hide any number of transgressions, but they kept their eyes out. Maybe they should post the land as private property—but that seemed a bit like overkill.

They didn't get a whole lot of trespassers. At least, not yet.

A coyote snagged her eye, feeding on something. She grabbed the single-bolt rifle from the rack, stuck a bullet in the chamber and shot into the air to scare him off. Most ranchers would have just shot the coyote, but that went against her grain. They all had a right to survive.

The coyote stopped feeding and eyed her. She stuck another bullet in the chamber. The coyote jogged off almost leisurely as she strode through the sage and scrub to see what was left behind. Making sure it wasn't anything of theirs.

No birds of prey circled overhead, which could be considered a good sign so far.

The carcass turned out a bloody and fresh kill. Just a rabbit that crossed the wrong coyote. Guts trailing out and half-devoured.

Lying on the ground sage and scrub covered range.

Emory rested the rifle on her shoulder and long-legged it back to the truck.

When she placed the unloaded rifle put back on the rack, the coyote displayed remarkable intelligence as it returned to its meal.

Checking the rearview mirror as she drove off and the feast continued, Emory thought about those two new calves she branded. They might be worth $3,600 as time rolled on.

Pulling up in front of the house, hands loose on the steering wheel, she surveyed the outbuildings in their varying stages of decomposition with fresh eyes. They sure as hell needed work or knocking down. But that's obviously not what the Historical Preservation folks had in mind. Hell, they might actually penalize them in the process. She could always put Cade on repair detail if she chose. Something to keep him occupied and prevent him from heading into town too often.

She was the boss. Best to keep that in mind.

She chuckled. Maybe she'd track him down right now.

As if reading her mind, there he came around the corner, in a tight t-shirt. Broad shoulders and narrow hipped. Arm muscles flexed and tanned golden. *Shoot.*

Cade carried a bale of hay which he dropped in front of the barn, yanking out the hay hooks as she rolled her window down.

He saw her, all right.

"It'd be nice if we had a working forklift," he grumbled.

"That's called good exercise," Emory replied out the truck window. "People in cities pay money to do stuff like that. In gyms, you know. Seems you always want something to make the job easier, don't 'cha? Say, aren't you're supposed to be able to fix things?"

"Maybe."

"Yeah." Emory noted a groaning sound in the wind. A sound coming from the upper portion of the barn siding where loose boards had come undone. "The Historic Preservation people came back. They said there are grants to match improvements we make on the place. That barn needs some help."

Running his eyes over the structure, his attention

settled back on her none too pleased. "I didn't sign on to do any damned painting."

"Didn't say it had to be you." She jumped out of the truck.

But he was the best option, by process of elimination. It sure as hell wasn't going to be her up on that ladder.

He pushed his hat back, watching her as she walked up. "You want others wandering around here?"

"Just what do you think we're doing out here that is so bad?"

He spat on the ground. "Well, those two calves come to mind for starters."

"They could have been ours," she countered.

"Seems to me all of the Daughter calves were accounted for."

Shaking her head, Emory offered a dry laugh. "Just who's to say how many pregnant heifers we had."

"I am."

"Is that a threat, Cade?"

"Nope," he replied, standing his ground. "Just stating a fact."

"Yeah, and it's your word against mine. Word's getting out you are up to something."

He shook his head and cricked his jaw like he found that funny and walked away disgusted, hay hooks still in hand.

"Don't you want to know what they're sayin'?" She called out after him.

"Don't care," came the reply flung back at her.

Flung over his shoulder and without breaking his stride.

If Cade ran drugs, he sure as hell didn't run scared. Not around her at least.

Either way she looked at it, a budding problem grew.

PART II

Own the Finest Colorado Has to Offer

The Lonesome Elk Ranch features an exceptional experience that rivals the finest properties found at nearby ski resorts but stands out as unique footprint of over 6,500 acres of unparalleled beauty and seclusion. The ranch boasts a multitude of year-round activities and offers the chance to relax in luxury and savor the amazing scenery that Rimrock County offers. Despite boasting a very private and pristine setting, the ranch is surprisingly close to the town of Stampede and the jet strip utilized by other large landowners in the area. All while the ranch remains secluded and secure. This is a generational property that will be enjoyed for decades. Own your piece of history and make it your own.

Asking price, $35,000,000.

BARROOM BRAGGING

THE SHERIFF DROVE THROUGH THE RANCH GATE, A PLUME of dust billowing up behind his approach.

"We've got company," Lance Cross announced, flat. The arrival wasn't exactly unexpected, it never was. Some years, visits from the sheriff were downright commonplace. But this wasn't supposed to be one of those years. "You know what this is about?"

Likely one of two options, and both amounted to about the same thing. Cade's half-threat sprang to mind, but Emory didn't want to go there. Yet.

"I didn't get those calves turned back onto the BLM land."

He eyed her, dead serious. "Don't go parading them under his nose whatever you do." Nine forty-six in the morning, he took another swig from his beer. "I'll do the talking."

"With beer on your breath."

"Who the hell cares? He ain't gonna kiss me."

Together they stood shoulder to shoulder on the sagging front porch and watched the sheriff's progress.

The sirens weren't on, the lights weren't flashing, and he wasn't driving particularly fast.

The car pulled up in front of the steps and Robert Preston emerged, standing between the car and the door until he gauged their reception. "Lance. Emory."

Her father struck a casual pose by leaning against one of the porch posts, almost non-threatening. "What brings you out this way, Bob?"

The sheriff took a few steps closer but didn't set foot on the stairs. His politeness allowed them the advantage of height. "Oh, there's been some talk."

"Talk, huh?" Her father repeated, still casual.

Well, that's usually how those types of conversations started out. Every player reluctant to show their cards.

"Talk." The sheriff stuck his thumbs through his belt loops.

"You came out here to tell me there's been talk? You never struck me as the kind to listen to gossip." Her father spat off the side of the porch. "Heck, why didn't you just call—isn't that what most people do nowadays?"

More words strung together than Emory had heard her father offer in a long time. A *very* long time.

"They might, but I don't." Sheriff Preston cast his attention over the yard, a far cry from casual.

"Fine. What's the talk?"

They couldn't see the sheriff's eyes hidden behind his sunglasses. Either way, Emory sensed his eyes were bolted onto her father. "Most of it centers around Cade Timmons. Seems he likes to go shooting his mouth off in the Ace-Hi."

Her father shifted, ever so slightly. "Shootin' his mouth off about *what* exactly?"

"Questionable accounting, for one. I'm going to need

you to pull all of your stock off of the BLM land so that we can recount them."

"Recount them?" Emory took a half step forward. "We just filled out paperwork not two months ago. Those cattle are likely scattered by now."

"Yep, more than likely." Preston wagged his head. "Unless you're telling me that you put some of your head onto another parcel where they aren't supposed to be. Is that it?"

"No," her father spat again off the porch and into the old, struggling rosebush. "We aren't saying nothing of the kind. Ain't that the type of things the BLM inspectors do? Didn't think the local sheriff got involved..."

"Well," Sheriff Preston half laughed. "This here is a courtesy call."

"Is that what you call it?" Her father scanned the horizon.

"Yep, that's what I call it. There's investigators as you might know. BLM investigators and brand inspectors. How many head did you file on, and how many head do you reckon you have? And don't try to feed me a line of bull."

Her father paused. "I'd say the count came back about two hundred and twenty-five, give or take. We might be a few short. Let me go get what we filed."

The sheriff rocked back on his heels. "Well, that's just it, Lance. Cade says you've got about twice as much as you filed on."

Emory cut in. "Don't suppose Cade was talking to a table full of blonde tourists, was he?"

Her father snorted. "And who the hell cares about a thing like that? That ain't got nothing to do with this."

The sheriff's eyes narrowed, focusing in on Emory. "I

know whatever he claims was overheard at the Ace Hi and called in. One of them anonymous tips."

Emory's heart felt stuck to her stomach. "Anonymous tips that go against us. Say, haven't you ever heard of bar-room bragging? That's likely the size of it. Shooting his mouth off and trying to make his job sound out to be something bigger than it is."

"Was," her father corrected. "After this stunt, looks like we might be short one hand."

Emory felt her eyes widen, panicked at the prospect. "I'll need him to help me bring all of the stock in, if we're really going to do that." She tried to keep the desperation out of her voice, but it didn't go down too well.

Lance's glance brushed over his daughter. "Come on, Bob. You know we don't have any four hundred head. I mean, *look* at this place."

"Plenty of good grazing," the sheriff remarked, half watching her father, and half admiring the land.

The senior Cross waved off the notion. "It looks like good grazing because we're grazing the BLM land. We're plannin' on cutting all our hay and storing it for the winter months."

"That very well may be, but your hay situation doesn't change anything about the allegation right now." The sheriff made it sound final. "I'll need you to show me your records."

Her father resumed leaning against the porch's pillar. "No can do," he wheezed. "The computer's broke."

The sheriff gave a dry, pained laugh. "Now how did I know you were going to tell me that? Don't suppose you have written back-up."

"Oh, bits and pieces here and there."

Which was a lie. There was no way they were that disorganized.

Emory kept her face hard and close to expressionless as the sheriff's attention raked over her.

"Emory, what is your count, and where are your records? I cannot believe that you would let things roll like this. You know, you HAVE to hand over livestock records when requested. And I'm requesting. Failure to do so, means more fines on top of the ones you're already starin' at."

Emory gave a half shrug in her father's direction.

He nodded his permission.

"I have a written partial copy I can show you. I don't know that it's right. I bought the book at Murdock's." That last part sounded mighty young, but at least it rang true.

Although she doubted the sheriff would catch it, her father was marginally backing down, his defiance waning. All of which told her, this time the accusation struck dead-center.

Lance Cross sniffed. "Look, we don't want any trouble here. We'll round up the cattle, bring them back in, and you have your inspectors ready."

The sheriff nodded. "Well, a couple of inspectors are going to be riding along with your outfit. Otherwise, it'd be mighty easy to leave some behind, once that two hundred and twenty-five number got reached, don't you think?"

Her father didn't like any of it, but he didn't rise to the bait. "I'm going to go get the filing records. And I'll show you my permit, too. You wait here."

He returned into the house.

The sheriff drank in the views. "Sure is pretty out here."

"So's the entire valley." Emory corrected, stomach clenching.

Sheriff Preston removed his sunglasses, squinting in the glare. "I personally took you for smarter than this is all turning out. Is this how you're planning on living your life—running cattle around underreported? You ain't lazy, Emory. And off the record, Cade sure was shootin' his mouth off to some peroxide blondes. He's building quite the string in town. I'd hate to see you falling into that line."

Icy ghost-fingers brushed across the back of her neck. "He's not important."

"Glad to hear it," the sheriff replied almost casual, as if he found it all a common-place conversation. "You know, ever since you fell off your bicycle, bit through your lip and bled all over me, well, I've kept my eye out for you. Always good grades, always working hard, and no one really has a bad thing to say about you *other* than the family you were born into. Why I'd even…"

Her father clomped back out onto the porch, holding out a pile of papers. "Here. Take a look."

Sheriff Preston reached out for the odd assortment and scanned them. "I see what it says, Lance. But we still need to do that count. I'll give these back to you, once that is done."

"Fine. Have it your way. Anything else you want? I've got some chores that need doing. Provided you don't have any objections to *work*." His natural defiance flared again as he snatched up an old, abandoned bucket that waited nearby.

"Go right ahead. Don't let me stop you," the sheriff said, plenty dry. "We'll be back tomorrow at seven o'clock in the morning."

"We'll be waiting," her father called out as he trudged to the barn.

The sheriff watched him walk away. Another long-eyed stare. "I sure hope you ain't attached to that cow-prod. Sooner or later, I'd wager he'll end up behind bars for one thing or another, if he hasn't already. What exactly do you know about him?"

"Nothing really," she shrugged. "He hired on about six months back, if memory serves. He rides well and doesn't shirk. Maybe he signed on for a fresh start."

A weak argument in the best of times, she figured. "Maybe his history is none of our business."

"Yeah. The Lost Daughter is kind of famous for those types of get-ups. A few fingerprints, and I would likely know more than anyone ever wanted, especially your father. Hiring the lone wolf passing through. It just adds to the reputation, doesn't it?"

Emory shifted her weight from one leg to the other. "People have long memories around here, don't they?"

"Yeah, but you don't have to go along with it. Striking out on your own would prove something. People might judge you on your own merits instead of history."

A bemused laugh. "Like that's going to happen."

"Watching the company you keep would go a long ways toward helping. Get a job in town or work for another outfit. Make your way—I have every confidence in you." With that decree, the sheriff launched himself toward his car.

Emory called out, hitting him square between the shoulder blades. "I can't see how working at the Kum-And-Go is any better than this."

"Set your sights higher, then," he didn't break his stride.

He didn't face her until he reached the car and opened the door. "There's a local scholarship, you know. Ag studies, range management, rural services. That type of thing."

"I'm already twenty-three." That admission stabbed. Twenty-three shouldn't mean that her life was set in concrete. "That's a bit old for starting college, isn't it?"

"Suit yourself," the sheriff replied, not seeming terribly concerned one way or the other. "But I'd start studying if I were you. And look up that scholarship form on the computer—that is, if you can figure out how to get it working. If not, the library has one you can use."

"What are rural services? Never heard of those."

"Oh, that's because there ain't that many of them out here. You know, social work, social services, law enforcement. There's a shortage of rural *services*, as I'm sure you've noticed."

"People don't much like the government meddling," Emory countered.

"There's people hurting, Em. You've probably run across that yourself. Shit goes on out here, the same as in the cities. We've got less funding, less resources, and less of everything."

Yeah. She knew all of that was true.

"I'll think about it," she said at length.

He nodded. "You've got the aptitude, and you meet the requirements."

He patted the roof of his patrol car twice, before starting up the engine and driving off.

The dust still floated back down toward the road when her father emerged from the barn—the pail still as empty and dry as when he first grabbed hold of it. He just hung on to the handle and watched the trail of dust lie back down and settle into the dirt ruts.

He stared straight ahead. "Tell Cade I want to see him."

"Yep," she eyed him. "But we'll need him to ride tomorrow. We'll need you, too." A longer pause as she stuck her hands in her Levi's and pretended not to care. "How much do you really know about him?"

"All I need to about now," he bit off the words like a plug of tobacco. And as with tobacco, he might just spit in her direction.

She backed down. For the time being.

The tension partially passed. Lance broke down a bit. "And I'll ride. Now go get that cow-prod and bring him here. Hell, you can even bring him inside the house this time."

Emory eyed her father.

That last part had to be the stinger.

NUMBERS ARE ENOUGH TO MAKE SOME PEOPLE DRINK

Fortunately for her, and almost certainly unfortunate for Cade, his pick-up truck remained parked alongside the bunkhouse.

Music blared, loud. Just the way he liked it.

Emory pounded on the door hard enough to carry across George Straight.

The music died down a few notches, but not all the way. The door opened a fraction, and Cade leaned out, blocking her view. Intentional, on his part.

They locked eyes. "You see the sheriff drive up by chance?"

A flash of something. "No. I was just chilling out and listening to music."

"You sure that's all you've been up to?" She half-laughed at the notion.

He peered down the road like he still expected to see the dust billowing, but the plumes had long since settled. "What's that supposed to mean?"

"Nothing," she replied, biting her lip. "Dad wants to

see you up at the house. Now. Might be best if you buttoned up your shirt. He isn't in a pleasant mood."

He grinned despite the warning, and Emory's heart tugged. She tried to rein in her feelings, but it didn't always work.

Running his fingers through his hair, he acted every inch the bad boy he wanted to be.

She turned to go, not wanting him to see her blush.

Trailing behind her, that latter-day James Dean buttoned up his shirt, taking his own sweet time.

Likely sizing up her ass as she walked.

If she hadn't been the boss' daughter, he probably would have made some comment about how nice she looked walking away.

While she felt his admiration linger, she didn't let on that she noticed.

Who was he, and why was he hiding out at the Lost Daughter anyhow?

Cade's past, or whatever the hell his name actually was, could be dealt with later, and his past likely had little-to-nothing to do with her.

The immediate predicament of the cattle reported to the BLM, did.

THE SCREEN DOOR banged behind them, the TV for once switched off. The silence echoed. The set-up felt like a trap closing, make no mistake about it.

"Back here!" Her father's words came as a shouted snarl from the back regions of the house. One thing came across as clear—there was nothing wrong with that man's hearing.

Emory swore Cade blanched a bit around the edges,

and she took that for a good thing. A reasonable response given the circumstances.

The living room, lit only by the fading light outside, came across dingy in the twilight. Preferable to the kitchen table illuminated by the overhead fixture, casting harsh light onto the mess below.

Papers and what-have-you blanketed one side; a small portion burrowed out on the other side where Emory took her meals. Pretty damn pathetic from any angle, but there was no time for that now.

She refused to acknowledge any reaction coming from Cade. She didn't have time to clean when she had a ranch to run. She didn't want to see the pity or disgust she figured she would find. As a hired hand, tradition held that he wasn't entitled to an opinion, but that didn't mean he didn't entertain them anyhow.

Single-file they crossed through the kitchen maze and through the tacked-on nook that served as the mud room. The mud room door opened out into a disused part of the yard; bare hard-ass dirt as bleak as they came. She noted a few straggling stands of grass as she passed. She also noticed how the door's half-cocked aluminum window didn't shut square with rags stuffed in the gap to keep the draft out.

If she was lucky, Cade'd be nervous enough not to notice that part.

On the far side of the mud room trailed another linoleum-floored passage. A passage that led to what should, by rights, be the most important room in the entire get-up.

The ranch office.

Hell, theirs didn't even have a door. Just a large desk awash in papers and crammed into the space. Outdated phone books, and old receipts scattered about and filled up the littered corners.

Not to mention the computer monitor had to be twenty years out of date.

Her father sat in the midst of it all, grizzled but belonging behind the stacks of bills and fishing magazines, stock reports and random scraps. Of course, he had made no effort to clear the area, but just sat there, lording over the decay and debris.

"What in the hell have you got to say for yourself?" He aimed his question right between Cade's eyes.

"Sir?"

The rancher leaned forward, coiled, and ready to strike. "The sheriff came out here. Talk's getting passed around that we have two hundred extra head more than we actually do. Instead of the two twenty-five we filed on. See the problem? Just how many cattle do you honestly reckon that we run?" The thundering statement brooked no argument or back talk.

A nerve in Cade's cheek throbbed.

"Two hundred and thirty-seven," Emory volunteered.

"Including those two mavericks?" Her father shot across.

"The two *former* mavericks. They're branded now," she corrected.

Still scowling, his glance landed cold in her direction before training back to land on the cowhand. "Certain on that number?"

Her father's eyes no longer made contact with hers, but they all knew she was the only one who could supply numbers and quantities.

"Certain." She hesitated, calculating. "Unless we find some more."

Lance Cross slapped the desktop, glaring at both of

them. "We sure as hell won't be trying to do that tomorrow, now will we? That's the very last thing we need. The BLM investigator and likely a brand inspector will be paying us a visit. That's a whole lot of oversight and a whole lot of trouble."

His eyes continued to travel from one to the other. Cade was smart enough not to say a word. So was she.

"Listen. If either of you see some of ours that you can reasonably pass by without drawing suspicion, do so. Otherwise round them up, bring them back in, and tell everyone that Emory don't do so good a job of bushwhacking on her own."

Stunned, she backed up half a step, like she'd been physically struck. Slack-jawed and uncertain, maybe she hadn't heard that last part right.

Her father still glared.

She refused to cower about an accusation like that. "I'm the one who told YOU how many head you have, Old Man."

His eyes turned mean, but she wasn't about to back down. She didn't think he'd hit her, but violence seethed. On something like this, she'd take her chances. She took a step forward and glared right back.

Her father refused to yield as well.

"And I'm telling you, as the youngest AND a female, that you're going to have to take the blame for this mix up."

She poked the desktop, defiant. "Mix up! Why that is not what this is at all, and you know it."

Cade's eyes first darted in her direction, then her father's.

"I know no such thing," Lance Cross thundered.

Emory shook her head. "Well, if I'm so hopeless, I don't see exactly how I can be expected to ride tomorrow. I'd probably make some sort of feeble-minded mistake and give everything away, once and for all."

"You'll ride, Emory," her father growled. "You'll ride like nothing is wrong. Now get out of here, the pair of you. Be saddled up and ready at six forty-five and I don't want to hear another word about it. And Emory, you try not to be too competent. Efficiency will only throw everything off even further than it already is."

She'd sassed back as far as she dared to that time, none of which stopped her from shooting daggers at her father to make sure her point was taken.

Turning away disgusted, she stomped out of that shambolic room, Cade following behind.

"People pokin' around our business..." her father muttered, like some impotent old man.

Angry, embarrassed tears threatened as she led their way through the maze and back out through the front room.

"Don't let the door hit you in the ass," she jeered at Cade. "You're the one that dropped us in this mess in the first place.

Him and his easy bar talk and lingering bar flies.

"Em, I didn't mean—"

"Save it for someone who cares," she spat.

He took two steps. Spun about to face her, about to say something. About to offer an excuse or a lifeline.

She cut him off, words tumbling out. "I want to know just one thing. Did you lie about the number of cattle we are running?"

He wagged his head slow, turning options over in his mind.

"I'll not lie to you. I did." He stood there, waiting.

"But why?" She all but croaked.

"I guess that was the booze talking," he replied, as if that explanation would settle matters."

"If that's truly the case, you might want to stop drinking."

She shut the front door, miserable and temper running high with a whole lot of other emotions thrown on in for good measure.

Who ever said she wanted to be a part of this damned outfit, anyhow?

No one *ever* asked. Her last name made sure of that one.

14

THE BLOOD SPORT OF CALCULATING RANGE FEES

THE MORNING LIGHT SKEWERED THROUGH A TEAR IN HER window shade.

Zero dark thirty might come early for her father those days, but the murky hours were no stranger to her. From her bedroom window, she checked for Cade's truck. Parked by the side of the bunkhouse, he had foregone his usual escapades into town and for once kept close to hand. That restraint was as near to an admission of guilt as she was ever likely to see coming from him. Of course, the flipside was there as well. He might feel guilty, but his admission also stemmed from a belated sense of self-preservation.

As of late, it proved hard to read anyone's motives with certainty, and at times, that included her own.

Her father's alarm went off and his groan carried as he struggled to his feet. Chances were he'd cut out beer the previous night, not that she knew anything about it firsthand. Whether he bothered to notice her mood or not, she was still plenty riled.

Riled or not, her anger wouldn't have made the

slightest bit of difference to that out-and-out stubborn man.

And that stubborn man probably felt better that morning than he had in a long, sorry while. Physically speaking. She wondered if he would notice the correlation between lack of booze and clarity. Statistics. Now there was a math that had some practical uses.

She pulled on her jeans, noting the sunrise filling window. She'd be damned, but she beheld a *red sky in morning, sailors take warning.* True, Colorado might be a thousand or more miles from any ocean, but signs, warnings, and portents had always served her family well.

"Ain't that just dandy," she muttered, taking the red sky as a harbinger in league with the coyote she almost ran over.

A niggling thought bother her, and it wouldn't settle. She could apply for that scholarship like the sheriff said, knowing it offered a way out of the Lost Daughter's limitations. A way out of the constraints that bound her into place. Uncertain she wanted to embark upon a course of studies, she dragged on a clean, faded red plaid flannel shirt, first one arm and then the other. The biggest problem would be leaving Kai behind. They were a team, and he was her only true friend. Abandoning him in favor of a new life had the taint of Judas about it. Maybe she could load him up into the trailer and board him close by to whatever she landed. *If* she got that scholarship. *If* she applied. Nothing felt certain, but all the points of consideration involved money one way or another. Well, hell. If she needed to work for anyone other than the ranch or herself, Kai had the next strongest claim.

Fully dressed, she headed downstairs to the kitchen

to get the coffee going before heading out to check on those calves.

Coffee started, Emory stepped outside into a morning cold enough to see her breath. What she didn't see were the calves. They must have ventured deeper into the pasture.

If she wanted to check on them, it would be fastest to ride Kai.

Cade, already up and about and inside the barn, worked with the door open. Straightening out tack, checking on his horse, and tidying things up as any good hand ought to do.

Glancing over when he heard her enter, his expression came across as sheepish.

"Sorry about last night," he said. "For what it's worth."

"Doesn't matter," Emory replied, still smarting and face averted. She and her father had aired out some very private dirty laundry. Laundry best kept hidden away and out of sight from unwelcomed witnesses. Witnesses like Cade.

"Guess that's all he thinks I'm good for. Taking the blame."

The cowboy shook his head, slow. "What he wants is the easiest way out, Em. Nothing more."

"Don't much care, and he can saddle his own damn horse. Right now, I'm going to go check on those calves and see how they're healing."

Cade stopped all movement. Serious. Deadly serious. "That's exactly what I wouldn't do. Don't check on the calves right now. You don't know, but the law may be watching the house and our movements with binoculars. Nothing's wrong with those doggies. Don't draw attention is my best advice in this situation."

"The situation you got us into."

"Yeah," he didn't flinch. "And I sure don't feel good about it."

Out of habit, she wanted of offer assurances, but she bit them back. Offering salve for his conscious would only make her come across as weaker than she already appeared.

"Too late for all of that now," she snapped instead. "You should have thought about that when you were hitting on your buckle bunnies."

He bit back an annoyed laugh, grasping around for something but coming up short. "Please just follow my lead on this."

Pissed off, she stared him down, hand on hip and plenty put out. "Whatever you say, Einstein."

The entire situation already had plenty of bad judgement to go around.

THE CAVALCADE of law enforcement barreled down the ranch road, a cloud of dust rising and them pressing in fast. Seven o'clock on the dot, Emory, her father, and Cade all stood on the porch, watching. Waiting.

"A bit of rain would take care of one problem," her father remarked, but no one commented in return.

The sheriff, two deputies, BLM inspector, brand inspector, and who knew what else, pulled up into the ranch yard, acting for all the world like they were preparing to either circle up the wagons or mount an attack. It was hard to determine just which eventuality they aimed for. Equally difficult was deciding who all the players were in this mess, but suffice it to say, Emory didn't feel like she would end up on the winning side. The Lost Daughter outfit was poised to be proven as liars unless every single one of them kept their wits at all time.

In actuality, no circling took place either.

All the trucks, cars, and horse trailers, fanned out to form a half-moon. Metal hitches clashed and groaned as the trailer doors swung open and horses unloaded, already tacked up and ready. The law enforcement men were raring to go, and they weren't green. They checked their mounts' girths and applied fly spray while the Crosses and Cade watched in silence.

The saddled Lost Daughter horses, tied to the hitching post, watched the newcomers and their mounts, stamping with impatience.

The sheriff walked up to the porch, rested his foot against the lower step, all nice and casual-like. Holding a clipboard.

"Lance."

"Bob," her father replied.

The sheriff noted the activity taking place behind him, stretching out his back as he turned. "Seems to me this all could have been avoided."

Her father merely shrugged, acting unconcerned no matter how events veered. "Don't see how. The paper-work got messed up somewhere along the line. Or someone don't like me. You ever consider that aspect? That type of history dies hard around here."

"Yeah, I thought of that." The sheriff didn't act overly concerned for his part, either. "But you guys don't do much to help live it down." His gaze landed square on her father.

"Before we get started, a round of introductions wouldn't hurt. The BLM inspector is Marcus Lindquist. The brand inspector is Terry Overholzer, called out from the Greeley Sale Barn…"

"Marcus," her father interrupted.

"Lance," the BLM inspector acknowledged.

So, her father didn't know the brand inspector. That meant he was a wild card, for all intents and purposes.

The sheriff resumed introductions, irritation rippling. "Deputy McMahon."

"Rusty," her father responded.

"Lance," he tipped his hat.

The sheriff set his jaw. "And Deputy Nelson."

"Joe."

"Mr. Cross."

"You're old enough to call me Lance." That was as close as her father came to flirting with charm.

"Lance, then." The young man appeared willing, at least, to give them the benefit of the doubt.

The inspectors acted by-and-large impassive, but the sheriff failed to be amused by the pissing contest of who-was-who and who'd-been-in-the-valley-the-longest type of bullshit. The sheriff's family had been around plenty long as well. "Let's just get done what needs doing and get this episode over with."

He held up the clipboard for inspection. "This is the computer print-out of your reported cattle tags. We'll be checking them off as we find them and round them up. I take it you all know the rules, but just to be on the safe side—an Animal Unit per Month is figured as one cow and calf unit or the equivalent. A calf is up to six months in this definition. A bull is one unit. A steer is one unit. A cow is one unit, wet or dry. Any transferred ownership of cattle to be grazed on BLM land has to be recorded and appropriate fees paid…"

Yeah. They all knew the rules. Abiding by known rules often turned out to be another matter entirely.

SADDLED UP, they all rode out into the clear morning blue. The lush hay meadow rippled unmown, the mountain peaks pierced the sky, and the rimrocks stood guard as they had for the last millennium.

Not much talking going on. Just the steady *clop, clop, clops* of the horseshoes thudding along. The occasional random strikes as the metal shoes struck rocks, ringing out. A whole lot more clopping than usual, but matters were out of their hands.

Together the factions rode through the ranch yard and passed by the stoved-in pioneer house. The ramshackle assortment of buildings and pens looked about the same as almost any other ranch in the district. The Lost Daughter just had more of them and often, in worse condition.

The back gate the opened out onto the BLM land came into view. Her father rode in front, stopping at the gate but making no move to dismount whatsoever. Instead, he waited.

Cade sat fairly glued in his seat as well.

Irritated, Emory dismounted and opened the dang gate. The men rode through without paying her any heed. She clanged the gate shut loud enough to make her point, threading the chain in the slit and doubling it back out the round hole for added security. Security against what was hard to say at this juncture. Her focus darted to the two mavericks grazing in the small pasture, brands scabbing over nicely.

For the time being, no one took the slightest notice of the pair.

A favorable condition that might change on a dime.

One of the deputies had the courtesy to wait for her

to remount, which is more than she could say for her father or Cade. She nodded at him once back in the saddle, and he tipped his hat before riding off. At least the law had manners, which is more than she could say for her own outfit.

She nudged Kai forward, following the string of riders. Emory wondered how much longer they would travel in a line like a bunch of donkeys. The posse passed the bend where the fly-fishing tourist popped out of the bushes, the sound of water growing stronger the same as any other day. The river's fording spots were the logical place to start rounding up cattle.

But she volunteered nothing, waiting to see what someone in command would do.

If the person in command was her father, well, he just kept on riding.

The sheriff, for his part, settled into an annoyed countenance. "Hold up, Lance. What's the plan here?"

Her father turned Draco, his good cattle horse who squared off nicely. "I planned on going to the back end of the BLM patch, and riding dragnet forward. You got a better idea?"

The BLM investigator spoke up. "There isn't much out there that would attract cattle, and there are plenty of tracks to follow right here. Let's ride the river first and flush out what we find."

Her father made his silent disagreement clear, and Cade made damn sure to mirror that stance. Emory waited as the men postured.

The sheriff glanced at her as he rode up to her father. "Lance, you and I will go this way. Cade, pair up with Deputy McMahon. The BLM inspector can do as he pleases and Emory, I'll ask you to ride with Terry."

The brand inspector.

Her father got half a word out, but the sheriff cut him off.

"I'm done talking," he advised in a tone that left no quarter.

The riders dispersed, the BLM inspector choosing to ride along with Cade. *Smart choice* Emory thought.

But she had her own problems to contend with, mainly the brand inspector. "Where'd you like to go?"

He eyed the ground like a hunter in pursuit. Intent and single-minded. "Let's cross here and get on the other side of this creek. Plenty of tracks heading that way." And, sure enough, there were.

In the thick coyote willows, they first found a stand of three. Emory read the brands. "Well, there's three of ours to start."

"Move them back to the other side of the creek to Deputy Joe Nelson."

She nudged Kai into work mode, pushed the three head toward the basin and back across the creek that ran about a foot and a half deep.

There weren't any problems to speak of getting the three heifers across to where the deputy waited.

"Three," she said, like he couldn't count.

Stupid.

"Noted," he grinned, with a clipboard salute.

She returned to the brand inspector who pointed at a nearby draw.

"You wait here, unless I call you."

A small trickle of water ran at the bottom. Less than five minutes later, he drove out eight Lost Daughter brands ahead of him.

Again. And unfortunate.

Lowing and thudding approached from the far side of the creek, along the more travelled side. Cade yipped and hawed, driving about twenty head. As far as the Lost Daughter outfit was concerned, the roundup was going fast. A little too fast.

More cattle were flushed out along the riverbanks, and the size of the herd mounted. Her father and the BLM inspector drove in a sizeable number to join the rest.

The brand inspector sized up her reaction, which she held tight in check. "All right, we'll take note of all the tag numbers, drive what we have back into the ranch. Then we'll make a second trip out," he said. "Later, we'll double check those tag numbers against a computer run once we've got them all in."

It was going on ten o'clock in the morning, when the first pass completed. The riders returned out into the open range, this time penetrating deeper and following tracks. Of course, they found more cattle, and the entire process repeated until they had about one hundred head waiting. Writing down the tag numbers took longer, but the deputies were efficient. Emory had to credit them with that much. The Lost Daughter outfit helped keep the cattle moving forward in a line, which they drove through the back gate and into the hay pasture where they all promptly fanned out and started grazing.

"Those cattle are feeding on the crop we need for this winter," her father bellyached.

"Should of thought of that before you under-report-ed," the sheriff countered.

'We didn't under-report," her father argued, although the lie had become obvious.

Her father gave Emory a glare, displeased and most certainly unsympathetic to any of her feelings on the subject.

Which pissed her off further, but she knew better than to show it.

"In the future you might want to keep a muzzle on that hired man," the sheriff suggested, in not an entirely helpful manner.

Her father took in the words and spat out phlegm.

15

A STRANGE AND SINGULAR TALENT

THE AFTERNOON RAN OUT AND WOUND DOWN INTO THE early evening. The heat of the day spent at altitude pressed down, dirt and dust sticking to sweat, gritty and uncomfortable from all the time spent in the saddle. Cade, the BLM inspector, and the accompanying deputy came driving in last, having done hard riding, judging by the sweat on the horses, their shirts, and the layer of dust that blanketed them all. Worse, they drove another twenty head. And those twenty looked kind of rough. Stringy old steers.

Blackjacks.

The blackjacks were completely unexpected. Emory eyed the brands, riding closer. Among the twenty, she cut out specific ones from the rest.

"These don't carry our brand," she called out to anyone who cared to listen.

The BLM inspector chewed on that fact while surveying the blackjacks with a practiced eye. "Those are old hummers, halfway toward wild and those brands are pretty faded. Terry, what do you reckon?"

He turned his horse in their direction and eyed the blackjacks. "Those ones might have been out on their own long enough to be counted as dead. They'll be hard to handle whatever the case."

But Emory wanted that 'death' credit saved for some animals belonged to them.

She cleared her throat, seeking the brand inspector for confirmation. "That's a sideways H. Don't you see it?"

"Hang on everyone," The brand inspector rode next to her angling to get a closer view. "I'd say she's right. You know whose that is?"

She would have been a piss-poor rancher not to. "The Highline outfit on the other side of the BLM land."

She turned her attention on Cade. "Just how far out did you two go?"

The deputy squirmed. Cade sat a bit taller and squared his shoulders, proud of something. Emory felt prickly, tired, and sick of all the bullshit.

Her father shifted on his saddle, strained about the edges. Probably sore from a long day riding. This was the most time he'd spent on horseback for many moons.

The cowpoke stayed silent. Like he didn't have to answer to her. That rubbed her the wrong way.

"Cade. You'll have to take them back at least halfway. It's not their fault that we're having this mess."

Poised to argue, her father cut him off.

"Do as she says. Emory, you see any others that ain't ours?"

Now it seemed the wind came blowing in from a different direction as far as he was concerned. Still, it remained important to keep everything level and civil.

"Not to be funny, but isn't that the brand inspector's job? I mean, I don't want to get us into any more trouble than we already are."

The brand inspector nodded at her. Odd. "Go on. There's no more trouble to get into, I don't think."

All the men seemed to be waiting on her response. Another oddity. "I haven't been examining all the brands that close—especially not the earlier ones brought in." She drove Kai into the middle of the cattle, cutting out first one and then another. Finally, she had five, which she pushed to Cade.

Not all of the brands belonged to the Highline's. The Bennett's and the Rocking A showed up as well.

"This one goes to the south, and those four need to go to the west," she said.

The brand inspector nodded and took down a few notes and the ear tag numbers. Emory intercepted a glance between the sheriff and the brand inspector, but she couldn't read it.

Feeling a bit too tired, when it came right down to it, to care as much as she ought.

"Let's go see what we have on the ranch," the brand inspector said, specifically to her.

She didn't bother to argue as she nudged Kai forward behind the inspectors, riding drag. Watching her father repeatedly shifting his weight in the saddle. *By golly, would he be sore in the morning.* That thought lifted her heart for the merest of moments.

Whatever the case might be, any discomfort served him right.

He'd let too many things fall out of shape. And one of those things was himself.

AFTER A FULL DAY of riding and eating warm granola bars out of their saddle bags, the law enforcement appeared satisfied with the effort made. To a point. Seasoned men, they still harbored doubts.

"Anyone think of some place we missed or that we ought to go check out?" The sheriff scanned around. Everyone shifted in their saddles, waiting for someone to offer up a distant destination that no one wanted to ride to.

As a result, everyone held their tongues. Predictable given the circumstances, yet sometimes an overly enthusiastic newcomer might volunteer and drag them all along for the long, sore ride. Thankfully, there were none of those types in attendance.

The brand inspector waited everyone out, and the BLM Inspector joined the sheriff.

"Take these back to the ranch and put them in the hay meadow with the others," the Sheriff called out.

Her father reared back. "But I don't want them in the hay meadow. We're going to mow that for this winter's feed."

Bob remained unyielding. "Again. None of this would be going on if you had been reporting right. Anyhow, seems to me that the haying should gotten done already, if you were serious about it."

Lance Cross grunted. "Cade was going to get on that today, until this came up."

It was all Emory could do not to shake her head in irritation.

She'd sure as hell get Cade on that chore tomorrow. Why did every damn thing have to fall on her shoulders?

"Fine," the sheriff said at length. "Put what you can in the corral, and the rest in the pens if they won't fall down around the livestock and injure them. Better?"

"I guess," her father exhaled, put out and showing it.

They'd still have to put some of the cattle in the

hayfield because that was all they had open. But the sheriff was right. If they had been on top of their game, many things would have been different.

Like everything else, taking care of the hay fell by the wayside. Just another chore that hadn't quite gotten done.

Everyone settled into position and set the herd moving toward the Lost Daughter's back gate.

ANOTHER ROUND OF SORTING COMPLETED, and it became rapidly apparent that a lot of the pens weren't in any condition to hold anything. Another sting of shame at just how far things had fallen.

Anyway, released into the hayfield, they grazed away,

The brand inspector called out to her, friendly enough. "Emory, why don't you help me check these brands, or at least make sure that what we've rounded up all belong to your outfit."

Starting with the cattle in the hayfield, all the brands marked Lost Daughter cattle as feared.

Finishing that segment, she eyed the two inspectors. "If we count these, there's no harm in putting them back out on the BLM land, is there?" Emory did her best to appear contrite.

Remarkably, it worked.

"Fine by me," the BLM man agreed. "It's not like we are going to impound them or anything."

Everyone made their accountings, dividing them up into groupings as best as possible. Two hundred and seventeen head counted and returned onto public land.

Next, the three of them rode into the corral examining the brands.

The two mavericks weren't accounted for. Yet.

Working her way through, the brands on some very old heifers and steers had faded. The two inspectors remained hanging back. Emory rode forward, cautiously making out the indents. She puzzled.

"These aren't ours, but I don't know who they belong to."

Terry nudged his horse forward to get a better view. "Well, I know what I see…but what do you see?"

He acted like an older school teacher quizzing a student, but not coming right out with the challenge. Probably he thought he was being supportive.

Emory shrugged. "It's no one I know. Looks like it's been rebranded at some point, and not the same brand, either. The older mark is pretty faded, and this heifer is an old girl. Maybe it started out as a KH to me but got changed to a K8 somewhere along the line. Hard to say. Could be they just weren't good at branding. It's possible, you know."

Uncomfortable at the implications, she shrugged. Whatever was going on there didn't appear too upstanding, but that idea remained circumstantial without proof. Just as long as those goings on weren't of their doing. Sympathy twanged due to past history, but she kept any further opinions on that matter to herself.

History pressed down, and she tried to ward it off.

But there was no denying the old vented cowhide hanging in their out-buildings, dating from sometime in the 1880's. From the reverse side of the hide, it was easy enough to see that the original brand had been altered. The older brand stood out as the deeper and clearer of the two. It didn't start out life as belonging to the Lost Daughter Ranch.

Glancing at the mottled brand again, she left this call

down to the brand inspector who snapped a couple of pictures with his phone.

At length, he shrugged. "If we were in a place where we could keep her a bit, I'd try to figure out who the original owner was. But for now, release her back onto public land *after* we figure out if any others go back besides."

Everyone who had anything to do with cattle knew rustling was still alive and well and living in the West. But the brand inspector didn't actually come right out and say it. *Professional tact*, she figured.

She remained more of a 'call an ace an ace' type of girl, but it wasn't the time to go shooting her mouth off.

Emory kept to task and found another seven head that didn't belong to the Lost Daughter. In time, Cade drove them out the back gate, heading them down the trail toward the river. The rest of the cattle, however, indisputably carried their brand.

Ninety-four head more.

Together, that brought the total to two hundred and forty-two head.

"There are two calves up in the back field," one of the deputies said, riding along side of them.

Stomach plummeting, Emory nodded.

The Sheriff didn't ask any details. "Fine. Get their tag numbers and let's try to wrap this up. My dinner's waiting."

The deputy turned and trotted to the gate that opened onto pasture number two. He rode up to the calves, examining their scabbed-over brands. Face obscured by his cowboy hat, she was able to tell what caught his attention by the direction of the tilt. At length, he moved up towards the calves' heads and wrote down the tag numbers.

He opened and shut the gate using a determined care, afterwards raising up his clipboard in a clear signal to the sheriff.

The sheriff trotted to him, intentionally keeping his back toward the Crosses. The men conferred for what came across as a long time, but in reality, lasted only a few minutes.

Matter determined, in their minds at least, only the sheriff returned down to them. "The brands of those two calves are fresher than the rest. Don't suppose they're listed in your records, are they?"

The sheriff out-and-out refused to make eye-contact with Emory, so trained instead upon the patriarch.

For his part, Lance Cross's humor was about half an inch from giving out. "Yeah. Well, if they aren't, we know who the dam is, if that's what you're asking."

The sheriff's eyes narrowed. "Who's in charge of your records, for heaven's sake?"

"Emory *was*," her father replied. "Don't seem she has the aptitude for it."

The sheriff shook his head, pressed his lips into a thin, pale line.

Emory concentrated out at the mountains beyond, heart thudding stronger. Temper flaring.

"That true, Emory?" The sheriff asked, steady.

It took a moment to gather herself. "It's true I kept the records in the Murdoch's book I already turned over to you. The calves are listed in there. Listing dam 1805 as their mother. And you're right. I made that entry only a few days ago. I guess I forgot to tell my father."

There was no sense in saying another blessed word, not when in-fighting would be the unravelling of them all.

Distracted, she nudged Kai into a slow trot—a trot away from the sheriff's scrutiny.

Off-count from the 237 number she had been so certain of. Off by seven.

"Emory!" The sheriff's voice cut through the distance. "We need you back here, please."

A hell of a thing.

She turned around and rode back for the reckoning, knowing it couldn't be good.

16

ALLIANCES ARE MEANT FOR BREAKING

THE SHERIFF, INSPECTORS, AND DEPUTIES, HUDDLED together on horseback comparing notes. At length, the brand inspector and the sheriff dismounted and walked over to the Crosses, who began dismounting as well.

Her father grunted as he swung off Drako, swaying when he hit the ground. Embarrassing for a so-called working cattleman. No matter how hot and tired they all were, that dip and sway sure got noticed, and not in a good way.

He wouldn't be remounting any time soon, at least not if he could help it.

"Well, Mr. Cross," the brand inspector began, noticing the dip as had the others, but ignoring it out of professional courtesy. "You see which way this is headed. We're going to take all our notes back to the office, enter them into the computer, and see what we've got by tag number. Next we'll cross reference those tags from ones reported in previous years and see what pops out."

Her father shifted his weight from one foot to the

other. "Yeah, it appears the record keeping got a bit out of hand."

Happily, the conversation stayed among the six of them. The inspectors, sheriff, and the Crosses, including Cade, all locked stares at each other—away from the deputies who groomed and loaded the horses.

"We'll be in touch," the sheriff said at length.

"We'll be here," her father replied.

The sheriff, heading toward one of the trucks, paused and turned back around.

"Emory, I'll want to see you in my office at nine o'clock tomorrow morning."

Mortified, she only nodded.

"Em's not in charge here, I am." Her father came across as stern, but something inside of him deflated.

"Em's the one whose recent records we have. What you handed over was three years old, Lance. So as I was sayin', Em. Nine o'clock in the morning. Sharp."

The Lost Daughter outfit exchanged guarded glances in silence. At least until the enemy drove off.

Without a way to dress it all up, the accusation leveled against them amount to the next thing to cattle rustling. Underreporting. A type of theft all the same.

That was a hard indictment to gloss over.

Afterward, the Lost Daughter contingent stood shoulder to shoulder.

Cade, unbidden but knowing his job, untacked Drako before staring on his. Kai stood waiting for her.

"What happens now?" She posed her question in a low voice.

"Depends how bad it is," her father replied with a pointed glint directed at Cade.

They waited for him to disappear inside the barn, carrying two saddles, one in either hand.

Emory swallowed. "When did the records *start getting out of hand?*"

"Oh," he gave her the long-eyed stare. "About three years ago, like he said. I didn't have all the money to pay the fees."

Now that confession shocked her. "You never mentioned anything about money."

"No reason to. And, that's not the type of thing a man wants to advertise."

She turned toward him full on, momentarily forgetting about Cade's part in the scrutiny. "There will be a monetary fine, I'm guessing."

"No doubt," he replied, eyes still trained on the barn door. "We'll see what they come up with and deal with it then."

"You have the money for it?"

Cade reemerged and sized up the two of them. Whatever he saw didn't prevent him from approaching. "What are you thinking?"

Her father shook his head. "I'm thinking we might just pull through, although I don't like it. I especially don't like them asking for Em in the morning."

Cade's eyes travelled from her father to her, and back again. "Anything I can do to help?"

"Yeah," her father replied. "Keep your damned mouth shut and your pants on. And that advice is just for starters."

Cade's nostrils flared, and a vein in his neck throbbed. He didn't take kindly to getting called out, even if her father had a valid point.

Plenty sore, the cow prod took about five paces toward the bunkhouse, spun around and came back, charging.

"Don't tell me how to live my life," he spat. "All of this

trouble is not down to me. It's down to you and the lack of interest you take. Everyone knows that Emory is practically running this place, and you had no call to cast suspicion upon her abilities. Out of all of us, this isn't her fault, and you know it."

A vein in her father's neck took up throbbing as Emory's heart quickened. Her fluttering heart didn't result from the unexpected outburst. Almost beside herself, it was hard to believe, but Cade was actually standing up for her. Against her father, of all people.

She looked from one man to the other. Fighting among themselves would only make matters worse.

"Dad. Please. It's been a long, hard day. I think we can all agree that we need to band together. How about I get dinner started, and Cade comes to eat with us tonight?"

Lance Cross eyed his errant cowhand. "He's probably got other plans."

"No, I don't." Cade shot across.

"Fine," Emory interjected. "That's settled then. Cade, can you come over in about forty-five minutes? We'll have microwaved food at its finest," she said. "And salad."

Like that would sweeten the offer.

Cade tipped his hat and headed toward the bunkhouse. Finally, some semblance of manners coming out of him which made him even more dangerous where she was concerned. His flashing eyes, crooked grin and bad-boy swagger combined with a trace of old-fashioned western manners struck to the bottom of female hearts. Chances were Cade had a plan, and that plan was aimed straight at the 'real' money crowd. That real money crowd didn't include her.

Together, she and her father stared at Cade's back.

"You coming in?" Emory asked him, actually waiting for a response.

But he still tracked Cade as the cowboy walked into the bunkhouse.

"Keep away from him, Em," he said, set on the matter.

Dead set. All the while knowing such commands likely fell on deaf ears.

Especially when girls turned giddy.

Inside, Emory cleared off the table so three people seated wouldn't be surrounded by piles of cast-off crap. Everything pretty much fit in a liquor store box laying abandoned in the corner. Her father sat down in his chair, looking older than he had that morning. His hair stuck up in tufts from his hat that he didn't bother to smooth down.

For once, he didn't turn the TV on.

"Aren't you going to take a shower?" She asked, leaning to see around the corner of the doorframe between the dining and living rooms.

"For Cade? That sonofabitch is the reason why we're in this mess, and don't you go forgetting that part. Invite him to dinner! What the hell is this ranch coming to, is what I'd like to know."

"Fine," she called, moving back into the kitchen and dampening a cloth to wipe down the table. "I'll get in the bathroom right now. I was just giving you first shot, that's all. I'm plenty hot and sweaty, that's for dang sure."

He hefted himself up from the chair and made his stiff-gaited way to the refrigerator. "I'll help myself to a beer while I wait for you to finish."

"Suit yourself," she replied. "Sore?"

"Now, what do you think? But probably not as bad as you was hopin'. Now git. I don't want to have to sit here and make small talk with Cade. Who is on my shit list, in case you couldn't tell."

Emory paused halfway toward the stairs, and looked at her father, closely. "I thought I was on your shit list."

He softened and shook his head. "Nah. That's just the part you had to play in all of this."

———

EMORY KNEW BETTER than to dawdle, so she made it one fast shower.

She drew the line, however at rushing to get ready. Instead she took her time styling her long brown hair, putting on make-up, and choosing the right clean clothes including her favorite pearl-snapped shirt that nipped in at the waistline nicely. Probably no one would notice the effort she made, but company was a rare commodity in that house.

Especially single male company.

For the occasion, she added a few quick squirts of perfume as she consulted the mirror. The hated freckles across the bridge of her nose didn't strike her as loathsome as usual.

Cade knocked on the door and the sound carried upstairs. She moved away from the sink after one last glance to check her appearance.

"Come in," her father bellowed.

The front door opened, the hinge protesting at a slow entry. A mumbled greeting only halfway toward audible.

"If you want a beer, you'll have to get it yourself. I'm going upstairs to take a shower while Em gets dinner ready."

Well, that part came out clear.

Em and her father passed each other on the stairs.

He eyed her, taking everything in. She felt a blush rising and darted past him.

"Dinner will be on the table in twenty minutes," she said to her father, bounding down the stairs.

Cade's eyes lit up when she burst into the living room, and self-consciously, she suppressed a proud smile.

DINNER TURNED out a strange and silent affair. If Emory had expected uplifting dinner conversation, she was sorely mistaken as the men tucked into the microwaved lasagna. Glancing at them both, Emory noticed how they kept their eyes fixed downward, focused on their plates.

Focused away from each other.

The only sounds were the clinking of the cutlery and chewing.

Without conversation, the next morning's impending visit weighed upon her mind.

"Don't suppose either of you been in a mess like this before?" She asked.

She posed her question not out of curiosity, certain that she had the answer. She posed the question because the silence and the strain were getting to her.

Cade looked up from his plate and met her eyes, shaking his head 'no'.

Her father didn't bother to hide his expression—the one that said "dumb-ass."

"Don't you think you would have remembered something like that if it happened afore?"

Yeah, she would have remembered. And the table once again sank into silence.

AT EIGHT-THIRTY, the following morning rolled around too fast for comfort. Or too slow. Hard to say which, other than time didn't act like a friend to her.

Not this time. Not this problem.

Emory managed drinking a cup of coffee down, but her stomach felt far too clenched to eat.

Whatever the sheriff wanted to say to her was bound to be bad.

Even more notable, her father had been up since before daylight, silently drinking coffee that he made himself. His forehead was creased—a sure sign of his worry.

"I'll drive in with you, Em," he announced, studying the clock on the wall.

Stubborn pride on her part won out. If she wanted to be truthful, she partially refused his offer as a type of punishment that she felt he deserved.

"I can handle it myself. Just answer the phone if it rings. It may be my one phone call, and I'd sure hate to have you miss it."

A gallows laugh. "I'll pick up the phone, but I'd feel better tagging along."

"Well, I doubt they are going to arrest me for bad counting…" But half of her thought exactly that. The other half said she borrowed trouble.

It stood to reason that this time the sheriff would likely give her a warning, but even that was bad enough. It rubbed against her pride in her ability to help run a ranch.

"Emory. Now you listen to me. The taxes have nothing to do with you. You've never prepared them, you haven't seen them, and you don't know a thing about them."

"True. You've always done them."

Her father nodded. "That's right, and I've never shown them to you. No reason to. Now don't go getting all rattled. You've done nothing wrong. I have. And don't you forget it."

She edged her way over to her father's side.

"I'll stay by the phone, Em. But don't you worry. You've done nothing wrong."

"Except the mavericks."

He rubbed his knuckles, considering. "You reported them and handed that book over. If they want to examine that dam, well. We'll handle that when we get to it."

Emory did a double take. "But she *had* a calf. It died." She frowned. "I thought I told you that."

Sheepish, he shrugged. "Maybe you did. Guess sometimes I get a bit beer fogged and whatnot. That's perfect then. We're back to you haven't done a damned thing wrong."

He widened his arms. She threw herself into them, clinging. Clinging and nowhere near as certain as she would like to be.

He patted her on the back.

"Now git," he said. "Never keep the law waiting without a useful reason."

17

BACK DOOR OPPORTUNITY

THE SHERIFF'S OFFICE OCCUPIED A LOW, ONE-LEVEL BRICK building dating from the 1970's. Hunkered down on the outskirts of town the main road passed by in front. The building stuck out like an outpost of a sort. Main Street was also County Road 10 and remained the only thoroughfare of note in town. The location couldn't be considered strategically placed strategically placed other than for keeping an eye on who came into town, and who left. But maybe that was good enough. Probably the builders availed themselves of a vacant lot at the time. Whatever the case, the building boasted its own parking lot—a rarity in town other than for the Kum-N-Go and the school. Actually the parking lot acted more as an asphalt-covered wasted expanse than a necessary feature. Nine times out of ten, it stood empty except for the sheriff's truck and the vehicles driven by the deputy and the office help. Judging by the appearances of the staff's vehicles, those jobs didn't pay anything much to get excited about.

Regardless, whoever planned the asphalt lot expected

a whole lot more activity than the town proved capable of producing. The meth-head's single gas pump stood straight in the line of sight from the front windows, but no one did a damn thing about it. *That* would be a reasonable place for law enforcement to start. But Emory had enough trouble of her own without offering unsolicited advice.

Unsolicited, not to mention, unpopular advice.

On that day, it was the one time out of ten when there were four cars in that parking lot, hers being, unfortunately, the fourth. It was embarrassing enough that people would note her truck there and of course, they would assume the worse.

Probably figuring that she had it coming, one way or the other.

She parked in front of the entrance, stepped down one leg at a time and faced uncertainty like she never had before. Squaring her shoulders, Emory strode in through the double glass doors pretending a confidence that she most certainly didn't feel.

An aging woman, sporting a mile-high bouffant, seated behind the reception desk guarded the entrance. Likely she was one of the owners of one of those beaten-up cars. Emory didn't know her, though the woman seemed mildly familiar. Hell, everyone in town looked familiar one way or another.

"I'm here to see Sheriff Preston," she explained, catching the pervasive smell of bleach and disinfectant.

"You're Emory Cross?" The woman asked, eyes too sharp for comfort.

Emory nodded, miserable enough but hoping to come across as nonchalant. Of course, she failed that mission, too.

"His office is straight ahead the first right as you enter the hallway. He's expecting you."

Emory crossed the linoleum floor and passed a set of mustard colored, vinyl covered chairs. There was also a magazine-strewn table displaying hunting and fishing galore across the laminated top. The woman at the desk must not have gone in for much for tidying, and good for her. She slowed in front of the former sheriff's gallery, engraved nameplates screwed onto the wooden plaques and frames.

To hear her father tell it, most of them were assholes. There was a prevailing indifference to the law in their part of the state.

Some of those assholes trying to change public sentiment and failed, at least from what she had heard.

Considering all the black and white photographs would get her nowhere. Just another form of dawdling; and besides, the woman at the desk watched and didn't even try to hide it. Emory felt the woman's eyes on her back as she knocked on the sheriff's door.

"Come."

She opened the door about five inches and threaded her way in sideways.

"Take a seat, Em."

She slid into the waiting chair without saying a word.

"I'll bet you're wondering why you are here." The sheriff settled straight down to business.

She swallowed and squared her shoulders yet again. "Not really, considering."

He blinked. "Oh, the business yesterday. No, I want to talk about the scholarship and some options."

Hands between her knees, she turned her attention out the window, miserable. "That probably won't work if I have a criminal record."

Tearing her eyes away from the comfort of the mountains, she met his direct.

Those eyes glinted. "No. You're right. It actually wouldn't. Which is why I want you to think about your future. Hopefully all of this has scared some smarts into that head of yours. If going to higher education doesn't appeal to you, there's something else. You managed to impress both of the inspectors, one way or another."

"Impressed them how—my inability to count?"

The sheriff chuckled. "We all know you were taking the fall for your old man."

She sighed, bothered about the undercurrent, both at the ranch and in the sheriff's office. "To be honest, I don't understand how things got so out of whack. What's going to happen now?"

The sheriff pushed back in his chair, never once taking his eyes off her face. "I don't know, Em. I'm sure there will be a fine of sorts, but that's not my jurisdiction. That would be up to the BLM inspector."

They locked eyes, a thought flashing through her mind.

One that the sheriff read loud and clear.

"Don't call him, Emory, and I mean it now. Not about the fines, not about your ranch. *Not* about this case. Besides, that's not why I've called you in here today. I wanted to get you away from the Lost Daughter and talk to you, one on one. Seems to me your lot don't need two lost daughters to boast of."

"What's that supposed to mean?"

"Don't play dumb. It doesn't suit you. The brand inspector came away impressed with your abilities. He said people can either see brands or they can't, and apparently you can."

Emory suppressed laugh, surprised and warming

toward the topic and safer ground. "Yeah, I can see brands all right. Still beats me how people can't. I mean, they are right there."

"What's being offered," Sheriff Preston leaned forward, cutting her off, "is a job that offers training with the brand inspectors at the sale barn. Best of all, you can even bring your horse."

Kai! She wouldn't have to leave him behind.

She blinked and sat forward, wary. "A brand inspector. Me?"

"You'd be working for Terry Overholzer, and you already met him. He's good. Think that would suit you?"

She couldn't believe her ears. "I'm not sure. What would I need to do?"

The sheriff gave her nod and pulled out his cell phone, scrolled through the contacts and pressed a button. "Terry, I've got Emory Cross sitting right here…"

Possibilities beckoned and remarkably, they didn't involve jail terms.

Stunned, Emory left the sheriff's office in a daze. She eyed the town as she drove through, poised to leave the only home she had ever known.

Her feelings scattered all over the board, drifting between excitement and hang-dog guilt at the very same time.

She didn't deserve this break but she'd take it, by golly.

Excitement bubbling up, she pulled out her cell phone to give her dad a call.

Dead.

Once again she'd forgotten to charge, so she pocketed the phone with a shrug.

Whether the opportunity as a brand inspector intern was deserved or not, Emory Cross drove back to the ranch at odds as to how she would explain the remarkable chain of events.

She pulled up in front of the house and burst into the living room.

True to his word, her father sat waiting, cell phone in hand. Visible relief showed in the release of his shoulders when he saw and read her face. He stood up slowly from the chair.

"What did they want?" He didn't even growl it. Just sounded tired, like any scared dad who had waited up too late. But the clock told the time as ten-fifteen in the morning.

The strain of everything took its toll upon him.

"My cell was dead, or I would have called from the truck." She checked it again. Still dead. "There's a county scholarship to go to college, but that doesn't sound like what I want to get into."

Confusion rippled through her father's expression. He jutted his head forward, like he hadn't heard her quite right. "Scholarship?"

Emory stopped. Inhaled, and waited for her words to catch up inside of her head.

"I've been offered a job and training at the Greeley Sale Barn, learning and working alongside the brand inspectors."

His eyebrows shot up, and his mouth hung open slightly. He shook his head, never once taking his eyes off of her. "He didn't want to talk about the count or the mavericks?"

"No, Dad. He wanted to talk to me about my future."

For a moment she thought he'd get mad. Really mad. But the darkness in his expression lifted, and he ran his fingers through his hair.

"Think you'd like that?"

Confusion hit her. "Why, yes…but I guess it's foolish. I know I'm needed here."

He sat back down, stunned, but she could tell the wheels in his mind slowly clanked together and shifted into gear. "Not so fast. This could be a blessing in disguise."

She waited.

He thought, expression stony and remote.

"This last go-round cut too close to the bone for comfort. I don't want you wrapped up in all of this." He met her eyes.

That caught her. All of a sudden, nothing felt certain. "I always planned on running the ranch one day. You said…"

His steel gray eyes didn't waver as they bore into hers. "And one day you will. But times, they are a-changing. It wouldn't hurt to make something of yourself before you're stuck here."

"I didn't think you'd like the idea." She searched his face, wanting assurance.

But he wasn't paying much heed to her at all. Instead, he stared into the corner at something no longer there. A ghost or a memory, it was hard to say which. "Knowing the ins and outs of brand inspection couldn't hurt. It might put us on the inside track for a change."

Uncertain how to take that comment, she tried again. "I'd just be checking brands, like I tend to do anyhow. I don't know what inside track there would be for us to get on."

"It's a start," he countered. "Having someone in law enforcement might prove an asset in the future. You're a smart girl, Em. Always have been. It's about time I got my ass moving again. Time's up for drinking the outfit away and letting the hired help run roughshod."

Emory double-checked to see if he was kidding, but he looked serious enough.

"It's not exactly like the FBI for heaven's sake," she corrected. "And Cade's not exactly running roughshod over the outfit. I see to that part."

Her father barely listened, but he caught onto part of that first one. "Law enforcement is exactly what it is, mark my words. That might be good, considering. And the last thing I need is to hear that you're involved with that cow prod. You deserve more than just falling for the first guy you run into."

"You never said." Em's mouth stumbled over the words.

"'Course I did," her father replied. "You just weren't listening right."

18

MELANCHOLIA

AUGUST 2020

IT DIDN'T TAKE LONG FOR THAT FINE TO COME IN. TWO weeks later the envelope arrived demanding $3,500 and some change. $3,500 they didn't exactly have lying around and unspoken for.

"That's the price of a steer," her father groused.

"Seems to me like we might be getting off light," Emory countered.

"Now you sound like one of them! But mebbe so. Mebbe on account of how you are on the road to reform." He seemed to find that last bit funny.

Still, her father had to make the trip into town and throw himself at the mercy of the bank. The exact situation that most of those buzzards wanted. Nothing hit the bank's bottom lines better for their portfolios and profit margins than to have ranchers trailing in, tails between their legs and pleading for small loans to tide them over. Small loans with large acreages to act as collateral. Loans they might just default on when those better days didn't come.

That stark reality provided another good reason for Emory to get a paying job. As long as they had cash for payments, nothing would get repossessed.

"What did you have to sign over?" she asked.

Her father knuckled the two-day growth on his chin. "The cemetery parcel."

She eyed him. "You did no such thing."

"And that's where you're wrong. I did," he gloated, not fooling around. "I showed 'em a picture of the views. If they want bodies, I'll give them bodies. Damn them all to hell and the horses they rode in on."

"Those graves are family, Dad…"

He didn't seem to care, or at least not much.

"Yeah, well. They'd understand. And people get squeamish about building on top of graves, or so I've heard."

Yes, that they did.

He winked. "Don't worry, so. We'll make the payments. Just wanted to get a line of credit established."

"What for," she asked. "Wouldn't it have been better just to sell off a few of the old cows?"

"I always told you, you was smart. Let 'em think we're hurting. It will only play in our favor at some point along the line. Keep 'em guessing. That's the plan. Especially if we take them history people up on the improvement money."

Dang.

Her father was wilier than she usually credited.

No one told Cade much of anything at all for obvious reasons.

His blood wasn't theirs, and he would never truly be one of them. He was just paid help and paid help that had screwed up royal.

Emory remained shut in the house following that strange morning trip into town. She knew full well that Cade would be waiting to hear what had happened. Now he likely assumed the worst based on her failure to appear.

Let him sweat.

She caught him glancing at the house from the shelter of the barn more than once. He went about his chores that day, with an eye on the lookout. For her part, she remained on the lookout for him as well, spying through windows but careful to remain out of the line of sight.

The sheriff was right.

No sense in having two lost daughters, not that she ever planned on being considered as such. As for Hapless Susan, there was no helping her now in this century. Perhaps that's what the brand inspector offered, a strange lifeline of a sorts. Local people sure remembered the matter of Emory's absconding mother and more than a few tragic stories to go around. All stories involving the ranch.

She didn't care to think about her mother. Why would she? She abandoned Emory and her father when Emory was a thin eleven year-old, all gangly limbs and broken hearted. Crying on the porch until her father carried her back into the house.

The subject of her missing mother would stay behind a locked door, never to be opened for discussion. At least, not by her.

There were plenty of ways 'lost' could happen.

Instead of dwelling on the melancholia lingering in the corners of her bedroom, she returned downstairs. She had chores to do.

Times had indeed changed within the Cross household. The TV wasn't on, and her father was nowhere in sight.

"Dad?"

"Back here."

She traced her way through the maze into the ranch office. Her father sifted through papers, making headway through the piles. He glanced up when she entered.

"Thought I'd try to make some sense of this," he said. "Clear off a spot if you want to sit down."

Emory picked up a pile of random papers covering the seat of an old barrel-backed office chair. It dated from back in the day when actual meetings might have occurred in that very office.

"When did this room get tacked on, anyhow?" The walls were thin, and likely didn't do much to keep the winter draft out. But it was summer now, and a breeze was somewhat welcomed.

Make a note. Another thing to fix.

"Maybe in the 'thirties. Before the war. My grandpa told me the original office was that old square-logged cabin."

He pointed a gnarled finger through the window, to an old squat building of square-cut logs.

"That had to be warmer than this," she replied. "Back in the day."

"Yeah," he admitted. "Until the time come he almost frozed to death coming back to the house in a blizzard."

Emory frowned.

"You go ahead and look like that all you want. Those were the days before yard lights."

She settled into the topic. "He should have tied a rope the distance to the house."

"Said he did," Lance Cross nodded. "Someone untied it, he claimed. But I've also heard it got cut."

That earned another long-eyed stare from Emory. "Any idea who?"

"There were suspicions."

Papers filling both of her hands and frankly stunned, she sat there for a moment, but her father resumed sorting. Conversation closed, at least in his mind.

"Want me to help you go through these?" She held up the assortment.

"If you want. I'm sorting them out by type: vet bills, feed bills, those damn historical preservation people. You get the picture."

"You tried firing up that computer?" Glancing over the edge of the desk, she had already dropped down to the floor, to set out her papers into piles on the rough planks.

"Told 'im it was broke."

"You know it's not. Just takes a while to boot up. He didn't exactly believe you anyhow."

Scowling at her, Lance Cross twisted to push a button on the floor console. The monitor flickered to life and he squinted at it, index-fingering in his name and password. She sure had her doubts on that password part.

It clunked a fair bit, but the computer came on after a time. A fairly long time.

"Don't suppose you want to buy a new one?" Emory asked.

"Nope," he replied.

She didn't even pause the sorting. "Let me take a look once I get these done."

"What are you back here for, anyhow?"

She paused, sitting on her haunches. "What'll I tell Cade?"

"Tell him you're outta here," his eyes twinkled.

A half-barked laugh from Emory. "That's not very father-like."

"Should do the trick," he countered.

Casting around the office, she felt a tug. Misplaced perhaps, but a tug all the same. "You know that I'll still come back to help when you need me, don't you?"

"You're a good girl Em. Glad you're doing something with yourself."

She eyed him. "You haven't answered my question."

"Time will tell. Sometimes things have a way of not working out, but I won't hold it against you none."

"I'll be back when needed. Straight or crooked." Mind made up on that matter at least, she would.

Her father cleared his throat and stared into the computer screen, throwing up error messages as it tried to function.

Maybe that's what they all did. Tried to function and throw up messages along the way.

STRAIGHT OR CROOKED.

That's how the Lost Daughter ran. She'd grown up under the shadow of that saying as a type of family pledge. A pledge that carried them all through all the decades and across century lines. That 'straight or crooked' probably carried them since the whole spread was carved out, fought for and won. True, the fighting hadn't been against the Utes, who'd already been relegated to the reservations—but they didn't always stay where they were supposed to.

Kind of like the Crosses themselves.

No, the Crosses fights had been more along the lines of struggling against the weather and conditions, the land itself, and the outlaw element. An outlaw element which they may, or may not have been, a part of. Hell, they struggled against the law, too. A long shadowy history. Unmarked graves. She wondered if the family even knew where most of the bodies laid buried.

For one, she didn't know. Hoping for a full accounting was a lost cause even before she started.

There was no denying the important fact that her father was the last family member standing, beyond her.

One thing remained for certain, a lot of those unmarked graves weren't in that now- mortgaged cemetery plot.

The afternoon and time itself wore on heedless of the dead and departed. Finally Emory made her way outside to find Cade.

She didn't see him in the yard, so she tried the barn. Nothing more than empty stalls, tack racks, and a few bales of hay, probably from last season. Lingering at the barndoor, she took a gander to the side of the bunkhouse. His truck was parked alongside where it ought to be, but she didn't want to go knocking on his door.

Instead, she checked for his horse, and it was gone. They were out riding somewhere.

With a shrug, she whistled hard. She waited, listening for a reply.

He couldn't have been that far out—he had no reason.
She waited some more and whistled again.

Nothing.

Absolutely nothing came back in reply.

19

REGRETS TO REMAIN
UNSPOKEN

LATER IN THE DAY CADE RETURNED, RIDING BACK INTO the ranch yard like nothing in the world was amiss. Nothing except for a haunted expression held in the lines around his eyes.

She'd only have been flattering herself if she truly believed she was the cause of his concern.

All the same, she wondered the source of his bother.

Her father remained in the back of the house, still occupied by shoveling out his office. With light, quick steps, she hastened out of the front door to talk to the cowboy.

He pushed back his hat when he saw her walking in his direction.

Her heart shifted, but she didn't act like it.

"How'd everything go at the sheriff's?" Saddlebag slung over his shoulder, he at least stopped moving long enough to listen.

"A bit unexpected," she answered truthfully. Swallowing as she tripped over the next part.

He came across as guarded. "Unexpected how?"

Another swallow. "I'm leaving the Lost Daughter."

Incredulous brown eyes widened. "They're putting you under arrest?"

Emory shook her head, half glad for the scare she inspired. "No. Nothing like that. They've offered me a position as a junior type brand inspector in Greeley. Kind of like an internship, I guess, but I get paid."

His eyes darted. "You're pulling my leg. I don't think—"

"It's not a joke. I can read brands. You know that as well as anyone."

"What the hell! What does your father say about all of this?" Cade looked like he'd been hit up alongside the head and hit hard.

Emory eyed the saddlebag still slung over his shoulder, sharp. "He's glad I'm being given a chance at something new. He's busy cleaning his office now. I guess this entire episode snapped him out of whatever funk he was in for the last few years."

What she really wanted was a reaction from Cade's reaction. *A reaction about her.* "You'll be working with him now, as far as I know."

He didn't rise to the bait but instead found a barb of his own. "Guess they don't know about them two calves of yours. How do you square that away?"

"I don't," Emory snapped. Still, their origins remained a thorny issue. Almost good enough for blackmail material. She'd have to find a better answer to that question or make amends somehow.

But for the time being, she wasn't saying a damn thing.

"Maybe, in time, I'll ask if anyone was missing two calves that didn't come in." That would be swallowing a big slice of crow pie, but she'd do it if she had to. Another option was to butcher the calves for the food bank. Just because they lived rural, didn't mean that hunger didn't go around.

"Sounds like we've come to a fork in the road," an exasperated half-chuckle from Cade. "And you're planning to take the high road. Or trying to. How do you think that would ever work out for a girl like you?"

A girl like her.

In the current of innuendo and half-truths swirling about them, she figured she'd never have an answer as to what Cade Timmons actually felt for her. Or thought about her.

At the moment, the expression on his beautiful masculine face fished for something.

Common sense told her not to supply anything he searched for.

"What's in the saddle bags," she asked instead.

"None of your business," he snapped, pulling himself up that much taller and trying to stare her down.

"Everything on this spread is my business," she replied, strong.

Cade spat, and grinned. "No, it ain't. Not anymore."

She took a step closer to him. Nothing more than a foot of space between them.

"I'm a Cross until the day I die. The Lost Daughter is my legacy. Not yours. Not anyone else's other than my father's. And let me tell you what. He won't allow backtalk or shady dealings that aren't of his own doing. He's taken an interest in how things are run. And he blames you for this mess."

Cade's eyes narrowed, although he acted unconcerned. "We'll see about all of that," he replied.

She wouldn't back down. Not now, not this time.

"One of your buckle bunnies said you dealt drugs."

Those brown eyes trained on her, right fast. "That's what you think I've got in them saddle bags—drugs?"

She waited. Said nothing, offered nothing, but stood there waiting.

He threw the bags down at her feet. "Go ahead," he muttered in a deathlike calm. "Take a damned look for yourself."

Tempted, Emory considered the pile of leather lying at her feet. Temptingly easy to reach down and open one of those flaps.

Instead, she took one long-legged step over the jumble and proceeded into the barn. Conflicted and mad.

A truly brave person would have opened those saddle bags, but she sure would have felt stupid if there had been nothing in them other than a bottle of water.

Weak. She cursed herself as weak, not having the backbone or fortitude to call his bluff.

Afraid of bottled water.

BY THE TIME SHE REEMERGED, Cade had skedaddled and his horse turned out into one of the paddocks, grazing. Mad at her insinuations—or hell, accusations—he likely was plotting a way out of dealing with her father. Things were going to change around the Lost Daughter, sure as shootin'. For Cade, that meant his job was about to get harder.

In the meanwhile, she had packing to do.

For all the times that she had imagined what it would be like to leave, actually preparing to do just that had a strange finality that she hadn't counted on.

Peering down a steep precipice. Never mind the opportunity at the bottom.

She'd only known life at the Lost Daughter and the world felt suddenly wide and strange. She'd learn more along the way, and probably take a few lumps as she went.

Flinging open the closet door, the contents therein were sparse but Emory would live to tell the tale. The wooden floor stood practically bare except for a sweater laying in a heap, fallen from a wire hanger. Dress boots, athletic shoes, and a pair of flat blacks, were all that she had for shoes in the closet. Work boots remained out in the mudroom or on her feet. She considered the scarred and battered boots she wore. Well. They worked good enough for stomping through pens and corrals.

Five western work shirts hung on wire hangers, a bit threadbare and faded from sunscald and washing, but still serviceable and would do the trick. One white blouse, a prim black A-line skirt, a prairie dress, and a fancy black dress that she bought for herself, but never should have. No place to wear black other than for funerals, and the low neckline guaranteed it sure as heck wasn't a funeral-type of dress.

Removing each garment from its hanger one by one and folding them, she'd never been good at that type of thing. The wire hangers hung empty on the mottled rod, the closet bare.

Her pending departure strikingly real.

Emory slowed down, pulled open the battered dresser's top drawer and removed the contents one drawer after the other.

Jeans, underwear, t-shirts, and socks, and not much else.

Emory had precious little to show for a young

woman her age. Small heaps of clothing piled alongside the suitcase proved that very point. She figured out too late that the jeans should go in first. So she took everything out and started over. Placing her fancy dress on top once again, she considered the expenditure, seeing as how the price tags were still attached. One-hundred and fifty dollars that dress had cost her. A waste of rare, hard-earned cash.

She'd never heard much about Greeley being fancy, but she'd give it a try.

At least Greeley was a place where no one had ever heard of her family or the Lost Daughter Ranch.

That would be a first.

BUCKSHOT

SEPTEMBER 2020

THE MORNING OF HER DEPARTURE, THE LIGHT CAME THE same time as always, but this time it rose up onto a morning unlike any other she'd lived through.

Her father stood gazing out the window over the dripping sink, coffee cup in hand.

"You all right?" Emory asked when she saw him.

"Maybe, yes." He tore himself away from the view and fetched her a cup and poured out the coffee. His handed her the cup then looked away, self-conscious.

He seldom served anyone but himself.

She swallowed a couple of extra times, her throat constricting.

Together they headed out to the porch, sitting down on the old time-faded furniture, bleached from the years of strong sunlight. The floorboards warped, rippled and pulled, still bearing traces of peeled ribbons of robin's egg blue paint. Above, the swallow's mud nest lodged in the eaves. Images she intentionally seared into her mind, knowing there would be no returning to this exact moment and space in time.

As much as she tried to capture the moment and essence, she knew it would fade like a photograph left in sunlight too long. But it would remain in some form, and she would carry it with her, forward.

Beyond the sunbaked fence rails and outbuildings listing from age, the sprawling green pasture still grew thick with unmown hay.

"When are you going to get around to that?" She nodded at the meadow.

"Right after you drive off."

"Sure?" She asked out of habit, knowing his assurances didn't mean it'd get done.

"Sure," he replied.

This all was home, the good and the bad and the past. The rippling hay carried the future and that hay needed tending. The mountains stood blue in the remote distance, guarding the valley the same as they had always done.

"Do you remember the last time this porch floor got painted?"

A dry, wheezing laugh. "As a matter of fact, I do. 1975 'cause I did it myself. Never saw fit to paint it again. Or any other floor, for that matter."

That sounded about right.

Her father palmed his denim-covered thighs over and over again in an absent gesture.

"Well," he said at length, "I guess it's about time. You don't want to keep the Oberholzers waitin' on you."

"Overholzers," she corrected.

"Huh," came his only reply.

The fence posts shimmered before a few quick blinks dammed up unshed tears. No matter that she would only be about three hours away, she somehow felt condemned. In a brief phone conversation earlier, the Overholzer's offered both her and Kai room and board while she found her footing.

Still, they couldn't offer her a true home, and she'd never had her own apartment. She wondered what it would be like, living on her own.

Emory tried to corral her erratic thoughts.

"You going to try to figure out what Cade is up to?"

A shrug. "Mebbe. Last thing I need is more trouble turning up for no good reason." He eyed Emory's truck, troubled about something. "Hang on a minute."

He went back into the house and returned about five minutes later, a 30-30 repeating rifle in hand. "Take this," he said holding it out for her.

"Why?" She stammered, completely taken aback.

"You got a rifle rack and a permit. What's the problem?" He eyed her like she ought to know better.

"I don't know," she replied. "That's likely pushing some boundary don't you think?"

He shook his head. "That might not, but this likely will."

He dug in his pocket and pulled out a wad of bills and thrust them toward her, his voice a tether grounding her to the here and now. "Take this, you'll need it at some point. Rent deposits and that type of thing."

Blinking back the tears, she mumbled. "What's that?"

"Two thousand and fifty dollars."

Emory didn't think she'd heard right. "From the bank loan?"

"Nah," came the reply.

"Where'd you come up with something like that?"

"From the sale of those mavericks," he grinned. "Had

Cade take them to auction yesterday. And I threw in a bit more, besides."

Though her stomach turned cold, she reached out for the money. "It's kind of stolen money, then."

"You bet," came his reply. "Part of it is."

He eyed her close to gauge her reaction.

She pocketed the bills. "Maybe just this one time."

"Give 'em hell." He winked.

A TIME AND PLACE
HOMESICKNESS

Armed and loaded, Emory peeled out of the Lost Daughter Ranch with Kai in the trailer behind. Cade stepped out of the bunkhouse to watch her leave. In the rearview mirror she saw him lift up his hand a split-second too late to wave.

He dropped his hand down by his side, limp.

Just a gesture—but maybe she meant something to him one way or another.

Nothing was ever certain at all concerning Cade. Not where females came in, not where accountability mattered.

She turned on the radio. Not a blaring good time, but enough to distract. The guitar twanging lifted her mood, but the steel sky hung low and stern.

Checking the horse trailer from her side mirror, she pulled off of the ranch road onto the paved county road.

Those dollars in her purse carried 2,050 blood-deep accusations right alongside them.

History ran hard.

Emory entered the garden city of Greeley three hours later, stomach in knots from the burgeoning thrill of freedom. The agreed-to plan stated she would drive to the sale barn to meet Mr. Overholzer, and from there he would take her to his home. She'd never been anyone's guest before, and that caused a fair measure of concern that she shrugged away.

She'd do chores around their place. She figured that was likely the best way to repay hospitality. Not to mention, she'd only stay at the Overholzers a short while, until she found permanent accommodations.

As it turned out, the sale barn wasn't exactly in the center of town so Emory had the opportunity to look the city over. It was big. Bigger than expected. And she knew what everyone else knew—that Greeley was a town trying to live down its reputation as the home of the feed-lot stink. She rolled down her window and sniffed.

Partial success. Success likely dependent upon the direction of the wind.

The scenic Cache La Poudre River meandered and then lassoed the town, and the Greeley Stampede was certainly a major draw.

Probably a draw that caused a shit-ton more work for the brand inspectors, too.

But that was several months off into the future. Ten, to be exact.

In all likelihood the bright lights of the university town still turned off at eleven o'clock each night. The students contributed to a sense of life and possibility, of movement and excitement. Young blood had plenty to recommend it, and that included her.

She drove by churches, a museum, greenbelts and parks, and buildings taller than two stories. Real grocery stores! Peering through her windows she noted various feed and seed shops scattered throughout, banks rested on any number of corners, and there weren't all that many bars to distract. Emory had heard Greeley used to be a dry town, and while it might have remained proud of its grain elevators, but it aspired to something greater and succeeded.

Greeley had earned its place as a card-carrying member of the twenty-first century.

Enough sight-seeing, and she didn't need to do all of her exploring at once. Couldn't, in fact.

For some reason, Greeley's map wasn't all that clear when Emory consulted her cell phone for the sale barn's location.

Considering the flat landscape expectations, locating roads and the large sale barn should have proved a straight forward proposition. Yet the gradual prairie swells, managed to hide details in the false flats.

"There it is," she murmured, proceeding east after a couple of wide passes. "Straight ahead."

The map marked her as 'having arrived' when she hadn't arrived anywhere at all. Emory stared at the back of a building surrounded by pens. That part had to be right. On site, she gave up on the map and drove along a frontage road, took a left onto another dirt road, and came upon the nearly empty parking lot where she pulled to a stop.

Good grief. She'd have to be able to do better than that.

Two white trucks were parked off to the side of the entrance bearing heavy black lettering on the sides. Brand Inspectors.

Seeing those two trucks parked like that, official and clean, made her choices suddenly real.

No kidding around. Not this time.

The lot had painted parking spots, but they sure weren't big enough for trucks pulling trailers. What the hell, no one was there. She took up several spaces, horizontal and feeling unconfident. Jumping down from the truck, first thing she checked on Kai.

"You doing OK, boy? I'll be right back, and we'll see if we can get you out of here." Emory eyed the rifle in the rack, apprehensive to leave it on open display. She'd heard about widows getting smashed in cities but going armed into a new job probably couldn't be the best of ideas, either.

She locked the doors and checked them twice.

Long-legged strides led her to the sale room's double-entry glass doors. No lights were on inside. Stepping into the silent building, she paused, listening. Nothing. The Stockman's Café waited, closed off to the right. Her stomach grumbled. The wide-open entrance to the sale arena was covered with old black and white photographs of clean and proper men. Dignitaries of one form or another they were plastered on the walls, and she glanced at them smiling down on her. A rare swelling of pride followed.

The lights were off in the sale arena, dark except for the slivers of light that came in from the ceiling's ventilation fans. Lazy blades churned in the hot prairie breeze. Old hummers, they were coated brown from kicked up dirt and manure. A lot of livestock must have passed through that arena for them to get like that.

While the exhaust fans might not have looked all that great, they were a sure sign of success, business-wise.

Old movie theater seats ringed the arena on three sides, probably rescued from demolished auditoriums: a bucket for chaw set at the end of each row for convenience.

A hanging arrow pointed upstairs indicating the location of the brand inspectors' office. Following the arrow, she paused at a Xeroxed sign posted on the cheap wooden door. *Go in and don't bother knocking.*

Right.

Light off, she flipped the switch. Black flies shot up at the intrusion, and Emory swatted them away from reflex. The door opened onto linoleum covered stairs and she took those steps two at a time and hurried through another door at the top, which again opened into a darkened hallway.

They obviously didn't go in much for lighting.

Finally, an office stood visible through a narrow, shatterproof glass window—the kind that she had in school growing up.

Two men worked inside. Out of manners, she knocked.

Glancing up, a welcoming smile lit Terry Overholzer's face as he stood up from behind his desk, motioning for her to enter.

"I wondered what time you would arrive," he said, coming around to shake her hand. "And this here is Dave Worrell."

The average age in the room had to be about fifty, and that counted her at twenty-three.

"Nice to meet you," she replied. "You guys have a gun safe in here? My father sent me with a rifle, and I didn't want to hurt his feelings by turning it down."

Both inspectors' sets of eyes widened.

"Planning on having to put some cattle down, are you?" The man called Dave asked.

"Hope not," Emory replied. "But I can if needed. I've done it before."

Terry cleared his throat. "You can bring it up here and we'll put it in the safe."

"Yeah, I figured I'd better ask before I just hauled it up in here," she added.

"Good idea," Terry replied nice and even, although his eyes again widened at the notion.

"I'll go back down and get it," she replied, darting back out.

She heard a few chuckles as she left, but no matter.

First day jitters, she figured.

THE OVERHOLZER'S RANCHETTE, located on the outskirts of Greeley, felt more remote than expected. Like full-sized ranches, it started out as a distant dot on the horizon a couple of miles from the local gas station and convenience store. It turned out to be a two-story house painted yellow, neat and tidy standing in front of a large red barn. The property had three sheds and two shelters —one for hay and another for horses.

She pulled her truck up behind Terry's.

He approached her window, smiling. "Something tells me that you're more worried about your horse's accommodation than your own, so if you want to unload him, we'll get him settled first."

Emory returned the smile. "You bet."

She circled round to the back of the trailer, unbolted the door and backed Kai out, nice and easy. "I've trained him how to load in and out of trailers," she explained, although it was obvious.

Nerves, she figured.

At that point, the front door to the house opened and

a trim woman emerged wearing a flowered dress and sensible shoes. A broad, inquisitive smile lit her face.

"You must be Emory," she said stepping up.

"Yes, ma'am." Emory replied, holding out her hand, which the woman grasped in both of hers. "I hope I'm not causing you a lot of trouble."

"No trouble at all," the woman replied, still holding on to Emory's hand. "We have plenty of room. Now I've got dinner going, but is there anything you don't eat?"

"No," Emory offered. "Don't worry about me on that count. I'm so grateful that you have a place for me while I look for a place. And I'm planning on doing chores. Please."

The woman waved off her thanks. "You stay just as long as you like, and we'll talk about chores later. Now, I'll let you two get this fellow sorted. What's his name?"

"Kai," Emory replied, rubbing his nose. "He's a good boy, and I just couldn't leave him behind."

"No reason why you should," Mrs. Overholzer beamed and returned into the house.

"Come on and I'll show you what we've got," Terry said, leading the way. "We have a stall for him inside. Don't know how you want to handle this, but he can start out in the corral, or you can go ahead and turn him out with our two horses, or you can just put him in his stall."

"I have his inspection papers," a fact Emory slid into the conversation, to see how he'd take it.

"I'd expect nothing less," Terry replied.

The thought about the money her father gave her stabbed her conscience. Still, it was a dull stab, and not a sharp one.

She studied the two horses grazing in the tidy pasture, smelling of both hay and the distant stockyards.

"Let's try him in the pasture with your guys and see how it goes."

They led Kai to the pasture gate, removed his halter, and let him loose. Tentative, he approached the other horses. Not much happened. That, in and of itself, passed as good news where horses were concerned.

TUESDAY BROKE BIGHT AND CLEAR, and Emory awoke surrounded by ruffles and pink flowers. Ruffles on the curtains, ruffles on the bed skirt, bedspread, and pillow shams. Matching, no less. The off-white carpeting didn't show any stains. True, the Overholzers took off their boots at the back door, and it did wonders for the rest of the house as well. While their spread came across like more of a hobby-ranch, there was no denying what the man did for a living.

All of it felt a far cry from the Lost Daughter set-up.

She dressed in a clean shirt and jeans and headed downstairs.

"How'd you sleep?" The lady of the house already bustled about. "Coffee?"

"I slept great, and I never turn down coffee." Emory smiled.

The woman poured her a cup. "Black? And call me Janet. Mrs. Overholzer is Terry's mother."

"Black," Emory replied, thinking how the Lost Daughter's hospitality would never match these people's. Not in one hundred years of trying.

Terry came into the kitchen from outside. "Today we'll get you settled in the office, and we have a few stops at ranches to make. Tomorrow's the big day of the week with the sale and all. Normally we process a hundred head, in and out. You ever been to a livestock auction?"

Emory shrugged. "I've seen the ones at the Stock Show and at the county fairgrounds. Guess nothing like what you've got going on here."

"Well, you'll get the hang of it in no time."

THE WEEKLY SALE days fell on Wednesdays, and preparations started off early in the morning. Truckloads of cattle and dairy cows pulled up and unloaded into the holding pens. The Stockman's Café was open and bustling as ranchers, drivers, patrons, and whomever else, came into the building waiting for the proceedings to begin.

The brand inspectors alternated between shooting the breeze with people in the old theater seats and running flat-out on the rounds checking brands and paperwork. A network of catwalks passed above the livestock yard accessible by the aisle bisecting the arena.

Emory emerged outside onto the catwalk, watching. Riders on horseback directed the sale animals into a maze of alleys, pens, and chutes. Judging by the volume, there would be plenty of paperwork and checking to go around. The scene unfolding below was a type of bovine theater straight from the old days. Old days when all the participants knew their roles, with the exception of the cattle. Cattle who, frankly, were bewildered and frightened. And why shouldn't they be? They came down the truck ramps, were herded into the aisles, and driven into the pens by unfamiliar horse and rider teams. A few buyers viewed the lots from the ground-level fences, jotting down numbers and basic impressions in the decision whether to bid or not.

The sale kicked off at 10:30, though the inspectors had arrived at the office about 6:00 am just to get a jump on all the competing demands. Just because a sale was going on didn't mean that livestock wasn't getting transported across state lines, wandering off, or getting bought and sold elsewhere. The sale arena might be considered the icing on the cake.

By about 9:00 in the morning, trucks and cars pulled into the parking lot out front or to the pens out back. The early arrivals meant business on the selling end. For the most part, everyone knew everyone, the buyers and sellers casually regular. The inspectors checked the brands as the cattle were unloaded, every so often finding a stray mark in the herd. Those stray brands necessitated a discussion and a call to the rightful owner to come retrieve their property.

Everyone, other than Emory, knew the routine.

On this sale morning, Emory's first, she stood positioned beside Terry, watching the parade of livestock go by and catching brands. Knowing that all the markings would be checked again—more carefully the next time—as a condition of sale.

Dave wandered over, to stand beside them.

Surrounded by grit, dirt, riders, and flannel shirts, a clean, shiny new sedan pulled up. Three young men materialized, just as pressed and shiny as their car.

Terry nudged her in the side.

"Never seen those three. Keep your eye on them," he said, voice low.

Emory shrugged. "Sure. Any particular reason?"

"Do they look like cattle sellers or buyers to you?"

"Well, no," she admitted. "Not exactly."

"And why not?"

"Too clean, I guess. Clothes too new, like they've never been worn. Don't know what they'd want at the sale barn," she admitted. She searched the two brand inspector's faces. "That a Greeley thing, dressing up to come to a sale?"

"No!" Terry and Dave replied in stereo, a bit louder than expected.

THE GREELEY SALE BARN
WHERE FANCY IS OUT OF
PLACE

"What else do you see?" Terry pressed as everyone calmed down a notch.

Frowning, she took a closer look. "Two Yanks and one likely Mexican. All wearing fancy Mexican boots."

A flash between Dave and Terry.

"And how do you figure that?" Dave asked.

"Curled up needle-point toes and cut in heels. It's the heels that's the giveaway. Making judgments based on curled up toes might just mean they don't believe in boot trees. So it's the heels."

A flicker of amused confidence passed between the two men.

"And before you ask, I call them Yanks because I figure they're from back East. As in Yankee Doodle Dandy territory. You know…the song?"

A quick guffaw from Terry.

Dave shook his head and stared back out at the too-clean wannabes. "They ain't even driving a truck. Hope they ain't buying. We had someone try to load a calf up in a Four Runner. Definitely not recommended."

The men stood shoulder to shoulder scanning the area.

"What are the chances they might be working on a documentary or something?" Dave deadpanned.

Terry shrugged, bothered. "Anything's possible I guess, but one of them *Yankees* there sure looks like hired muscle to me."

"That he does," Dave agreed.

The two inspectors turned back to Emory.

"OK, sunshine, this is how it works," Terry instructed. "Dave and I are on hand to check the papers of all the sales that go through. Each and every one. Sometimes one of the sellers gets cute or makes an honest mistake and tries to sell on something that ain't his. We usually catch that after the sale at the paperwork part. During the auction, the riders push the cattle out of their pens and get them lined up for the sale room. That goes pen by pen. The guy running the saleroom pushes them on out the exit door following the bidding, and the riders pick them back up and push them down into the holding pens. Once the individual sale is done, we check the papers and make sure everything is in order, nice and legal. Then money changes hands. Got it?"

"Got it," Emory replied. "What do I do?"

"Today you learn. And keep an eye on those fancy guys. Feel free to view the livestock from the overhead catwalks and see if you notice any stray brands. When you ain't watching those guys, that is. And they'll likely be inside."

"Finding stray brands is going to be kind of hard to do unless they're branded on the top of their butts or on their heads." She figured they had to be pulling her leg.

"You'd be surprised what you can see from that vantage point. And Emory? If you see anything that doesn't strike you as right, don't be shy. Call one of us, and we'll be right there. You've got us programmed into your phone, don't you?"

"Yes, Sir!" Emory replied, wondering if she'd remembered to charge the phone.

"Show me," Terry said.

She opened up her contacts and *Terry* came up. "Good enough?"

"Good enough," he replied. "Since you passed that test, here's a key." Terry held it out. "It's for the gun cabinet, which we keep locked. You got that? We only take firearms to go out to remote ranches, or if a steer breaks his leg and has to get put down immediately here. And we don't like to do it. In fact, we try like hell to avoid disposals."

"Understood," she replied.

He looked at her to be certain, then nodded.

"You can also watch the sale room proceedings," he continued. "Make yourself known and meet some people. All of this will come in handy in time. You'll see."

Emory nodded.

Piece of cake.

MOST OF THE sellers and buyers were seated early, although nothing much transpired. They seemed content catching up on the news, making wisecracks and second guessing prices. When the auction kicked off and bidding sparked up, Emory watched the first five or so head pass through bidding and decided to give the catwalk a try. Reaching the door, she turned back to double check the locations of the pointy-toed boot wearers. They paid close attention to the action in the arena, a little too close.

Odd. Perhaps she just didn't know what she was looking at.

She proceeded out into the bright blue morning noting the full-scale operation with ranchers unpenning and riders pushing the cattle along. Terry, in his element, laughed with a fellow on the southern end of the yard, obviously shooting the breeze. Dave, stationed at the gate where the cattle came out of the sale arena and into the holding pens came across as the busier of the two, clipboard in hand and jotting notes. Emory waved at one of the riders, half-way toward jealous. That girl's job sure had to be more fun than chasing paperwork around.

Cattle passed through the pens into the aisles, the riders kept the livestock moving, and the gate men had everything under control. As far as she knew, everything *looked* fine on the surface.

She returned into the arena just to be seen, to get the pulse of the room. First thing her gaze landed on was the 'muscle' Yank leaning over to talk across the smaller guy. His shirt rode up in back. A gun handle showed, tucked into the back of his waistband.

That was one way to get shot in the ass.

For brand new pants, the fit left a fair bit to be desired. And concealed weapons had no place in a sale barn as far as she was concerned.

Ever so casually, the man tugged his shirttail back down. Didn't even pause in his conversation but concealed the weapon again, nonchalant.

She didn't stick around waiting for another sign, but hightailed it down the stairs, and out through the back pens. Dave directed riders for pen switches, while Terry was the closer of the two and still shooting the breeze.

"Terry," she interrupted the conversation with the rancher. "A minute please?"

"Gotta go Fred, this here is Emory. She's the new brand inspector."

"Intern," Emory corrected.

Terry smirked. "What have you got?"

"Mind stepping over here?"

Terry tipped his hat at the rancher and took a few steps closer.

She lowered her voice. "One of those Yanks has a gun on him. Stuck in the back of his waistband. I saw it when he leaned over."

"That a fact?"

Terry didn't seem as concerned as Emory had expected. Maybe guns were more common in sale arenas than she had figured.

"He might have a concealed-carry license," Emory supplied, "but I don't think I should go asking."

"He might," Terry agreed. "But no. Don't approach them. Just keep a close eye on him especially."

"Will do. It'll probably turn out to be nothing, besides. I'll watch them and the sale. Say, how much longer do you think this one will take?"

"Maybe another hour, when the fun of the paper-work begins. Once the bidding has ended and the arena clears out, come on out here and you'll help either Dave or me out to get a feel of it. Next time, we'll set you up with your own pens."

Emory turned to go.

"Say, Em? Call if something ain't right. OK?"

She nodded, heading back into the building. "It'll be fine, Terry," she called over her shoulder.

Nothing she couldn't handle.

INSIDE THE ARENA, Emory stood watch from the mezzanine, leaning against the mezzanine rails nice and casual-like. The three Mexican-boot wearers fidgeted as more numbers were called and paraded through the arena. Now it was number 135 that came jogging in, nearing the end of the auction.

The ring man took a quick run through his notes. In a strong, clear voice he sang out the auctioneer's song.

"Lemme lemme get you to bid on number one thirty-five. A fine-looking steer, what do you say? Well-fed and none too skinny. Who will start me out at a thousand? Thousand thousand thousand...A thousand-one, there a thousand-two? What'cha say, ladies and gentlemen? One thousand-three!"

The bidding finished: nothing spectacular but nothing disappointing either as far as auctions went. The final price ended up just shy of $1,750 which seemed respectable, all things considered. The arena guy snapped his flag a couple of times to keep the steer moving, and he trotted toward the open rear gate. Trying to catch the brand as the steer passed, Emory made out a Bar KS. The pointy-boot brigade came across as relieved. Definitely not buying but selling. Another steer came in and they cast their eyes down, shuffled their feet and exchanged smug grins. Then they shifted their attention back up, paying closer attention.

A little too close for men who sold livestock regularly, unless they were selling a prize bull. None of the animals that day fit that description.

Emory marked the second brand as Lazy 4.

Two different steers, two different brands.

Emory reached for her cell. "Those Mexican-boot

guys are selling, and the steers have two different brands on them, at least that's what I gathered. Lots number 135 and 139. One looked to be a Bar KS and the other, a Lazy 4."

"Got it. I'll tell Dave."

"The sale is wrapping up," Emory said in a low voice. "They're getting up now and heading outside to the pens, I guess. You need me down there?"

Another pause. "Keep watch on them. Go on out to the catwalk just in case. You'll have a better view from up there."

He hung up, just as the men headed down the stairs and out of her sight.

Emory considered the stairs leading up to the brand office. She knew enough to listen to her instinct, and her instinct told her that it was now or never.

She stole up those linoleum stairs nice and quiet. She wanted her rifle.

She unlocked the gun safe and pulled it out. She made sure it was loaded.

As discrete as she could make it, she carried the rifle across sale arena's mezzanine and out onto the catwalk, pretty certain that no one saw her.

And if they did, they had enough sense not to question.

Emory thought about the Range rules.

Absolutely no excuse to get caught flatfooted.

Whoever drew first, usually lived.

Upslopes tilted the odds and balance toward those positioned above, firing down. Rifle shots carried further than handguns.

Some of that knowledge was hereditary, playing out right there in the twenty-first century. Some of it came down to pure common sense. Not for the first time, she felt the long reach of the past pressing down upon her.

Telling her what to do, and how to do it.

Cautioning her against being too trusting and against giving the benefit of the doubt in a situation such as this.

The past rose up and offered her an inbred track for survival.

The catwalk door swung outwards, the mechanism weighted to shut automatically. In case that mechanism failed, a posted sign advised everyone to "Keep the Door Closed". Which was about the last thing she planned on doing in the circumstances. Grabbing a makeshift spittoon, she wedged it between the door and the frame to keep the entrance—or escape—open, as the case might be. Emory removed her cowboy hat and tossed it onto one of those vacated theater seats.

Brims had a habit of getting in the way at times.

Positioned outside, she had a fine view of the proceedings. Proceedings that so far, had nothing more than business as usual.

Terry, clipboard in hand, inspected the livestock brands, reviewed papers and wrote out permits. Dave did the same. Unhurried, they didn't come across as concerned or rattled. Just going through the motions, the same as they did on countless other sale days.

About that time, the three boot fellows emerged outside. They stood off to the side in an uncertain clump —standing together, uneasy and obvious. They didn't know where they belonged, or what they ought to do. Neither did they come straight out and ask for help like typical people might have done.

Emory stood in the shadow, behind the wedge of the door. Halfway covered and watching everything unfold down below.

The three men briefly conferred, and apparently came up with a plan of sorts. The smallest Yankee plastered on an 'aw shucks' type of grin and approached an old overall-wearing rancher. After a brief consultation, the older man pointed out the northern pens.

Two of the fellows hung behind, and the muscle approached Dave working the pens near to where the steers waited.

Dave said something. The muscle responded. The sound of their voices carried, but their words remained indistinct.

The muscle guy patted his pockets.

When Dave shook his head, both men stiffened and squared.

A split second later, the Muscle pulled his gun and pointed it at Dave. Everyone else nearby, if they noticed the danger, either froze or backed away.

Emory waited a split second to see if anyone else pulled out a weapon. They didn't.

One gun against an upslope rifle.

She eased the 30-30 from out behind the door, figuring she was supposed to yell out a warning like they did on TV when she got into position. Common sense made her decide against it.

The Muscle's gun arm extended fully, and straight out. No one stood in the line of fire.

She lifted up the rifle, found her line of sight and pulled the trigger.

The bullet ripped into his upper arm. He screamed and dropped his weapon.

Dave dove into the dirt to grab the gun and came up now aiming at the man who clutched his arm, blood seeping between his fingers.

Emory swung her rifle, drawing a bead on the other two.

The darker fellow made a move to draw.

"Don't! Your head is in my sights!" Her words carried and carried clear.

Confusion played out in her favor. For a brief moment, all movement stopped.

The ranchers, drivers, riders and the Mexican-boot gang in the pen area all turned in the direction of her voice.

They found the long blued rifle barrel pointing down.

A BLUED RIFLE IS A FINE THING

She'd shot a man.

The cattle panicked and churned from the shot, bellowing out their distress. Without room in the pens to stampede, they ran into each other, pressed up against the rails and roiled. Loud and wild-eyed as the dust churned up a fog.

While the Muscle clutched his arm and bled, the two other Mexican boot men surrendered in quick order, holding up their hands.

The ranchers and drivers pressed in on the men in their too-new store bought clothes like a tightening noose. In short order the dark man was rendered disarmed, and both of them were made to lay face down in the dirt. Right where they belonged. Dave kept the one gun trained on the Muscle and made him kneel down. No one made any move to bandage his wound.

"We've got the other gun," someone called out, "the other bastard is unarmed."

There were plenty of men crowding and pushing. The Mexican-boot gang members weren't going anywhere, and it felt like vigilante justice reared up as a real possibility in the moment.

And the Muscle's new shirt and jeans were ruined from the bullet hole and subsequent blood.

Knees locked and fighting off waves of nausea, Emory lowered the rifle a fraction.

Terry yelled up to her. "Everyone cool down, but no one go anywhere. Everything is under control. Emory, put that rifle down and stay right where you are."

She nodded, lowering the rifle all the way down. No one could hear a nod, but she didn't trust herself to speak.

Pulling out his cell, Terry had it pressed to his ear, talking. Within minutes, sirens approached. Faint at first and growing louder.

One patrol car pulled up in front of the building, and another three, trailed by an ambulance, pulled around back by the pens.

Screeching to a stop.

Emory's heart pounded in her throat, her breath came out in jagged rasps. She figured puking was in the realm of immediate possibility as well.

She'd actually shot a MAN.

The sheriff and deputies cuffed the three men in short order.

"That bitch shot me!" The Muscle shouted, blood dripping between his fingers clutching his arm. Rivulets of red flowing down his hand and into the dirt. This time his words carried, no problem.

"The scene is secure," the sheriff yelled, and the EMTs advanced to bandage the man for transport. But he wasn't going to be going to the hospital in the ambulance. Instead, he was folded and stuffed into the back of a patrol car like his buddies.

Terry went directly to the sheriff, and the men conferred for a moment. Both men pinpointed her exact location where she remained—not moving an inch as instructed. Terry took out his cell, and hers rang.

"Yes?" Her voice wobbled.

"Emory, a deputy is going to come up and escort you down here. Give him your rifle."

She swallowed. "I understand."

In no time at all, the deputy stood in the door.

"Easy now," he said.

"I'm handing you my rifle," she replied.

Together they walked through the arena and back outside to Terry and the sheriff.

"This is Emory Cross," Terry's voice carried measured and calm.

The sheriff was all business and locked into her eyes. "Did you warn him that you were going to shoot?"

Emory searched both men's faces. "No. Why would I do a thing like that?"

The sheriff cocked his head, thoughtful. "Well, it is customary."

She frowned. "That would have given my position away."

"True…" the sheriff agreed. "Still. You might have hit an innocent bystander."

"I seldom miss," she protested. "Like almost never. Besides, they had a better chance of getting shot if I *hadn't* fired."

The sheriff cleared his throat.

"She's got a point," Dave offered, as cool and unhurried as always.

"My father always told me to shoot first and ask questions later."

There was a masked admiration for that sentiment, but the sheriff cleared his throat at her words.

Maybe she shouldn't have admitted that part.

Three of the deputy cars drove off, prisoners loaded into the back seats and headed for jail.

"Still, you might have killed him," the sheriff muttered watching the cars pull out.

"And he might have killed Dave," Emory countered.

How hard was that to grasp for the people down here?

"Ballsy," the sheriff replied jerking his chin in her direction.

Emory knew better than to grin. And there would be reports to file. Plenty of reports. Not the least of which were statements concerning her, because she'd shot a man.

What's more, she fully admitted to it.

"When do I get my rifle back?" she asked, and the gathered men did a double take.

"Once you've been cleared," the sheriff replied, concluding the matter.

For the time being.

PART III

The Territorial Sons

The 'club house' amounted to nothing more than a downtrodden storefront on the wrong side of the tracks. Literally. The taxpayers never saw fit to get around to paving that side of the small, featureless town, so the street remained dirt. Once the Territorial Sons moved in and took over, the odds of paving decreased even further. Forget what the upstanding citizens might pretend about their town, the truth hurt. It proved damn near insipid except for that stretch across the tracks. The stretch where, in the Blue Law years, saloons and clip joints once flaunted convention in the staid town. Such high jinks faded into obscurity over time. So, the ghosts remained in the boarded-up old buildings, dust-coated and forgotten.

Until the motorcycle gang roared into town and took root.

The Territorial Sons Motorcycle Brotherhood established their presence in a freewheeling choke-hold of a business—club, flophouses, and other closed-door enterprises, without ever once asking permission or signing a lease.

A condition that didn't pass without notice.

Some of those good citizens owned the properties where the Territorial Sons squatted, and that's when things turned interesting. The proprietors of those non-income generating storefronts objected to the motorcycle gang's presence and tried to collect on rents.

The gang members sent the townsfolks packing in no uncertain terms.

A couple of punches thrown, a pistol-whipping or two, and the matter resolved itself. Unfavorably to the town.

Favorably to the one-percenters.

The townspeople might have thought about it, and to a person decided to drop the matter dead out of a sense of self-preservation. It wasn't like they were getting rent out of those buildings anyhow. Any meager income couldn't possibly be worth likely consequences, should they press the matter and bring in the law.

Fear and intimidation would surely follow.

So, the Territorial Sons squatted and their nefarious dealings expanded, all behind closed doors. When they took to the streets on their motorcycles, the noise vibrated pure thunder and adrenalin.

Who cared that the law-abiding citizens of the town might scowl, or simply look the other way? They didn't have the stomach to say anything to the wild men who shredded the small-town lull, motors revving, and whiskey-harshened laughter carrying.

When it came right down to it, very few people

wanted to know what transpired on the other side of the tracks.

History didn't make the townspeople feel much better, either.

Outlaws once were strung up in those big cottonwood trees that still dotted the plains, bodies left hanging and twisting in the wind.

One-percenters were modern-day outlaws.

But the townspeople simply shrugged.

The interior of the club house hung in smoke blue claustrophobic. Cigarette and weed tendrilled upwards, as pervasive as the stench of unwashed bodies. Spilled beer added to the aroma, occasionally laced with meth and crack. A permanent bar in the middle of the room lorded over cast-off couches, reclining chairs, and scarred tables, scattered throughout.

The Territorials were a tentacled organization that reached throughout the state of Colorado. Each of the club houses had their own 'turf' for generating income. Some dealt in methamphetamines; others fenced stolen motorcycle parts and fake IDs. Yet others specialized in prostitution. Gunrunning. Moving illegal commodities through the counties expanded their reach. For the plains of Colorado, all of it was going on: the dealing, the fencing, and the trafficking. Common belief held that the headquarters were located in Denver, as anyone might expect. The tiny outpost in a gasping town provided a harbinger of things to come.

There was a dark current running right underneath the surface, and a death rattle in the town with a thin line of law enforcement for protection.

Henry Alderson—known as Dirge—roared up to the clubhouse and parked his Harley alongside the others. Their bikes indisputably claimed that segment of street. Dismounting, he noted his bloody knuckles before opening the door and walking on in. Four o'clock in the afternoon on a Thursday boasted of beer drinking, pool balls clacking, and rough laughter erupting, as time drifted by. Not so commonplace was the huddle of three men in the corner, locked in discussion. Business dealings, from what anyone could tell. Often those turned unpleasant, but such matters played out as just part of the deal.

A biker called Gasser paused shooting pool as Dirge passed by, distracted him from the men in the corner. "How'd it go?"

The question broke Dirge's concentration, and he lifted up his bloodied hand in response. "Fine."

"You didn't kill him, did you?" Gasser was the sergeant-in-arms.

"Nope," Dirge replied. "Just messed him up. Broken nose, knock-outed out a couple of teeth." He tossed a wad of bills down on the pool table.

Gasser scooped up the cash and held a beer aloft in a silent invitation. He indicated the men in the corner with the slightest of nods.

Dirge caught the warning within that gesture.

"Didn't think he'd be able to pay," Gasser remarked holding up the bills.

Taking the beer, Dirge shrugged. "Maybe he's selling stolen farm equipment. If he tries to undercut us again, we'll take over his migrant run."

The Sergeant-at-arms smiled, displayed overlapping, discolored teeth.

The chapter vice president nodded at Dirge from the table in slow recognition.

The Territorial Sons were a one-percenter club on a mission, and the leader of that chapter was a biker called Roadhouse.

Roadhouse was the vice President, and he had a friend. A shadowy man who wore suits and was rumored to have a pipeline of money coming from back East. He lived up in Denver, or so the common assumption played.

No one talked about that guy. Ever.

Unless Roadhouse brought him up, and he didn't. Not very often.

And never, ever by name.

24

THINGS AREN'T ALWAYS WHAT THEY SEEM

EMORY'S CELL PHONE BUZZED BRIGHT AND EARLY. Somewhat up and moving, she frowned at the coffee cup held in her hand. Glancing at the phone, the name Terry Overholzer displayed on the screen. At five past six in the morning, whatever he had to tell her couldn't be good.

"Mornin' Terry."

"Hi Em. Say, I know it's early, but I'm headed out to the Pruitt's ranch. Something sounds off, and a dead calf's been found. They called for a brand inspector, and it wasn't us."

Odd. "How'd you come to hear about it then?"

"The other district made what they termed a courtesy call. Some Texan who's up bright and early and adjusting to Mountain Standard Time, I guess. Anyhow, the ranch spans two counties, but normally we handle them. Want to ride along?"

"Sure. I'm already up and dressed." *A partial truth.*

"Meet me at the office in twenty minutes?" More of a

statement than a question, she had her chance to slow things down a bit if needed.

"Yes. I'll be there." Her apartment located on the outskirts of town, was a five minute drive, and she felt lucky to have a suitable roof over her head. The building was the closest decent place located near to the sale barn available when she needed it.

Hanging up the phone, she didn't have time to ponder the strange request, other than in passing. Very few incidents required multiple brand inspectors—well, two brand inspectors and one trainee—to look a dead calf over. It might be one of those learning or testing moments.

In Terry's mind, at least.

Terry usually drove straight to the point and called it as he saw it, but for once it came across like he just didn't know.

Obviously, a dead calf couldn't be considered good, but it seldom raised a commotion in most cases. There had to be more to the incident than everyone was being told. Or letting on.

INTO THE LAND of double lettered farm roads, they drove in the Ford pickup, BRAND INSPECTOR painted above the front tires. They took backroads that wound along to the ranching outposts dotted across the landscape. Back in the day, the Homestead Act allotted 160 acres to each homesteader. But most of those smaller concerns had consolidated over time. The smaller, therefore deemed weaker, spreads succumbed as larger controlling interests moved in. Those small holders weren't always forced out; some gave up when the Dustbowl hit. Other homestead tracts were sold by heirs who wanted no part in ranching or farming. Some even sold back in the day, right after they 'proved' up. Especially if they discovered a profit to be made.

Whatever the case, those half-number and double lettered roads were buried deep within the prairie swells or sprouting out from the flat, hard-packed dirt. They warned of a remote existence, a far cry away from even the small towns in the broad Colorado expanse. They remained outposts where help often came too late.

One thing hit her as certain—the low horizon of the eastern plains stretched wide and far. Daunting in its sheer magnitude, Emory still couldn't quite comprehend the vastness. As far as the eye could see, there was plenty of horizon to go around. That morning, the dawn slashed the eastern sky in vivid hues of peach and indigo rising. The landscape, at least to Emory, appeared next to featureless. The mountains reduced to nothing more than a distant afterthought, waited spread out in a low blue ridge to the west.

The Cheyenne and other tribes knew how to read those prairie swells, but she sure didn't.

For the settlers, it must've been easy to get lost and be swallowed up whole. Just another pile of bleached bones to stumble upon when it was far too late to do any good at all.

She sighed at the notion.

Terry's eyes darted to her. "Problem?"

"No. Just wondering how many people used to go missing out here in the early days." She stretched out a bit.

"That's kind of morbid, ain't it?"

"Maybe," she replied. "But practical. No mountains to

go by." A pause. "You hear anything about the Mexican-boot guys, like what's going to happen there?"

Terry shifted in his seat. "Two posted bail, and the one you shot is cooling his heels in jail. Waiting for his trial date to come up, I suspect."

Emory tried to act cool—keep her tone even. "So, two of them are out and roaming about. When did you hear that?"

"Last night after you'd already gone home. I planned on telling you today."

"Well, you sure took your time about it," Emory snapped.

Terry studied her. "I was figuring on what to say."

She took a breath. Waited a moment so her voice didn't wobble. "You think they'll come looking for me?"

"Nope," Terry said, firm. "You want to move back to the house for a while?"

She would have felt a whole lot better back at the Lost Daughter, far away. "Nah," Emory replied with false bravado. "I'll just keep my eyes open."

"Yeah. You do that. And no heroics. You see something, you call the sheriff. Got it?"

"Got it."

The drive out to the Pruitt's place fell silent in short order. The brand inspector never did talk all that much, but rather the words had to be half-dragged from him in the best of times. This trip wasn't one of those times.

"Don't worry, Terry."

A half-strangled laugh. "Never do."

A claim which, in this instance, was a bald-faced lie.

Silent or otherwise, Emory knew he was bothered. She kept giving him the eye from the passenger seat but if the brand inspector noticed, he gave no indication at all.

Finally, she couldn't stand it any longer. "Well, are you going to tell me anything about this before we get out there, or did that earlier conversation scare you off?"

Now she got the side-eyed stare.

He cleared his throat. Sniffed. Took his time about it, choosing his words.

"No, it didn't scare me off. Just don't get a good feeling about the Pruitts, that's all."

All of that for that. Absolutely ridiculous.

He had to be messing with her.

"Whoever you talked to must have said something to get you out here, and that set off some type of alarm because *you* called *me*."

"It was more of the tone," he admitted.

"The tone," Emory parroted.

"Yep," he said flicking on the turn signal and peering through the windshield, taking a right. "You got to listen to the tone."

Pursing her lips, she resumed her watch out the window. His explanation didn't cover the entire story, and they both knew it.

She set a foot up against the dashboard like she would in her father's truck, getting comfortable. Wheels turning in her mind as she studied the horizon and pondered the topic of blizzards come winter.

"Get that dirty boot down off of there!" Terry snapped, only half in jest. "Didn't they teach you any manners where you came from?"

"Nope," Emory claimed, smirking.

"You hear anything more about that scholarship?"

Again, a one-word answer. "Nope," she replied.

The Ford turned off the county road, rattling over the wash-boarded dirt. A low-slung ranch house and a bigger barn came into view, nestled into a tiny swell that would offer next to nothing as far as protection from the winds were concerned. As they neared and details came into focus, the property's buildings were painted and cared for. Old-lady flower beds clung to life against the house and a green bench adorned the front porch. Frivolous, and no sign of weathering to speak of.

That actually took a fair amount of doing.

A jumble of rusty old farm gear welded together made a strange sort of totem pole, crowned by an old tiller wheel that rested atop a shortened windmill tower that hadn't weathered properly to match. Yet. Various old generator parts were welded on at intervals, apparently added for good measure. The brand inspectors pulled to a stop, her thoughts unformed and scattered.

None of it was her business, anyhow.

Both feet professionally on the floor, Emory picked up her clipboard and followed Terry out, a split second later.

For an older guy, he moved pretty fast.

An even older man in overalls came out onto the porch and stepped down to meet them.

"Hey Lloyd," Terry stepped forward, hand outstretched. "Guess I beat the other one out here. This here is Emory. She's learning how to be a brand inspector, down from Rimrock County. and I'm showing her the ropes."

The man's eyes flickered. "Didn't mean to get you dragged out here."

An uncustomary steeliness ran through Terry's manner that she couldn't quite put a finger on.

"Not a problem," Terry claimed, like he hadn't noticed anything amiss. "Someone called from the other livestock office because they'll need a verification of the brand."

The owner nodded, sticking his hands deep into his pockets. "Yeah, we have to report suspicious deaths you know."

Terry rubbed his jaw. "That's right. But normally don't you call our office? Why go to the other county—not that it matters all that much. Something got you bothered?"

"Things ain't what they used to be," the rancher agreed, readily enough. "The ranch straddles the county line. Heard they had a new brand inspector. Thought I'd give 'im a whirl."

Give him a whirl. What the hell was that supposed to mean?

The conversation ended up in a showdown of stares. Everyone watching each other's faces, and none of them blinking. Em cracked first on account of how all that staring felt rude. In the meantime, the rancher's expression remained closed down, but a struggle continued in his flinty eyes.

At length, he sparked back to life. "We're getting kind of old, me and the wife, and we're a fair distance from town."

The motor hum of an approaching truck reached them, and Pruitt's eyes flickered past. "This must be him coming now."

Indeed, dust plumed up behind the other brand inspector's pickup.

No further words or explanations were offered. They all watched in silence as the truck grew larger and pulled into the yard, stopping right behind Terry's truck.

A young, trim man emerged—handsome and wearing mirrored sunglasses.

The new inspector walked up, hand outstretched for

the rancher. "Hugo Werner. I'm the new guy fresh from the Texas Panhandle."

Yep, he had that Texan drawl. Blame it on southern charm, but Emory's stomach took a small flip.

"Lloyd Pruitt," the rancher replied. "Sorry to call you out here."

The Texan turned to her, hand extended.

"Em—Emory...Cross," she stammered, heat rising.

"Terry Overholzer," the senior brand inspector offered when his turn came around, more interested in Emory's reaction than anything else.

"Pleased to meet everyone," Hugo said to all, but his eyes darted back to Emory.

Pruitt hooked his thumbs under his overall straps and didn't seem in all that much of a hurry.

"So how do you like Colorado so far," he asked, and everyone shied, surprised at the frivolous question.

"I like it just fine for now. Waiting for winter to come around to see what happens," Hugo Werner replied, smile nice and wide.

Conversation drying up about the same as the creek beds in those parts, Terry's eyes narrowed at the wait, and he toed the dirt, making a pattern of no particular merit.

Kind of like a silent standoff, but Emory, for one, couldn't figure out the purpose of all that squaring.

At length, the rancher broke the silence. "Well, I'll show you where he is. Come on, and I'll lead the way." Already moving off in the direction of his GMC pickup, Pruitt gestured northeast, climbed into the battered truck and kicked it into gear.

The Texan returned back into his truck, revved up his engine and peeled out following the old rancher.

Terry, finding amusement at her expense, tailed

behind taking his own damn time, and her with her cheeks stinging.

"Seems he's new in town like you," he commented, climbing into the truck.

"Yeah. It seems to be something going 'round," she bantered, opening her door. "Mr. Pruitt sure looked surprised to see you at first."

"So you noticed." Terry turned the ignition and followed the trail of dust.

The Texas Panhandle drew up flat too, and Hugo was probably more at home in the Colorado plains than she was. How was that for an injustice?

25

THIS AIN'T EXACTLY DORITOS

ABOUT ANOTHER HALF MILE DOWN THE DIRT TRACK, TERRY and Emory pulled up behind the two pickup trucks alongside the road, listing toward a drainage ditch. Circling crows and their rasping caws to each other proved a dead giveaway.

All the interest—man, beast, and insects—centered upon the motionless black lump.

The Texan squatted down about two feet away from the carcass, pushing back his hat, considering. Outside of the truck, Terry and Emory were met by the strong stench of rotting meat.

The constant low drone of flies peppered the air.

It didn't take much in the way of an education to see that half of the calf had been hacked away. Chain-sawed in fact, and a sloppy job of it at that. The best meat portions removed without much skill, with plenty left just to rot in the sun and the open air. The calf's eyes filmed over, attracting insects and blue-bottle flies. Terry waived his clipboard to disperse the glistening insects.

"I'd say this calf has been dead for a while," the Texan

twanged at length. "What's he doin' outside of the fence?"

"See them cuts?" Pruitt asked.

Indeed, the barbed wire fence had been cut, but only the lowest row.

Anyone could cut a fence to cast suspicion.

Terry frowned, fingering the barbed wire, considering the implications of the severed ends. He eyed the rancher, sharper. "And you just reported him today."

No comment to that statement came, and it kind of thudded as it hit the ground.

"Well. Let's flip him over to check the brand." Terry moved over to the carcass.

"When did you say you found him?" The Texan took a hard look at the rancher, adjusting his hat back to the customary position, eyes returning to the barbed wire.

"A week ago," the rancher admitted.

Terry squinted at the information. "Why so long Lloyd?"

The rancher took off his baseball cap and scratched his balding head with gnarled, work mangled fingers. "Like I said. We're far away from town. Need the report for the insurance."

"Insurance, huh." Terry didn't seem convinced.

Insurance was a rarity right there.

The Texan took notes and snapped some pictures of the wire, but they wouldn't amount to much in all likelihood.

Terry, hands on his hips and still holding the clipboard, took everything in. "But we come to you, you know that. Why take so long to report this? Do you know who did it—is that the problem?"

The rancher struggled, caught someplace between the truth and a lie. "Sure, it's part of the problem. No, I don't exactly know who they were. Don't wanna know, either. Might be some of those potheads from Denver who wanted a BBQ."

Terry spat. "Shoot. You ain't afraid of no potheads from Denver with a case of the munchies. And this ain't exactly Doritos."

The Texan stood there, not missing one word of the conversation. "This is a crime, as you already know. Did you see what they were driving—or can you provide any information at all?"

The rancher's eyes appealed to Terry for help, who didn't act predisposed towards giving any. "It came about last Wednesday night. They had a U-Haul. That's all I know."

"And you waited until this morning to call."

"My wife made me. She talked to Dustin, and she wants that insurance money. Me, I'd rather just leave it be."

Head quirked, Terry stepped forward, still displeased. "You have insurance on your cattle? All of them?"

"Yeah," Pruitt replied. "Just got it a couple of months ago. Some deal Dustin's got goin'."

"Who's Dustin?" Hugo squinted.

"Our son," the rancher explained.

The Lost Daughter cattle didn't carry any insurance. Too expensive, for one.

Terry chewed that part about Dustin over. "He working for an insurance company?"

"Nah. Said he did some readin'. He's got a friend in the business."

At that point, Terry dropped his line of questioning knowing it wouldn't get them anywhere at all. "Em, give me a hand here and let's get this turned over to check the brand."

"I'll do it," the newly arrived inspector offered, approaching the calf ready to pick up the front legs.

"Let her do it. It's part of the job," Terry countered in a steady voice.

The Texan backed off, good-natured.

Terry pulled on his gloves, and Emory did the same. He moved to the back end and expected Emory to manage the front.

She inhaled, pretending to find it all an ordinary task.

The worst thing she could do was come across as squeamish. It wouldn't have been so bad if the witnesses were just Terry and the rancher, but...Hugo. Why, he put a whole other layer of complication into the proceedings right there.

Terry had already grabbed the back legs. "Ready?"

She bent down and grabbed the front legs, meeting Terry's eyes. "We're going to pull the legs up and over, right?"

"On the count of three," Terry nodded. "One—two—three."

The ripping sound of membrane separating the meat from the hide.

Emory struggled, gagging, as more flies flew upwards like buckshot. Maggots and larvae were at work in the wounds, wriggling. She dropped those legs right quick when they were positioned for gravity to do its job.

Hands on knees and bent over, did her best not to throw up in the ditch. She knew the men were watching her, trying not to laugh at the notion of her puking her guts out.

She pulled herself together enough to find the brand and pointed at the back hip.

"This ain't yours!" Terry exclaimed.

Pruitt leaned in to get a better view himself.

"No, it sure ain't." Now the rancher came across as bothered. "What do you suppose that means?"

Terry's watered-blue eyes were sharp and calculating. Once again, choosing his words. "It means, most likely, that this is a stolen calf from some another outfit. Someone brought it out here to butcher. Why do you suppose anyone would bother to do a thing like that?"

Offended, the rancher blustered. "Why'd they do something like that? How the hell should I know?"

Emory kept her silence. The rancher's reaction seemed at least partially an act. The Texan stood hands on hips, lips pressed together, while the Colorado folk were leaning in and about ready to exchange words.

Serious words.

But something held Terry off. Eyes narrowed, Terry shrugged, more neutral than expected. More neutral than Emory felt prudent. "That's probably the eighty-four dollar question, and we haven't had reports of any calves stolen lately."

He consulted with the Texan. "You?"

Hugo Werner shook his head. "No. Not in the six days I've been up here. Nothing's been called in. Well, nothing like this."

Terry took careful pictures of the brand. "This one's not from around here, I don't think. You got everything you need from your end, Tex?"

"My friends call me Hugo," he corrected, a wary edge added that hadn't been there before. He turned to Pruitt.

"It would've helped if you had called this in sooner. That way we might have gotten foot prints or something, but with the rain we had earlier this week and the wind...well. Any traces are all gone now." Doubts flew clear.

The rancher saw everyone's expressions but offered nothing to shore up opinions on the matter.

"I'll get a tarp," the Texan said, walking back to his truck. He paused, and turned back to the rancher, like a thought just occurred to him. "You haven't seen any others like this one by chance, have you?"

"Nope," the rancher spat. "Don't you think I would've said?"

The Texan flicked back his head like a stallion. He returned carrying a folded Kelly-green sheet underneath his arm. "Load it up?"

"I guess," Terry replied, "unless you've got a better idea."

The two men exchanged glances over the torn-up carcass. Then they unfolded the tarp and hefted the calf onto the green surface lugging the burden by the corners to the truck and slung it into the bed. The load thudded down, hooves coming free and clattering against the metal.

Pruitt, bothered by the suspicions circling in his direction, didn't say anything further.

The rancher knew details—critical details—that he left unspoken and had no intention of sharing.

Terry stated the obvious. "Lloyd, I expect you know that we can't sign off on this. Meaning that the insurance money likely ain't coming."

The rancher only shrugged and shook his head.

Disquieted and puzzled, Emory loaded back into the truck. The unfolding half-evidence reminded her of one of the dodgier Lost Daughter deals she'd been on the edges of. But she couldn't figure out the angle being played on the Colorado plains.

She would have even asked.

But for once, Terry didn't look in the mood for questions.

Most ranches had a charnel pit, boneyard, or scrap heap of varying levels and degrees.

The Pruitt's place turned out to be no different.

There were a few ways to dispose of livestock carcasses: a removal service (cost money), burial (might leech into the water table), and the time-honored tradition of dragging the carcass to a remote site. A site away from the direct line of sight from the kitchen window and preferably downwind. Authorities favored the modern-day removal services, but they didn't always get a vote.

The Pruitt's chose the most economical method, espousing the traditional boneyard common throughout time.

The three pickup trucks drove up to the edge of the pit, which appeared the same as a thousand other ranch pits throughout the West. At one point in time, a depression had been dug, about two feet deep. A long time ago. Carcasses were left to rot in the sun, bones protruding and bleaching. The sickly, sweet dead animal smell of rotting meat carried.

"What happened to that cow there?" Terry asked.

"Old age," the rancher replied. "No need to report, if that's what you're asking."

The pit had plenty of dirt clods and a sprinkling of ag lime to help matters along, dampening down the stench to a point.

"It's old fashioned, but it passed inspection," the rancher offered unbidden, a shade on the defensive side.

The men lifted the calf out of the truck bed and tossed it into the pit with the other refuse.

Terry's blue eyes sharpened. "I gotta tell you Lloyd, I don't like any of this."

The rancher shrugged, preferring the horizon to the brand inspector's eyes. "And that's why I called you out here," he replied.

But he'd called out the new brand inspector, and they all knew it. Likely attempting to play the new man as a dupe, with the threadbare hope that he was none too bright or experienced in such matters.

That unspoken fact was left hanging and the Texan didn't enjoy playing the part of a fool.

"You gonna press charges, Lloyd?" Terry asked.

"Against who?" the rancher replied, tired. "Not my brand, so not my battle."

"Let me give you my cell number," Terry said to Hugo. "How about I'll call yours. What number've you got?"

He rattled off the digits, and Terry punched in the number and tried it out.

Hugo's phone rang. Both men checked their phones and cut off the call.

Turning toward the rancher, Hugo thrust out a hand. It didn't mean there were no hard feelings in this case, but the Texan chose the professional route. "Take care, Mr. Pruitt. Call us if anything else out of the ordinary happens. Maybe a bit sooner the next time."

The rest of them shook hands more reserved than the first time around. Without anything else to add, the inspectors settled in their trucks and pulled out, the Texan leading the way, and all of them passing the metal totem pole for the fourth time that morning.

"What the hell is that thing, anyhow," Emory asked, staring at the composition.

"Art," Terry deadpanned.

A blank stare.

"That's Dustin's work. *Found object art* is what they told me it's called the last time I come out here. They act like sunshine radiates out of that boy's be-hind."

"Uh-huh," Emory replied, turning to stare back at it through the rear window of the cab. "Wonder how he ended up involved with insurance if he's an artist. Think that totem pole is worth anything?"

Terry snorted. "It's worth whatever the Pruitt's paid for him to go to that Denver art school I suppose."

"Live around here?" Emory still stared at the diminishing object through the rear window.

"Denver," Terry replied. "Comes back now and again. I heard they built him a studio in one of them outbuildings. Can't say that he helps out much. More the other way around."

He pulled his cellphone out of his pocket and hit the recent call button.

"Hey Hugo. Hold up at the intersection of the two county roads a minute, will you?"

A pause.

"Yep. Out of the line of sight from the Pruitt's. Thanks."

The brand inspector's eyes darted over to Emory. "And to your unspoken point, yes I think there's plenty Pruitt ain't saying."

Emory nodded. "With an operation that size, wouldn't he know if a calf went missing?"

"Uh-huh. Maybe a calf of his did go missing."

She turned to search his eyes. "The brand didn't belong to him. Come to think of it, you *really* didn't recognize that brand?"

"Nope. It's nothing common around these parts, meaning whoever it's registered to hasn't been running livestock through the sale room. At any rate, sounds like you'll be searching through brand books for a while."

"Fine. I like looking at them." She shrugged, still bothered. "But I'll start with the computer, first. You know, the website?"

26

THE DEVIL'S AFOOT AT
CROSSROADS

At the intersection of the two nearest county roads, the Texan waited, pulled over. He leaned against the side of his truck, long and lean. Neat and masculine.

The Greeley inspectors pulled up right behind his truck, rocks crunching under the tires before locking in a slight skid.

Hugo approached Terry's window.

"What'd you make of that tangle?" Terry asked.

Hugo shrugged, eyes alighting on Emory before surveying the expanse of nothing-much flat. "It's a crime scene that got reported too late to do anyone much good. You know him?"

Terry half-shrugged. "In passing. But, something's bothering him."

"Hell, something's bothering me, too," the Texan deadpanned. "I'm not stupid, and he said he called us out for insurance purposes. What did he think, that I wouldn't check the brand and just sign off? How's that supposed to work?"

"Not well," Terry laughed. "We're returning to the office to see if we can figure out who the calf belonged to. But there's more to it than that. I'd say Lloyd's afraid of somethin'. Before you arrived, he mentioned *twice* about how they are far from town, which I assume means they are far from help if needed."

"Yeah," the Texan still scanned the horizon, pride a bit dented. "So it seems. And insurance is real expensive, ain't it?"

Emory couldn't help but notice the Texan's nice, clean-shaven jaw. The memory of Cade darted into her mind. One on one side of the law; one on the other. She squashed Cade right back down.

"We can't afford it," Emory interjected. *Maybe that wasn't something to go around admitting.*

Terry nodded. "I wondered about that part myself. That cut fence is suspicious. Think he done that?"

"Probably," Hugo drawled. "That's why only one row was cut. That lessened the chances of other head wandering away. So that's kind of a given I'd say. What I don't get was the surprise at the brand. You?"

"That calf's been dumped from some other outfit. Maybe it's some sort of insurance scam. He won't be able to collect without the paperwork in any case. Unless the claim adjuster is in on it."

Hugo peered down at his boots, waging his head. "Anything been going on out here that's been reported crime-wise? It doesn't seem to exactly be a hotbed of activity."

"Nope," Terry replied. "Didn't you do your research before you came out here?"

"I did," the Texan agreed, lifting his face and flashing an even-toothed smile. "Nothing since last year and that involved a couple of teenagers drinking beer and a fence that bore the brunt of it. But we all know there's plenty more that goes on. It just doesn't get talked about in these types of areas. Not enough people to go around, I guess."

Stretching his shoulders, Terry agreed readily enough. "That's true. Can't help but guess the Pruitt's had a calf stolen somewhere along the line that they failed to report. In any case, all our evidence is back in their ranch pit."

"Yeah," the Texan drawled. "That it is. Remember the cut wire. Let me know if you hear of anything, and I'll do the same."

He patted the truck like that solved matters and made to walk off.

Emory burst out. "What about the son? The insurance was his idea after all...And the mother warmed to it."

Terry stiffened. "Hard to believe he talked Lloyd into getting insurance without good reason. Hell, they're just average like, you know? Not sayin' anything against the livestock but..."

"They're average," Emory shot across.

Terry's eyebrows lifted a fraction.

"Anyone can see that much," Emory shot back across those dang eyebrows. "Might as well call it as it is,"

"Shoot," Hugo grinned.

Terry sighed. Old, local information welling up. "Their boy's always been in and out of trouble, but nothing his parents couldn't handle. I wonder if the size of the problems have grown. Hard to say which. Moved up to Denver. Hard to say what he got into up there."

The Texan shrugged. "I'll get in touch if I run into anything interesting."

"Likewise," Terry replied, and the Texan tipped his hat in Emory's direction as he turned back to his truck.

He sure looked nice walking away. Wide shoulders and narrow hips always made her heart jump.

"Guess your job just became more interesting." Terry eyed her, not exactly poker-faced.

"Thanks for not telling him that I shot someone," Emory muttered. "He must not have good sources, 'cause I thought that story made the rounds already. Besides, Coloradoans and Texans don't mix."

And to that piece of wisdom, Terry shook his head and chuckled. "Whatever you say, girl. Whatever you say."

Dave acted fidgety when they returned into the office.

"Mail came," he nodded in the direction of her desk.

Sure enough, an envelope with SUBPOENA printed in bold ink across the front waited.

"Here we go," she said, tearing the envelope open and scanning the contents. "It's for the preliminary hearing."

Dave and Terry exchanged glances.

"It'll be fine, Em." Terry encouraged, but his words fell flat.

To make matters worse, the trace of doubt stayed hanging.

There was nothing further to be done, other than to let the judicial system and courts play out.

"Never figured to be in a witness box for something like this," she admitted.

Well, not for the prosecution.

And the two brand inspectors just nodded, accepting her words at face value.

They were awful trusting, she decided.

Emory wanted to make good. For damn sure, she didn't want to disappoint them.

SIGNATURES OF IRON

It wasn't a sale day at the barn, thank heavens.

Upstairs they climbed the stairs up to the office. Shut off from the sale arena proceedings, a door separated the brand inspectors kind of like an agricultural separation of church and state. The same sign on the door said to go on up, and that's what regulars did. Just headed on up, climbing those dang 1970's linoleum-covered stairs—light switched off in a continual attempt to keep the black flies down to a tolerable level.

Whose tolerance remained another one of those debatable points.

"It's like running a dang fly gauntlet," Emory grumbled.

"They'll die out soon enough, come winter," Terry offered.

The top door opened into a darkened hallway. To the uninitiated, it might look like the brand inspectors weren't even open for business considering how dark it was. But the third door showed signs of life—lights were on inside the office.

"You think they'd figure out a way to get rid of these file boxes one of these years." Emory remarked to Terry, intentionally yanking his chain. She knew exactly how the men felt about their papers.

"In time," Terry said sitting down behind his desk, and mind elsewhere. "Right about the time I say *adios*."

That was probably the size of it.

"So, where do you want me to start?" Emory asked, unwilling to succumb to lamentations.

"Where do you think you should start?" Terry eyed her.

"*I* might as well try the computer, but if I don't find the brand listed there, it's over to the books. Brands that don't make it on to the website mean they haven't paid their registration renewals. Yeah, I was listening. What are you going to do?"

"Call the sheriff," he said. "Never hurts to have a conversation."

That sounded plenty interesting, but eavesdropping was low, no matter how carefully conducted. "Can I listen in?"

"I'd expect nothing less," he agreed. "While you're searching for the brand, that is."

Emory dragged out the brand books while Terry connected to the sheriff's office, number stored in his phone.

"Good morning, Maxine. Terry Overholzer here. Say, you got the sheriff handy?"

A pause.

"Hey Frank. Terry here. Say, I think something's going on, at least out at the Pruitt's place. You haven't heard of anything out that way, have you?"

A longer pause. Terry leaned forward, elbows on desktop. "How's that?"

Another dart in her direction.

Terry spoke into the phone guardedly. "Yeah, well. Not exactly what any of us wanted to hear."

He cricked his neck and for all the world looked like he regretted saying Emory could listen in. No matter, since he sure as hell wasn't saying much.

"I understand," he said, glance darting in her direction. "Oh, what I wanted to discuss with you is the Pruitt ranch. Lloyd Pruitt called out the new brand inspector, instead of calling into here on account of a chain-sawed calf that isn't even their brand…"

More waiting.

"Don't like it much." Terry rubbed his forehead. "You see where I'm going?"

Another short silence.

"Yep. Bye."

Terry leaned back in his chair, visible thoughts travelling in his mind.

"Did he know anything?" Emory prompted.

"A great many things, Grasshopper."

"Is Karate Kid really your favorite movie, or do you just like the sound of that?"

He placed his hands on the back of his head, training his attention onto her too close for comfort.

"You know them Mexican-boot fellows?"

"Yeah." Her blood chilled, running not exactly cold, but darn near close to it.

"Two of them got released from all charges. Bernie Mendoza and Michael Q. Holmes. The third, the guy you shot, is still behind bars and awaiting trial. Name came back as Russell Van Hoon. Long rap sheet. Mainly larceny and bodily harm."

Emory's breath caught. "You know where those other two are?"

"Not exactly. Probably took off for Denver or decided to winter in Cancun." He eyed her sharp. "They have a record of fencing stolen goods."

"You don't say."

A man's figure approached through the darkened hallway.

"Here comes Dave. I *think*. Might help if we switched the light on out there," Emory groused, tone coming out harsher than she meant.

Dave opened the door and sized up the pair of them. "What?"

"Those damned boot guys." Terry explained, sounding concerned. "The one who pulled his gun on you is still behind bars, but not the other two."

"Figures."

"We all need to keep our eyes open. They've got ties to the Territorial Sons, and heaven knows what else might crawl out from underneath that rock. Anything strange, you say something. Anything suspicious, you report it. Got it?"

"Got it," Dave replied.

"Menaces, that's what they are."

"Son of a bitch," Emory spluttered. "I knew I should have winged those other two."

"That would've been harder to explain," Terry said, dead serious on the matter. "Badges only go so far in this day and age."

"Do you suppose they saw me?" Her stomach hurt, although she would never admit as much.

"Don't know. I hope not."

Yeah, but there were plenty of lonely roads and empty fields.

Emory shook her head. Changed the subject. "What did the sheriff have to say about the Pruitts?"

"Just more movement throughout the county than usual—people passing through that no one knows."

"Oh my goodness," Emory deadpanned. "Where I come from, they're called tourists."

Terry cocked his head. "Where I come from, they're called suspect when they have no purpose for being out here in the first place."

"Welcome to Colorado," Emory crowed.

"Bullshit," Terry replied.

That was a fine bit of bravado, but the fact of the matter was that she was spooked.

Like a spooky horse, the best thing to do was get their mind and attention focused elsewhere.

Brand books were an excellent source for that type of thing.

Since she'd been snarky, however, she searched the computerized database first. It would have been quick work, had the brand been there.

But nothing matched up.

Halfway relieved when the brand couldn't be located, she turned to the brand books hoping to lose herself for the next half hour. At least.

Forty-five minutes of rifling-through-pages later, she located a possibility.

"Let me see those pictures again."

Terry pulled them up on his cell and she scrutinized the images.

"See right there," she scrolled the picture larger, comparing it to the recording in the book. "That's what's throwing me off. I'd say that brand's been run over with a running iron, wouldn't you? The T's stem is tilted a bit."

Terry squinted at it. "Maybe."

A half shrug. "Might belong to Earl F. and Patricia J.

Alderson over Ft. Morgan way. Should we call to see if he's missing any stock?"

Terry refused to provide a quick answer. "Don't know yet."

Emory studied him as she handed back his cell. "What's stopping you? Here. I'll show you what I found." She brought him the brand book from her desk.

Her very own desk. That part was still new and cool.

The senior brand inspector just sat there chewing on the notion and the brand drawn out in black and white.

He offered nothing more than a shrug in response.

The wiry man said about as much, or as little, as Terry did himself.

Terry eyed him. "What do you know about the Aldersons over by Ft. Morgan?"

"Nothing much," Dave said, returning to his desk facing Terry's.

She hovered near their desk sides. "You guys act like the two old men on The Muppets. Remember that show?"

A suppressed guffaw as Terry pretended to ignore that comment.

"What," Terry began, "do you know about the Pruitts?"

That elicited a bit more seated consideration. "They think the world of their boy, but that ain't what you're asking, is it?"

"Not exactly." Terry stretched a bit. "I'm more asking about how their business prospects are faring."

While he might have appeared unconcerned, Dave was taut as wire. "Ain't heard anything of note. Why?"

"He reported a dead calf to claim the insurance money. Seems to us," a nod in her direction finally included her in the conversation, "that he would have noticed he wasn't missing any calf in the first place. So, I'd say there's something strange going on."

"Insurance? You sure about that?"

The brand inspector's office wasn't exactly a place to go throwing accusations around.

"He said so. Said he wanted to collect on the insurance money. Or rather his wife did."

Dave scrutinized the view beyond the window, and Terry scrutinized Dave. "Don't sound like him, at least by what I know. Didn't know he carried insurance, neither."

A half-shouldered shrug from Dave. "Might be an honest mistake."

Strained, no one believed that conclusion either.

"We should skin that calf and see if the brand's been altered," she burst out.

Two sets of eyes immediately rotated toward her, startled.

The heat of color shot up in her face. But it was now or never. She met their eyes straight on, and without flinching. "Surely you've seen a vented hide at least one time or another."

"Know much about that, do you?" Terry replied in a mild tone, but it wasn't exactly a mild question.

She took a breath in, truly wanting to explain about the old hide in the outbuildings. But that was a closely held secret. "Oh, guess that's just regional stuff we know. Outlaws and all. But when the original brand is altered, the newer marks will be less pronounced on the reverse of the hide. Obviously, you'd only do that on a carcass, but we left one behind in the Pruitt's pit. Likely it's still out there and we could go get it. Just to make certain."

Dave went a bit bug-eyed. "You want to skin a calf? You do a lot of skinning up there?"

"I don't personally, but I'm willing to give it a try."

In any event, she'd seen it done.

"Rotting out in the sun for a week doesn't sound so great..."

"Surprised you know about reading hides from the reverse." Terry commented, gauging her response a little too close for comfort.

Emory nodded, hopeful he didn't see the twinge. "Like I said. And, I've read about it in history books. That's how they used to catch cattle thieves in the Brown's Park area back when. The stock detectives would search outbuildings for hides. Vented hides were usually all the proof needed for conviction."

She ventured absolutely nothing about what lurked in the Lost Daughter's outbuildings.

"And based upon that reading, you're thinking we should skin that calf in the Pruitt's charnel pit. Is that what you're sayin'?"

"That's the size of it," she replied. "It couldn't hurt. Especially since I can't find that exact brand online or in the brand books. What have we got to lose?"

"Maybe our lunches," came Dave's poker-faced reply.

TERRY AND EMORY drove back out to the Pruitt's that same afternoon. Without calling, without requesting permission. Terry's set jaw and lack of a twinkle in his eye meant he took the matter to heart. Delivering a serious unspoken accusation all the way around. No one felt comfortable accusing ranchers that had never caused a speck of trouble in the past.

Known trouble, that was.

A hawk circled overhead, soaring and gliding on the currents and hunting for prey, keen-eyed and watchful.

Emory admired the grace and the dapple colored under-belly, wondering how the world would appear from such lofty vantages.

A hawk would certainly be able to spot dangerous people hiding.

"Bothered, Em?"

"A bit," she admitted. "Don't like it."

"No," he replied as the rusted sculpture came into view, marking the periphery of the ranch yard. Emory shifted in her seat.

"You done anything like this before?"

"Not exactly," came Terry's caged reply.

Pulling up, the house stood quiet and with no visible movement inside.

"I'll go knock," Emory offered, getting out and heading for the door.

She rang the bell and waited. She rang the bell again.

Finally, footsteps approached.

Mrs. Pruitt opened the door, short hair curled in the manner of traditional grandmothers.

"Yes?" Her blue eyes blinked, travelling to the truck.

"We're brand inspectors ma'am, and my name's Emory Cross. We were here earlier."

"Have you found something," the woman asked, now opening the screen door. "Would you like to come inside?"

"Thanks, but my boots are likely dirty. Say, did you talk to your husband about the calf?"

Her watery blue eyes darted to the truck then returned to Emory.

"Yes. It wasn't our calf. Or that's what he said." The ranch wife glanced behind her into the silent, orderly house that held little more than fading memories. "Lloyd's out driving the perimeter right now."

"It's a good thing to do," Emory replied.

"It's a necessary thing to do," the woman corrected. "Every morning and every evening, he drives the fence lines. Sometimes more than that, even."

That part seemed a bit extreme. She checked Terry's reaction.

The brand inspector was intent.

"Expecting trouble?" She asked, leaning slightly forward, focused upon the answer.

"It's the way of the world these days, it seems." Mrs. Pruitt claimed, sounding resigned.

The Pruitts didn't seem like the type to file false insurance claims, but assumptions were risky at best.

"Ma'am," Emory started, "the reason why we are here is that we want to haul that calf away and skin it. Even that originating brand isn't true."

"It's not?" Pure, unadulterated surprise rippled.

"No, ma'am. Nothing's currently registered that matches. That's why we need to take it. Do you mind?"

Terry fidgeted in the truck behind her, but she ignored him.

Mrs. Pruitt searched Em's face. "I don't see why not. I'll just call Lloyd and let him know."

"Sure, that would be fine."

The woman travelled about five steps into the interior when she paused and turned around.

"We had a calf stolen a month or so back. I thought we would just make up for that one. Lloyd didn't want to call it in."

"Now since you're bringing it up, that's the part we don't understand. Why wouldn't anyone report a stolen calf? That way we'd watch for it, and with luck return it to you. Especially if someone had the idea of running it through the sale barn."

"I guess he just didn't want to go courting trouble," she replied.

Emory stiffened. "Trouble with who?"

The woman smoothed down her shirt, liver-spotted hands capable and strong. "I guess with the men who drive the roads out here. Not that I know for certain, but I'd say they're some of the men who run migrant workers." Mrs. Pruitt inhaled. "But like I said, that's just an assumption, you know. They aren't from around these parts."

Or if they were, no one wanted to admit as much.

CARCASSES AND CELL PHONES

EMORY MOTIONED FOR TERRY TO ROLL DOWN THE window, and she leaned in. "She's calling her husband to make sure it's OK for us to take the calf."

Terry shrugged. They would take it anyhow, one way or the other, and all of them knew as much.

No warrants needed in brand inspection work.

Manners, however, were another matter altogether. Emory glanced back at the Pruitt's open door and lowered her voice. "Thing is, she gave me a bit more background. She—"

Then Mrs. Pruitt emerged from the house, barreling straight for the truck.

"He'll be right back, but he said you can take the calf. You can load it up now if you want or wait for him and he'll help. He won't be but about ten minutes."

Emory included rancher's wife in the conversation intentionally. "Mrs. Pruitt told me how he drives the fence lines each morning and night." Emory made sure to make it sound like an exemplary practice.

Standing a bit straighter, the woman nodded. "It's the only way to keep on top of what is going on."

Terry nodded genial, but his eyes sharpened. "Are you having problems out here, Mrs. Pruitt?"

"Irene. And it's nothing we can't handle." She stiffened. "I shouldn't have said anything about it at all."

Emory held her tongue knowing men sometimes blamed their wives for airing grievances they didn't exactly want aired. She wondered if Lloyd Pruitt was that type of man.

"Guess I was just letting my imagination run wild," Mrs. Pruitt added, a challenge aimed at Emory.

"A dead calf is enough to get anyone going," Emory agreed. "Especially a chain sawed one."

"Chain sawed?" The woman blanched. Her husband obviously hadn't seen fit to share that detail with her.

"Chain sawed," Emory repeated emphatically.

Terry cleared his throat, but Emory refused to yield.

"I've got chores inside." Mrs. Pruitt's voice came out much tighter and smaller than it had only a moment before. "You going to wait for Lloyd?"

Terry leaned forward. "Yeah, we'll wait if it doesn't take too long."

Offering a brief nod, the woman returned inside the house. Never once looking back to the problem in the yard as she shut the door.

"Now," Terry chided, "what did you go and do that for? And why didn't you listen in on that conversation with Lloyd?"

"First of all, I don't like eavesdropping," Emory

sniffed. "Second of all, I only told her the truth. What of it?"

"What of it? You scared the crap out of that poor lady."

"Yeah," Emory countered. "The poor lady who wanted to collect on the insurance money. Now I have something more to tell you, but now is not the time since here comes Mr. Pruitt."

Indeed, an ATV revved toward them, heading fast. Mr. Pruitt's body sure filled up that front seat.

He came to a stop and hefted his bulk out. "Irene said you want to take the calf?"

"Yes. If you don't mind," Terry replied. "It's got us bothered."

"Well, hell. It's got me bothered, too. Go ahead and take it. I can get the backhoe if you want. It'd be easier that way."

Without waiting for an answer, he headed around the back of the house toward the pit, leaving Emory and Terry to follow.

His overall-covered backside climbed into the cab, cranked it up and drove it to the pit and down the dirt ramp to scoop up the calf into the bucket. Slapping the machinery into reverse, he pulled out and rumbled toward their pickup truck complete with calf legs dangling over the bucket sides, like fragile spider legs.

Tarp unfurled and already spread out, he dumped the calf unceremoniously hitting dead center. Again, that sickening stench of rotting meat wafted.

Mr. Pruitt turned off the motor and climbed back down.

"What do you think?" He asked Terry, man-to-man.

Frustrated, Emory did her best not to show it, a female in a traditionally male role.

"I'm concerned about the fact that brand's been altered," Terry said. "There seems to be an underreporting of missing livestock these days and I can't understand the reason why."

"Haven't heard of anything like that," he claimed, unknowing that his wife had admitted that they'd done the same. "Whose brand do you think it is?"

"There's a similar brand registered to an outfit near Ft. Morgan, but it doesn't match up one hundred percent."

"That's about forty miles from here." The rancher took off his cap and scratched his head. "That's a long way to go to dump a carcass."

Terry nodded. "That it is."

Emory tried to cover the dead calf with the free part of the tarp, but there wasn't enough to go around.

"We'll be in touch once we figure something out," Terry told the rancher, opening the truck door. Followed by an afterthought.

He was just pretending it was an afterthought.

"You don't suppose that calf is some sort of warning, do you?"

"Shoot," the rancher said, pretending—and only pretending—to find the question funny. No humor reached his eyes, and that was for dang sure. "You've been watching too much TV."

Terry shrugged it off. "Maybe so. It's my wife. She likes those crime dramas. But Lloyd, if there's something troubling you, I sure wish you would come out and say it."

"Things just ain't as they used to be," came his foregone reply.

"LET'S HAVE IT," he said pulling out of the ranch yard.

"She said they are worried about the men who run the roads. Something to do with migrant workers."

"She said it exactly like that?"

"No, not exactly like that," Emory replied, "but men driving around on the roads was the gist of it. Strangers. Where are those migrant workers that she referred to, anyhow?"

Terry scratched the back of his neck.

"Well, she could've been referring to darned near anything—transient workers, temporary workers, or the true migrants. Not to mention the illegals. But how'd you get that out of her in the first place?"

"Women talk to each other." Emory said, scanning the plains thinking just how lonely things might get out there. Life got lonely at the Lost Daughter as well, but at least she had the mountains for company.

"Uh-huh," Terry replied.

"Don't you go rolling your eyes. She also admitted that they'd had a calf stolen a month or so back. They just figured they'd make up for it with this one and the insurance."

"Did she come right out and say that?" Terry stuck a toothpick in his mouth.

"She did." Emory let those words sink in. "These people are certainly on edge, if not out and out afraid."

Those released lowlifes might be some of those slow cruisers.

"Yeah. Got that part."

Silence descended between them. Emory flicked on the radio, and Terry flicked it right back off.

"I'm thinking, if you don't mind," he said.

"And you can't do that with music on?" she asked.

"Correct."

The one-word answers were annoying. "Now what?"

The forsakenness of those lone cottonwood stands bothered her as they occasionally slipped by. Hanging trees. She could also imagine a girl sitting beneath them, crying.

"I guess talk to the sheriff again."

She stared out the rear window at the lump of covered calf. "Do you hunt, Terry?"

"Occasionally. Why?"

"Because I might need help taking that hide off. My father did that when we butchered a beef or an elk."

"So, the truth comes out. You backsliding?"

"I'll do it," she snapped, before ratcheting down a notch. "I got a bit ahead of myself. I just need someone to tell me what to do. That's all."

"That's plenty. Seems you might want to quit exaggerating unless you don't mind getting yourself in a bind."

He just didn't know about the Crosses and the Lost Daughter. Getting out of binds was their specialty. She wondered how everything up in the mountains was faring.

BEHIND THE SALE BARN, stood an iron crossbar rack mounted into a concrete pad. Welded together, the rack strong enough to manage hanging up almost anything, and that anything included chain-sawed calves. The crossbar stood about five feet off the ground; Terry pulled up beside the iron and eyed her.

"If you thought flipping that calf was bad, wait until you see what comes next."

Emory didn't have a clever response to give. One

thing struck as certain: her undignified retching hadn't gone unnoticed.

Outside of the truck, they lowered the tail gate and tugged at the tarp.

Terry assessed her, assessed the calf. "Hell. You ain't going to be strong enough. Call Dave, would you?"

She pulled out her phone. Much to her horror, it was dead.

"Well?" Terry asked.

"Needs to be charged," she replied, trying to make light of it.

Terry eyed her cold. "Think you should plan ahead better?"

Emory chaffed, becoming mighty tired of getting into so much trouble that day. "Yep. Got no defense for this one."

The lead brand inspector resumed tugging on the tarp, eyeing the cross bar and measuring the carcass by sight. "Go on up to the office to get Dave and plug your phone in while you're at it."

"Can't you just call him?"

"Yup, *I* sure can," he stopped moving, rested his fore-arms over the side of the truck bed. "Think you can keep your phone charged and usable?"

She didn't need to be a mind reader to see the outcome of that particular conversation. Without further comment, she jogged back into the sale barn and up the linoleum stairs, ignoring the buzzing flies. She burst through first the door at the top of the stairs and darted in through the office door.

Dave glanced up at the commotion. "There a bear chasing you?"

"Well, of a sorts. I need to charge my phone."

Dave kept eyeing her like he found her predicament

interesting. Emory concluded that he was good at inspecting more than just brands. "Uh-huh. Not a favorable condition."

"We also need your help downstairs. Terry sent me up to get you instead of calling and making things easy. Teaching me a lesson, I guess."

"Yep, he sure could have called seeing how his phone ain't dead." Dave narrowed his eyes. "Guess he thought you needed to figure out how modern technology works or responsibility. One or the other. Having your phone inoperable is no laughing matter out in the field."

Dave, while no whiz at the computer, religiously plugged his phone in every time he returned to his desk. Whether it needed it or not.

"Very funny," she replied. "Bring your gloves along. You might want them."

He gathered his gloves and followed her out of the office, stopping to lock the door. "Say you need help in a remote area. How are you gonna get that without a phone?"

"Radio," Emory supplied, hurrying through the dark hallway, and opening the door to the stairs.

"Good answer. Which frequency?"

Halfway down. "If you are so into preparedness, why aren't these lights ever on? Anyhow, I'd have to consult the chart."

"No lightbulb. So, you'd have to look at the chart. Let's say we're all out in the field. Then what?" Dave followed behind in no particular hurry.

"I call one of your numbers," Emory admitted.

"Which you cain't do, unless your phone's got a charge."

"Got it, Dave. I'll plug in my phone." She opened the bottom door out onto the arena's mezzanine.

"Sure seems like you ought to."

Together they crossed the arena and went out through the door to the pens where Terry waited like he hadn't a care in the world.

Dave long-legged it up to the pickup truck, taking a gander over the edge.

"What's the plan?"

"Hang it up by the back legs and get the hide off of him, I guess."

Dave chewed on that for a second. "This has gotta be a new tactic in 'we'll go you one step further.'"

A half chuckle from Terry. "Don't be a smart-ass."

Lashing its back legs together, it took both men to heft the carcass up to hang on the hook, head hanging down.

"Emory's really going to do this part?" Dave asked, doubtful.

Terry answered, eyeing Emory. "She said she would. Now, do you think you can manage this or not?"

Em eyed the carcass, not overjoyed at the prospect. "If I said I'll do it, I'll do it."

At that same moment a white pickup truck came driving up, the driver craning his neck to see who they were. Instead of taking the bend into the parking lot, the truck drove straight up to them.

Shit!

Emory set her mount in a grim line, hoping against hope that it wasn't who she thought it was.

But, of course. It was none other than the Texan, Hugo Werner. And he couldn't have picked a worse time to show up.

Long-legged, he emerged from his truck, noted the hanging calf, and smirked. "What are ya'll up to? That the calf from this morning?"

"One and the same," Terry replied. "We're giving Emory a lesson in skinning. That is, unless she's changed her mind."

They were riling her up and having a laugh at her expense.

"I can manage," she snapped.

Great. Now she sounded bitchy.

Terry handed her a skinning knife—handle first—and a pair of latex gloves. Hugo and Dave stood off to the side, waiting, watching and coming damned near close to smirking.

She didn't care about Dave. Or Terry, for that matter.

Terry cleared his throat. "Now. Start down the metatarsals of each leg until you reach the intersection of the two cuts on the underside."

Breathing through her mouth, she stabbed the tip of the blade into an indent on the calf's leg. Cutting through the hide and gaining purchase proved a bit harder than she expected.

She stole a quick glance at the men, then back at the mangled carcass.

Sweat formed on her forehead and the back of her neck, unpleasant and prickly. Intent and grasping the knife in both hands she tugged downward, cutting through the thick hide. Once the cut was established, she sliced the length of it. As to the nasty details, she ignored them to the best of her ability.

Hitting a hacked-out patch where the meat got butchered, she continued onwards, making do and extending the line to the other side of the gaping hole.

She shirt-sleeved the stinging sweat getting into her eyes.

Just wonderful. He'd think she sweated like a pig.

Next, she progressed to the right leg, running the cut

down toward the stomach, meeting the other incision in the gaping mess that made up what remained of the calf's belly.

"This far enough?"

"Yeah, for our purposes," Terry replied. "Now, from the back legs, pull the hide down until the brand is peeling off."

It didn't come right down. First, she had to cut at the pale blue fatty connective tissue so the hide could pull free.

The sound and sensation left plenty to be desired, but the hide gave way.

"Now?" She forced the single word out, gagging at the end. If she puked, she'd never live it down.

"Yeah, that'll do 'er."

Scrutinizing the carcass from all angles, the branded part of the hide had to be removed, nice and clean. "Do I just cut across now?"

"Might as well," Terry replied.

The hide came away and she examined the reverse. Sure enough, the original brand stood out clear.

She held it up for everyone to see, gloved hands covered in gore.

"Looks like the calf started out life as a *7 Lazy S* but got added to. Somewhere along the line it got changed to a *T Lazy S-S*. On a calf, it's harder to tell which marks came first, BUT that's what it seems to me. No wonder we couldn't find this brand in the database. It hasn't been registered." Emory's voice came out stronger than she felt. Vindicated, but wobbly-kneed all the same.

The Texan nodded his admiration straight out, but approval from her partners was grudging and veiled.

All because of that damn phone.

Terry considered at the hide she held. "Let's go check

up on this other one and see who that belongs to at least." He turned back to Hugo. "What brings you over this way anyhow?"

His eyes darted to Emory, then returned to the men. "Just passing by. Wanted to hear if you found out anything. Obviously, you have."

"We've heard mention of SUVs driving slow on rural roads, making multiple passes down the same stretch, back and forth in front of the same houses. Maybe something to do with migrants. Gets people on edge, and that's the truth."

"Migrants, huh? They're hard enough to track at the best of times. Well, I just stopped since I was nearby. Holler at me if there's anything I can do."

And with that, Hugo drove off.

It would be a fine thing if the ground just swallowed her up.

"I'd say you made quite the impression there," Terry ribbed.

If she'd been empty handed, or if her hands hadn't been covered in membrane, flecks of meat, and blood, she might have just hauled off and belted him in the arm.

With the hide slung over one of the corral rails, Dave and Terry took pictures of the underneath where the brand showed through, eyeing her surreptitiously.

"I guess your reading didn't lead you astray," Dave said at length. "It's kind of a singular thing to be reading about, wouldn't you say?"

Emory's cheeks stung and insecurity flared.

"It was about Brown's Park. Anyhow, it struck me as interesting and—"

Terry held up his hand, cutting her off. "You don't owe us any explanations."

The implications hung in the air, bold and brazen.

"I figured Sheriff Preston told you about us," she mumbled.

Terry and Dave exchanged glances, but they weren't unkind. "People can change…if they want," Dave offered.

As usual, Terry proved more direct. "Past histories can die hard, but it doesn't mean that some skills can't be put to good use."

A half-laugh escaped from Emory. "It takes a thief to catch a thief, is that it?"

Both men stiffened. "I don't know I'd exactly put it like that," Dave said.

"Well, if you don't, others sure as hell will." Emory replied. "In fact, they already do."

A LOT OF CURIOUS COINCIDENCES GOING UNANSWERED

Up in the office, her phone dinged with an unheard message.

Emory pulled out the charge cord and frowned, weighing the phone in the palm of her hand. The message had the ranch phone's number.

A familiar voice came through.

Hi Em, it's your father. Nothing is out of the ordinary except I twisted my ankle bad and am laid up on crutches. Don't suppose you might be able to come home this weekend, could you? Let me know.

She must have looked bothered.

"You need to tend to that?" Terry asked.

"Yeah. My father's had a slight accident. Or so he says. I'll be right back."

She'd meant to call her father at least once a week. Sometimes that happened, sometimes it didn't. Taking her phone into the darkened hallway, she gave half-hearted thanks that the lightbulb hadn't been replaced.

The phone rang twice.

"Dad?"

His voice warmed. "How you doing, Em?"

"I'm fine. What happened?"

"Well, them preservation people came out, and I fell off the bottom step of the porch. Tore ligaments and Cade nowhere to be found. Those people had to drive me into town to the doctor's."

"What cause you to fall of the porch—did they get you riled?" Emory asked, having trouble imagining it.

He chuckled. "No. Nothing like that. Got distracted, I guess."

That was strange right there.

"Well, did you ask Cade where he was and what he was doing since he wasn't around to help?"

"Yeah. Said he was checking on cattle in the upper pastures, but I don't believe him none."

Emory felt like she was dragging information from the man. In fact, she was. Maybe things weren't going as well on the ranch as she had assumed.

"Are those preservation people causing problems?"

A bit of a groan. "They'd like to if I let them."

She felt like she was getting nowhere. The bottom line remained that her father had asked her to come home. "I'll be home tomorrow night after work." She hesitated a moment. "Say, none of those people are young and blond, are they?"

Her father chuckled. "Same crew as you saw the last time. Well, that Peterson woman is blonde, and probably outweighs Cade by fifty pounds and twenty years, not that he's choosy. She's smarter than he is, too." A long pause. "And so are you, Em. That's why I need you to come home."

She thumped the edge of an old cardboard file box with her boot. "Her last name is Paulson."

"Ha! I'd call her Peterson, and she'd say 'Paulson', and I thought she was talkin' to me, so I'd say Lance…"

"*Dad.*"

An amused sigh. "She's bossy."

"You think all women are bossy. Anyhow, don't tell Cade that I asked."

"Wouldn't dream of it. Anyhow, you figure out what he's up to. I've got a ranch to run, and now I'm laid up. Say, you find a boyfriend there yet?"

She thought about the Texan. "No," she replied. "They're kind of…straight-laced."

Yeah. Not exactly the Cross kind of prospects.

"Don't sell yourself short, but you ain't getting any younger," came her father's only reply.

"None of us are," she countered. "Now Terry and I have gotta go drive out to a ranch to check on a missing calf."

"Well, listen to you," he drawled. "See you when you get here."

The phone went dead.

Her father didn't truly understand. She probably had options, and a lot of baggage to bring into any relationship. No one would be too keen, not when they knew what she came from.

Unless they were after the Lost Daughter itself.

That pointed to the dark heart of the matter. It was always about the ranch.

THE PLAINS of eastern Colorado slipped by as the brand inspectors drove out to the Alderson's ranch. Mile upon mile of flat grass nothingness stretching wide. Occasional outpost towns still lingered: ghosts of their former selves, vacant, boarded up, or scratching by. The brand inspectors drove straight through, as did everyone else. Populations dwindled as young people took off fast at eighteen, and likely never returning except when Thanksgiving and Christmas rolled around. While the mountain towns boomed and sprawled, the towns in the eastern plains struggled in their death-throes, closing down shop after shop, as their lives bled out and spilled across the land.

Emory sighed as she considered the false-fronted main street nine-tenths of the way dead. "Do you think these places are ever going to make a comeback?"

Terry took stock of the view outside. "Oh, you never know, I guess. Some movie star might blow in through town and buy up the whole thing, lock, stock, and barrel."

They both knew the likelihood of that ran small to non-existent. And if some movie star actually happened to snap one up, the towns wouldn't be restored to their pasts—not really. Any of the towns would be a shell of its former self—just a rich person's plaything to be discarded once it ceased to amuse.

"You know, I saw something about that on the news once. An entire town being for sale somewhere out here. Did anything ever come of it, I wonder?"

He sniffed. "Can't say that I recall, so probably not."

"Where are your people?" Emory asked.

"Lamar," he replied.

She nodded. "That's a bit bigger. Didn't they get that National Park for the Indian massacre?"

"National Historic Site," he corrected, turning onto a smaller county road. "Nothing to be proud of there. But, it's important. Don't know if it'll help the economy. Maybe it will, but maybe it shouldn't. It's a pilgrimage site. The Indians probably don't feel like bedding down in any of the local motels where their ancestors got slaughtered. Can't say that I'd blame them on that count."

Conversation dried up on that note, and miles of barbed-wire strung fenceposts rolled on by.

A left-hander down a long, straight road signaled they neared their destination and small dark smudges of buildings punctuated the distant horizon.

A side-eyed stare. "Now this is more delicate than our other visit," Terry cautioned, "and they don't have any idea we're coming."

"Meaning I should keep my mouth shut," Emory supplied.

"Meaning it wouldn't hurt, unless you get the woman alone."

He wasn't kidding.

She scrunched up her nose, like he'd farted. "Some women might say that's chauvinistic you know."

He grinned and stuck a toothpick in his mouth. "Sounds just like a plain statement of fact to me. And didn't you just say women tell each other things, woman to woman?"

The truck rumbled over the rutted road, kicking up the ever-pervasive autumn dust as they approached another dried up ranch ready to blow away in a strong wind.

"Need rain or snow," Emory said. "It's dry. Dry, dry, dry."

Terry lifted his finger off of his steering wheel to agree.

Forget about the next strong wind, but the Alderson's out buildings appeared unlikely to withstand another century of trying to eke out a living.

That hardscrabble ranch sure reminded her of the

Lost Daughter, and she shifted in her seat as they pulled up into the ranch yard.

A curtain twitch that said their arrival hadn't gone unnoticed. A female twitch, meaning their knocking might easily go unanswered.

They both emerged from the truck, but she dawdled by her door.

Terry's glance posed an unspoken a question.

"No need to go ganging up on people," she said in a low voice.

With a halfway defeated shrug, he went up to the door and knocked.

Emory scanned the windows for further movement but saw nothing.

He knocked again, harder. "Brand inspector," he called out, aiming at the crack between the door and the frame.

Glancing back at her, Emory index-fingered, pointing upwards. Gesture small and hidden.

Terry caught it all the same. He waited another moment for the door to be answered. It wasn't. Right at the time he turned away, the front door opened approximately three inches.

"Can I help you?" The woman asked.

When she saw Emory and checked out the writing on the truck, she opened wider.

Reddened hands and expression tired, the same as any number of harried and work-hardened ranch people across the state.

Terry turned around to face her. "Mrs. Alderson?"

"Yes."

He tipped his hat. "I'm Terry Overholzer, the brand inspector from the Greeley Sale Barn. This is Emory

Cross. We've run into a strange situation. Is your husband around as well?"

"Do you need him?" she asked. Puzzled and distrustful all at the same time. A combination that was becoming more and more frequent from what Emory gathered.

"It might be best," Terry replied.

"He's out checking on the livestock and doing whatever needs done, but I can give him a call if you really need him. What's this about?"

"We found a calf in another county that had an altered brand. It looks to have started out life as one of yours, but the brand was tampered with along the way. Are you missing any calves?"

Her long hair was pulled back in a ponytail as severe as her expression. A few wisps escaped at their own risk. "I'll go call Earl," she said, abrupt.

She abandoned Terry on the stoop.

Door ajar, he appeared uncomfortable enough to return to the truck, giving the woman a measure of privacy.

"You can't really hear from here," Emory muttered. "Go on back up there."

"No need to eavesdrop as they work out whatever they are working out."

"Hmmm. That's the exact opposite of how you expect me to operate."

Busted. "Couldn't hear the exact words, but it didn't sound too pleasant.

Mrs. Alderson rejoined them a few moments later. "You might be wondering what all the discussion was about," she said, color rising in her wind-chapped cheeks. "My husband and I are having a slight difference of opinion on how to go about things in this instance. And I'm only telling you this because he's too damn bull-headed to tell you much on his own. Not without prodding."

Both women stared at Terry, who had enough sense not to say a damned thing.

Emory jumped into the breach. "Is there a particular line of questions you would suggest that we take?"

"Well, you could ask him about that bull that keeled over dead and the coyotes won't touch. I'd like to hear the answer to that one myself."

The woman's expression a determination settled in the lines and wrinkles. Her faded eyes shining and the color still hot in her cheeks.

A dead bull untouched by scavengers was out of the ordinary at the very least.

But the bull, no matter how concerning, wasn't the reason for their visit.

Terry tried again. "Sure. We can bring that up. We're enquiring about that missing calf I mentioned."

"And I'm enquiring about a bull in the bone yard," she shot back.

Terry suppressed a sigh, and offered a question asked out of habit. "How long has the bull been out there?"

"Three days," the woman replied without a trace of uncertainty.

"Well," Terry frowned. "Did you report that one?"

She stared at him. "Did you see a report of anything like that coming from here?"

"Deaths from possible contagion must be reported. Likewise, deaths from trauma or criminal activity."

She stared at Terry and said nothing in response.

The implications were left out in the open, hanging in the wind.

SUSPICIONS AND PREDATORS
OR LACK THEREOF

THE HUM OF AN ATV MOTOR DRIFTED TOWARD THEM, building in strength the nearer it came.

The rancher pulled up in front of the three assembled together, trained his eyes upon Terry, and didn't give a word of welcome. His expression reminded her of her father.

"Yes?" He asked, barely civil.

Terry took a step forward, hand outstretched. "Terry Overholzer, and this here is Emory Cross. We responded to a Weld County ranch for a dead calf report. It wasn't their brand, but upon inspection, turns out the original brand belonged to you. The brand was changed along the way."

"That a fact," he said, still not getting off of the ATV. "Changed how?"

"Brand got added to. You have any calves go missing lately?" Terry took a few steps toward him clipboard in hand.

"Nope," the man said, but for a stray second his eyes darted to his wife, uneasy.

She stood her ground, arms folded across her chest.

"We'd like to take a look at your bone yard," Terry said.

The man still didn't act convinced of anything, other than an intrusion took place on his land. "What for?"

His words came across close to a demand.

"Inspection," Terry replied, flexing his shoulders. "You can show us, or I'll go find it myself. Your choice, and you know we don't need a warrant."

The rancher sat back in his ATV seat, eyed Terry. Again, locked eyes with his wife. He rubbed the back of his neck like it pained him.

"All right," he conceded, backing down a notch. "We lost a calf about a week and a half back. So what?"

Terry sure weighed that reaction. "And you didn't report it. Why not?"

"Didn't seem worth it."

"Not worth it?"

A disgust-tinged sigh. "Some runners showed up a couple of weeks back. Seemed easiest and best just to keep quiet."

There it was. Again. Runners, slow-drivers or however they were labeled, likely all amounted to the same thing.

"Seemed easiest how? What kind of runners are showing up?"

Exasperation rippled.

"How the hell should I know? It's not like they come up to the door and introduce themselves. And if they did, I'd be forced to shoot them on sight. And I would, too."

"That sounds a bit extreme," Terry said.

"Maybe so. You ever met any at your place?"

"No. Now why don't you tell me what's going on out here, now that the conversation's started?"

The man pointed to one of the roads. "They drive by real slow. You notice them. At first, we just thought they was lost. But they came back at night. *That* night. We saw lights across the field. The next morning, one of the calves was gone. About a week and a half ago, just like I said." He consulted with his wife. "That right?"

His wife nodded.

Terry cleared his throat, scanned the horizon. "The rancher who found your calf thought it was his at first. The darndest part came down to how it had been butchered using a chain saw."

The rancher took that in. "Calves are easier to steal than full grown ones. But you said the brand had been changed? Can't figure why that might be."

"Nope, that's a puzzlement," Terry agreed. "And what's that about a bull in the bone yard?"

"To use your word, that's another puzzlement." The rancher shrugged, less defensive and more apprehensive, if that were even possible.

THE BULL ROTTED in a depression far away from the house.

Black flies swarmed around its anus, over his mouth, and on his eyes. No readily identifiable sign of trauma visible, the bull's hide had only been torn at in a few places. The dead animal smell, sweet and metallic at the same time, sure hit when the wind shifted.

The Alderson's alighted from their Kubota and joined Terry and Emory, standing at their side.

Everyone fixated on the stinking carcass.

Terry hopped down into the depression to get closer, putting his boot on the bull and pushed. Flies shot up in a swarm, then settled back down to feed.

"You know what happened to him?" Terry asked, although he had already heard Mrs. Alderson's impressions and opinions on the matter.

"Well," the rancher started, "he was old. Don't know why ain't nothing but the flies feedin' on him."

"Poison?" Terry asked.

A sigh. "Yeah, the thought crossed my mind. Didn't want to get her worried," he jerked his head toward his wife, who didn't seem inclined toward either nerves or worry.

"Poison would explain it," she said, drawing near the edge to stand by Emory. "But why would anyone poison one of our bulls. Earl?"

The 'Earl' part came out sharp.

"No idea. Doubt that's what happened."

Terry tried again. "This is the only loss to death, correct?"

"That's right," Alderson answered, monotoned.

"You call a veterinarian or anyone?"

"Nope," Alderson pronounced. "Costs money."

"So, no necropsy, is that what you're saying?" Terry continued. "Got it insured?"

"Nope. I'm saying I don't want to know at this point." Alderson shrugged. "Don't carry insurance. Besides, like I said. That fellow was old."

"Still, his death is a significant loss, wouldn't you say?"

"I would," Mrs. Alderson replied.

Her husband, still bothered, didn't act so sure. "They don't last forever, you know. His time was up."

"Still, you two don't have any idea what might have happened here, is that right? Where'd you find him?" Terry pressed.

"In the far pasture that direction. We dragged him over here."

Terry and Emory each stiffened.

"You know," Emory began, "this is the second time we've heard about people driving along the out of the way roads. Each time those people come around, something happens to cattle. I'm from Rimrock County, and I know we'd be sharing that information up there. Terry and I are stationed in Greeley, and we'd have to get pretty lucky to come upon some of those drivers. Don't suppose you might consider helping out a bit here, would you?"

Earl Alderson's expression came across like he played a game of scrabble and had a hard time spelling.

Plenty of concentrating going on there.

A slow wag of his head, but a spark lit his eyes.

"These people won't play nice, I'm fair on convinced. In a certain nearby town and on the wrong side of the tracks, there is a motorcycle club. And that motorcycle club attracts a rough clientele. In fact, it says Territorial Sons right on the front. Go ask them if you want to know so bad."

"You think they're behind this?" Terry asked, watching the Aldersons close. Real close.

"No," Mr. Alderson interjected, cutting his wife off. "But they might know who is."

His wife nodded. "Last any of us heard, motorcycle gangs were running drugs, prostitution, and raising general hell. At least that's what they said on *60 Minutes*."

"Yeah," Emory agreed. "I saw that show, too. It didn't make me feel too good."

"Rimrock County?" Mrs. Alderson asked, interested.

"Yes, ma'am," Emory replied.

"Why, we've got a cousin up there. Leroy Timmons. You know him?"

I'll be damned.

A laugh from Emory. "And we've got a hand that goes by Cade Timmons. You figure they're one and the same?"

"That sounds about right," Mr. Alderson shifted. "I got another dip-shit, useless cousin who claims he's running with the Territorial Sons. I suppose I could listen to his bullshit to see if he knows anything of use, which is highly unlikely."

His wife went a little bug-eyed at the notion. "Well, you aren't setting one foot over there. Call him on the phone if you want, but you aren't going to any dang motorcycle club house. Especially not the Territorial Sons. What is this state coming to, is what I want to know."

They all stared at the bull and the flies collecting. Silent.

"I'll write down the tag number," Terry said, snapping the stalemate and approaching the bull, hand covering his nose and mouth until the time he had to start writing. He checked the brand, and indicated it was as should be.

"Want me to send in the report?" he asked the Aldersons.

"We'd be obliged," Mrs. Alderson said. "That's just one less thing we'd have to do."

"Guess I'll give Henry a call," the rancher remarked climbing back into the Kubota. "But, that bull died of old age."

His wife, unconvinced, took her seat alongside him.

Mrs. Alderson clearly didn't care who knew she had several gripes going on that afternoon.

A rough night and a cold dinner looked in store for Mr. Alderson.

NO STONE UNTURNED

THE DISQUIETING SHADOW OF THE TERRITORIAL SONS
faded. As did the whereabouts of the Mexican-boot guys
released into freedom. Each passing westward mile and
closer to the mountains, a weight lifted and she felt dang
near light hearted on a Friday afternoon. Kai loaded up
and both of them headed home into the west.

Preoccupations about the Lost Daughter and what
she might find didn't weigh in. Until they did, right
about the time she passed through the Eisenhower
tunnel.

Three hawks glided along the thermals. Emory knew
Native Americans believed that the raptors were
messengers of warning from their ancestors. Chiefs
relied upon hawks to guide them through trying times.
They represented honesty and clear vision.

Two things she certainly had need of.

The worry and realization came as a stab, somewhere
in the middle where her conscience ought to be. A
notion wormed its ugly way into her brain.

The Lost Daughter. Her father. That $2,050 maverick

dollars which hadn't been touched even though the calves were long gone. What would she ever do about that money?

None of it sat well. Not on her current trajectory into the law-abiding world.

She could give part of the money back, pretending it was a loan with an obligation to repay. Sure, her father'd see right through that act, but it might work. Details vague enough that they could both pretend it was no big deal.

She cast her eyes toward mountain peaks searching for answers, knowing none would be forthcoming. The mountains stayed silent and aloof, apart from man-made misery.

Those damn, sprawling, and oversized houses took their toll on the western side of the tunnel.

Sizing up and dismissing the prolific crop of 'McMansions' out of hand, knowing they were built for people who bought and sold where ever their current desires led them, unlike her family. Unlike the other ranchers. The likes of them that settled those valleys in the early days could never match that kind money, not even in a good year. Unless they sold their ranches to the newcomers with deep pockets.

That was the catch-22 right there.

The rich settlements had clustered around Colorado's resort towns, grasping and strangling the landscape like bind weed. Every newcomer purchased his slice of paradise; and each rancher lost a tract of production. For an insane amount of money, the ranchers had no clue of handling. *Really* handle.

Back to the rustlers and safer ground.

It stood plumb unlikely that true, dyed-in-the-wool rustlers of western lore ever worried, or even thought about, spending or not spending their proceeds. If they didn't use their ill-gotten gains for their own advantage, what in the hell was the point? Unless they were far-thinking planners, and that would have been rare. Mighty rare. Sure as shooting, outlaws never opened up bank accounts unless they were casing the banking operations.

Emory chuckled to herself, but none of it was all that funny. A way of life was changing, if not disappearing altogether.

Now she found herself working on the other side of the law. A card-carrying member to boot; she had her identification and a badge to prove it.

Driving always gave Emory time to think. Just like riding, just like chasing cattle.

Mavericking.

A historical occupation local to the region. While those days *likely* were done for her now, habit died hard. Some of the old ways still served them in the 'new' days. Thanks to the prevailing indifference to the law that her family held close to their hearts, she was able to come up with ideas the law-abiding citizens couldn't imagine. Still, half of her wondered if she shouldn't confess to branding those mavericks. The smarter half told her to leave well enough alone.

The blue shadows of early twilight fingered their way across the land and down from the mountain spines and ridges. The distant peaks to the west still gleamed in the cool autumn sunlight. The radiance would fight to the last before settling down and succumbing to darkness.

Emory's soul didn't thrill anywhere near the same at the lower elevations, and that was the truth.

Once past the Eisenhower tunnel and taking the familiar highway headed north, she traveled through Cross territory.

Deeper into the heart of Colorado.

The land of Zane Grey.

Damn. There she went again.

He wasn't from Colorado but Ohio, for crying out loud. Probably would have wanted one of those McMansions as well while he was at it.

She oughtn't confer on him a status he didn't deserve. He never fought for the land but just skimmed along top. One thing for certain, she hadn't had cause to think of him for a long time. She cast a critical eye over the sage in the twilight just to check.

Still not purple, but dark gray.

Purple sage my ass.

She grinned at the notion, shook her head and turned the radio on. Loud.

THE CLEAR VELVET night fell deep, littered with cold, glinting stars. The mountains' shadowing sentinels of midnight blue ran deep—impassive and deadly in a biting night. The moon lit the sky and snow stood out a paler blue despite the porch light's defiant attempt against all the darkness. All the danger—and the beauty — had tethered the Crosses together for years to come.

They knew what was in those mountains and in the gullies and the draws. On the flats.

Emory noted that a couple of lights were on in the house, and none of that damn ghostly flickering from the television.

Cade's truck stood parked beside the bunkhouse. It was a Friday night, and his presence struck as downright odd.

Cade. What to do about Cade.

Make that Leroy.

No matter how she turned the issue around in her mind, he was still another problem.

Pulling to a stop near the center of the yard and near the barn, her truck triggered the yard light to come on, ending the spell and the magic. She sprang out of the truck and unbolted the horse trailer.

"We're home, Kai-Kai!"

He nickered and blew, recognizing the familiar surroundings. With a pat, she led him over to the pasture gate, pulled off his headstall, and turned him loose. Head high and mane flowing in the breeze, he ran toward the other horses, happy to be home with his herd.

The other horses whinnied their recognition.

At that same moment, the house door opened wide. So did the bunkhouse.

Over the distance between, judging from their postures, the two men stared each other down. For the moment, no one paid the slightest bit of attention to her.

Her father hobbled out onto the porch.

"You let Cade deal with them horses, why don't you. It's what he's paid to do, ain't that right Cade?"

A pause that lasted a fraction of a second too long.

"Yes, sir." His voice came out sharp with an unlikely enthusiasm. "I hoped to have a word with Emory now that she's here."

"Why don't you let her get some supper first," her father replied.

"Catch you later, Em," he called out. "And I'll take care of Kai, so don't you worry. On *that* count."

Lance Cross crutched his way back in and waited for the door to close.

"What the hell was that supposed to mean?"

She shook her head. "How am I supposed to know? I've been in Greeley, remember?"

"Yeah, I remember," he poked at her using the crutch's rubber tip to get a rise.

"Cut that out," she scolded, and gave him a hug. "How's that ankle feeling?"

"I've had worse," he replied.

Emory sniffed. "What's for dinner? It smells good."

"Some boxed potato thing. I've got a couple a steaks to throw on the grill, too."

"They aren't slow elk, are they?"

His eyes twinkled. "Hell no. I've reformed. At least partially. Ever since I have a daughter who joined law enforcement. Them steaks came from the Mercantile, although they ought to be ashamed of themselves for the prices they're asking. It sure don't equate to what us ranchers get paid. I've probably got some of that slow elk in the freezer, but it would take a while to defrost."

That earned a closer look to see if he was teasing, but the last part sure had the ring of truth to it.

He winked at her. "Carry these out for me, will you?"

"Sure. I can grill them if you want," she offered.

"Hell, no. There's nothin' wrong with these hands."

She laughed and carried the tray, her father trailing behind.

Outside and in the night air, the stars seemed so much closer than they appeared in Greeley.

A spangled black more precious than any diamonds, at least to her. At least on that day.

She wondered if she would feel the same way if she ever had a diamond engagement ring, and figured she was doomed to remain alone.

Her father, a shock of gray hair falling into his eyes as

he grilled, acted relaxed, content that his daughter was home.

She didn't want to ruin it by debating the merits of slow elk. *Stolen beef.*

But slow elk might be a preferable conversation than talking about the life stretched out before her. She would run the ranch when the time came, even if she had to do it singlehandedly, but she hoped that wouldn't be the case.

Old habits died hard, all right. Real hard.

Her father pulled the steaks off the grill, and she carried them on a platter held out like an offering. She pulled the potatoes out of the oven and carried the dish to the table. Her father had already put a steak on her plate and when she set the hot dish down, stuck a serving spoon straight up in the potatoes.

"What's that job of yours got you doing, anyhow?"

"Brand inspection stuff. I look at a lot of hindquarters." Her laugh had an unintended hitch.

His fork stopped halfway to his mouth. "Out with it."

Not ready to deal with the shooting. Not yet.

"There's one strange case we haven't sorted out. A calf from one ranch was reported stolen on another, and the brand got vented. So, we go out to the originating ranch, and they tell us that a steer keeled over dead without warning. They didn't report the missing calf either, and all that comes to their minds as far as suspects go are, and I quote, "the men who drive slow on the roads." They think they have something to do with migrant workers. Oh, and get this. They're related to Cade."

Her father resumed chewing, eyes clear and sharp. "That a fact?"

"Yep. Said his real name is Leroy."

Her old man chuckled at that nugget. But he remained a cattleman at heart, first and foremost. "And you don't know what did the steer in."

"Maybe some type of poison, but the Aldersons didn't report it and the man doesn't want to know. The rancher says he likely died of old age, but we'll never have proof."

A deep, considered inhale. "Sounds like warnings or a grudge to me."

That caught her.

"Warnings for what? The calf got hacked up by chain saw, and the best meat taken. Whomever did that was sloppy, but they knew their cuts."

She had more than a passing interest in her father's reaction to the *Leroy* part.

Since he offered none, she'd just have to let that sink in.

She returned to the mystery. "The first rancher sure acted traditional, but he said his wife wanted to file for the insurance. They aren't big enough not to know when a calf gets stolen, I'd say. And it's pretty flat. It's not like they're running on BLM land or anything. No ravines or draws like here."

"Insurance, huh? Expensive. Fancy beef?"

"Nah. Average. But they still can't file on calves that aren't theirs." A quick change of topic. "Why do you suppose Cade changed his name?"

"Guess he didn't like Leroy. Can't blame him there. It's kind of old fashioned, ain't it?"

Emory shrugged. "Maybe he's hiding something. You ever wonder about that?"

"Have I ever wondered about Cade? Hell, yeah. Like every other day." He acted like it was one heck of a joke.

Emory glared back at him and refused to laugh. "I'm serious, Dad."

Her father shifted in his seat. Like she'd said something unpleasant. She changed course.

"So, back to the insurance. They won't get anything for it. Don't know why they would try to file a claim on something that wasn't theirs."

"Maybe his wife just wants money and goaded him into doing something."

That sounded like the voice of experience to Em, but she didn't say anything of the sort and stuck to the topic. "She seemed straight enough. Said getting insurance was the son's idea."

"You don't know what type any of them people are. Hell, people can seem to be one thing, and are another entirely."

The topic had obviously veered off path in her father's mind.

"You talking about Cade now?"

"No, but I could."

Yeah, he was talking about her mother. Change the subject and change it fast.

"What about the Historic Preservation people?"

"They got damn peculiar ideas, and that's no lie. But speaking of *Leroy*, some biker came sniffing around his truck last week, and I had to run him off. Didn't come from around these parts. His eyes bugged out a bit at the rifle."

"You have to stop running people off armed, Dad." Emory sighed, knowing she couldn't change him. Not in a hundred years.

Lance Cross shook his head at her. "I'll bet he was packin'. Just wasn't prepared."

"Even worse," Emory replied, smarting a bit at her own hypocrisy.

"It's how I get my exercise. Besides," he drawled, "it's kinda fun."

She chuckled and her heart swelled. "People are going say that you're a crazy old man."

"*A crazy old man with a rifle.* Darn straight. That fella sniffing around Cade's truck weren't up to no good."

A cold feeling travelled her spine.

"Well, who was it?"

"I didn't ask to see his driver's license! Some of them motorcycle riffraff I'd guess, not to put too fine of a point on it."

Emory's stomach tightened.

"That's something we might want to talk about, Dad. Did you say anything to Cade about it?"

Her father's fork and knife didn't even stop. "Yeah."

"And?"

Wary and tired, he snapped down his utensils and pushed back into his chair. "I mentioned it to him, never you mind."

If she wanted her father to level with her, she'd have to level with him as well.

"You didn't ask me if I brought the rifle back with me."

A quizzical expression. "Didn't occur to me. Well, did you?"

"No."

Her father shrugged. "So…"

"It's been taken as evidence. I used it and shot a man. He's still behind bars, but the other two were let loose."

All movement stopped, except for his throbbing jugular vein. "And you're just telling me about this now. When did this happen?"

Now came Emory's time to shift in her seat. "A couple

of weeks ago. I didn't want you to worry. The sale barn's got a catwalk over the pens. I was up there, and a guy trying to sell two stolen animals pulled a gun on one of the brand inspectors, so I shot him in the arm. Simple enough."

"Huh," her father said, eyeing her with a new respect. "Did you give him any warning?"

"Hell, no," she replied. "I just shot him."

Her father grinned. "Good girl. Now what about them other two?"

"Don't know, and I'm not supposed to do any more shooting until I'm cleared. All of which leads me to the next thing we ought to talk about. What *is* Cade up to? I got the impression he wasn't exactly happy to see me."

Her father stopped chewing, gray eyes turned serious. He gestured with his hand for her to get on with it.

"Think he's dealing drugs?" The accusation hung between them.

Shifting in his chair, Lance Cross peered through the kitchen in the direction of the ranch office.

"I believe in keeping a man's dealings his own," he claimed at length.

"On *your* spread? Noble, old fashioned and a few other things besides. And the man poking around Cade's truck? What did he say about that?"

Her father looked a type of bothered that he tried to keep hidden. "He probably lied about that one. Swore it had to do with hard feelings over some girl."

"And you said…"

"Told him to keep his troubles in town where they belonged."

"That's it?" She felt herself go slack-jawed. Her father couldn't be called naïve. "If he's dealing drugs, he might bring down the rest of us right along with him, easy. I'm sure you've thought of that."

"I have." The way he held himself was clear. Any more on that line would only cause hard feelings, and either stone silence or a heated argument to solidify that position.

Emory backed down a notch, seeing as how it was her first night back and all. "Want me to get some of those no trespassing signs in town? I've thought about it before but decided it wouldn't do much good. Pain in the ass, but I might be wrong."

"Don't think that would deter them bikers." Lance Cross shrugged. "But sure, why not. At least if it turns real western, we can say we had it posted."

"Don't like the sound of that. You think *Leroy* knows about 'real western'?"

A spark. "I'd say if he continues carrying on, he just might have the chance to find out. Patience don't grow on trees."

She wagged her head, slow. "Cade even own a gun?"

"No idea. But if he had an ounce of smarts, I guess he would."

That left quite a bit up for debate.

One point stuck out as certain, at least in Emory's mind. The last thing the Lost Daughter needed was another shootout.

A shootout of the modern kind.

SNAKE CHARMER

OUTSIDE ON THE PORCH, STARING UP IN THE COLD NIGHT
sky, Emory felt comforted by the midnight blue draped
across the landscape, blanketing the ranch. The night
provided a cloak over the ranch, a sense of familiarity
she'd sorely missed.

A light shone through Cade's window.

She'd check on Kai before going to see the cowhand.

Kai stood in his stall, relaxed in the familiar
surroundings and dozing. Nothing needed doing in the
barn. Clean and neat—more so than usual—she
wondered in passing whether that newfound fastidious-
ness came down to Cade's own initiative, or her father
cracking the whip. She had a pretty darn good idea
which side of the coin landed up on that one.

Maybe a clean barn turned out as one of those
preservation people's 'strange ideas', but it remained
unlikely that her father wielded a shovel, throwing out
old garbage and broken-down tack.

Walking to the bunkhouse, no visible improvements
had taken place there. There used to be at least five

hands, but that had dwindled down to the one. Music played within, the bass vibrating.

When she knocked on the door, the music immediately died down. Cade answered, shirt unbuttoned low.

"If it ain't the brand inspector," he smirked, standing aside so that she might enter. "Come on in."

He halfway bowed as she crossed the threshold.

"How've you been, Cade?" Emory asked as he shut the door, heart jumping a bit.

"How do I look?"

She refused to rise to the bait. "Where were you when my father fell?"

"Well, then," he said, leaning back against the closed door. "Straight to the point. I've been fine, by the way."

Emory smiled none too pleasant and hoped her fangs showed. "Dad wasn't. I guess those preservation people drove Dad into town since you were nowhere to be found."

He offered an irritated laugh and a fine profile. All the while posing, like good-looks might actually solve something for him. "Had business to attend to. How long you down for?"

Emory considered the sagging couch that had probably seen more action than she wanted to know about. She claimed a seat on an old barrel-backed chair without being offered.

She shrugged and stretched out her legs in front of her. "No set duration. I'll leave when I'm good and ready."

A prickly wave of dismissal and a sneer. "For the record, I told your father I needed that afternoon off. He forgot. Seems he forgets things more than he used to."

Her father had a mind like a steel trap, especially when sober.

"Bullshit," Emory replied. "He also mentioned scaring off some trespasser messing around your truck. What was that about?"

"Well, I've missed you too, Sunshine."

"Cut the crap, Cade. What's going on?"

His eyes sparked. "He figure out that we're a few head light?"

She quirked her head at the notion. "Not that I know of. Are we?"

Cade's arms folded across his chest, and he stared at her. "Likely. There were tire tracks. Not that it is going to be my battle much longer."

"You quitting on account of tire tracks?"

"Not because of tracks. He needs to ease up on me."

"How many head do you reckon we're missing, and did you tell him any of this?"

"Didn't seem advisable. Happened last Wednesday." He eyed her up and down. "He can be pretty temperamental at times."

"Hope you called the brand office."

Agitated, he stood up and started pacing. "Hell, I don't know their tag numbers! I'd have to pull in every last head to do that one. Might be retaliation for the mavericks. You ever consider that might happen? That'd be down to you to straighten 'im out."

"You're the lead hand—"

"I'm the only hand," he cut in.

She pretended like she didn't hear him. "We'll have to get the theft reported. That's likely a case of rustling. And what's that bit about the trespasser? You know he doesn't like people nosing around."

Cade, hands planted on hips, tried to stare her down. Met her square in the eye and pointed at her like she ought to know better. He dropped his hand and finger, then re-upped them. Pointed again, like he had a pistol.

Little did he know.

She stared at him, making it cold. Hoping to make him feel small. "You even own a gun, Cade?"

A vein in his neck throbbed. "I got a .45 and a cross-bow. Make you feel better?"

"Don't rightly know. What are you tangled up in, anyhow? You might as well spill it."

"Tell you because you're a junior brand inspector? Let me see your badge."

"Give me a twenty," she snapped.

"You can be kind of a bitch, Emory," Cade drawled.

"Take me out to those tire tracks tomorrow morn-ing," she said, rising up and moving to the door.

"And if I'm busy?"

"You aren't busy. And it's not exactly like I'm giving you a choice in the matter. Good night, Cade."

He shut the door without giving a response.

Outside in the ranch yard, the stars in the deep sky were indeed biting and cold. Emory stood in the center of the yard, arms folded across her chest and allowed the night and the history sink back into her bones.

Enemies watched and waited. She *felt* it.

She would be on her guard, wondering who to watch out for and what signs to read.

A HALF -HOUR LATER, a knock came on the front door.

Cade stood on the porch, hatless and hands in his coat pockets. Some of the fight gone out of him. She stepped outside and closed the door behind her.

"You here to see me?"

"All right, Emory," he said in a low voice. "You win on part of it. I've had a bit of trouble with my truck payments, and making ends meet. The wages paid here ain't great. But I've got that part sorted out now."

Alarm bells went off. "Sorted out how?"

"Guiding during my free time, which ain't all that much either, the way your father's going about it. Taking out hunters. That type of thing. Scouting."

"And how do you meet these . . . hunters?"

"Word of mouth," he pronounced, turning proud.

"Bullshit. Your reputation ain't great around town, and all that anyone respects about you is your cowboying and riding abilities. I can't see how anyone's going to be doing you too many favors."

A dry, humorless laugh. "The foreman at the Heritage Ranch and I have an arrangement. You know, the flocking place of the rich and the famous? He sends work my way."

Emory narrowed her eyes. "And what do you send his way?"

"Expertise. Knowledge of the mountains and the wild game. Ability to get them what they want, whatever it may be on a given day. And what is it you do for the brand inspectors?"

Hell. He was a flatlander. He just didn't know what she knew.

"I help them keep track of livestock. What'd you think?"

"I thought maybe you'd miss me. I said I missed you, in case you didn't notice."

Emory didn't flinch, she didn't blush, and she certainly didn't allow herself to believe any of the crock of shit he was selling.

"Oh, you're just saying that because five head were lost on your watch."

"You can be kind of a bitch, Emory."

"So you've already said. Comes in handy at times." She bit back. "And calling me a bitch doesn't bode kindly for you."

An inkling of trouble danced through his eyes. "You know I would never do anything to hurt you, your father, or this ranch. You should be aware that there is talk. And that talk is untrue."

"Do I? Talk about what?"

"I'd rather not say."

"You brought it up. Something got you scared, Cade?" Searching his eyes, she thought she detected fear hidden just below the surface. "Is that fellow going to come back out here?"

"You have my word that he will not." He puffed up at his claim.

That part made her doubt grow even stronger. "And who was he exactly?"

"Some type of repo man, I guess."

"Oh yeah. Those types come around all the time," Emory made sure her words came out as sarcastic. "Dad said he was motorcycle scum. If you're *truly* having trouble making payments, why don't you just stay out of town for a while—"

He cut her off. "It ain't that type of payments, and it's not that type of repo man. But it's nothing I can't handle. A few more trips to help out my cousin, then we'll all be square and this episode will be ended."

Emory searched his face for an opening, a clue. But his guarded eyes made it clear that he'd said all he would on the matter.

Episodes often spawned sequels.

"Be ready to ride tomorrow," she called out after him.

He lifted his hand in response as he kept has back toward her, walking back in the direction of the bunkhouse..

Instead, he flung open the door of his truck and hopped in like he couldn't wait to get away.

Like he couldn't wait to get into town.

RERUNS AND CATTLE

HER FATHER HADN'T MOVED. STILL SEATED IN HIS TV chair, watching flickering reruns, he shifted when she came back in

"Good to see some things never change."

"Huh." His bandaged ankle rested propped up on a cardboard box. Gray eyes traveled to her face.

"Cade says he thinks five head were stolen. He ever tell you that?"

Her father chuckled without mirth. "Ain't that just dandy. He *thinks*. No, he didn't say nothin' to me. When'd that all happen?"

"I guess Tuesday night sometime," Emory said, watching his reaction. "He said he saw the tracks on Wednesday."

"I scared that fellow away from his truck on Tuesday about four." Her father stretched out, flinched. "All the cattle are *supposed to be* in, and none running on BLM land. Guess we'll take a look tomorrow."

"You can't ride like that," she said, distracted. "He also said the theft might come down to the mavericks."

Her father's eyes turned cold. "He sayin' them two got stolen?"

"No. No details. Just made mention of my part in it."

Her father snorted. "I'd say that biker nosing around his truck had a better chance of having something to do with this. Don't let Cade get you riled. Besides, those two calves are long gone."

"So, we need to take stock. Again."

"Yes, we do."

"Shit," she spat out. "I never thought anyone would rustle from us."

"Well, they don't know us I guess," he agreed. "Once we figure out IF we got rustled, it might be time to introduce ourselves. In no uncertain terms."

The following morning Em strolled out to the mailbox in the mountain morning air. More practically, she figured collecting the mail had a high likelihood of being one of those "things" her father didn't get 'around to' with any regularity. The mountain sides glistened shot-through with the fading, tarnished gold of spent aspen trees. A frayed ribbon of mist threaded its way through the valley below.

In the crisp, clean morning she took her time, taking it all in and letting the image soak into her soul.

She pulled open the door, and sure enough, found plenty of mail, fliers and whatnot jammed in there. He obviously hadn't gotten around to collecting in a week. Pulling out the magazines, catalogs, envelopes in clumps, at that same moment, a BMW rounded the curve, skidding and engine racing.

Aimed square for the mailbox.

Emory jumped aside just as the car righted its course and sped off. Sure as hell, they weren't locals. They didn't stop to apologize for scaring the living daylight out of her. That would have required manners.

Assholes.

EMORY and her father ate breakfast, and at eight o'clock, Cade emerged from the barn leading her father's horse and his. Both bay horses, they ambled into the ranch yard, unconcerned as he tied them to the hitching post.

He didn't bother to tack up Kai. That meant he was trying to make the point that he didn't recognize her as being his boss. But she damn well was.

"Never mind," she called out like he had offered. "I'll get Kai saddled up myself."

He cocked a grin at her. "Didn't know you needed help, Em."

By this time, her father hobbled out to the porch, one boot on and one boot off. Just in time to hear the tail-end of what passed as banter.

He seemed interested in how she would handle the challenge.

"You're right. I don't want to get lazy. You might want to think about that yourself."

Emory sauntered across the yard to pull Kai out of his run. She lifted his headstall off the gate, went in, and grabbed him. Leading him into the barn, she saddled him up in nothing flat, mounting him and rode across the ranch yard.

She pointedly shot a questioning look at her father's bad ankle but didn't voice her reservations. Her expression was enough.

"I'll just mount on the right side," he explained, intercepting her glare.

He also had three clipboards in hand, and most remarkably, computer printouts of tags.

Blinking a couple of times when she saw the rows of tag numbers, Emory had a snappy comment on the tip of her tongue. But she stifled it, figuring ribbing might piss her father off. It wasn't the morning for it, and not with that particular problem looming.

Her father's eyes wore that hooded, guarded look to them, especially where Cade was involved. Dead serious on the matter, he obviously didn't trust the man.

That's the part that Emory couldn't truly understand. Why would he keep the cow prod around considering the clear lack of trust?

Lance Cross hobbled to her, holding out her clipboard. He hobbled over to Cade and did the same.

Then Cross mounted up, boot on the right foot, sock on the left.

"We'll use all the pastures to keep them sorted. Get the close ones first and drive them into the upper pasture. Once that gate's closed behind us, start checking off the tags you see. Then we'll feed them numbers back into the computer and see what we've got."

Each clipboard had a name on top of it, meaning two would carry more weight than the third.

He'd obviously put some thought behind it, and Emory tamped down a budding smile. Immediately. The issue at hand couldn't be considered a smiling matter, but her old dad was back from the brink. Back to the way he'd been before life, problems, and beer knocked him down.

That made the trip home worth it, right there.

Still in command, he pointed each in a direction along the perimeters. "There are plenty of cattle up in the higher pastures already."

Easy pickings. The Cross specialty.

Excited, Kai's ears flicked.

Emory held the reins in one hand and scratched his neck with the other. "Good to be back home, boy, isn't it? Both of us working and a job to do. Rounding up the cattle as we see them. Easy."

"Cade—you go through the draws and ravines. Emory, you go through the brush and river. Push the cattle where they need to go. If you run into trouble, whistle." A strength carried in that voice that she hadn't heard for a while.

The cowboy's back strong and straight in his faded plaid shirt as he wheeled away, pressing forward for the outer reaches of the ranch. They would all work together in that slow pushing—like a noose tightening around the neck of a bad guy in one of those 50's movies. The ones where the good guy always came out ahead.

That was another thing. The good guys didn't always win in the real west, and they sure as hell seldom came out ahead.

Tracking Cade, she felt the twinge of an insult as he didn't return the favor.

She and Kai would do their part. Neither one of them ever considered not trying or stopping at 'good enough'.

Dogged determination some called it.

She called it ranching.

Four and a half hours later, the tallying came to a close. Too many cattle pushed into the upper pasture to keep them there for long.

The mountains stood cold and stark and the cattle called.

Her father collected Cade's reckoning and handed her both clipboards. "Em, go stick these in the computer and see if we have to ride out this afternoon."

"Sure. Let's agree on one thing before we start. We

will file a report if some are really missing. That way the sale barns are alerted and inspectors for cattle shipments crossing state lines will be notified. Chances are good we'd get them back."

"Ever heard of real rustling?" Her father wasn't angry with her, although his words came out harsh. "I'm talking about the kind where they don't take the highways and don't go through any friggin' sale barn. Those head will be sold on for slaughter in a couple of days at most. Shit."

Of course, she had heard of real rustling.

She eyed her father, wondering if he didn't understand the magnitude of her job. *What a question.*

THE TABLES TURN–AIN'T THAT A HOOT

THE FINAL TALLY CAME UP TWO HEAD SHORT.

They reported, just like they were supposed to do. All legal and above board.

The mountains witnessed a fundamental shift in the Lost Daughter operations. Maybe the day had dawned upon a new era where a select few rules from the outside world might be adhered to and upheld.

Still, a general disregard for law prevailed.

That didn't mean her father wasn't smoldering, but he'd hold his fire. Those beeves might still turn up somewhere along the line.

Driving into town and passing down Main Street, she peered through the windshield at the second story of the old hotel where Zane Grey reportedly stayed. Rumor had it he'd written the *Mysterious Rider* in one of those very rooms. Somewhere along the line, he'd used the phrase *sage-tired eyes*, and that one sure stuck with her, and not in a good way. Emory most certainly took exception to that description. Once again, the words sounded good, but didn't hold up to closer inspection the way she saw it.

Man, she'd missed the sage-covered land when she was away on the plains.

The plains had some scrub, but it wasn't the same. And if eyes truly tired from sage-looking (which still wasn't purple no matter what ol' Zane said), surely the rimrock, the mountains beyond, or the wide-open sky with a deep blue so bright it made anyone's eyes hurt would have provided beauty enough to distract. A person didn't have to dwell on the sage if they didn't want to.

Unless some easterner kept calling it purple.

Emory shifted in her seat as the truck rumbled down the main street and past said hotel. The vacant street was hanging onto life by a thread despite the cavalcade of tourists passing through. Perhaps they stopped for a cup of coffee in the sparse town if the mood hit, took a few pictures, or stopped in the only shop worth mentioning. The businesses had whittled down to the mercantile, feed store, auto parts and vacant, empty shop windows that needed a gust of life blown into them.

Those windows revealed nothing more than echoing caverns, dead flies, cobwebs, and debris. One thing came across clear, if buildings had souls, those souls had long since departed. Only the most stubborn lingered and moaned.

Pulling up into a space in front of the mercantile, she hopped out and darted in to get whatever signs possible. She passed the refrigerated cold drinks and food stuffs, past the folding table that held jeans and sweatshirts, and passed further back the aisle to the motor oil and scant hardware supplies.

She stared at the empty shelf space where the signs used to be.

"Can I help you?" A pimply kid in a green vest walked up to her.

"You don't have any *No Trespassing* signs anywhere, do you?"

He shook his head. "Nah. They sell out almost as soon as we get them in."

Well, that part sounded about right. She nodded her thanks to the kid and left.

Driving back out of town, she passed the sheriff's building and noticed his truck parked outside.

What the hell, she might as well stop in for a visit.

The receptionist must have stepped away from her desk, so Emory walked straight back to the office. Glancing at the table—yep, still hunting and fishing magazines strewn about. The sheriff's door stood open, and she walked up and leaned against the door frame.

"Howdy," she said.

Sheriff Preston looked up, surprised.

"Why, Emory! What brings you here?"

"Oh, just home for the weekend. I *tried* to buy 'no trespassing' signs at the mercantile, but they were sold out."

The sheriff nodded, taking that as a given. "How are you settling in as a brand inspector?"

"Pretty good." A wisp of trouble must have passed over her face because the sheriff jutted his chin, ready to hear her out.

Emory squinted. "There's a couple of strange cases. A vented calf for starters. Told my dad about it. He said it sounded like some sort of threat or warning. The more I think about it, it sounds like some weird form of intimidation. And I winged a guy who pulled a gun on one of the other inspectors."

"What was that?" The sheriff's brows knit together and he sat forward.

"Don't worry. I've been cleared." She offered a broad, toothy grin.

Sheriff Preston pursed his lips together and nodded, slow and measured.

Emory shrugged, acting breezy.

The sheriff cleared his throat. "Intimidation is a real thing, Emory. You know that."

"Are you referring to my family?" Emory countered, still leaning against the door frame and steel settling in her spine

"Don't know that I meant it that way. Venting is beyond rare these days. Mostly stolen cattle get loaded up and driven across state lines. What would you have said if the same thing happened on the Lost Daughter?"

Emory launched from the door and took a seat, unbidden. Considering.

"I'd say someone had it in for us, but I guess that's what we always think. Or at least my father does, given the history. I'd start riding around armed, at least for a while. Until everything got sorted out."

"Fine. Let's say you did that. How would you expect things to get sorted out?"

"I'd expect to catch someone doing something they oughtn't be doing," Emory replied.

Like sniffing around Cade's truck.

"Well," Emory added. "I didn't come here to spill my troubles. How are you? How's everything in Stampede?"

"About as to be expected." A shrug. "Prices have gone crazy, people are going crazy, and probably there's no end in sight until we get a really bad winter."

A laugh of agreement from Emory.

The sheriff leaned forward. "You seen the real estate prices?"

She shook her head.

"You might stop at the real estate office and take a gander. You're sitting on a fortune. Hell, we all are."

"You really believe that?"

"No. No, I don't. But the visitors, tourists, transplants and what-have-you don't know that part. And until they learn, the prices will be sky high. Say, did you ever put in for that scholarship?"

"I did. It's been awarded to someone else for this year. It's OK—I have my hands full with the brands."

"Apply again next year, Em. Give it some serious thought. Take law enforcement courses. Those sure wouldn't go amiss."

"You know I already wear a badge," she grinned.

"And so you do. Next get a weapon to go behind it."

That part sounded kind of tempting.

CURIOSITY COULD PROVE A FINE THING, and in this case, a motivating force.

When she finished up visiting the sheriff, instead of turning right, she turned left and back through town. She pulled up in front of an old dusty storefront that served as a fairly makeshift real estate office. It'd been there a while. Hell, others might crop up by then, but she knew about this one now. A scribbled note was taped to the inside of the glass door.

Gone to take care of the cattle. Call my cell.

The cattle part sounded about right, but he probably

wouldn't get too many calls, seeing as how the scrawled number was practically illegible.

Crouching to read the placards propped up on a bottom ledge visible through the plate glass window, she almost choked.

Hideaway Ranch. Pristine. 350 acres. $19,000,000

Why, he'd gotten the number wrong by a zero or two was her first inclination.

She studied the next placard.

Winding River Ranch. 500 acres. $12,000,000.

And so it went, one after the other. Ranches cut up and parceled for gain. Some being offered lock, stock and barrel. The lowest price in the window hovered around $500,000 for a swatch of land she knew like the back of her hand and wouldn't have paid a dime over $50,000 for it.

But she didn't even have that kind of money.

One thing struck her as a certainty: large amounts of money caused trouble, and nothing good would come from it.

Half of her wondered what the Lost Daughter would go for and the other felt guilty for even allowing that thought into her mind. She knew the truth. Someday the ranch might be foreclosed for taxes or taken by time and inheritance. The likelihood of another generation running it when she was dead and buried in the cemetery plot would be her lasting contribution.

The Lost Daughter wouldn't be sold off for gain.

Not while she or her father remained alive.

PART IV

Hard Prairie Towns Are Dying

The hard-ass prairie towns were dying and dying in droves. Drying up and blowing away like the tumbleweed in a mid-winter storm.

Most crossroad towns had once sprung up from the raw grassland. Usually a single-track road, whether county or state, bisected the town, and buildings sprouted up on both sides of that divide. The inhabitants of these buildings and granges clung to the misplaced notion that their hard work and industry would ensure survival, and in time, provide the very foundation for their success. A lot of those notions changed during the Spanish Flu epidemic, only to be further whittled away by the Great Dustbowl years. Progress often passed the prairie people by. Industries changed, the railroads died out, preferences shifted, and it seemed not many wanted to do agriculture anymore, or at least not out on the plains. Especially not during the blizzarding winter months that beat the fragile spring straight into summer.

Take Wild Horse, for example. A town with a post office meant it hadn't rolled over all the way dead. Yet. Wild Horse began life as a cavalry outpost, so named by Wild Horse Creek nearby. When the cavalry left, the railroads came, and the town expanded and grew. Fine by all accounts, until most of it burned down in 1917. Everything cascaded downhill from there. People no longer wanted to live in outposts, scratching in the dirt or chasing cattle around in hard, dry years. They moved into the cities when their circumstances allowed. Their dreams faded into the prairie, just an old collection of wind-scoured buildings clinging to an outdated notion. Well, those hopes and dreams packed up and left for Denver after a time.

That abandonment marked a shift in an era when only the Great Plains' cemeteries grew.

35

SADDLING UP

MONDAY MORNING FOUND EMORY BACK AT WORK, SEATED at her desk in the sale barn. She smirked, proud of the fact that she'd managed to beat both Terry and Dave into the office.

"Mornin," Dave greeted, heading for the coffee maker. "Thanks for getting that started."

"It used to be my job at home, but Dad's taken it over. Thought I'd get my hand in before I forgot how."

"Aw, maybe he was just glad to have his little girl home."

Emory shrugged, smiling. "Anything happen round here this weekend?"

"Yep," he stretched out, pretending a casual he probably didn't feel. "I'm kinda waiting on Terry to come in. He met with the sheriff."

Her coffee cup hovered half-way to her mouth. "About what we've got going on here?"

"10-4," Dave replied, sitting down and effectively killing the conversation.

A quarter of an hour later, Terry's footsteps made their way up those linoleum steps.

"You made it back at least," he said to Emory. "Morning, Dave."

"Never any doubt," Emory countered for a half-smile in return.

Terry didn't talk much until he had his morning coffee, so they had to wait for him to get situated.

"Well?" Dave asked after a time.

"Frank Aranda? Yeah, had a powwow with him. The general consensus is that a bad element's come into the area. Some woman got beaten on. At least she made it into the clinic."

Dave chewed on that. "What does that have to do with the calf or the bull? Or the two released idiots for that matter."

"Don't know. No one knows the woman, and she refused to say who beat her. Migrant. Spoke Spanish. The common thread we're following is strange behavior."

"Where are those migrants?" Emory asked. "That seems a likely place to start."

Terry frowned, took a sip of coffee and rifled through his notepad. Checked the call log, scratching the side of his face as he scanned the page. Most of their day's work amounted to little more than stock certifications.

"Maybe," Terry muttered. Right about the time she almost lost the thread of the conversation, he said, "Guess we might drive out to those shacks on the way to our regular calls. Keep in mind, the migrants ain't exactly our battle. Unless we see something out of place."

Dave stared out the window saying nothing, but the wheels in his mind were visibly turning.

Terry rose from his desk. "You ready to saddle up?"

"Ready," she replied.

The overriding sense Emory picked up on was that they were heading into something tangled if they intended to act upon any migrant issues.

She was enough of her father's daughter to know that poking around meant uncovering nasty truths. For once, Emory felt pretty sure that's how everything tilted.

Seated inside the truck with Terry driving, Emory couldn't help but notice the brand inspector acted more focused than his normal custom.

"Yeah," he said after five minutes of silence elapsed. "I want to talk to you about this migrant stuff."

Emory considered his profile. "OK…"

A thoughtful inhale as he searched for the spot where he wanted to begin. "You know how there is that debate in New Mexico? The one about how brand inspectors might carry guns to bolster local authorities, say with suspected DUIs, disturbances, and traffic accidents? That type of thing."

"Vaguely."

"As you notice, we don't carry weapons as a matter of routine. The bad guys do. Don't you never forget that. You can't always make it back to the truck to get a rifle. That is fundamental. Next thing," he stared at her to make sure she took his point. "I ain't planning on stopping at those shacks, but we might. Depending on what we see. I'll tell you that I don't feel comfortable horning in on domestic or immigration issues, and problems like that. But we will, if we have to. We all work together out here with limited resources. We've got big territories to cover, and we don't turn blind eyes. We also pick our fights. But while we pick our fights, that don't mean we don't share information. Understand?"

"Got it." Emory figured that amounted to the longest speech Terry'd ever given her.

A speech that came down to one solid fact. He was worked up about the migrants.

There came a time for everything, she supposed.

But Terry hadn't finished. He kept trying to read her expression. "Now, if anyone asks, and I don't know why they would, we're on our way out to the Reynolds spread to verify cattle getting shipped. We're just taking a little longer way to get there. That's all."

"Got it again," she replied, her stomach clenched more than it had only three minutes earlier.

Nerves. And she wondered what Zane Grey's Lassiter would do in that situation.

Damn Zane Grey. He didn't belong out on the plains of eastern Colorado.

Outside of an almost dead crossroad town, a line of shacks broke up the horizon. Clinging on to an old drainage or irrigation ditch, the picture struck as barren. Without so much as a few scraggly trees for a windbreak, the clapboard hovels resembled something straight out of *The Grapes of Wrath.* Constructed in the 1920's, or maybe even earlier, those dwellings sure hadn't benefitted from basic improvements that most people took for granted. One thing for certain, there wouldn't be much insulation in the thin walls, no matter the time of year.

The gray skies announced that the weather turned colder and the building winter gathered strength.

"If they're migrant workers, shouldn't all the crops be in?" Emory asked, sizing the tinderboxes up.

"Oh, there may be some late ones. Carrots, onions, potatoes. Maybe beets. You know, hearty vegetables. The things your mother told you to eat."

Nobody talked much about vegetables on the Lost Daughter, at least not after her mother ran off. But to that, Emory said nothing. The truth would only make Terry feel sorry for her, and she couldn't bear that. Sympathy could be akin to drinking turpentine at times.

"Then what for them?" Emory persisted, throwing the brand inspector off the scent of the unfortunate business about her mother. "We're already in November."

"Meat packing plants hire people holding permits. The vast majority of the migrants simply want to work, but don't know their options. They get taken advantage of by the people running the crews."

"And what about the woman who was beaten up?" Emory wanted that unspoken truth acknowledged. As a female, it felt very important. Like all women, she *knew*.

Terry tilted his head, bothered by the notion. "Likely, we'll never get to the bottom of that one."

That notion still didn't sit so well.

Over the years she'd seen the tell-tale signs: blackened eyes and deep arm bruises. Jawline discolorations. Haunted eyes. People never questioning for fear of what the answers might bring. If such revelations escaped out into the open, the truth would seep into common knowledge. That seepage would mean that something would have to be done, and fragile ties might sever. Hell, usually everyone knew at least *of* someone.

The familiarity bred a strange silence.

A dangerous type of silence.

"Maybe she came from one of those shacks. Looks

cold," Emory commented. "They don't live there in the winter, do they?"

"They might. You'd be surprised on how some folk live. Probably pay for the privilege, too."

"That's not right," Emory glowered.

The disgusted bark from Terry said she still had a lot to learn. "We need to get going to the Reynolds, but let's stop by the Aldersons afterwards."

Emory nodded. "You ever consider that calf and the steer might be some kind of threat or warning?"

Terry rubbed his knuckles across his jaw, considering the implications. In the end, his exhale was his answer.

The shacks retreated through the rear window, reducing in the distance until they were swallowed up whole by the dry grass of the windswept plains.

"We're just checking paperwork at the Reynolds?"

"Checking and certifying brands, making sure the paperwork is straight." A pause. "Since we're out there, we might ask them if they've noticed anything strange."

"10-4," she said, imitating Dave.

Then they'd get on to the interesting parts. She could feel it coming in her bones.

THE REYNOLDS RAN A CLEAN OUTFIT. Nothing much going on—just the way everyone liked it. Business as usual, and all on the up and up. Nothing strange, with a daughter getting married in an anticipated and popular match.

Afterwards, the brand inspectors drove out to the Aldersons. Unannounced.

They pulled up in front of the ranch house, and they

both alighted from the truck and approached the door together.

The rancher answered that time, though Mrs. Alderson was visible at the kitchen table.

"What brings you back out this way?" Mr. Alderson shook hands with the brand inspectors.

He shook Terry's hand first.

"Looks like our timing is bad," the senior brand inspector apologized, nodding toward the table. "We were in the area."

Mrs. Alderson stood up and came to the door, unperturbed.

"Two things," Terry continued. "Did you ever get hold of that biker cousin of yours, and second, do you know of any migrant gathering places nearby?"

"Nah. To be honest, I forgot to call him. He's OK as long as you stand down-wind of him. I mean those guys don't shower or wash."

Emory grimaced. "We drove past some possible migrant shacks, but I sure hope they don't live there in the winter. Never seen anything like them in Rimrock County."

Mr. Alderson's eyes narrowed as he honed-in on Emory, rocking back a bit on his heels. "Your lot is Leroy's employers, huh? I didn't exactly latch onto that the last time like I should have, dealing with the calf and bull and all. Well, you see that he works hard. That boy's got a streak of something, alright. Bound and determined to take the easy way unless there's no other way to be had."

Emory cocked a smile. "I was just up there this weekend. He said my dad was running him hard."

Alderson seemed to take that under advisement. "How long has he been with your outfit?"

"Oh, about seven months, if memory serves."

Mrs. Alderson's eyes twinkled. "Just make sure you don't go falling in love with him. He's a bit of a ladies' man. I can tell. Never did like the name Leroy…"

Mr. Alderson turned to his wife. "Anyone can see straight off that she's a smart girl. Smart enough not to give him the time of day." Turning back to Emory, he said, "Or at least I hope you don't."

If Cade's relatives thought he was lazy, that reflected bad on the Lost Daughter operation as a whole.

"He rides really well," she offered.

"That he does," Mr. Alderson grudgingly agreed. "That he does."

"Any nearby migrant camps?" Terry prompted again, drawing the conversation back around.

"Depending on the season, Greeley's outskirts might be a place to start." Alderson shrugged, disinterested but acting polite. Trying to be helpful. "A lot of the workers with papers find jobs at the meat packing plant, you know. Those without papers, well, who's to say. But yeah. They had some sort of camp down by the river-bend. They might still be there for late harvest. Don't know. Have no reason to go down there, myself."

"Maybe we'll go check it out," Terry replied with a casual shrug.

"You still want me to talk to Henry?"

"It wouldn't hurt. Obliged." A tip of Terry's hat.

But Emory stopped halfway toward the truck and turned back. "You don't take the theft of a calf and the bull keeling over as some type of a threat, do you?"

She could have sworn that Mr. Alderson turned a shade paler beneath his rancher's tan.

He stood silent under his wife's darting glanced. As the silence held, she ended up answering for him by making light of it with a forced laugh. "With our cattle? Now why would anyone want to do a thing like that?"

Her laugh snuffed out, abrupt.

That remained the eighty-four dollar question. Mr. Alderson had acted like he had a secret or a suspicion he wasn't sharing. His wife suspected it too.

The old west code of silence held and held fast.

The silence would continue to hold until something was proven or said that couldn't be taken back.

Those types of catalysts tended toward fighting words.

36

WIDE OPEN PLAINS STILL HAVE PLENTY OF THINGS TO HIDE

That same week, Terry's cell rang as he sat at his gray metal desk just like countless other brand inspectors had over the years.

"Overholzer," he answered.

Long pause as he listened.

A wary hand rubbed his forehead, finger joints arthritic and work thickened. "Don't suppose he's willing to tell me that face to face?"

Another long pause.

"OK," Terry said. "We're on our way."

His attention travelled the expanse of his desk to Emory. Dave was already out on calls and checking shipments. "We're heading out. Once we get this all wrapped up, I'm going to start sending you out on your own to check shipments. You're about ready, I'd say."

"I'd say so, too," Emory replied, uneasy. "Which ranch are we going to now?"

"Not a ranch. A crossroad."

"That doesn't particularly sound good," Emory commented.

"No, it don't. But it'll have to do. Oh, and Emory, don't go meeting people at crossroads on your own. It's a dangerous type of thing to do."

BACK INTO THE land of the double-lettered and half numbered roads, the brand inspectors pulled up. The first to arrive. Nothing but wind and sky for company.

Emory's phone said 8:39 in the morning.

She glanced at Terry, question unspoken.

"They'll be along."

Terry climbed out of the truck and leaned against the side, putting his elbow on the hood. Emory followed suit lacking anything better to do.

"Nothing's better than space," he claimed.

"Unless it's mountains," Emory countered, grinning in the breezy bright morning.

"You ready for that court date?" Terry asked.

She shrugged. "I guess so. That's next week. I'm meeting with the prosecuting attorney at three, day after tomorrow.

"At least you didn't quit." He made it sound like an accomplishment.

"Over shooting a man? Nah."

Pretty tough words that she didn't exactly feel.

That bravado earned her a long-eyed stare of disbelief. A stare only broken by the sound of an approaching motor in the distance, faint at first but building. Their attentions shifted, marking the sound's direction. A motorcycle popped up on the horizon, coming over a small hillock.

"Guess that's the cousin," Terry said. "Earl said maybe he'd show."

Emory stiffened.

"Did you bring your rifle?" She asked.

This all might be a plain bad idea, a voice cautioned in her brain.

"No need," Terry claimed, giving her another long-eyed stare.

A chopper roared up, fringe on the handgrips streaming until it came to a stop. The large-sized man wore intimidating black leathers topped by a dirty jean jacket. Sleeves ripped off and plenty of patches. To complete his outfit, the biker wore goggles that reminded her of Snoopy, but any other comparison stopped right there. She sure as hell kept such notions to herself.

The biker's beard was a fearsome bush, and when he took off his helmet, long hair flowed. Long, straight brown hair that needed a wash.

Terry walked forward, hand extended. "Terry Over-holzer," he said.

"Dirge." The biker didn't extend his hand but pushed his goggles up revealing a pair of clear blue eyes.

Eyes that traveled to Emory, who remained next to the truck.

"That's Emory," Terry explained, dropping his hand.

"Inspector Cross," she corrected, snagging both men's attention.

"Ma'am," the biker replied.

Whoa. An unexpected trace of manners. Or was is sarcasm? Didn't matter either way, she guessed.

The biker turned his attention back to Terry, glare rising.

"Want to wait for your cousin, or do you want to get started?" Terry sounded amiable.

Likely a practiced act.

Emory took in the hillock. They stood around, collected in a bit of a hollow—never the best of plans. A white Ford pickup approached.

"Is that Mr. Alderson?" She asked.

"Yep," Dirge inhaled, not getting off his bike.

The truck pulled up, and the rancher emerged. Displeased with his cousin, the feeling appeared mutual judging by the look Dirge shot back in return.

"Terry," a nod. "Emory," another nod. "Henry."

"Dirge," the biker corrected.

"Say that on your birth certificate?" Alderson shot back.

The biker shifted his weight. "I don't have to be here, you know."

"Yes, we know," Terry hastened to add. "What's behind the calf, if nothing else?"

"Money," Dirge replied. "And boundaries."

"Yeah, well your lot owes me $350," Alderson spat. "Minimum."

"No, they don't. That calf was already hacked up. We just used it to convey a message. That's all.

Terry held up his hand to silence the men.

"Message?" What kind of a message and why?" Terry kept his voice neutral. A practiced neutral.

The biker half-shrugged. "Dustin Pruitt got a fondness for blow. Couldn't keep up on the payments and decided to come up with a counteroffer to getting his leg broken. A runner said they wanted beef for some migrants in a goodwill gesture. Guess Pruitt took one of Earl's."

Earl spat.

Terry motioned for Dirge to continue. Dirge, for his part, shot a glance at Emory who pretended not to notice.

"Them assholes hacked up the calf. Somehow it got dumped back at the Club House—men on drugs do strange things. Yeah, I saw the brand all right. It was supposed to be one of Pruitt's, but I guess he got clever. Anyhow, we came up with a plan to fix the brand and dump it over at Pruitt's. A kind of calling card. *T Lazy S S*. Territorial Sons, or as close as we could make it."

"You do the branding?" Terry asked.

"Nope," Dirge replied, but it was a lie.

Terry didn't stick on that fine point. "Is Dustin Pruitt's debt cancelled then?"

"Doubtful," Dirge replied. "Especially not when he paid with one of Earl's."

"This all is your doing, Dirge." Alderson flung the accusation at his cousin.

Dirge drawled, "Maybe you'll get one from the Pruitts."

"Like hell I will," Earl countered.

The exchange deteriorated and deteriorated fast.

Terry eyed him close. "Your lot have anything to do with the bull that keeled over?"

"Keeled over? Nope. Don't know anything about that." He eyed Emory. "Send my regards to Cade, will you?"

That hit like a gut-punch. *How did he know she knew Cade?*

Dirge started up the motor, wheeled around, and took off on the open road.

Yep, a big old patch on the back. A circular Territorial Sons with mountains in the middle. Guess that meant something at least. A pride in the state that apparently spawned them.

"That just pisses me off no end," Alderson swore, uncaring about patches or the mountains on them.

"Yeah," Terry agreed. "It wouldn't make me none too happy, although it didn't sound entirely personal. You think he's telling the truth?"

"For the most part," the rancher replied.

Earl Alderson turned dead serious on the matter. "I sure wouldn't go passing no messages to LeRoy if I was you."

"And how did he know that I knew Cade?" Emory asked plenty bothered—a condition she did her best to conceal.

A sheepish look stole over Alderson. "Guess I let that part slip."

Not that it mattered. As it stood, she had no intention of telling Cade anything at all.

Everyone loaded into their respective trucks, one headed north and the other south.

Emory had concerns. "I don't believe the part about them not targeting the Aldersons, considering how easy that brand got altered. Seven becomes a T and another S gets added. Simple."

Terry sniffed. "That'd be my take."

"Thought I'd feel better once we learned the story, but I'm not sure that I do. Don't know what the deal is between Dirge and Cade beyond the fact that they're cousins. But I gotta tell you, I told dad about the calf bit, and he pegged it as a warning. Turns out he got that right."

"Interesting. How's that cowhand of yours, by the way?"

Emory shifted. "Ain't that the burning question? Don't like the fact that he's got ties to a biker gang."

"Coincidences happen," Terry commented. "You can't help who you're related to."

No joke.

Emory diverted the topic. "Why do you suppose Dirge told any of us that?"

"No idea. Maybe tryin' to help his family."

They both chewed on that unlikely notion, watching the Colorado plains roll on by.

THAT NIGHT AFTER WORK, Emory drove out to the Overholzer's to exercise Kai, a plan forming in her mind. Evenings spent sitting around her apartment became more monotonous by the night. The same old grind. Get up, go to work, verify a bunch of brands, check the paperwork, go ride Kai, stay for dinner at the Overholzer's or not, go home, and read or watch TV, go to bed. Repeat. And repeat again.

That night she'd decided to make a break for it. To change things up a bit.

She pulled up in front of her boss's house and headed out toward the paddock. Mrs. Overholzer saw her through the kitchen window and came to the back door.

"Can you stay for dinner, Em?"

Emory shook her head. "'Fraid I can't tonight. But thanks for the offer. Tonight Kai gets a quick ride before I go home to get cleaned up."

That caught the lady's interest. "Oooh...who's the lucky fellow?"

"I don't know yet," Em laughed, "but as soon as I find out, I'll let you know."

Mrs. Overholzer joined in the laughter. "Oh, my goodness, I remember those days," she teased.

A lot of lonely nights in front of the TV.

The image of her father watching the flickering blue

light most nights flashed through Emory's mind in a glancing realization.

More than likely that TV was just a diversion, and her father was lonesome, too

---

THE SPOKE and Wheel had the best reviews for dancing.

The large building stood out in an empty expanse of pavement—a neon sign atop a pole stuck in the parking lot. Plenty of parked trucks and cars meant the evening was already well under way and hopping.

With no girlfriend to accompany her, Emory placed her bets on the simple hope that the clientele went in for plenty of line dancing. That way it didn't matter if she was with someone or not. Dressed up in clean jeans, her good boots, a plain shirt and a blinged-out belt, she caught her reflection in the darkened windows as she entered through the door. The place looked nothing more than a dressed up honky-tonk…music blared and a couple of guys noticed her entrance.

Trying to catch her eye.

Feigning indifference, she went up to the bar. "Coors Light, please."

Right as she paid, a line dance struck up so she downed it, leaving the empty bottle on the bar. She joined in the rows of strutting, pivoting, and stamping good fun. If nothing else, if felt good to move, and it didn't matter if she was all that good at dancing or not. At least she was out of the apartment, alive and trying to have a good time.

At the end of the dance, Emory went back to her empty and held it up as a flag for the barman.

"Can I get that for you?" A man's voice asked behind her.

She turned, holding the bottle of beer. "Hugo!"

A big, wide grin. "I thought that was you! How are you keepin'?"

"Oh, just fine. Needed to get out tonight, that's for sure. You come here often, Cowboy?"

"A couple of times. The mornings roll around mighty early, but I am sick of staring at the same four walls."

"I hear you. Tomorrow, first thing, I'm going back out to the Pruitts to check some brands. They're selling a few of their head."

Hugo shook his head at the memory. "That mess still bothers me. You guys figure anything out?"

"Oh, we figured out the original calf belonged to Earl Alderson's operation, and the calf was dumped at the Pruitt's as some type of warning."

"That doesn't sound good."

"No, it sure doesn't."

"Let's not talk shop," Hugo grinned. "There's music playin'. Wanna dance?"

Emory didn't need to be asked twice and headed for the dance floor. "Yes. Yes, I do."

37

MODERN DAY OUTLAWS

CADE, ALREADY SEATED AT THE BAR, WATCHED THE motorcycle pull up out front, visible through the dark plate window. That was the thing about those tinted windows, they made the daylight come across as night which was probably how everyone wanted it. Neon signs buzzed bright on the walls, the smell of spilt liquor permeated everything, and no one would bother the drinkers hunched over their bottles or glasses, bleary-eyed and hopeless.

It was three o'clock in the afternoon.

"Give me two beers." He turned to lean over the worn bar, catching the bartender's attention.

"Same?" The question came across tired.

Cade picked up the bottles and claimed one of the vacant booths. He sprawled out in a casual manner; however, his actions were anything but spontaneous. Keeping watch on the door with the lit EXIT sign above. Just in case bleary-eyed patrons couldn't find their way out, which probably happened more than once.

The door opened revealing a silhouette, haloed by daylight and peering into the dim interior—Dirge.

He spied Cade and walked over to the staked-out booth, wallet chain swinging at his haunches and long brown hair pulled back in a ponytail.

"Cade," The biker said, sliding into the other side of the booth.

"Dirge. Have a beer." Cade held out a bottle.

Dirge grasped the beer, took a swig and eyed his cousin. He set down the bottle on the table and thought about something just beyond reach. "Met someone you know. Did she tell you I said hello?"

Cade stretched out further, resting his arms across the back of the booth. A dismissive flick of his wrist.

"Nope. Not that I recall. Who are we talkin' about?"

Suspicion came clear and unhidden. "A brand inspector. I forget her name. How's that supposed to go?"

Cade sighed as he pulled himself forward. Took a swig of beer. "Emory." He shook his head. "She ain't one of my string."

"Well, cousin. That kind of gives off the wrong idea, don't it? Which I've already got, by the way."

"She's kind of cute, ain't she?" Cade's heart thumped, but he made light of it. "It goes like this. When I got out on parole, I answered an ad in *Craig's List*. Her old man's got a bad reputation himself and don't ask too many questions. Better still, people don't drop by that spread without a reason. A *good* reason. And check it out, the ranch borders on BLM land to boot."

"Huh," Dirge chugged half of the bottle down and belched.

"Don't you see?" Cade gestured grand. "It's the perfect set-up. Get this—I've worked my way in with an outfitter for the rich and famous. I can get them damn near anything they want. A built-in customer base. What do you say about that?"

Dirge didn't appear entirely convinced. "I say maybe. The plan never was to deal to individuals. Need a dealer for that, and that dealer ain't *you*. We just figure out transport over the divide and make connections into the resorts. Just like shootin' fish in a barrel."

Cade leaned in, eyes glowing. "Think of the possibilities. Your club does more than drugs. Maybe they want women. Maybe they need things...fixed. What could be better?"

"Not having someone in law enforcement in the mix."

"Aw, shit, Dirge. She's just some sort of junior brand inspector. She reads brands and fills out paperwork. There ain't nothing more to it."

"You like her?" Dirge eyed his cousin close.

"Em? Yeah, she's all right. For the most part. She can be a bitch, too. Trust me." Cade shook his head, bothered somewhere as he took a pull of beer.

"Seems to me she's smart and rumor has it, she's got good aim."

"Yep," Cade agreed. "A regular can-shootin' smartass. But she ain't as smart as she thinks she is."

"How's that?"

"Well," Cade pointed to his visible chest, shirt unbuttoned farther down than fashionable. He flashed one of his lady-slayer grins. "The Crosses are going to need a man to run the Lost Daughter one of these days, so Emory needs to have children. Why, I'd be doing them a favor." Cade ran his fingers through his hair, eyes sparking like he'd figured out something pretty damned clever.

Dirge inhaled, raised his eyebrows unconvinced.

A waitress walked up. "Two more beers?"

"Sure thing, darlin'," Cade flirted. "And two chasers. How about Jim Beam?" He eyed her ass as she walked away.

Dirge eyed Cade and couldn't have cared less about the waitress.

"So that's how you're going to get your ranch. Is that the plan?"

"Maybe," Cade admitted. "Unless something better crosses my path. Which is possible up there. There's a hell of a lot of money walking around on two legs. It's a hell of a sight better than what you're doing—riding around Colorado and making money for some…club. What's in it for you?"

"The brotherhood of freedom," Dirge drawled. "I'll get a cut. With my cut, I might ride down to Arizona and get out of the snow, once and for all."

"And if you do time?" The cowboy didn't come across impressed with that plan.

"Well hell, Cade. You didn't have any troubles on the inside. Or at least that's what you claimed when you got out. Which way is it?"

The waitress returned, and the two men cut off the conversation as she set the drinks on the table. "That's seventeen dollars 'cause it's happy hour," she said.

Cade pulled out a twenty from his shirt pocket. "Keep the change," he said, puffing up.

"Well? Which is it?" Dirge asked again.

"It wasn't bad, but I was in for selling stolen parts. Selling other things raises the stakes. Don't it?" Cade rubbed his chin.

"Yeah. Guess it does." Dirge took a swig, his eyes drilling into his cousin. Weighing his answer. Weighing Cade.

"You still in or are you having second thoughts." Cade asked, trying not to flinch.

Dirge laughed without mirth. "I ain't allowed to have second thoughts on club business," he replied, shooting the whiskey down. "But I ain't a fan of maimed cattle."

"Maimed cattle?" Cade snickered. "What the hell brought that on? Never mind, you need to toughen up. Cattle get slaughtered all the time. What do you think happens at feed lots?"

Clearly Dirge didn't agree, but he didn't argue either.

AMERICAN SCOURGE

THE NEXT MORNING ROLLED AROUND PRETTY EARLY, BUT Emory didn't mind. In fact, she awoke smiling with music swirling in her head.

That happiness carried as she pulled into the sale barn's parking lot, radio bass loud and pounding, and feeling as carefree as the sun on her face. In fact, she was settling into the job and getting her feet underneath her. Remarkably, the Colorado plains felt near-enough like home, almost like someplace she wanted to be. She whistled into the office, took the linoleum steps two at a time and ignored the ceiling light that couldn't be used.

Not bothered one whit about the fact that she came in last that morning.

Terry smirked. "The Pruitts'll be expecting you. Guess you won't have time for a cup of coffee."

"Just getting the paperwork," Emory half-sang, grabbing the clipboard on her desk, and flicking through the papers. "Says they're selling five head."

"Yep," Terry eyed her. "Call if anything seems strange

out there. I have half a mind to go along with you myself."

Emory stopped her humming and flicking. Terry fidgeted, like he just might insist on riding shotgun.

"You said I could handle routine inspections on my own," Emory countered, checking the papers in her hands once again.

True, surface impressions of the Pruitt ranch didn't foster much trust. The three brand inspectors knew as much, four if they figured in Hugo.

She definitely wanted to count Hugo.

Emory shrugged the suspicions off, unwilling to let any dark clouds settle on her horizon that morning.

"I'll be careful," she rushed to say, bolting out the office before anyone could really protest.

She bounded down the stairs, burst onto the mezzanine, and out into the parking lot. Driving off to loud music Emory sang along, hoping against hope that the Pruitt's might have called out the Texan as well.

She nodded and sang along in places, tapped the steering wheel in time with the music.

Sometimes a girl struck it lucky, and that girl might as well be her.

———

THE PRUITT'S junk-metal totem pole stood out stark, marking the ranch road and location. Coming at it from any angle, the strange lightning rod interrupted all the flat. If the sculpture's purpose was to provide a notable marker, it worked. If it was meant as true art, Emory harbored doubts.

Most people drove by landmark out there, and in that

way, it filled the bill and contributed to a few conversations besides.

Emory pulled up in front of the ranch house and hopped out, grabbed her clipboard, and shut the door behind her.

The sound alerted Mr. Pruitt, who came out on the porch while his wife hovered in the doorway shadows.

"Isn't Terry along?" Mr. Pruitt asked, not bothering to keep the disappointment from his tone.

"No," she replied, light and cheerful. "I'm handling cases on my own now." She eyed the couple closer, her cheerfulness draining. "Why? Is something wrong?"

Mr. Pruitt scratched his head. "We're just used to seeing him, I guess."

Sure. And that's the reason why he called in Hugo the last time. Only she didn't know him as Hugo then. Mind on the task at hand, girl. Mind on the task at hand.

"This is just a routine check and signoff on the five head you're selling, isn't it?"

Pruitt motioned to his wife, who reluctantly ventured out in the yard to join them. She acted as if the effort cost her somehow.

Emory took a closer look.

Sure enough, a bruise formed along her jaw.

"What happened to you?" It was a question Emory didn't want to ask but had to. She kept her voice neutral. Nothing was going any further until she received an answer. A *direct* answer.

"Dustin," Irene Pruitt admitted, eyes red and watering.

The old man, a ball of angry and helpless intertwined, looked like he wished someone would put him out of his misery. "That's why we was hoping Terry'd come out."

"I can get him," Emory offered.

Mr. Pruitt nodded his assent, and Emory turned back to the truck where she'd left her phone on the front seat.

She opened the door with a strange feeling. It was there alright. There and waiting. There and completely dead.

Her stomach turned cold—she had failed to charge it the night before. She pressed the button in a last-ditch effort, but sure enough. Dead.

Sucking in her breath, she braced herself and grabbed the radio and pressed the transmit button. "This is Emory, over."

The sound of emptiness before static brought it to life.

"Forget to charge your phone? Over." *Dave.*

"Where's Terry? We've got a situation at the Pruitt's, and he's been requested. Over."

"10-4. Don't hang up. Over."

A long moment before Dave came back on.

"He's on his way. You OK? Over."

Emory lowered her voice as she spoke into handset. "The son hit Mrs. Pruitt. Over."

"Roger that. Be careful. That's a domestic. Over."

Emory returned to the Pruitts, sheepish at her blunder. Mr. Pruitt put an arm around his wife's shoulders. A kind gesture of protection that had already proved ineffective no matter the chain of events.

"I take it your son is still here?" Emory said it soft and kind, but Dave was right. It was a domestic.

She sensed danger.

"In his art studio, probably sleeping it off." A nerve near Mr. Pruitt's mouth twitched as he let go of his wife. He blew his nose into a red bandana.

Emory considered that complication. "And where is that studio exactly?"

"I'll show you," the rancher said.

Together the three of them went around the corner of the house and stopped when another building to the northeast came into view.

"That's it there," Mr. Pruitt said, pointing a gnarled forefinger. "But I'd think we'd best wait for Terry."

He then turned in the direction of five steers waiting in the trap. "Those are the ones we're selling, but I'll be damned if I sell any more."

His wife put a restraining hand on his arm.

Emory scanned the landscape. Dustin's parents didn't act concerned for their safety, but a worried undercurrent churned all the same. "Has he done something like this before?"

Mrs. Pruitt shook her head 'no', miserable.

A silence descended down. Silent except for the wind, the drone of insects, and the plaintive song of the longspur.

It should have been peaceful.

"Do you want me to check the brands while we wait for Terry? That is, if you're still going to sell them."

The Pruitts shared strained glances. "Yeah," Mr. Pruitt fairly spat. "I gave my word. The truck'll be here in about an hour anyhow."

Relieved at having something normal to do, Mr. Pruitt pulled out the papers from his overall's front pocket. Reading and cross-checking, Emory recorded everything down nice and legal on the forms.

"These are good-looking cattle," Emory said, not able to entirely mask her surprise at the quality.

"The best we own," he agreed, with a slow wag of his head.

Mrs. Pruitt again patted his arm but addressed

Emory. "We might as well wait for Terry out front. How long do you think it will take him?"

Emory didn't wear a watch either. "Just a few more minutes," she replied.

Terry pulled in about fifteen minutes later. Emory and Mrs. Pruitt sat on the immaculate green bench while Mr. Pruitt leaned against a porch post. They all stood up and straightened at his arrival.

More handshaking followed, the brand inspector's eyes flickering over the bruise on Mrs. Pruitt's jawline.

"Are you going to press charges," Terry asked the couple, jerking his chin toward the bruise.

"Oh, heavens, no. What an idea." She averted her face and rubbed the bottom fringe of her hair in an empty gesture.

"Don't suppose you have any coffee, do you?" Terry asked.

The question startled Emory, but Mrs. Pruitt brightened. "Of course we have. Emory, do you want to come inside and help me make it?"

The slightest of nods from Terry let her know that she ought to take up on that offer.

"Just lead the way," she replied.

The two of them walked back to the house, Emory noting how the men standing in the yard waited for the women to leave.

Irritated, not only would Emory not hear what they said, she got the decided feeling that the men thought the women couldn't stomach the truth.

Two steps into the house, Emory backtracked. "I should take off my boots," she said.

Mrs. Pruitt shrugged. "This is a working ranch, hon. If you don't drag it in, someone else will."

A huge, vibrant red painting dominated the sitting

room's far wall. In fact, it stopped Emory in her tracks. Deep red slashed with vibrant blues, greens, and gold then splattered with black droplets. Vivid and bold.

"Wow. That's some painting," Emory exclaimed. "My, look at those colors. I don't think I've ever seen anything like it."

Mrs. Pruitt puffed up. "Dustin made that as a Christmas present a couple of years back. That boy is so creative…"

Her voice trailed off. "Well, he wasn't in his right mind when he done this." She fingered the bruise.

"No," Emory replied with a helpless feeling that brought her low. "I'm sure not."

She noted how the woman silently counted each spoonful of coffee into the filter like it made a difference under the circumstances.

"You see," Mrs. Pruitt sounded more tired than anything else, "when Dustin first went up to Denver, it came as an adjustment for him. But he made friends at the art school. At first, they were all real nice. Kind of quiet kids from what I could tell. We went up to one of their shows and met those early friends. Somewhere along the line, he started running with a fast crowd. Drank liquor more than we ever did at home. Said that everyone smoked pot to enhance their creativity, but I didn't buy it. Still, I went along. Figured I didn't know city ways. Shouldn't have, as it turns out."

Emory leaned against the counter.

The art studio with its unfinished wooden walls stood prominent and visible beyond the kitchen window.

"I still don't understand that bit about the insurance," Emory murmured.

"That was another thing I should have said 'no' to."

The woman laughed harsh and bitter. "He was all keyed up on insuring the herd. It costs a lot. But he said we would be safer that way. Safer from unexpected losses."

"Sounds reasonable, I guess," Emory sighed at the futility rising. "Our ranch can't really afford that."

An ashamed glance. "Well, neither can this ranch. Not really. At the time, Dustin convinced me that we could just put in claims as needed. In the case of the butchered calf, we figured the insurance company wouldn't know the difference. Said he needed the money again, and we figured insurance was the best way to get it. Dishonesty is a bad thing to get into, and we should have known better. The insurance said we needed the brand inspector's report. We never figured on that part. As far as Dustin was concerned, oh, I knew he'd gotten himself in trouble somehow. I just didn't know the details then, and still don't now."

Emory wasn't entirely unsympathetic. The Lost Daughter tried to scrape out advantages as well. "If your son does hard drugs, that might be the cause of everything we're considering here this morning."

The woman nodded in a way that shut the door on that conversation.

They waited for the coffee to brew, staring out the kitchen window beyond the studio to the plains, as if the prairie might provide them with answers or solace. Now and again their attentions snagged on the studio, the women more intent upon the person shut within.

Both intent, but for different reasons.

Emory and Mrs. Pruitt carried out two mugs as they rejoined the men.

"Well," Mrs. Pruitt began, "now that you all will be properly caffeinated, what needs to be done to sell those steers?"

"Already got the papers signed, Mother." He watched his wife's expression closely. "We're talking more about what *needs* to be done next."

"Next?"

"About the boy. Now before you go getting upset, we've already called the sheriff. He's on his way."

"I won't press charges, and no one can make me," his mother flat-out announced, color flying high in her cheeks.

Mr. Pruitt scuffed in the dirt, but locked eyes with his wife. "No one's sayin' you have to do anything of the sort. But it wouldn't hurt to scare some sense into the boy."

Flicking her head back, her eyes brimmed but no tears spilled. "I suppose not," she blurted. "Can't go on like this much longer."

Her husband took the first sip from his coffee cup, eyes trained in the distance. "Not when we have to sell good steers for no reason other than irresponsibility," he complained. "That chaps my hide."

The sheriff's car approached in the distance.

Terry drank his coffee, a study in neutrality. Emory didn't fall for it but kept her silence.

With the sheriff's car approaching, Terry addressed the rancher. "Lloyd, if you have a way you want to go about it, you might want to say right now."

"Guess beat on his door and see what he's got to say for himself. Just seeing the sheriff should drive the point home that this is serious."

"Does he have a gun in there?" Emory asked, sorely lamenting the still elusive District Attorney's clearance. The one allowing her to carry arms.

"Don't know exactly," Mr. Pruitt replied, "but he does know how to shoot."

The four of them watched as Sheriff Aranda emerged from his car.

"Thanks for coming out, Frank," Terry said. "This all is a bit beyond our normal jurisdiction."

The abbreviated account was repeated.

The sheriff sized up Emory. "You bring your rifle?"

"Don't have the DA's letter yet," she replied.

"I've got a rifle for you in the car, but you're going to provide cover, nothing more."

Emory's heart hitched, ready to argue that she shouldn't break the law. *Another first.*

The sheriff cut her off before she could even start protesting. "Now, I'll take the flack if something goes wrong. The son may not be armed, but I'm not too willing to take any chances due to dumb-ass technicalities. I filed that report two weeks ago. And you Pruitts? I think it best if you wait in the house. Whatever you do, stay away from the windows and lock the doors."

"I don't want Dustin hurt," Mrs. Pruitt warned as her husband turned her back toward the house.

"And I don't want ANY of us shot," came the sheriff's reply.

CLEAN SHOT RULING

TRUE TO HIS WORD, THE SHERIFF HANDED HER A RIFLE AND ammunition. Emory stuck the bullets in the chamber and tried out the sight. It would do, even though she liked hers better.

"It's fine," she replied.

Sheriff Aranda's eyes focused on a very specific location. "Now, you're going to stand behind that far corner of the house. Check the view. When you're ready, give us a sign."

Emory jogged to the position he indicated, placing the artist studio across the yard in her sights. She gave them the thumbs up.

Terry and the sheriff walked the other way around the house, bulletproof vests on. Nothing happened in the approach. The sheriff pounded on the door.

"Dustin? Welfare Check. This is Sheriff Aranda. Open up."

Silence.

Terry waited, intent. Nothing happened.

The sheriff pounded again. "I said open up, and I ain't going to ask you again!"

Emory inhaled, lifted the rifle and took aim. Holding it level, steady and ready.

The door cracked open a few inches.

"Come on out, hands where we can see them," the sheriff barked.

"What's this about?" Dustin called out, words slurring together. He sure as hell didn't open the door any wider.

"Welfare check, like I told you," the sheriff replied.

The silence hung between them all.

A long moment of distrust and consideration passed on Dustin's part. He opened the door and stepped out, taking his own sweet time about it. His mouse-brown hair stuck up in tufts all over his head, and his face covered in a patchy beard that most men would be ashamed of. His clothes hung loose on his skinny frame, dirty, unkempt, and slept in.

"I'm fine," he said.

"Well, your mother isn't," Terry countered.

"What d'ya mean?" Dustin took a tentative half-shuffle forward.

"Let's see your hands, Dustin," the sheriff commanded. "Hold them up above your head."

Emory hadn't lowered her rifle. Just stood stock still, propped against the corner of the house, waiting. Eye against the sight.

Slowly, Dustin raised his burn-riddled hands.

Had to be due to drugs.

The sheriff went up to Dustin and patted him down to verify no concealed weapons on his body.

Emory stood at ease at that point.

The timing of lowering a rifle was another one of

those inbred things she knew, without ever having once to be told.

The semi-truck arrived for the cattle. Emory left her post to deal with the transportation and paperwork, as they were paid to do, all by the book and above board. She retrieved the signed papers from Terry's front seat, summoned Mr. Pruitt to oversee the loading, which turned out as a good thing. Putting him in the role of overseer gave him a job to do while waiting for the other two men to finish their conversation out back.

That conversation sure didn't take long, and the timing of everything meant a whole lot of activity in a short period in a place where nothing much ever happened. Make that, nothing much was ever *supposed* to happen.

Terry came back out from around the house in time to see the back-end of the semi; the sheriff following a couple of paces behind the brand inspector, his arm on Dustin's and half-propelling him along.

"You give him the papers?" Terry asked.

"I did," Em replied.

The old rancher looked ready to beat the shit out of his hung-over son. "Those were five of our best head sold off to bail you out of whatever shit you've gotten yourself into—"

Mrs. Pruitt stepped between her husband and her son. "Lloyd…"

"And take a good look at your mother's face. Takes a lot to hit a woman, don't it? Especially the woman that gave birth to you." The old guy stepped around his wife and leaned in for a fight.

Dustin's hands remained stuck deep into his pockets, miserable. He wouldn't defend himself, if it came to that.

When his father pulled back, Dustin pulled his hands

from his pockets, half-opening his arms to hug his mother. He took a couple of tentative steps forward. "I'm sorry, Ma. I didn't mean…"

Mr. Pruitt intercepted him, blocking his path.

Mrs. Pruitt's blue fear-widened eyes watched the two men in her life.

To Emory, none of it exactly came across as a first-time event.

"Everyone," the sheriff cautioned angling between Dustin and Mr. Pruitt. "Stand back and let's get this settled peaceably."

Terry and Emory stood to the side, her rifle still loaded but barrel pointed down to the ground.

"Now," the sheriff continued. "Your mother has the right to press charges against you for striking her. It would be a domestic violence charge for starters."

"That won't be necessary," Mrs. Pruitt interjected, quick to defend.

The sheriff acted like he expected as much.

"Brand Inspectors," he called. "Do you have any questions for Dustin Pruitt?"

Terry stepped forward. "I want to talk about the insurance policy you have. You can only file on livestock registered under the Pruitt name and brand."

"So?" Dustin shuffled. "There ain't no insurance policy."

He turned to his parents. "If I didn't get that money, the drug dealers would break my legs," he whined. "They have bikers that use chains on people who don't pay up. I seen one guy get mauled in Denver. Please, Mom…he couldn't ever walk again…"

Lloyd Pruitt roared. "I *trusted* you!"

The sheriff held up his hand. "I counselled your son to stop doing drugs and get his ass into a rehab, because the next time he lays a hand on either one of you I'm hauling him in and throwing him in a cell whether charges are pressed or not. I've seen enough of this bullshit going around and am getting mighty sick of it."

Terry cleared his throat.

"Pardon my French, Ma'am", the sheriff apologized, tipping his hat.

Like manners mattered at this precise point in time.

Mr. Pruitt's jaw set, and his wife fluttered her red, work-roughened hands as she looked away. Their son had lied to and cheated them. Again.

"One more time," the sheriff said to the Pruitts. "Will you press charges?"

"No," Mrs. Pruitt replied, emphatic "I'm the one who got hit so what I say in this matter, goes."

And that was the end of it. Dustin slouched back to his art studio, and the Pruitts remained in the yard to see everyone off.

"You go finish your calls, Em," Terry told her.

Upon finishing her rounds, Emory pulled into the sale barn's parking lot and jogged up to the office.

Both men wore serious expressions, sitting at their desks and barely moving.

Eyes riveted toward her.

"What?" She hesitated near the door.

Dave dipped a nod in the direction of her desk.

Sure enough. A letter from the District Attorney waited on her desktop.

"Look what we have here," she sighed. "I'm half afraid to open it."

Terry leaned back in his chair, assessing. "You already know that Frank did the investigation and cleared you."

"Yeah, well. You can never be too sure until it's

spelled out in black and white and legal." She tore open the envelope and scanned the contents.

"A clean shot," she exhaled, knees buckling forcing her to sit down, hard. "It was ruled a clean shot."

"Never had any doubt," Dave said. "We would have fought like hell if it came back different."

Terry nodded. "You know they're going to want you to testify at that trial."

"Figured," she replied. "I probably don't have that much to say."

She thought about it for a minute.

"Other than I made one hell of a shot," she added, grinning.

The trial was scheduled roughly seven weeks after the shooting, now in two day's time.

Emory drove into the heart of Greeley, where she met with the silver-haired attorney named Collins leading the charge.

"You'll have very little to worry about," he assured her. "Under the letter of the law, all you need to do is describe the events and details of the day at the sale barn. Answer questions. Do long silences bother you?"

She almost laughed. Silence was the Cross' code. "No. They don't bother me at all," she replied.

"Then you're ahead of the game," the attorney said. "Be decisive. If you don't know, you don't know. And if there are silences, don't feel the need to fill them."

The image of an open grave shot through her mind. *A grave that needed filling.*

"That won't be a problem," she offered back, a bit hasty on account of a feeling.

Uneasiness traveled up and down her spine as she left the attorney's office. A bad enough feeling that she wanted to call her father, to hear his familiar voice.

Once inside her truck with the door closed, she picked up her phone.

His cell rang a few times. "Howdy!" he answered.

Emory smiled at his voice. "Hi. What are you up to?"

"Riding along and admiring God's country," he said. "Wanna talk to the horse?"

"No," she laughed. "I don't want to talk to Drace. Are you any place nice?"

"The whole damned place is nice. I'm in the upper pasture, riding the fence line. Cade's slackin'. So, why are you calling your old man?"

She hesitated—a hesitance that swirled with conflicting emotions. Her father would pick up on the unspoken current. She swallowed. "You know that trial I told you about? Well, it's coming up the day after tomorrow and I have to testify."

"Uh-huh." The wind blew in the background, rushing through the pines like a fast flowing river.

"Testify against the man I shot."

"Yeah, I get that. He had it coming. What's the problem?" Her father's voice tightened.

"Just a bad feeling, I guess."

A silence. The space it took for him to formulate a plan. He didn't say anything, but she knew he was calculating. At length he offered, "You want me to come down?"

"No. It's OK."

Another silence. Another calculation. "I've never been to a real trial before," he said. "Just one of them preliminaries, or whatever the damned thing is called."

That caught her. "Never heard about that one…"

"No reason why you should. Just another round of mudslinging. This time they claimed we stole and hid a neighbor's bull. Free semen and all that kind of shit."

"And were you?"

A pained laugh. "It all came down to circumstantial evidence. That bull just liked our ranch better. Came in of his own accord and decided to stay a spell. Besides, you weren't even thought of back then. That entire escapade stemmed from your grandfather's dealings. Still," another chuckle, "I'm the one who got hauled in for it."

"And you find that funny?" *What was wrong with their family?*

"Well, I'm still standing to talk about it," came the dry-offered reply.

Emory sighed. "No, you don't need to come down. I should be OK."

A pause. "What *exactly* has you rattled?"

She rubbed the back of her neck trying to get the tension to release. "Those assholes from the sale barn don't strike me as being from around here. I think they're trouble. And I don't know how well I'll do in a witness box."

"Yeah," her father agreed. "Crosses have a history in witness boxes. I'm fine to come down, Em."

"Did anyone show up when you testified?"

A pause. "Well, no. Hell, I didn't want them there anyhow."

Emory swallowed, driving away the old cautions. Again.

"It's OK, Dad. I'll just keep up that tradition, if you don't mind. No one that matters to me personally can watch me testify. That means you."

"Hard-ass," he chided.

"Saves time," she replied.

THE TRIAL STARTED ON A THURSDAY, the first week in December. Held in the county Courthouse, the impressive building carried the weight of law and order as intended from the moment of construction. Emory eyed it a bit askance, given the family history. Nevertheless, she was on the right side of the law, and she'd be darned if she'd let a bastard like Russell Van Hoon get away with threatening one of her co-workers.

Law wasn't always the enemy.

She stood outside of her truck and gazed up at the massive building, taking its measure finding it far more impressive than anything up in her part of the state. Greeley's founding fathers sure wanted to get the point of permanence across. Permanent, upstanding pride that would last generations.

They got that part right.

Hell, they'd built eight huge columns marking the entrance. Possibly even more impressive were the massive doors carved in bronze. It was enough to provide one hell of a distraction, and Emory found herself caught up in the display enough to almost forget the real reason for her being there.

Inside, she checked the directory. The courtrooms, located on the third floor, were accessible by a massive staircase or a small bank of elevators.

Emory chose to climb.

The stairs led into a hallway where the bailiff met and escorted her into the courtroom and gave her a seat in the first row. Once settled, Emory assessed the people assembled. Ranchers spruced up and clean for the occasion held the majority—ranchers who might have witnessed the events on the day. Spectators also added to the courtroom contingent, and not all of them casual. Seated at the back, those other men didn't come across near as friendly or as clean. In fact, they radiated a cloaked hostility barely held in check. Unsmiling to a man, their sole occupation centered around staring down people.

One of whom was Emory.

The judge hadn't entered the courtroom yet. The proceedings were a bench trial, and those didn't have a jury. Which was a good thing under the circumstances. Those men were the type to intimidate jurors beyond the shadow of a doubt.

They would, however, be have a good shot at unnerving the witnesses whose testimony they did not like.

The judge came in, entering through a door behind the dock, and Emory noted with satisfaction that he appeared solid and unlikely to spook easily.

The charges against Van Hoon started the proceedings.

"The People of Colorado vs. Russell Van Hoon. The charge is assault in the first degree and larceny of livestock.

On October 17th at the Greeley Livestock Sale Barn, Russell Van Hoon, drew a gun with intent to cause serious bodily injury to a peace officer. The peace officer in this case was brand inspector David Worrell, who was engaged in performing his duties as brand inspector. The defendant is also charged with the attempt to sell stolen livestock."

The bailiff asked, "How do you plead?"

"Not guilty," Van Hoon replied, staring straight at the judge.

He saved one very threatening scowl for Emory as he took his seat.

Making a conscious refusal to shift or move a muscle, she locked eyes with him.

Crosses didn't back down.

Still, this was shaping up worse than any of the charges her father once faced. Especially if those long-ago charges even had merit.

Opening statements given, the bailiff announced. "The court calls Emory Cross to the stand."

When she took the stand and turned around to swear the truth, she didn't mean to, but her gaze fell upon the men staring her down. Staring daggers and something even worse, in fact.

She put her left hand on the *Bible* and raised her right, swearing to tell nothing but the truth before sitting down in the witness box.

A rumbling of muttered comments came from the back row.

The judge struck his gavel. "Silence!"

He glared at that back row. "This is a caution. You will be held in contempt of court if I detect any malice or attempt to intimidate the witnesses."

The courtroom guard moved a few steps closer to the men, keeping an eye on their actions.

"State your full name," the prosecutor began.

"Emory Idella Cross."

"And on the day in question, October 17, how did the defendant attract your notice?"

"His and his friend's clothes."

A ripple.

"Can you be more specific?" The prosecutor asked.

"Boots. They all wore Mexican boots." Emory replied.

A definite ripple of laughter.

The judge glared at the courtroom.

The lawyer leaned in. "And more specifically, what caused you to watch them?"

"I was in the arena behind the seats, watching the

sale. When the defendant leaned forward, I saw a gun concealed in the back of his pants."

The attorney paused to let that sink in. "What did you do next?"

"I called Terry Overholzer. He's the supervisor."

"And did he instruct you to go get a rifle?" The attorney's question came out flat and calm.

"No sir," Emory replied. "I did that on my own."

The spectating men in the back row glowered. She stared at them in return, refusing to waver or cow. Emory wondered just how much protection the strong the arm of the law truly offered.

Dave was called up next, followed by Terry and the sheriff.

There wasn't all that much for the defense to dig into.

Russell Van Hoon was found guilty in due process. A process that only took one day. Three hours and forty-two minutes to be precise.

The sentencing hadn't yet occurred, but the going rate lasted six to twenty-four years.

"He'll do two years, tops," came Dave's arid assessment.

Van Hoon stared her down as he was led from the courtroom.

"Kind of feels like the OK Corral, don't it?" Terry muttered.

It sure did. And everyone knew what happened there.

40

SULPHER GULCH

A DARK BLUE PICKUP WITH COLORADO PLATES LISTED ON the usually deserted road.

Taking the 'scenic' route back to the sale barn, Emory slowed down. The truck was parked on a noticeable decline, banking downwards toward a dry gulch. All the gulches that time of season were dry and without water flowing unless there was a spring nearby, but she hadn't heard of too many of those. Whoever owned the truck was probably another rancher out chasing wandering cattle around.

Unclear as to who might own the draw, it never hurt to meet a local. Especially if assistance was needed.

She pulled the Brand Inspector truck up behind the other. Taking note of her surroundings and the dark clouds gathering above, she was on GG, a single-lane road on the northern edge of the county.

Stepping out, she eyed the locked rifle box and decided she didn't need it. The scent of burning wood and brush carried. The campfire wood fragrance puzzled her most. Trying to locate the source, a faint smoke wisp rose from the draw—tendrils caught on the wind, dissipating.

Burning brush or debris carried a different scent altogether. A scent different from pine campfires. Pine was a mountain scent, a purchased scent.

Brush and tumbleweed came free.

Checking her cell phone signal, it read fully charged. Satisfied and relieved, she pocketed it again and headed downhill toward the smoke. Peering over the embankment, Emory located an old rutted track that traversed the embankment and led to the secluded creek bed hidden from view. Barren cottonwood trees ringed the upper reaches, while the scent came from the obscured the bottom reaches. Sparse dried grasses grew out from the drop-offs at awkward angles and rippled in the wind.

Wind wasn't always a friend. Any burn, intentional or not, might easily get out of hand.

Cautiously, Emory chose her footing with care as the terrain listed steep and unstable.

The faint sound of voices carried along with the smoke as the wind insisted. Words were indistinguishable, blocked by the faceted sand embankments and drop offs.

Some of the laughter sounded harsh.

Maybe the ranchers were having a party, and that was ill-advised if they were burning and the wind was blowing.

The track hair pinned down a steep, eroded embankment. When she dodged an old chokecherry bush, she stumbled upon a black motorcycle parked on a dry flat streambed. The kind with the tall handles. A chopper, she thought they called them. Tracks were visible in the sand, where it had driven up on the same creek bed.

She took a few steps further in.

Another motorcycle rested on its kickstand.

A warning rose up between her shoulder blades.

Turn around, before anyone sees you.

Hard to say why she didn't that time. Maybe she'd grown too cocky about her abilities. Maybe she simply lacked judgment.

She followed the tracks as they bent toward the right and out of the wind.

Five men in black leathers gathered around a fire-ring, flames licking and them passing a bottle of booze. Drinking as the flames snapped and the firewood crackled.

She froze.

One of the bikers noticed her at that exact same time.

"Well, well, well," said the man, turning to face in her direction, cutting off the conversation. "What do we have here?"

She left her rifle in the truck. Damn.

"I'm a brand inspector," she answered.

They all stared. A few chuckles started. Laughter erupted.

Emory's heart fell. She stared at the five. Two sure as hell appeared similar to, if not the same, as men she noticed in the courtroom.

"Judging from the truck, I thought someone might have needed help."

"And you thought you'd be just the one give it, is that right?" The voice came from behind.

She spun around.

Mexican boots, cut-in heels.

"You want to offer, ah...help." He taunted. The others hooted.

Her airway constricted. "Which one are you?"

"The one that got away," he laughed, harsh and threatening.

He took a couple of steps closer, circling. He looked her up and down—slowly—violating her with his dark, menacing eyes. Eyeing his prey.

He walked up to her and leaned down to peer into her face.

The gleam in his eyes told her plenty.

"Is she the kind of girl to screw and tell, Hammer?" One of the bikers called out to him.

"I dunno," he shouted back. "Should we find out?"

"What happened to the other guy?" Emory stammered.

"He went back to Mex-i-co," Hammer replied.

The others, hanging back until this point, started closing in.

"Wanna belt of whiskey?" One asked, snide.

She didn't dignify that with an answer.

Hammer came up closer to her. He brushed a lock of hair from her face. "Those sure are pretty earrings," he drawled.

"Leave me alone," she snarled, slapping his hand away.

"Make me." He grabbed her arm and pulled her into him, grip vice-like and bruising.

The other men pressed in like a pack of predators, circling and intent on the kill.

The crack of a gunshot fired.

"Hand's off!" A man's voice shouted from above.

Emory wrenched out of Hammer's grasp. The sun stood at the wrong angle for her to see her savior. All she could make out was an indistinct figure in black. The voice struck her as familiar.

"Piss off," Hammer yelled back.

Another shot hit the dirt, missing his damn Mexican boots by inches.

Hammer held up his hands. Not in the air, but shoulder-height. Signaling defeat of a type. But did he mean it?

The rest of the bikers eyed the man at the top of the embankment, wary and calculating.

Emory took a few tentative steps, backing away toward the trail that led out of the draw.

A root caught her heel, and she unexpectedly tripped and fell.

Scrambling to her feet, she grabbed a hand-sized rock.

Two the black leathers broke away and lunged toward her.

Another shot rang out. "Next one goes into someone's gut. Now you let her go." Then, "Inspector, get your ass up here, NOW."

Emory ran, but Hammer's arm snagged her. She drove the rock hard into his temple. He pitched sideways, stunned. Blood flowed.

She ran.

She reached the tracks and hurled herself uphill. The man at the top provided cover, one gun against five men.

"Don't you move," he shouted down towards the bikers.

Emory clawed her way to the top.

It was only a matter of time before someone else pulled a weapon.

"Dirge!" Emory gasped when his features came into focus.

"One and the same," he replied.

She dove towards the truck to seize her rifle from the

lockbox. Her hands tremored as she fumbled with the damn lock and key.

Slow down! A voice inside commanded. *Nerves could have lost the West.*

The lock released. Emory pulled out the 30-30 and grabbed the box of bullets. She loaded six into the magazine.

"Go," Dirge shouted. "Drive away NOW."

Drop-jawed, Emory hesitated. "And leave you here alone?"

"I'll be right behind you. Get driving. If something bad happens, don't stop. DO NOT stop."

41

SCREAMING BACK TO GREELEY

EMORY STUCK THE KEY IN THE IGNITION, SLAMMED THE truck into gear, and peeled out. No help would be nearby. She called into the radio.

"It's Emory. I've got a problem. Over."

Silence.

"Over. Do you hear me?"

No response. She eyed the rearview mirror. Dirge followed behind, black leather fringe streaming. Riding like hell was a-poppin'.

Rattled, she pulled out her cellphone, selected Terry's name and let it ring.

One ring. Two rings. Three rings.

It was taking him too long to answer.

She stifled back a panicked scream.

Four rings.

"Hi Em."

"Terry! We need help. I'm on road GG approaching Country Road 115."

"What do you need?" Terry held his voice level, as cool and steady as a block of ice.

"The sheriff. There were men in a draw. Thought they needed help. Dirge came and held them off while I escaped."

"Hold on Em. Which direction are you travelling?"

"Toward Greeley."

She checked the rearview mirror. Dirge remained behind her, but a distant speck approached, gaining on him.

"Don't hang up," Terry instructed. "I'm calling dispatch now."

She heard him on calling in on the other frequency. "Overholzer here. This is an emergency. Over."

An answer.

"Requesting armed sheriffs, state patrol, whatever can get there fast on Road GG approaching country Road 115 travelling southwest. Over."

More radio sounds.

"Brand Inspector in distress. Being chased by bikers."

Watching in her rearview mirror, the second black speck grew larger. Closing in and gaining even more on Dirge.

Emory yelled into the cell phone. "Dirge held them off. They are closing in on him."

Dirge told her to keep driving no matter what.

In the mirror, another biker was gaining behind the third.

"Stay calm," Terry instructed.

"How far away is help?"

"I'm driving. We're all driving. Ten minutes away, tops" Terry replied. His voice cracked a bit on that last part.

Emory gasped. "We don't have ten minutes."

They were on their own.

She took a deep breath, slowed the truck, and spun it

to block the road, leaving a small gap for Dirge to shoot through.

If he made it that far.

Emory slid across the seat to the passenger side and jumped out. Rifle in hand.

She crouched behind the truck bed. Taking a breath, Emory raised the 30-30 and aimed it down the road. Time slowed as she squinted through the sight.

Another slow inhale to calm her jagged breathing. Her heart pounded. Slower, slower. She had to bide her time. Hold her fire.

Dirge grew larger.

The other biker chased, joined by the second dark figure riding. Nearing and closing.

A single shot rang out, but Dirge kept on coming.

Another shot and a metallic ping sounded on the truck.

Dirge rode his bike through the gap.

He jumped off, dropping the motorcycle while the other bikers closed in with no signs of slackening.

Emory's heart slowed even further.

She held her breath, aimed for the chopper's front tire, squeezed the trigger.

The crack of the report and her shoulder took the recoil.

Nothing.

Oh, shit!

Then it happened. The tire and wheel exploded, disintegrating and the chopper spun out of control. The biker crashed onto the asphalt, the motorcycle skidding another ten feet down the road, metal crunching and grating.

Dirge joined her, crouching at the side of the truck. His handgun pointed toward the road.

The black-leather form lay motionless—his gun lay about ten feet away in the road.

He made no movement. Another gang member roared up but stayed a cowardly fifty yards behind them all. The third biker stopped even further away than that.

Again, Emory took aim and waited.

Better they just ride off than her having to shoot them.

The biker considered the body of his fallen comrade in the road, turned around, and left his companion like bleeding roadkill.

"You see that gun in the road?" She asked Dirge, pointing.

"Yeah," he replied.

"One of us needs to go get that. Make sure he can't reach it. You want me to go since he's one of your friends?"

Dirge gave her a strange look. "He ain't one of ours. That's a rival gang. Keep me covered."

In a crouch, he ran with his weapon drawn and pointed, and kicked the other gun away. Off from the road, and out into the brush.

"What did you do that for?" Emory shouted. "I didn't tell you to kick it away!"

He approached the body, stood over the man in the road. "That's more than road rash," he called out. "There's a big pool of blood spreading. I think he's dead."

Dirge looked at something. "He's got weird boots on."

Emory heard what he said, likewise she heard the faintest sound of a siren approaching.

"We'll need to find that gun you kicked away," she called out.

"Well, I wasn't about to get my fingerprints on it! No, thank you."

Forget the argument, Emory started to tremble, shaking worse than when she winged Van Hoon.

Emory gripped her rifle, white-knuckled. She continued to aim down the road.

"You can put that down now. He ain't gonna get up," Dirge said, weighing his options. "Do you mind if I leave?" he asked.

She blinked. "Hell yes, I mind."

Emory tracked the direction of the sirens. "Aren't you worried about the others?"

He searched her eyes. "Not too thrilled about being here when the police arrive. They take a hard view on club colors."

To her horror, she welled up.

He shook his head, uncomprehending. "You got a scare, that's all."

"That was more than a scare," she hissed.

Dirge watched the car approaching in the distance.

"You got off easy," he muttered, displeased. "But you're right. Others might be waiting down the road."

Emory nodded. Willed herself to get control and her confidence back. "I'll vouch for you."

A state patrol trooper pulled up behind her angled truck still blocking the road, lights flashing. He pulled out his weapon and aimed at the two of them.

"Hands up where I can see them!"

Both Emory and Dirge raised their hands. "Officer, I'm Brand Inspector Emory Cross. This man helped defend me against the man in the road. That man, however, needs an ambulance."

The lump in the middle of the road just lay there.

"I have my badge in my righthand pocket," she said.

Dirge added, "Pretty sure he's dead."

The trooper glared at Dirge as his radio went off.

"Ambulance required," he replied. "One of the people here is a brand inspector. I'm going to check her credentials. She's armed."

Terry's white Ford roared up.

He walked alongside the state trooper, flashed his badge.

"She's one of ours," Terry said, eyes registering Dirge.

"You all right, Em?"

She burst into tears. "Yeah," she said. "I mean, sort of." She swiped at her face. "Thank you for coming."

Terry held her for a moment. "Everything is under control."

"You know what happened here?" Terry asked Dirge.

"Only a part of it," Dirge glowered, covering up a trace of shame.

ROAD KILL

THE BIKER DID, INDEED, REMAIN SPRAWLED IN THE ROAD, dead.

The sheriff approached the body lying in the road and said something into his radio. Two state patrol cars pulled up, lights and sirens going. They didn't even get out of their cars but tore around the truck and headed off in the direction the bikers likely turned.

Emory, Terry and Dirge walked over to the body. Sure enough, Mexican boots.

Terry raised an eyebrow.

Emory shook her head, staring at the pool of blood. "I knew this wasn't over with."

Terry shrugged. "Where's his weapon?"

"I kicked it away," Dirge said.

Sheriff Aranda called over to the deputy. "There was a weapon this man says. You two try to locate where it landed, but only the deputy touches the weapon to bag it. Understand?"

"Understood," Dirge replied.

When the two men walked off, Emory turned to Terry again.

"I shot his tire and he lost control," she said through jagged breaths. "Is this going to be prosecuted, too?"

"You've sure got good aim," Terry replied, dry.

She sniffed. "What about Dirge?"

"Don't know." Terry replied.

Sheriff Aranda motioned for the ambulance to come through. He took a few pictures of the biker and location with his phone.

The ambulance pulled up and carted the biker off.

"He'll likely survive," the sheriff remarked, watching him wheeled off on a gurney. "We'll see what others the boys bring in." Then turning to Emory, "You're a regular Calamity Jane, ain't you?"

"Not meaning to be," Emory mumbled.

"So, what are we looking at, besides the obvious?"

Emory's hand tremored as she pushed back a lock of hair. "I thought someone needed help, and I was introducing myself to the district. Turns out there was a bikers' drinking party going on, and a fire. Someone ought to go back to check that part. It's dry enough the whole prairie could go up in flames."

Wildfire in Colorado and the entire west was no casual matter.

"Where was that again?"

"GG. Mile marker 49."

"Trooper," he called over to the man standing nearby. "Check out the fire but don't enter the site. It's a possible crime scene."

"Go on," The sheriff turned back to Emory. "What's the bit about the rifle shot?"

"He was shooting at Dirge, and he would have been shooting at me," she explained.

"Do you know that the shots fired were aimed at you?"

"No," Emory admitted. "I don't know where the shots were aimed, other than it seemed fairly obvious. There were two shots fired. One, I think, hit the truck."

She eyed the sheriff. "Is this going to be something where I have to go give evidence? That's how this all got started. Some of those bikers recognized me from Van Hoon's trial. The man you got there? He was one of the two that skipped his bail."

The sheriff took the rest of Emory's fractured statement, distrustful of Dirge, still looking for the gun.

Emory followed where the sheriff's eyes travelled.

"Dirge...I mean, Henry Alderson helped me. This would have been a much uglier story if he hadn't stopped to help."

The sheriff nodded, approached Dirge using more respect.

"Found the gun!" The deputy called out, lifting it up through the trigger with a stick.

The sheriff nodded and approached Dirge. "Got any ID?"

Dirge pulled out his wallet and handed over his driver's license.

"I gotta call it in," the sheriff said by way of an apology.

Dirge shrugged. "Rules, huh?"

The sheriff nodded. "Rules," he replied, heading back to his car.

Emory, Terry, and Dirge exchanged glances.

"I don't think they'll catch any of the others. They had one hell of a head start," Emory remarked.

Dirge searched her eyes. "Why do you think crime is moving out here?" He asked sounding like a lesson.

"Takes law enforcement a real long time to arrive, as you can see."

Dirge didn't have any active warrants out, so the sheriff told him he was free to go with a couple words of added warning.

Before motoring off, Dirge returned to Emory's side. "Don't exactly know what to say."

"Well," she sighed. "I do. You saved my hide."

He nodded. "Well. Looks like it was all for the best. Glad nothing much happened."

"Yeah," she replied. "Guess I might want to be smarter how I go about things."

He offered a quirky smile that reached his blue eyes and made her feel like she mattered.

Put it out of your mind, girl. He's not your type, and he definitely needs a shower.

Dirge revved up his chopper, waved a high-handed farewell without a backwards glance, and rode off. A solitary figure on the dark ribbon of road.

"This job is a bit rougher than expected," Emory admitted.

Terry found that almost funny. "Sure is, at least the way you're going about it."

She glared in response then burst out in laughter which ended in tears.

The men shifted when she started crying again, uncomfortable.

She thought in that moment, maybe she'd try to just stick to livestock and leave the two-legged varieties alone.

"Come on Em, I'll drive you back. Dave and I will pick up your truck later."

THE CODE OF SILENCE

FOUR DAYS PASSED. EARLY ON A THURSDAY MORNING, Terry's cell rang as he was seated in the office. "Overholzer," he answered. Listening. Glancing at Emory.

"Yeah, I'll be right there."

He shoved the phone in his breast pocket. "That was Lloyd Pruitt," he told both Dave and Emory. "Dustin Pruitt's dead."

"Dead?" Emory exclaimed. "That's unfortunate, but what's he calling you for?"

Terry shook his head. "The coroner's been summoned. Dustin was found in the drainage ditch running through their property."

"Still don't get it," Emory replied.

"Lloyd wants to give the Alderson's a calf to make amends," Terry shrugged. "Wants to do the paperwork before he changes his mind."

"Bad business," Dave mused. "Does that mean he believes Dustin was tied up with the dumped original calf?"

"Yeah. Or at least something like that. I wasn't about

to ask him straight out. Not now, not under these circumstances. Feel up to driving out there, Em? I know Mrs. Pruitt'd be glad to see you."

"Sure," Emory croaked. She hadn't left the office for the last four workdays, and the men had been covering for her.

Guess they thought it was time she got moving. But the job was getting to her. She didn't want to act rattled, but rattled she was.

THE DRIVE to the Pruitt's ranch remained largely silent. Emory's nerves jangled despite being safe in the truck. Terry mainly kept his eyes focused straight ahead.

"I'm not sure what can be offered in these circumstances that would improve upon the situation," Emory watched the plains slip on by.

Finding nothing but the wide-open empty and feeling the heartache ingrained in the land and upon the people. Emory fell silent.

The prairie and plains proved a hard land, one that didn't suffer fools lightly.

Like the rest of Colorado, everyone on the plains knew that the ill-prepared usually found that lesson out the hard way. She'd made a serious, rookie mistake the day she went down into the draw.

"I thought I was doing good you know," she finally muttered at length.

Terry cleared his throat, catching the reference. "Good intentions don't always cut it. My grandpa always said the road to hell was paved with good intentions." He waited for her response, but she offered nothing.

Her silence got to him. He tried a different way.

"Don't make the same mistake again. You're doing a good job. Don't suppose you'd believe me if I told you that nothing much happens out here."

She gazed through the passenger window, noting a sentinel stand of cottonwood trees on an embankment. "I would not," she replied, deadset on the matter.

Terry scratched his neck and offered nothing further. But nothing at all struck as funny on that day. Not after what had almost happened to her. Not going out to see about cattle, and more importantly seeing about a dead young man.

THE CORONER'S van and Sheriff Aranda were already at the Pruitt's when they pulled up.

"Not good," Emory mumbled under her breath.

"No," Terry replied.

The brand inspectors walked around the side of the house toward the back where Dustin's art studio was located. Yellow CORONER tape created a boundary segmenting the yard around the studio and down a ravine to where, upon inspection, a trickle of autumn water ran through the bleakness.

Dustin's body lay sprawled, face down.

They went to stand next to the sheriff. Mr. and Mrs. Pruitt held on to each other, silently crying into the cold wind.

"Foul play?" Terry asked the sheriff.

He shook his head. "Don't think so. There's drug paraphernalia in the studio that's recently been used. Damn drugs."

"Why's he out in a ditch then?" Emory asked softly.

"Who knows? Out of his mind, I guess. That's for the coroner to decide."

The coroner came climbing up from the short bank, heavy and older. Tired.

Sheriff Aranda provided the introductions. "Emmett Franklin, meet brand inspectors Terry Overholzer and Emory Cross."

"Didn't know this was a livestock matter," the coroner stated, but he didn't mean it unfriendly.

"The family called on a related matter, I'd say." Sheriff Aranda shrugged.

The coroner lifted his eyebrows.

All of them covertly assessing the Pruitts.

Emory took a deep breath and approached the grieving family. "I'm very sorry this happened. You are good parents." She refused to put it in the past tense.

Still, Mrs. Pruitt broke down at her words.

Mr. Pruitt held his wife. "Dustin didn't always act like it. We knew things had gotten bad, but not this bad."

Terry came up behind Emory. "My condolences," he offered, allowing silence to fill the moment, and waiting for that same moment to break.

Lloyd Pruitt let go of his wife A thin and frail figure the wind could almost pick up. Instead, it blew her hair into her eyes and the skirt about her legs."

"You need a coat on," Emory said to the woman, gentle.

Irene Pruitt just shook her head.

"You said you wanted to transfer ownership of a calf to the Aldersons," Terry began. "Why might that be?"

A nerve throbbed in his cheek below Mr. Pruitt's puffy, red eyes.

"Just tell them, Lloyd," his wife snapped, angry.

"There ain't nothing left worth hiding. Well, other than shame."

The rancher inhaled, his lungs and chest filling up his overalls. "Dustin got addicted. I guess that's the only way to explain it. We knew more than we was saying the first time Emory came out. We didn't feel good about lying to you, but we thought there was no better way."

Emory nodded. "A lot of people would have done the same."

"Well," the rancher continued. "We knew we didn't have no calf that went missing. I mean, look at the size of this place. You've got our records. One hundred and twenty-two head. Well, one hundred and eighteen, now. Dustin owed money to drug dealers. Said he'd been invited to some biker gang's clubhouse. Was going to do some artwork for them, or some damn thing." The rancher choked up.

They waited.

"We want to sign over one of our better ones to the Alderson's. We'll deliver it to them, if you'll tell us where. Maybe you'd consider calling ahead to explain we want to make amends. None of this mess had anything to do with them."

"We can manage that," Terry replied. "Emory, you want to take note?"

With a nod, she entered it into her phone, biting her lower lip.

"Is there anything else that we can do for you?"

"Light a candle," Mrs. Pruitt said, voice flat.

"Don't know when we can hold the funeral," Lloyd mused.

"Don't be in such a rush to get him into the damned ground," his wife snapped. Then crumpled down to the ground. "I didn't mean that," she screamed in a whisper.

The coroner came up behind them. "This shouldn't take too long. It's obvious your son was another victim of the drug scourge."

"Why do you suppose he got started?" Mrs. Pruitt asked.

"Why, that's what they do up in Denver, of course," her husband replied.

The coroner and sheriff exchanged cynical glances, brows raised.

"How does any kid get started?" Terry countered, exasperated. "It feels like the whole damn country is either runnin' drugs or takin' them."

Mr. Pruitt pulled out his papers from his overall's front.

"Let's go pick a good one out," he said to Terry.

And the two men walked out into the pasture where the cattle stood waiting around the feeders. They singled out a handsome black angus calf, and Terry filled out a form for Mr. Pruitt to sign.

Emory gave Mrs. Pruitt a hug. "You're about the same age as my Dustin. Don't you ever get started with them drugs," the woman cautioned. "Not even at parties."

"No. Of course not," Emory replied.

She never was invited to many parties in the first place. Drugs seemed far from her realm, and out of the question. Not that she had the slightest inclination to ever try.

"I THINK I might go home for a week," Emory mentioned when she and Terry left the ranch. She fell silent when they passed the metal totem pole. "If that doesn't cause too many problems for you."

"Nope, sounds like a fine idea. The Pruitts get to you?"

"Yep, in a manner of speaking." She shifted in her seat. "Dustin's death didn't really solve the root of the problem."

"Nope," Terry replied.

"How do you suppose he kept getting those drugs? Remember what Dirge said in the crossroads?"

"I do." Terry stared straight ahead.

"Well?"

He shrugged. "There's drug pipelines and highways crossing the entire damn country. Biker gangs, organized crime, and low-level junkies distribute. That's what they do."

"Seems like courting trouble to me," Emory said.

"Yep."

"Did you ever consider that maybe someone involved in drugs saved me last week? Dirge had to be the one that vented that calf as a warning, but I guess you figured out as much yourself. Nothing is straightforward it seems."

She thought about Cade, wondered what to say. Wondered if the code of silence should even hold. He wasn't a Cross.

"Maybe silence isn't always so good of a thing," she offered at length.

Terry long-eyed her. "Now what are we talking about?"

"I wish I knew," she said, sinking down further into her seat.

The Lost Daughter was off the table for discussion. The old west code of silence held steady and won.

HER TAIL WASN'T TUCKED,
NOT EXACTLY

THE PLAINS PLAYED A ROUGH OLD GAME.

Drugs, bikers, rustlers, migrants, and heaven knew what else, all roiling beneath the placid surface. Emory was relieved to be heading home despite the veil of snow.

Kai was packed up in the trailer towed behind.

She took the familiar right-hand turn on the western side of the Eisenhower Tunnel and considered her options and predicaments. Her tail wasn't tucked, but it felt close. Emory felt far more unsettled and lost than expected. She didn't even warn her father that she was coming—just packed up the horse, a few belongings, and hit the road home.

A swatch of white caught her attention along one of the empty ranch segments.

That white plastic fluttered, caught on a barb of the wire fence. A surrender flag with the hell beaten out of it, and Emory drove into the headwind nearly gale-force.

Fencing meant, in Colorado, to fence livestock *in* rather than to keep livestock out. It was all in the interpretation of free, or open, range. Cattle had the right to roam. If you didn't want them on your land, you fenced your livestock in.

People were another matter entirely.

Truth of the matter was that there wasn't really any true open range any longer.

The cross bar came into view, and Emory slowed the truck. Stopped, in fact, taking a deep breath and considering the implications right there. Her blood quickened. She had inherited one hell of a Legacy.

T H E L O S T D A U G H T E R R A N C H
Established 1888

Her father made at least one improvement while she'd been away, and it was notable. Beyond the declaration, the sign carried the deeper message that Lance Cross was acting upon the advice and the tax grants the Preservation people offered.

Something to drag the Crosses into the twenty-first century kicking and screaming.

Emory passed underneath the sign with a spark of pride, picking up the truck's speed before pulling into the ranch yard. She stepped out into the cold air, her breath hanging in a cloud in front of her. Precious little movement about the place, she couldn't help but notice.

At the house, Emory climbed the still roughened stairs opened the unlocked door.

"Hello?"

Her voice fell flat in the silence.

The house appeared empty. Her father's dirty dishes perched on the recliner's arm. Ketchup and eggs. His favorite. The TV was off. She returned outside onto the porch, scanning the surroundings.

Her gaze followed the ridges above. Then something caught her periphery. After a slow double-take, Emory realized she was now staring at the severed head of a steer propped up in the far corner of the porch. Film-covered eyes stared straight at her, empty and dead. Emory switched on the outside porch light and took a few steps closer. It wasn't cleaned, boiled, or treated. The hide remained attached. The familiar stench of rotting meat. If she turned it over to see the underside, she knew what she'd find.

Emory's stomach sank lower and fear shot through her spine—but she rolled the skull anyhow.

Tell-tale maggots wriggled. One vertebrae still clung, attached to the skull. Another chain-saw hacking maybe a day or so old.

Emory's first instinct was to throw the head back down, get away from it and whatever brought the message onto the Cross' porch. Instead, she studied the ranch, her eyes searching for other changes.

What in the hell was going on this time? Had the plains trouble followed her home?

Had her father seen the skull? Or worse, had something happened to him, and the skull was left as her warning?

Summonsing all the control she could muster, she set it back where and how she found it. Reflexively, she flipped off that porch light right quick, and decisively moved through the dim house interior. Her footsteps careful and near silent, she moved fast to retrieve a rifle from the gun cabinet. It was already loaded and ready.

Emory paused in the living room to stare overhead at the ceiling, as if she could see through floors and walls. Perhaps the house might warn her. Emory listened close for any out-of-place sounds.

Only the house settling as the temperature dropped.

Emory stole into the ranch yard—with hesitation.

Eyeing the horse trailer, she realized she needed to unload Kai. Another quick scan, but nothing stood out.

When Emory approached the truck, Kai nickered and blew. The trailer latch groaned and protested. The 1,000-pound plus horse clattered down the cold steel ramp, announcing Emory's presence despite her caution. Her pulse thudded, strong.

Emory led Kai to the pasture to turn him in with the other horses. But Draco, her father's horse, and Cade's nameless horse were nowhere to be found.

Dread began building.

Emory eyed the bunkhouse. Was Cade even there?

Pointing the rifle down, she knocked on the bunkhouse door. Silence as she cracked opened the entry. Her grip tightened on the rifle. The inside of the bunkhouse was disorderly—beer bottles standing out, an unmade bed, and the general debris of a guy living on his own who cared little for anything else than his immediate needs. Whatever the case, she gathered the distinct impression that no one had been there for a few days. The antique armoire provided the best clue, as it stood empty with a few wire hangers, an empty shoebox, and nothing more.

Cade had obviously lit out. Why hadn't her father said?

She turned around, retraced her steps, and went back to the house for a pair of binoculars. Her father's truck remained parked at the side of the house as usual.

Emory scanned the mountainsides again but only saw the long blue shadows of night unfurling.

Suddenly, a thought sprang up. Likely Lance had ridden out into the upper pastures to check on the cattle.

She whistled twice, hard. Waited. Nothing.

Glancing up, she noticed the old dinner bell. The one she had shot at as a girl.

Emory reached up and rang the bell, long and hard. She waited.

A whistle came.

Her father was coming back in.

Nerves still jangling, Emory leaned against the porch post, watching the snow fall silent and thick in the blue hours of twilight. From the lengthening shadows, her father rode in on his horse, lifting a hand to her in greeting.

"Hey Em!" He called.

"Hey Dad. I'm home for the week. Got kind of nervous when no one was around."

"A lot's been going on," he said, dismounting. On his hip he wore a holstered .45.

"Like that head stuck in the corner?"

"Saw that, huh?" He eyed the rifle, approving. "Yeah. Like that steer head. It got hectic, and I haven't had time to deal with it. Things are getting more western by the night."

"Where's Cade?"

"Gone."

"Gone where?"

"Hell if I know. Don't much care, either. He was mixing up in things he oughtn't."

She waited for her father to say more, but of course, he didn't.

"I'll go put your horse away," Emory took the reins and led Draco to the barn. "Don't suppose you have a new hand," she called over her shoulder.

"Not yet," her father replied. "Unless you're planning on staying."

Emory shook her head and kept on walking.

"Not this time."

———

LANCE CROSS EMPTIED two cans of soup into a pan on the stove, stirring water into the contents. "That clean?" Emory asked.

"What do you take me for," he replied, stirring paused momentarily.

Emory leaned around him to fire up the oven before placing some refrigerated rolls onto a cookie sheet. That sheet needed a good scrubbing, which would have to wait.

"I always wondered why you kept Cade on."

"Good enough hand," he answered.

"But didn't you wonder when we learned his name wasn't his name, and suspicions were swirling like white water?"

Her father stood in profile, stirring the soup.

"I figured he'd be grateful or loyal. Something. I was wrong on that count. What are his people like? You said you met some of them."

"Nice enough. Guess Cade's their cousin, and they don't seem to think too highly of him in balance. One of his cousins runs with a biker gang, but he helped me out of a tight spot. A real *tight* spot."

"Soup's about ready," he said, ignoring that last bit, but he'd heard it all right.

"The rolls need ten more minutes," she offered.

"I'll go wash up real quick," he squeezed her shoulders gently as he passed by. "We'll talk over dinner. Ain't that what them fancy people do in Greeley?"

Emory laughed. "They aren't as fancy as we might think."

Her father had a spark in his eyes. "Good to see you home, girl. And just in time."

Emory pursed her lips and held tongue, fairly certain the dinner discussion would take a bit of warming up to.

On the table, a pile of papers encroached inwards. An onslaught of receipts, bills and fliers.

"Guess you've been collecting the mail," Emory commented, wry.

"How come you're home? Not that I mind...and frankly, I need the gun power."

"Gun power?" She asked, spoon stopped mid-air.

Her father, however, continued to butter his bread. "You go first."

"I came home because I got a scare. The guys figured I needed a change of scenery."

Lance Cross chewed his bread with thoughtful movement. His eyes rested on his daughter. "Uh-huh. What happened?"

"Busted up a party."

"Did you get hurt? Are you going to court again?"

"No, I didn't get hurt. And I hope I'm not going to court again," she admitted. "But, I'll do what I have to do. Shot the guy's tire out and he crashed. What do you mean you need gun power?"

"You're sure you ain't hurt, or I don't need to go crack some skulls?"

She bit back a smile. "I'm sure. I took care of it myself."

"Well," he drawled leaning back. "You got a scare and I want to give a scare. Simple."

"Not really," Emory replied. "What happened to Cade, and what's that head about? The full story."

"Cade got sloppy. Also, he was in over his head with something, and he was running at the beck and call of them people on the hill. That resort shit. Hell. Let 'em pay his damn wages."

"The head?" Emory eyed her father across the expanse of the table.

"A warning, like that chain-sawed calf you had. Hell, this steer got chain-sawed, too. I'll tell you what," her father chuckled, "when old Cade saw that head, he lit out like hell was chasing after him. I sure didn't know that boy could move so fast."

Emory just stared at him.

"Figure that head belonged to one of those steers that went missing last time you was home. They left it on the front porch like in *The Godfather*. Glad it wasn't a horse's head. That would have really pissed me off. That's what drove Cade off. He got scared and ran." Her father laughed, dry. "'Course, I wasn't too thrilled of the fact they made it onto the porch, either."

"So what's the gun power part?"

"I was getting to it," her father said leaning forward. "I've got a plan…"

THIS I WILL DEFEND

Four o'clock in the morning surely rolled around early and dark.

Neither she or her father turned their bedroom lights on, for that would show across the distance and would alert anyone on the periphery that they were awake and moving.

They kept the bathroom and kitchen dark as well. It took them about fifteen minutes to get dressed and ready, and to bolt a cup of old microwaved coffee. Emory went out to get Kai and Draco, Lance loaded the guns and rifles.

During the night snow had fallen, glistening mica chips under the full moonlight.

The moonlight might pose a problem, but it wasn't exactly as if they could command it to stop shining.

Horses ready and scabbards loaded, the Crosses took off toward the back gate that led to the BLM demarcation line.

"I think they want me to stop shooting people," Emory admitted to his back as Draco carried him along.

He father shifted. "Well, that's too damned bad," he replied. "Anyone complaining about your aim?"

"No," she laughed. "No one is."

"Now pipe down," her father said.

They rode the rest of the way to the back gate in silence.

Two squat, stone pillars stood guard on either side of the gate, another improvement. The same old steel gate had a stronger lock, too. She looked to her father in question.

He nodded, proud.

Curious as to the transformation, any questions would have to wait until events unfolded. Conversation carried in the clear moonlight. They dismounted, her father handed her the reins and pointed over to a stand of trees about twenty yards away near the flowing river. She tied the two horses each to a separate tree and made her way back to her father crouching behind one of the squat pillars. Hidden from sight and from anyone riding up on them from the BLM side.

She did the same, holding her rifle and waiting.

They both waited.

The faint morning light rose to the east, first a drained yellow then flaring into brush strokes of salmon. The sound of an ATV carried from below, threading through the trees toward the gate.

The motor drew nearer, until it sounded like it would come over on top of them.

Then the motor switched off. The crunch of sinking footsteps in snow.

Lance Cross signaled to his daughter. One-two-three.

He threw a stone in the opposite direction of the horses and hit a pine with a thud.

Lance and Emory Cross raised up, rifles pointed.

"Cade!" She called out, surprised.

"Whoa, whoa, whoa," he called out. Unarmed, he immediately raised his hands skyward.

"You want to explain yourself before I shoot?" Lance asked.

Cade's eyes were white and wide. "I'm coming to take that...that...steer head away."

"Bullshit," her father replied.

He pulled the trigger. The bullet hit Cade in the foot.

Cade screamed. "Don't shoot," he said, hobbling around. "You shot my damned foot."

"Next is your damned knee unless you tell me what you are up to." Lance said, sight against his eye.

Emory hadn't expected her father to actually shoot Cade, but she never moved a muscle. Still, shooting an unarmed man could not be good. Not the way the laws worked.

He turned toward Emory, hands held out in a plea. She kept the sight against her eye as well, unyielding.

"I need to drop off a package on the road," Cade admitted.

"And you thought you would come through the Lost Daughter to do it. Is that what you was thinking?"

"It's faster," Cade whined. "Look. You don't need to know nothing about this. Just stay out of it, old man."

"Don't shoot him, Dad," Emory said, low.

Lance lowered his rifle. "Tell you what I'm gonna do," he drawled. "I'm going to let you go back to whatever rock it is that you crawled out from under. You tell them the Lost Daughter, her cattle, horses, buildings, and what-have-you are off limits. Forever. Next time I ain't going to have a conversation about this. Do you doubt me?"

"No sir," Cade replied.

Lance pulled up his rifle again. "Emory, you go check him to make sure he ain't got any weapons."

She climbed over the back gate, patted Cade down, and looked in the ATV's compartment. A clear wrapped package was inside. White powder.

"What's this?" She asked him, shaking the package in accusation.

Cade shook his head, eyes wide like a wild-eyed horse ready to rear. "Just leave it, Em. *Please.*"

"You running drugs, Cade?" She asked, already knowing the answer. "What do you want me to do with this, Dad?"

"Throw it away," he said without the slightest hesitation.

"No!" Cade screamed, leaving red trails in the snow. "They will kill me."

Emory flung the package as far away as she could, marking where it landed in the snow and blended in.

"Now drive," Lance snarled at Cade. "Drive before I change my mind and shoot you again."

Cade got into the ATV and took off down the road.

"They might come back," Emory said.

Lance watch Cade's retreating form. "Maybe, but we'll be ready. And I can guarantee that Cade will try to stop them now."

"What if they try to kill him," she mused.

"It ain't our concern," he said, looking over at her. "And we're still not done."

"Hang on," Emory said, walking over to where she'd thrown the powder.

It took her a moment of searching, but she found it and brushed it off. She climbed back to her father. "We need to turn this in. That way, everyone will know that we don't have it. Otherwise, someone will come beating on the door for this, and the violence just continues."

"You sure about that?" Lance asked.

"I'm sure," she replied, thinking of Dustin Pruitt.

Together they went into the stand of trees, untied the horses, and rode back to the house.

It sure looked almost pretty with the fresh snow. Fresh snow that hid and softened most of the brutal edges.

"When did you put those pillars up?" Emory asked.

"Oh," her father sighed, "right about the time I got an inkling that we would need to defend the boundaries. About a month ago."

"And Cade didn't know?"

"He knew all right. He just didn't stop to think."

They rode into the yard. "Shall I put the horses away?"

"Yep," Lance replied. "We'll use the truck for the next part. Bring me out a big old headstall and a length of rope, would you?"

"What for?" She asked.

"You'll see," came his cryptic reply.

After the horses were unsaddled and curried, they were given hay and turned out into the pasture.

Lance Cross lugged out an object wrapped in an old rag, while Emory brought out an old, tattered headstall.

She had a pretty good idea what was in that rag.

Her father put it in the back of the pickup, and they drove out to the old cross beam. The one with the newly improved sign.

"Gimme that," he said, nodding to the tack in her hands.

She handed it over to him. He hopped out and went around to the truck bed where he pulled away the rag.

Sure enough, the head of the steer.

Lance made a few cuts and ties before fastening the headstall around the steer's head—filmed over eyes still staring straight ahead, unseeing.

He climbed out in the truck bead and flung the lead rope over the beam and tied it off with the tack.

The steer head hung down below the *Established in 1888.*

Crows circled overhead, ready to feed.

Emory looked at her father and felt a sense of pride, looking at the steer head hanging there, in all its gory, menacing glory.

"If that don't make them ass-holes think twice before setting foot in here, I guess I'll have no choice but to shoot them. How does that make you feel?"

Taking in the head, the cross beam, the mountains and rimrocks circling them, and the glinting snow, she felt tears threaten.

"It makes me feel wanted. Like I belong," she said.

He father put his arm around her and ruffled her long hair.

"Of course, you do. You always have, even before you was born. You're a Cross, and this is ours. And we'll fight to hell and back to keep it."

And so they would. They both climbed into the truck, and as they drove away, Emory checked out the rear-view mirror at crows already alighting on the head and pecking at the remains.

"People might complain," she remarked.

Her father laughed. "Let them come up to the door and tell us."

Emory sank down into the seat, shook her head and laughed. "It will only scare them away for a while," she said.

Her father winked at her. "And then we'll just come up with another plan."

THAT NIGHT, sitting up in bed and trying to read whatever book in the stack beside her bed, words couldn't hold her attention as her brain whirled. Damn *Riders of the Purple Sage*, instead she thought about the skull hanging from the cross bar. Zane Grey could never have imagined the half of it. Eventually she turned the light off, but her thoughts remained unquiet as she stared into the dark, restless at the magnitude of what they had done.

She had been an idiot about Cade. But that was all done and could have turned out worse. Much worse.

The solitary howl of a lone coyote split her thoughts.

That solitary howl received a response, followed by and another. Each song coming from a different point in the evening's dark. Answer followed answer until a whole chorus sang. A lonely, beautiful primal symphony, those predators were possibly better off than her, and that realization stung. Coyotes might be reputed as solitary by nature, but they had each other. She listened to their music for a good long while as the chorus rose and fell. In time, the choir broke off, and the coyotes went their single ways.

Emory settled in to sleep.

Maybe she and her father were like coyotes, and other ranchers dotted around offered a shared history.

A rugged determination.

Comforted by the song of the coyotes, she drifted off to sleep. Alone.

A SNEAK PEEK AT:
BRANDED GRAVES

DARK RANGE BOOK TWO

THE ROTTING STEER HEAD SWAYED IN THE BREEZE EVER SO slightly. Suspended from the ranch cross beams and dangling from an old, modified headstall, it got its intended point across, loud and clear.

It might not have been so menacing had the skull been weather-bleached like a Georgia O'Keefe painting, or even if it had been treated as a decorative emblem of the Wild West. But this skull hadn't been boiled clean or left out in the elements over time. No, the skull hanging from the sign *Lost Daughter Ranch—Established 1888* held another purpose entirely, and it sure as hell wasn't decoration. Its purpose wasn't to attract buyers into the valley. No, a steer cranium swinging in the breeze replete with rotting meat and withering eyeballs—well, the eyeball that hadn't been pecked out—was hardly a welcome mat.

The remnants of the remaining eye had dried and withered, folding back into the depths of the eye sockets. Hide remained attached here and there, but the brains were devoured or dried up—the elongated jaw stretched in a gruesome and cadaverous grin.

No, that skull didn't carry the promise of any hospitality, but rather a stark warning in all of its gore and carnage.

It offered a declaration of how the west used to be, and the message was simple—*Keep out* or be prepared to go down swinging.

The inhabitants down that ranch road weren't backing down. They *never* backed down. Never had in over 125 years of hard fought history. Never would, while they controlled and held that patch of ground.

It was nine o'clock on Saturday morning in the shallows of January.

The azure blue soared as bold and profound as a person could fathom, and another hundred miles beyond even that. Not a cloud marred the surface of all that brilliant, frigid blue. Below, the snow blanketed the land, flattening out the swells and drop-offs and glittering. Glittering like a scattering of a million mica flakes cast to the wind and glistening where they landed. The snow blew in wisps low to the ground, bearing the imprint of the wind's currents and patterns. And the day shone blue and the sun blazed bright for the frigid morning and set the snow to dazzling. The valley sprawled out wide and clear and grand the same as it ever had. Back in the day when ranch founder Hank Cross first traversed the valley, sized up the landscape and filed his legal claim.

And some more claims besides.

Emory pulled up to a stop right before the Lost Daughter ranch sign and climbed out of the truck. She stood in front of the cross beam hands on hips and staring at the skull swaying in the wind travelling down from the high country.

Upon closer inspection, a single shot pierced the frontal bone dead center. She knew it had been a little over month since the fresh skull had been hung. She had seen it when she left. Now she was back and the skull remained. The fetid underlying flesh had succumbed to the birds and the weather. The meat no longer remained fresh or red. Taken all together, the display was hideous. Ominous. A declaration in no uncertain terms.

It was a wonder complaints hadn't risen to a level that demanded its removal from public view. If such demands had been ventured, however, she knew how her father—Lance Cross—would have responded. And so the macabre statement remained hanging from the ranch gate for all the world to see—and more importantly, to heed.

She stuck her hands into her back pockets and looked up at the cranium a while longer, turning notions over in her mind. If she were of a mind to be truthful, she would admit that there was something about that steer head hanging which felt about *right.* Justified, even. When she tired of considering the carnage, she tore her gaze away and focused upon the beauty of the valley in the winter. The tops of the rimrocks were blanketed in snow, their sheer cliffs and drop-offs boasting their original colors proud and bold. Long thin reeds of grass poked through the depressions where the snow'd been whittled out, low. Great drifts stood tall, caught against the wooden fence posts, rendering the strung barbed wire invisible beneath the snow crests and waves.

No other ranch was like the Lost Daughter, when it came right down to it. The rest of the surrounding valley probably took that knowledge and sighed with an apprehensive relief.

What the hell, she thought to herself taking one lingering look at the skull.

She'd come home.

———

AT THE SOUND of the truck pulling up out front of the ranch house, the door opened and Lance Cross came out onto the porch.

"Have trouble finding the place? It took you long enough to get here, and we've got work to do."

"Nice to know you missed me. Gotten any complaints about that skull?"

Her father's eyes twinkled, and he cocked a grin. "Nah. Why would anyone want to complain about a thing like that?"

Emory shook her head. "Let me get Kai out of the trailer and settled. We've been on the road since before six. What's the plan for the rest of the day?"

"Ride the fence lines before the weather comes in." He stuck his hands halfway into his pockets as he scanned the Never Summer range before turning his attention back to her. "You might want to consider boarding Kai here now, if you really have to put in all them hours at the Stock Show like you say."

"Might be a good idea." Flat-out, she hadn't thought of that possibility. "That will be one less concern. Terry said the hours at the show are long, and while it might be hopping, it's tiring, too."

"We'll make it work then. But I'm glad you've got a few free days before you start," her father drawled. "I've got plenty of work for you to get caught up on."

She shook her head, moving around her vehicle and unlatching the trailer. "I should have opted for Hawaii," she muttered.

Her father laughed at the notion.

———

AFTER A DAY FENCE-LINE riding and making sure the water troughs weren't frozen solid, father and daughter wound down as the evening hours took hold. Emory cleared the dinner dishes as her father folded himself down into his chair while pressing the remote at the same time in one practiced move.

"Anything you want to watch?" he called out in the direction of the kitchen.

Emory remained by the sink, drying dishes and giving the place a once-over. For an old bachelor, her father wasn't doing bad, but cleanliness and organization were slipping.

"I don't care," she called back. "I've spent enough nights in front of the TV in Greeley that it's all the same to me at this point." She looked around at the clutter. "When's the last time you cleaned out some of these cabinets?"

A grunt was the only response to her question—a grunt that could have meant any number of things. But the evidence stared straight at her. Glasses were shoved onto the shelf any which way, and the plates below weren't arranged according to size, but stacked haphazard, and the cereal bowls listed at an angle. Running her finger along the shelf edges, dust collected there and in the corners. The best plan would be to take all the contents out, wipe down the shelves, rearrange the contents, and to start over.

As she poked around, she also found a chipped cup with random nails and metal parts, rusting and manky.

"The dish cabinet isn't for hardware, you know," she said.

"Don't bother me none," came his reply.

Draining the water out of the sink, she noticed the faucet still dripped into the same brown rust stain with a permanency that never should have been allowed in the first place. She could try to bleach it later.

That was part of the problem. Routine chores didn't always get done, and it showed. It showed every and anywhere a person cared to look.

Flipping off the light switch, Emory admired the darkened view through the window—the mountains settling into a dark and velvet sleep while the stars glinted as cold as ice fragments in the clear winter sky. Shades of the darkest midnight blue contrasted with the brightness of the blazing moon high over-head—the snow a pale bluish gray, the skies spangled with stars and the shadows drawn out long and deep. A view she'd grown up with, but a view that still had the power to beguile. The old outbuildings listed and the stoic rimrocks guarded the ranch's parameters the same as they had always done, faintly illuminated in the moon-light. The scene beyond a quiet and peaceful night on the ranch.

The silence perfect, except that the television din always drove that notion away.

"I'm going to go check on Kai and Draco before I get too settled in," she announced, pulling on her coat that hung by the front door.

"The barn latch needs some work," her father said, slumped in his chair. "It's been hitching."

Emory stepped out into the cold air, feeling the dark

embrace of the ranch in the dark of night. She lingered on the porch for a long moment, inhaling the scent of the land and tasting the approaching snow on the breeze.

She stepped off the porch and took a few paces into the yard before stopping. The yard light should have flicked on, but it didn't.

Just another thing to fix.

The moon provided enough light to navigate, although she could have reached the barn if she were blind, it was so ingrained. Upon reaching the barn door, she struggled a bit with the latch, which indeed needed tightening and a shot of WD-40, but it came free after the brief tussle. The door cracked its protest as it swung open. Inside, she switched on the fluorescent overhead lights, blinking for a moment as her eyes adjusted. Those banks of lights gave off a harsh greenish glare that didn't leave much to the imagination, enabling her to catch the glimpse of a mouse tail as it scurried back into a hiding place near the hay.

Unconcerned about lights or mice, Kai dozed in his stall and Draco stood equally at ease and settled in his. Emory took a quick glance at their water to verify both were full and clean.

"Good boys," she crooned. Kai's ears flicked, but he didn't open his eyes.

Leaving the stalls, her attention snagged on the tack. Over to the side was a saddle she hadn't seen before. Not that there wasn't plenty of room to go around. The Lost Daughter used to host at least five hands plus the family. Now it was down to her and her father—and whoever the mystery rider was.

Pretty ordinary and plain, it had the look of a saddle unused for a long time. But it had been conditioned, hinting of the intention to come back to life.

She'd ask her father about it.

One thing of the many she knew about her father, he didn't collect or trade saddles for the hell of it.

Switching off the light, she shut the barn door and headed back toward the house. As she crossed the dark yard, she pondered on that saddle, however, her musing broke off, right quick.

In the distance, headlights aimed toward the ranch house. Her jaw set and eyes narrowed as she watched the headlights aim in her direction…then they switched off. It took a moment for her eyes to adjust. She had the firm sense that the truck still approached, and she could have sworn she caught a dark glimmer of the moon reflecting off metal.

No lights reappeared.

With a shrug, the lights must have turned off. She stood a few more moments, just to make sure.

Puzzling.

Back inside the house, her father's eyes were at half-mast. They needed to hire a new ramrod to replace the departed Cade.

She ruffled her father's hair, just the way he liked to do to her when he could.

"The yard light's not working," she said.

"Yeah," he said, waking up a bit and smoothing down his hair. "I'll take a look at it tomorrow morning."

"Has it been that way long?" It was a pointed question that she didn't bother to soften.

Lance gave a slight flinch, and shifted in his chair. "Only a day or two."

Emory raised her eye brows. "I've noticed a couple of other things. First we need to get another hand hired. Second—"

Her father raised up his index finger in the air to stop.

She cut-off mid-sentence.

Both Crosses listened past the noise of the TV. Emory looked askance at the TV, but her father shook his head to leave it alone.

With silent, practiced movements, he got up from his chair. He was suddenly spry and intent. He went to the back room off of the living room, leaving it in darkness. Looking outside of the window.

The TV flickered and droned on, the same as always —as if the inhabitants within were off-guard.

Swiftly, Lance moved back through the living room, headed toward the rifle safe.

She didn't need to be asked, but stealthed behind him, equally silent and intent.

"Who is it?" she whispered.

"Don't know," he whispered in return. "Truck lights are off."

A man shouted from outside. "Lance Cross?"

Father and daughter exchanged dark glances. Lance pulled out his rife.

"Who's asking?" her father shouted.

One of the porch boards protested underfoot.

Emory pulled out another rifle, checking it was loaded.

Her father primed his rifle and approached the unlocked door, standing to the side.

Crouching, Emory ran to the staircase right as a shot hit the side of the house. The shot was coming from a completely different direction.

"Don't shoot!" the man hollered.

Her father pointed for her to go to the second floor.

As quiet as she could, she bolted up the stairs, taking her position beside the bathroom window.

Another shot fired.

A crouching shadow in the distance running toward one of the outbuildings for cover. She opened the bottom window and took her aim.

A voice shouted from the porch.

"Holy cow, Lance! It's Iver Holstead from the Highland!"

"Why are you driving around without your lights on?"

"I was afraid you'd start shooting!"

"I ain't firing!"

The slightest of pauses. "Well, who is then?"

"Don't know. Get your ass in here if you don't want to get shot."

The crack of another shot, and the thud of a body falling.

"Iver?" Lance called out.

No answer.

He called again. "Iver!"

A groan.

"Someone is taking cover behind the outbuildings," Emory said in a low, urgent voice.

"What's the direction of the fire?" Lance's voice cut across the distance, low and measured. Dead calm.

"From the west. They're trained on the door. Don't go out there."

The glint of a gun pointing from around a building… the shadow of a shoulder coming into view.

Emory squeezed the trigger, the recoil thudded against her shoulder and a body fell.

"Damn," she cursed.

"You miss?" Her father questioned.

"No, I winged him," came her reply. "Don't really want to kill anybody."

True enough, a figure darted away, clutching his shoulder.

"He ain't alone," her father cautioned.

She heard his steps moving back toward the door to the mud room.

Emory again scanned the outbuildings. No more movement. She changed her position as well, moving to the bathroom window.

Against the backdrop of snow, a figure ran toward an awaiting truck.

A shot came from the house and the figure fell. Then he got up and hobble-loped to the truck. He pulled himself inside and drove off.

"Should I let him go?" Lance shouted up to Emory.

"Yes. For now," she replied. Finding her target, she aimed for the truck, and not the driver. She took one final shot, scarring the metal or at least the finish.

Emory returned downstairs, leery about leaving her vantage point. Lance had already headed out the front door to check on the neighbor.

"Call an ambulance," he barked. "He's alive. Get some towels or bandages. We need to stop the bleeding."

Emory checked her cell and was relieved at finding it charged.

She dialed as she searched the linen closet.

"911, what is your emergency?"

"We need an ambulance at the Lost Daughter Ranch outside of Stampede. There's been a shooting..."

COMING SOON

ABOUT THE AUTHOR

Randi A. Samuelson-Brown is originally from Golden, Colorado, but now lives in Denver. A passion for Colorado history was instilled by her father from early on, and she certainly latched on to the more notorious aspects of life in Colorado and the West. She was a finalist in the 2021 Colorado Book Awards.

When not writing in her free time, Randi is often riding horses and traveling around Colorado and the West, finding inspiration from people, places, and open spaces. She loves speaking at museums and organizations, and especially loves to meet readers.

Made in United States
Orlando, FL
15 June 2022

18839821R00217